Motherlove

Motherlove

Thorne Moore

HONNO MODERN FICTION

First published by Honno Press in 2015
'Ailsa Craig', Heol y Cawl, Dinas Powys, South Glamorgan, Wales,
CF64 4AH

1 2 3 4 5 6 7 8 9 10

A catalogue record for this book is available from the British Library.

Published with the financial support of the Welsh Books Council.

ISBN 978-1-909983-20-5
Cover design: Graham Preston Cover image © Corbis
Text design: Elaine Sharples
Printed in Wales at Gomer Press, Llandysul, Ceredigion SA44 4JL

For Liz

With many thanks to my editor,
Janet Thomas.

Prologue

The naked trees dripped, the tarmac paths ran black. The park had soaked up rain like blotting paper and the lake was full, spilling over the litter-clogged weir into the dark sewer that ran beneath the town.

Even in the clammy chill, the park had its occupants, heads down, striding through, taking a shortcut from one side of town to the other. Not many came to enjoy the park for its own sake at this time of year. No one except her came to pace every path, note every hump and hollow, count every skeletal tree.

Because somewhere here was the answer. Hidden. But if she kept looking, one day she would find it. She must.

'Good evening, Mrs Parish.' Lewis Damper, grey-haired, West Indian, warmed his hands on his mug as he emerged from his kiosk by the gate. He beamed, his friendliness simple and transparent. She valued him for that, she realised. Valued a guileless smile that conveyed nothing but a smile.

She smiled in return, welcoming the human contact. 'Good evening, Lewis.'

'Days drawing out. Still chilly though.' He put his mug on the sill of the kiosk and pulled the collar of his uniform around his ears. 'You keep warm now.'

'Yes.' She nodded, walked on, thinking of that bottle-green uniform, that pathetic display of civic concern for public order. Park wardens. Last year there had been a rape, in full daylight, a woman screaming and no one helped.

Lyford council had been forced to make a show of doing something, bringing back wardens after thirty-five years, closing the park gates at night.

After all those years with no one caring how dangerous the park was. Because little evils didn't matter. Her little evil didn't matter.

She dug her nails into her palms. No point directing her anger and resentment at the uniform. Certainly not at the man wearing it. Lewis was one of the good guys, even if there was precious little he could do about anything. There were still broken bottles and used condoms littering the concrete round the swings. Still obscene graffiti sprayed on the toilet block and supermarket trolleys in the boating lake. Still the gaps in the clusters of cherry trees where a gang had taken a chainsaw to them.

Still the emptiness, the unanswered question.

If only—

She walked on, briskly, keeping fit, keeping ready.

Through the chestnuts – ignore the expectant squirrels – to the knoll with the drinking fountain, smashed and dry now. Then to the playground, with its decaying timber shelter. Always empty. No one seemed to play any more on the rusting swings and the battered roundabout kicked clean of its colours. Children were all too busy at their Play Stations probably. Or at the brand new play area with rubber mats and garish plastic on the far side of the shopping centre.

She paused by the shelter, seeing the sheet of paper pinned there. A photocopied blur with the glimmer of two eyes. 'Lost. Trixy. Black and white kitten. Please contact Lucy Grayling.' And a number. The paper, ripped almost in two, dangled by one corner.

Anger and bitterness swelled up in her throat. She

searched on the ground, found the missing pin and secured the sad little poster. Someone should care. It was only a kitten but even so. Lucy Grayling was suffering. Someone should care.

She turned away, continued on her route.

Two women passed her, one with a pushchair, one with a cigarette. Their eyes took her in, then averted. Strangers did not make contact in the park.

She took her usual turn, over the footbridge that crossed the narrow neck of the lake, past the long-abandoned boating shed, past the stump of the old bandstand, round the head of the lake and back. Counting the trees, the bushes.

At her usual spot she stopped, gripping the railing. She opened her bag. Just a piece of burnt toast today. Even before she had reached inside, the ducks began to gather, streaming across the lake, querulous quacks building up to a cacophony as the birds crammed together, fighting for a place within reach. Some swam in determined circles, others clambered out onto the grass, waddling closer to the fence. Quack quack quack.

Every crumb fought over and devoured. When she had nothing left, she hesitated. Maybe this was the day her mind would be tricked into spewing out its contents. She turned, with the ducks still gobbling and quacking, to face the darkening park.

Empty.

No buried memory. No revelation. No exoneration or incrimination. Today, as ever, just an empty park.

'And I said to her, you do as you're fucking told.' The two women she had passed earlier. Again the hasty look, wary and dismissive.

Then a backward glance, a hesitation as memories

slipped into place. The one with the cigarette came marching back, eyes squinting in accusation. 'I know you.'

The mother with the buggy turned too, her infant lolling unaware. 'What's up?'

'I know her!' said the first, jabbing her cigarette in emphasis, near enough to be threatening. 'I remember you, in the papers. They shouldn't let you in here. You should be fucking locked up.' She spat.

Her companion glared her support.

'Keep our Kiera away from her. She's a murderer. Shouldn't be allowed in the park.'

Would they attack her? She could feel their hatred already battering her. Once she would have responded, shouted denial, faced them down, but now, after so many years, so many similar scenes, she knew better than to bother. Keep quiet. Keep dignified. Keep sane.

'Mrs Parish?' Lewis Damper was strolling across the grass, alert to trouble and ready to calm any tension.

The cigarette woman grabbed her companion to lead her away. 'You should keep her out of the park, you should. Keep her away from kids. Fucking child killer, that's what she is. Killed her own kid. Hanging's too good. They should have thrown away the key.'

Was she hearing all that, or simply filling in all the insults that had been hurled over the years?

'You all right, Mrs Parish?' She could sense the sudden chill in Lewis's voice, the suspicion.

'Child killer!' A last receding screech.

'I am fine, thank you.' She raised her chin.

'Park will be shutting soon. Best be on your way, yes?'

Out of his life, he meant. But she didn't care. She didn't care what foul-mouthed women said. She would keep coming back, until finally she was shocked into focus,

4

found the hidden memory that must be there in the corner of her mind, and grasped what she had missed, what she had done or not done.

Until she understood what had happened to her daughter.

She turned back to the lake, to the ducks who were drifting into the gathering gloom, the water rippling white in their wake. Rippling out and out, going nowhere.

CHAPTER 1

i

Kelly

The house was dark. It jolted Kelly Sheldon the moment she pushed the door open. Darkness like a hand raised in her face, halting her in her tracks. The house should be alight by now, a warm glow after the gloom of the early spring evening.

And her mother should be in the kitchen, cooking or brewing or bottling. But the cluttered kitchen was silent. A saucepan stood cold on the cooker, empty jars waited forgotten on the table. Kelly pushed aside pots of herbs on the windowsill, to peer out into the field. Sheep and lambs were milling about, disgruntled, by the gate. They hadn't had their usual feed.

What had happened to her mother? It wasn't in Kelly's nature to worry but a chill clenched her stomach now.

'Mum?' She tried to speak normally, keep her voice level.

No response. She tiptoed upstairs, wanting to shout, but afraid there would be no reply.

'Mum?' For a moment she thought that Roz's bedroom was also empty. No light. Silence. A jumble of bedding. That wasn't right. Messy bedding was normal for Kelly's room, but Roz always kept calm order in hers. Tantric harmony.

Kelly laid a hand on the quilt and felt her mother's arm beneath. She turned back the covers.

Roz was half undressed, one shoe still on, huddled in the tangle of cloth, shivering. She mewed as Kelly pulled the quilt, her eyes clenched shut.

'Mum? What's wrong? How long have you been like this? Christ, Mum.'

Roz's fingers closed round her wrist, as if Kelly could give her a transfusion of strength. She swallowed hard, opened her eyes with a wince. 'I'm all right.'

'How can you say that? Mum! I knew you weren't well. I shouldn't have gone out. Look, I'm going to get a doctor.'

'No!'

'But Mum, you're really ill. I've got to.'

'No. I'll be all right. You can get me some water. Some tea. Dandelion root. There's some in the kitchen. Make a—'

'No, Mum, this is serious. Look at you. You can't solve this with herb tea.'

'I don't want a doctor. I'm not taking their poisons.' Roz was struggling up, ready to fight, and Kelly saw her with new eyes. Not just slim and supple, as Kelly had always thought, but gaunt. Still in her thirties, she was looking nearer sixty. The effort of rising was too much; the nausea was clearly taking hold. Roz was waving her arm for support, so Kelly helped her, half carried her through to the bathroom, where Roz dropped over the pan and heaved. 'Just some water,' she said hoarsely.

Kelly hesitated for a second. 'All right.'

She raced down to the kitchen for a glass, because doing something, anything, gave her time to confront her panic. Think. She groped in her pocket for her mobile, and checked for a signal. Why was she bothering? She knew there was never any signal here, in the shadow of the hill. She would have to climb…

Joe. Her boyfriend. Of course, he was still in the yard. He had brought her back from The Mill and Tuppence on the pillion of his spluttering bike, and he always took time to see if the potholes on their mountain track had done any damage.

She flung the door wide, calling him.

Joe ambled over.

'Mum's ill.' She didn't like to shout, so she forced herself to wait until he was close enough. 'I think she's really bad. She needs a doctor. Call one.'

Joe was flummoxed. 'Doctor? I didn't think she had one. I thought she didn't believe—'

'She doesn't. But tough. She's really ill, Joe. Here, take my phone. Find a signal. Please.'

'Okay.' He took the mobile, confirming that, yes, there was no signal.

'Please hurry. I've got to get back to her.'

'Yeah, yeah, okay.' He wandered off and Kelly dashed upstairs with the water.

Roz was back in bed, shivering. 'No doctor,' she said.

Kelly held the glass to her lips. 'You've got to have a doctor. I don't care what you say. You're ill, and I'm scared and I don't want to lose you. Please, Mum.'

Roz's face, already creased with pain, frowned more. Then her resistance softened into tears. 'Kelly.' She squeezed her hand, then lay back and allowed her daughter to straighten her bedding and wipe away the sweat.

'I couldn't do without you, Mum,' said Kelly, unable to stop her voice quivering. 'So please, be good when the doctor gets here. Because I am going to do whatever he tells me to do.'

Again, Roz opened her lips to argue. Then stopped, smiled and sank back. 'You're the boss.'

'That's right!' She was going to play the boss and take a machete to one of Roz's strongest convictions; no doctors. Herbs and acupuncture and the correct balancing of Yin and Yang were all very well for sniffles, aching feet or sore eyes. But this was different. This, Kelly knew in her twisting gut, was bad. For the first time she imagined a world without Roz.

Kelly lit a couple of scented candles and sat on an embroidered cushion, holding her mother's hand while they waited for the doctor.

A siren. She heard it, muffled by distance and a bank of trees, the brief blast of an ambulance edging a car out of the way up on the narrow road. Of course, Joe wouldn't have had the sense to find a GP's number, he'd have gone straight for 999. Kelly gave her mother's hand another squeeze and went to the window. Blue pulsing light. Then she glimpsed the white van bumping its way along their track.

It was too drastic, an ambulance. Not what she'd wanted. But her instinct told her it was what her mother needed. She went down and out to the yard to greet the paramedics.

'All right, love? Where's the patient?'

Midnight. She had never known the house so silent. Which was absurd, because, if she chose to listen, there were all the usual noises of the night, the faintest creaks and rattles, the wind outside, an occasional bleat. Just like any other night. But there was an emptiness, something missing, so fundamental, the house seemed dead without it.

Kelly switched on the light, leant back against the door, out of energy. 'Go home,' they'd insisted. 'There's nothing you can do here. We've got her stabilised, just waiting for the test results, so you go home and get a good night's sleep.'

Joe had brought her back, thought he'd stay the night, but she'd waved him away. Joe wasn't the right companion for dealing with this – this thing. This was a lesson in being alone. As she would be, if Roz died.

It wasn't loneliness that Kelly feared. Happy and easygoing, she would always have friends, companions, lovers. But the loss of Roz would be the loss of a part of herself. She would have this place, but what sense would it make without Roz?

Carregwen, the cottage, battered and patched, tasselled cushions, wooden bowls and sandalwood and patchouli disguising the smell of damp, was Roz's home. Home in its deepest meaning. Kelly loved it as a comfortably unconventional retreat, a place to do her own thing, the good night's rest after adventure. But for Roz it was far more, totemic, something that had made her whole. Carregwen meant she was a home provider. She had filled it, obsessively, with little things, but most of all with the one prize that mattered – a family. Her daughter.

And now that daughter slid down the kitchen door, slumped on the floor and contemplated how meaningless the place would be without Roz.

'Of course your mother seems to have a comparatively healthy life style.'

Dr Choudry pulled up a chair for Kelly. She had spoken to three hurried doctors since her mother's admittance and received a dismissive grunt from a fourth. Dr Choudry had been the most convincingly human one, so Kelly decided to corner him for explanations. He was ready to oblige; Roz's medical notes needed some urgent padding.

'I gather she's a vegetarian.'

'Yes, these days.' There had been a burger and chip

interlude in Milford Haven, but mother and daughter had returned to the diet they'd enjoyed in the commune. 'But she's not a vegan,' she added. Roz would have been, but Kelly had insisted that it made no sense to keep chickens and goats if they didn't eat eggs and milk.

Dr Choudry nodded. 'She's certainly not overweight.' Tactfully put. Roz was skeletal. 'She gets plenty of exercise?'

'Oh yes, in the garden, you know, and she walks everywhere, and she teaches yoga. What's this got to do with her being sick?'

'It may have helped conceal her condition for a long time. Of course if she had been signed up with a GP, gone for regular check-ups, it would have been caught long ago. This sort of diabetes can often be dealt with by simple—'

'Diabetes? I thought it was a problem with her kidneys.'

'That is one of the long-term problems that can arise with diabetes. Your mother agrees she has been getting increasingly tired over the last few years. There are other signs. A lot of trips to the toilet in the night?'

'Those were symptoms? I should have done something earlier.'

The doctor smiled. 'I'm guessing your mother would not have been very amenable. She's not a great fan of doctors. As far as I can see, the last time she had any dealings with the orthodox medical profession was at your birth. Am I right?'

Kelly tried a smile that she hoped wasn't too apologetic. 'She likes to do things naturally. I didn't think it would matter if someone wasn't really ill.'

Dr Choudry raised his eyebrows in response. Enough said. Roz had been ill, but they had never known.

'It's called Maturity Onset Diabetes of the Young,' he explained. 'It usually develops in the late teens or in early adulthood – at about the time your mother disappeared off the NHS radar in fact. No rapid rush of symptoms, so she probably never appreciated them. Until now, unfortunately, when things have progressed to a relatively serious level. A very simple medication might have prevented this. No need even for insulin to start with. But now her kidneys are damaged. Eye problems too, but the kidneys are the real problem.'

'Will she need dialysis?'

'It may come to that. Dialysis or a transplant.'

'A kidney transplant? She can have one of mine.'

He smiled at Kelly's instant eagerness. 'Let's not jump the gun. She's a long way off being in urgent need of one. For now, we'll manage her condition by other means. She will need to stick to a careful diet, but I don't suppose that will be a problem.'

'No, no problem.' Kelly was sounding calm. Could he tell, she wondered, that her insides were dissolving in panic? She needed the toilet.

Dr Choudry's hand was on her arm as she started to rise. 'That's your mother. We also need to think about you.'

'I'm fine. Really. Never a day's illness. I can cope with one kidney. Wouldn't that solve everything? Wouldn't that make her better? Having one of my kidneys?'

He was calming her, a hand on her shoulder. 'Even if that were the best solution for your mother, it's not an automatic option. You might not be a suitable donor. We would have to see if your blood and tissue are a match, but first we would need to consider whether your own health would allow it.'

'I told you, I'm fine.'

'This type of diabetes is hereditary. Any child of a parent with MODY has a fifty per cent chance of inheriting the condition. You are, what, twenty now?'

'Twenty-two.'

'You should sign up with a GP, Kelly. A doctor to help you deal with any symptoms, or with any other medical complications in your life. Yes, conventional medical help, but I'm sure you can see the sense of having the option of both worlds.'

'Yes. Maybe. I'll think about it.'

'Think seriously. Meanwhile, there is a simple predictive test that we can do, to establish whether you have inherited the gene from your mother. That has to be the first step.'

The first step, so innocent. A simple blood sample, almost forgotten by the time the results came back. Roz was home, being nursed and bullied by her daughter, having good days, sometimes almost back to her old self, tramping the fields and counting lambs, talking to her herbs, serenely meditating. But having bad days too. While Roz had still been too weak and vulnerable to object, she and Kelly had signed on with the local surgery. As Kelly had explained, it didn't mean they ever had to see a doctor unless they chose to.

Free will. It was enough for Roz to allow Dr Matthews to call once or twice to check on her.

The surgery notified Kelly that the results of her test were back.

'I'm clear,' she said, bursting in on her mother who was pottering gently in the kitchen. 'No trace of your naughty genes.'

Roz sat down heavily on the farmhouse chair, dislodging the disgruntled cat. 'You mean – what did they say? That you and I—'

'It means I haven't got this MODY mutation. It was fifty-fifty, and I got the right fifty. Don't worry, I'm sure you've

14

passed on plenty of other nasties to me.'

'I have?'

'Who knows? Do you have any more nasties you haven't told me about? Sudden baldness at forty? We'll find out soon, won't we.' Kelly filled the kettle, feeling light as a feather herself, and baffled that her mother wasn't similarly elated. 'Anyway, this test was just for the one gene, so I may never know about the others.'

'Oh.' Roz was smiling at last. 'And you're clear. Oh, Kelly.' She was up and hugging her, with a small wince of pain.

'Come on, sit down again. What sort of tea do you want?'

'The nettle and parsley? Kelly, I am so pleased. But I knew that you would be all right.'

Kelly smiled. Back to normal – her mother sublimely confident again that things would sort themselves out. 'The best thing is that maybe I can help you.'

'You do help me, sweetheart. All day and every day. You help me too much.' There were tears in Roz's eyes as she reached out for her daughter's hand. 'You shouldn't be here, stuck with me. You should be away, at college, getting that degree, making a life for yourself.'

'I am making a life for myself. The life I want.'

'But you don't want to be nursing me for the rest of my life.'

'Yes, but maybe I won't need to. That's the point. Now that I know I'm not going to get this moddy noddy thing, there's nothing to stop me giving you one of my kidneys.'

'No!' Roz looked appalled. 'No! I won't hear of it.'

'I've got two, you know, both as healthy as the rest of me. I'll be just as good with one and if you have the other, you'll be back to normal. See?'

But Kelly knew that look on her mother's face. She didn't want Kelly to have a needless operation. The mere mention of it was filling her with an undefined fear. Kelly could feel it. She could read every fleeting nuance of her mother's feelings; the telepathy of their lifelong closeness. 'Surgery doesn't kill, Mum. It's all safe these days. You won't lose me on the operating table.'

'You can't be sure of that.'

'I am sure.' It was important to be firm and confident when Roz's anxieties took hold. 'Look, nothing's going to happen any time soon. I'm not rushing off to hospital tomorrow. But we can be prepared. They can at least do tests, to see how well our blood and tissue match. Then—'

'Don't, Kelly.' Roz stood abruptly. She leaned on the sink, staring out of the window. 'Don't let them do any more tests, please.'

'It would just be a simple test, Mum.'

'Don't do it, please. I don't want to lose you.'

'A test isn't going to kill me. An operation won't kill me. Nothing will kill me.'

Roz turned, tears streaming down her face.

Kelly hugged her. 'I promise; it's just a test to see if there's a match.'

Roz's breast was rising and falling like a stormy sea. 'What if there is no match?'

'Then they can't use my kidney, that's all. But I'm hoping there will be a really good match.'

'And if there isn't?'

'I told you.'

Roz pulled back, covering her face with her hands. 'I don't want tests. I don't want to know.'

'Mum?' Kelly took her hands, lowering them from her face. This terror wasn't about kidneys or operations. It was

16

something else. 'What's the matter? What don't you want to know?'

'I don't want you to give me a kidney.' Roz's blurred eyes were wandering, looking at anything but Kelly.

'No, that's not what you meant. What don't you want to know?'

For a second, she could feel the great wall of resistance in her mother, straining for survival, before it crumbled like a collapsing dam.

'I don't want to know if you're not my daughter!'

Kelly stared at her, aghast at the terror engulfing her mother. Then she absorbed the words. 'What do you mean? Of course I'm your daughter. Why on earth—?'

'Because.'

Roz returned to the chair. She sat, looking at her hands.

'When I was in hospital, in the maternity ward with you… They put labels on all the babies. I woke up one night. There was some row going on outside the room. I went out, stopped a nurse, asked her, what was the fuss about. She told me that someone had muddled up some of the labels. On the babies. She said it was all right, I wasn't to worry. I tried not to worry, Kelly. I tried. But I always kept wondering, what if they'd mixed up your label and given me another baby? I kept looking at you, looking into your eyes and I was so sure I knew you. But I couldn't stop worrying. I tried to tell myself it didn't matter. As long as I didn't know for sure, they couldn't take you away. I didn't want to know. But now… If you have these tests, I'll have to know. Don't you see?'

Kelly took this in, automatically tending the kettle and the tisanes and the mugs, mopping up spilt water. It explained so much – her mother's neurotic fears for Kelly, her perpetual anxiety. A seed of terror planted in a young

17

girl, in hospital, in a state of hormonal riot. A girl not capable of understanding that it didn't matter.

That was Kelly's sole thought, without a moment of doubt; it didn't matter. But then she was already much older than her mother had been then. More mature, less mentally chaotic.

She waited for Roz's eyes to focus on her. Eyes full of desperation, awaiting the executioner. Then Kelly smiled, as only she could smile. A broad beaming smile. 'Mum. Of course you are my mother. You've been my mother all my life. In every way that really counts. So maybe, supposing there really had been a mix-up, someone else had a claim on me for a few hours. But you've been my mother for twenty-two years. Nothing can change that. It's all that matters. Did you think, if I found out, that I'd stop loving you?'

Roz was looking at her like a child, waiting for reassurance. Wanting to believe.

Then the first worm of doubt in Kelly... 'If there was a swap, would you stop thinking of me as your daughter? Is that it? You'd want to find the other girl and claim her instead?'

Roz shook her head. 'No! You could never stop being my daughter. When I looked at you, when you were just a wrinkled red bawling baby, you were mine, all I wanted. But I've always been so scared that if you found out, you'd want to go and find her. Your real mother.'

'You are my real mother. Whatever. I promise you, whatever the tests show, I am your daughter and you are, always were, always will be, my mother.'

ii

Vicky

'I like it when they're unconscious. So much more co-operative.' Zoe Tyler's laugh distintegrated for a second on the laptop screen, as the Skype connection threw a hissy fit. 'I don't mind getting really hands on. Not nearly as squeamish as I thought I'd be. It's when they start talking I go to pieces.'

Vicky Wendle smiled. 'Maybe you should go for forensic pathology. They'll never answer back on the autopsy slab.'

'I hadn't thought of that! Brill. Except I really wanted obstetrics.'

'Perfect. Babies can't talk at you.'

'No, but their mothers can.' Zoe shuddered. 'I don't know how you coped in oncology. Doesn't matter what we've been taught, I just sound like I'm talking by rote. Mitchelson said you were a natural.'

'Did he?' Vicky knew she was far more communicative with the patients than with her lecturers and fellow students, but she hadn't expected anyone to notice. She felt quietly flattered.

'But then you're his star, you and James "Actually My Uncle" Danvers. Drew says – oh yes, Drew's party, Saturday, are you going? I thought, if you were—'

'I don't think so,' said Vicky, slowing the words so her haste wouldn't be too obvious. She was four years into her course, and her classmates still hadn't cottoned on that she didn't do parties. 'Think Mum's got something planned here. Look, she's coming. Better go. Talk to you about that Harper lecture this evening?'

The door of her tiny bedroom opened, and Vicky switched off. In every sense.

'Thought you'd like a cup of tea.' Her mother, Gillian, bustled in with a tray.

Vicky moved her books and files from one side of her miniscule desk to make way for it. 'Thanks.'

'Not studying too hard, I hope. We want to see something of you. But I suppose there's such a lot of work for your course.'

'Yes.'

'Oh.' Gillian frowned at the tray. 'I brought you biscuits. I suppose I shouldn't have done. Shall I take them away again?'

'Might as well.'

'All right. Well then...' Gillian hesitated, picked up the biscuit plate and an empty mug from the windowsill and added in a library whisper, 'I'll let you get on.'

The door softly closed. Vicky sat back with a sigh and picked up her fresh tea. Zoe was right, she could sit and listen to dying cancer patients with compassionate interest and discuss their most intimate issues with calm professional concern, but she couldn't speak to her mother about anything. Not properly. Not anymore.

It didn't matter. She had work to do.

And she should collect her medication. She could do that now, walk down to the chemist's. She needed some exercise, some air, even if it was only the air of Marley Farm.

Downstairs in the kitchen of her former council house on the Marley Farm estate, Gillian's mother Joan was topping up the teapot and coughing over her cigarette. Gillian watched the dangling ash about to drop off into the box of tea bags. There was absolutely no point in saying

20

anything, but she did. 'I wish you wouldn't smoke in the kitchen.'

Joan coughed again and flicked the ash, just in time, in the direction of the bin. It missed. 'My bloody kitchen, remember? No one's going to stop me smoking in my own home. Bloody Nazis, telling us what to do. We fought a war against that. Look at your father! And now they're bloody telling us where we can and can't fucking smoke.'

Gillian wanted to argue that smoking bans and the Final Solution weren't in the same league, but she held back, biting her tongue. 'I just want to keep the kitchen clean.' She wanted the house smoke-free too, but no chance with Joan there. Gillian had smoked, too, once. Long ago, before cigarettes became one of the many resolutely embraced sacrifices of her life.

Joan watched her slip Vicky's empty mug into the washing-up bowl and return the biscuits to the tin. 'I suppose you're going to be waiting on that girl hand and foot for the next month. Spoilt bloody princess, if you ask me.'

Gillian turned on the hot tap and washed plates with concentrated vigour. Concentration on something else always helped her keep her temper. 'I want her to be able to get on with her studies.'

'A bit of proper work wouldn't do her any harm for a change. Instead of all that messing about with books. Not what I'd call work.'

Gillian took a deep breath. 'Most of Vicky's course is done in hospitals, not with books. None of it is messing about, and she works a bloody sight harder than you ever did!'

'Ha! You don't know what hard work is. Slave labour in that factory. Keeping a house, and you brats, and a crippled husband on next to nothing. And what thanks do I get? This lot today—'

'Don't know they were born,' Gillian completed the sentence for her. Did Joan really believe a word of what she'd just said? She had spent her factory years happily slagging off the management, flirting with the overseers, skiving off down the Blocker's Arms with her mates. A slave to housework? Gillian would come home from school to find a ten bob note thrust into her hand to buy fish and chips, while her mother, without bothering to look at her, filled in the Pools coupon. A husband crippled enough for a scant pension, disappearing each night down the dog track.

Gillian thought of her daughter, diligently, obsessively working eighteen hours a day for her medical qualifications, and though it was pointless she had to say it. 'Vicky is a clever dedicated girl, who is going to make something of her life, and you should be bloody proud of her.'

Joan stubbed out her cigarette before it burned her fingers. 'Don't see why she's extra special just because she's got a few snotty exams. I've got seven grandchildren, and five greats. Proper ones, my own flesh and blood, *not like her*. Thinks she's so smart, but when's she going to get herself a man, eh? Not so clever in some departments, is she? I don't suppose you give a toss about grandchildren. Wouldn't be the same for you.'

Gillian stared at her, a chill in her stomach, realising, as Joan spoke, that they were not alone.

She turned her head to the kitchen door, where Vicky was standing.

'Vicky, darling, I thought you were working.'

What had she heard?

'I'm going out. To the chemist.' The girl's voice was as

emotionless as her face. Showing nothing, even when her grandmother glanced challengingly at her. 'I'll see you later.'

'Yes. I'll have lunch ready.' Gillian smiled, that bright, determined false smile that she had mastered over the years. 'Take care.'

Vicky left. Gillian stood still, tea towel clasped to her until she heard the front door click shut. Then she turned on Joan. 'Why can't you shut up? Why can't you ever bloody well shut up?'

Joan shrugged. 'Don't know what all the fuss is about. Well, I can't stand here gossiping all day. Meeting Bill at ten. You want this tea?'

Vicky walked. The one good thing about the Marley Farm estate was that if you wanted a walk, you could walk for miles, without getting anywhere. Only five hundred yards to the chemist on the Parade, but she took the long way round. And round. Walking fast. It was good exercise. She made a point of exercising every day. It was something that she could control. Drown out the past.

Drown out Joan. Surely she had learned to do that by now? She'd thought she'd reached the stage where the old witch was invisible to her, her snide comments nothing but the faint drone of distant traffic.

But Joan could still sting like a viper's fangs. 'Seven grandchildren...proper ones...my own flesh and blood, not like her.'

Gillian always called her 'Gran', as if endless repetition would make it true, but Joan would never be 'Gran' to Vicky. She had never behaved like other people's grans. This explained why not. Joan wasn't really Vicky's grandmother.

Vicky walked. Past the half-hearted multi-storey block

23

at the end of the Ring, through the equally half-hearted industrial estate that clustered round the link road.

Joan had never said it outright before, but there'd been ample hints about 'gratitude' and 'burden'. Snide remarks about Gillian and Terry's inadequacies in the baby-making department. In her teens, Vicky had thought she understood. Gillian and Terry must have had trouble conceiving. They'd spent – wasted, according to Joan – all their money on fertility treatment. Vicky had assumed sperm donation, meaning Terry wasn't her biological father. That made sort of sense. Terry had never rejected her in any way, but he never seemed to know what to do or say, to be hoping for someone to tell him. Once, when she'd asked him something, he'd reached forward and ruffled her hair. Like an experiment, to see what would happen. Then he smiled and shuffled away. It hadn't shocked her to think that he wasn't genetically connected to her.

But now she realised she must have it wrong. The egg must have been donated, not the sperm. Why was that so much more disturbing? Distressing. How could it hurt her to know that Gillian wasn't related to her? She had stopped relating to Gillian so it shouldn't matter.

It shouldn't matter.

Of course it didn't. Vicky was an adult now; she could cope. She wasn't a thumb-sucking infant needing maternal hugs.

She half-marched, half-ran across the link road, through a gap between the thundering lorries, to the bridleway onto the downs. Gillian used to hold her hand when she crossed roads. A loving mother, she'd thought. She didn't think it any more – but it didn't matter. She couldn't be hurt. Not by them. Not by anyone. She could look after herself.

So why was this upsetting her? Because Gillian, who had

failed her so unforgivably, was all she had, and it was so hard, so cold, to be alone.

As hard and cold as the wind on Brewer's Down.

Gillian, alone in the house, busied herself with housework. Time to vacuum, do the stairs, get the cigarette ash out of the carpet. Try to keep the dread at bay.

What had Vicky heard?

Of course she should have told her years ago. Why hadn't she done as everyone had advised and been honest from day one?

She had been put off by her mother, that was the truth of it. By Joan's comments, her constant belittling. Whatever Gillian had said to Vicky, Joan would have spoiled it. With the cat officially out of the bag, there would have been no stopping her. As if her heavy-handed hints all these years hadn't been enough. It was a miracle this hadn't happened sooner.

Landing done, Gillian reverently pushed open the door of Vicky's room. Nothing to do. Everything neat and tidy, in its place. It had to be; the room was so small. Years ago, when Vicky was doing so well at school, accumulating so many textbooks, needing quiet space to do her homework, Gillian had suggested that Joan, who had the big room at the front, should swap rooms with her. Joan was having none of it. The house was hers, wasn't it? Damned if she was going to be turfed out of her own bedroom for a brat who should be outside playing with the other kids, not burying her head in books. No matter that widowed Joan spent five nights out of seven away from home, with her succession of 'fancy men'. Even now she was eighty and her latest, Bill Bowyer, was seventy-seven, she wasn't a woman for a cosy cup of cocoa before bed.

Night after night the big front room stood empty, while Gillian and Terry shared the smaller back room and Vicky made do with the little one over the hall. A narrow bed, a tiny dressing table that passed for a desk, a chair tucked under it so that there was room to move. Shelves on the walls, bending under the weight of books. She needed more. She deserved more. But there was no point letting her use the big bedroom in her grandmother's absence. Joan's room stank of tobacco smoke, scent and used underwear. Vicky refused point blank even to enter it.

Gillian laid a hand on the books by the closed laptop on the desk, as if to draw strength from them. Medical books. Utterly incomprehensible to her. With all her might, she had catapulted her daughter into a future beyond her own. Only now she realised that she would be left standing, watching Vicky disappear from view.

Not yet. Please God, not yet.

She put the vacuum cleaner away, wiped down the bathroom, put her apron on to start on lunch. Something healthy. Ham rolls with salad. Would that be all right? She always managed to get something wrong.

She heard the front door open; she was listening for it. Footsteps on the stairs. Gillian peeled back the wrapper from a fresh block of butter, her chest so tight she was barely breathing. If she heard Vicky's bedroom door close, what should she do? Go up to her? Or leave her to get on with her work?

She didn't have to decide. She could hear her daughter coming back downstairs. The kitchen door opened.

'Ah, there you are.' Gillian buttered furiously. 'Did you get your medicine? I'm making some rolls for lunch. Is that all right?' The knife hovered. 'Should I be using low fat spread?'

'Is Joan out?'

'Gran? Yes, gone to Bill's. Don't suppose she'll be back today. Salad cream? I never know…' She felt compelled at last to face her daughter.

Vicky stood in the doorway. A blank mask. 'Can we talk, please?'

Gillian felt her insides shrivel. 'Yes, of course.' The floor was buckling under her feet as she followed her daughter into the living room.

She sank onto the brown velour sofa, looking up at her daughter. Tall and angular. Beautiful to her mother, even if other people didn't think so. Standing there, arms folded tightly. Gillian felt a twinge of pain merely looking at her. For all her academic success, there was something about Vicky that screamed distress. Some deep anger boiling within. Was it Gillian's fault? Was it all because of this, because she had been too cowardly to tell the truth?

'Could you explain, please? I would like to know. I know you had fertility treatment. I thought it was the sperm, but it must have been the egg, if Joan thinks I'm not her real granddaughter. Is that right?' The girl's careful politeness acidified. 'I'm not her granddaughter? Thank God for that at least!'

'Oh Vicky, don't be like that. Your gran means well.' What was she doing? Defending her mother, for God's sake, just so that she could postpone talking about anything else. She met Vicky's eyes, blank behind her glasses.

'Actually…' Gillian stood up, walked to the glass cabinet, opened a drawer. Why? Was she expecting to find the Answer within, tied up with a bow? She pulled out a tissue and wiped her sweating hands.

She turned, bracing herself against the cabinet. 'None of the fertility treatment worked. Terry and I couldn't have children. We adopted you, Vicky. Please, darling, don't think—'

'Adopted?' Vicky's voice was sharp with surprise.

'You mustn't think for one moment that you've ever meant any less to us. You're every bit as precious to us as if—'

'Precious.' She repeated the word as if it were too bizarre to have any meaning. 'You adopted me. Some other woman didn't want me, so you took me in.'

'Yes. You see—'

'To this family. I didn't belong, but you brought me here.'

Vicky's voice was so even that Gillian mistook her words at first for understanding. Then she saw the tremors in Vicky's hand, the tick under her left eye, and she realised that some seething molten emotion was about to erupt.

'We wanted to give you a loving home, darling.'

'A loving home. You spent every last penny trying to conceive, and when that was exhausted, you selected me, something another woman had discarded, and put me in this loving home.' Vicky's voice was rising, her fists clenching.

'No, Vicky, it wasn't like that! I didn't think of adoption at first because the doctors talked about other things, about trying this, and then that. If I'd known I would get you, I would have gone straight for adoption from the start. You're my daughter, Vicky, my darling, all I ever wanted.'

'I'm what you wanted?' Vicky opened her arms and looked down at herself, her face twisted with challenge.

She'd taken to doing this, selling herself as an unattractive, ungainly shrew. Why? Vicky might not have a face from the cover of *Vogue*, but she would look wonderful if she made the right effort. If she bought herself some nice clothes, had her hair done, put on a bit of make-up. It wouldn't take much. It was almost as if she took satisfaction from the snide comments Joan slipped in every day. 'Never going to get yourself a man, looking like that. What's this, you off to the frump's ball? What do you want to be wearing those specs for? Men don't need women to see. You've had your hair cut. Look like a boy. But you might as well. That long straggly stuff wasn't doing you no favours. Not that long or short is going to turn you into a fairy princess.'

Gillian had spent twenty-two years trying to shield Vicky from comments like that. All Joan's granddaughters had received the same, her daughters too. The others knew how to respond. But despite Gillian's attempts to protect her, Vicky had reacted with hurt and later with contempt.

Now that same contempt was being turned full force on Gillian. Perhaps it had always been there. Contempt for a mother who allowed Joan to victimise her. A hopeless and inadequate mother, despite all her efforts.

'Vicky, you are exactly what I wanted. You are the daughter I love. I will always love. I just want you to do well and be happy.'

'Happy! You brought me here to be happy? That's a new one. I remember you wanting me to do well. Nose to the grindstone. Someone for you to push into doing all the things you weren't allowed to do. Someone to live your life for you.'

'No, that's not what I wanted!' There was a flicker of anger in Gillian too now. It helped to quell the nausea of distress. 'I wanted you to live your life.'

'But you decided what that life was to be.'

'You mean you don't want to be a doctor?'

'A bit late to ask me that now, isn't it? You were the one

29

desperate for the top grades, the posh career. "My daughter is not going to be a hairdresser." That's what you said to Amy's mum. You never asked me if I wanted to be a hairdresser.'

'Did you?'

'That's not the point.'

'Yes it is! You had the brains, you could do anything and I didn't want you to throw it all away, like everyone else round here. I pushed because I loved you, and I'm sorry if that wasn't enough for you! I love you because you're my daughter, whether I gave birth to you or not.'

Her heated response took a little of the wind out of Vicky's sails. They stood for a moment staring at each other.

'Are you going to tell me who my real mother is, then?' Words deliberately calculated to hurt. Lashing out.

Gillian took a deep breath. 'Your biological mother? I don't know.'

'You mean you won't tell me. Stupid of me to ask. For twenty-two years you haven't even bothered telling me she existed. That I was just bought over the counter.'

'You weren't bought! You were found. Aban—' Gillian stopped, biting on the word.

'Abandoned? Oh great! Chucked away!'

Vicky put her knuckles to her mouth. Gillian reached out but she flinched.

'No! Don't – I need to think. Just – leave me alone.'

She ran, blundering up the stairs blindly, slamming the door of her room.

Gillian slumped onto the sofa, acid in her stomach, an iron band tightening round her head. For years she had shied away from this moment, dreading how badly it might go. Now she knew. This badly. Worse than her worst nightmares.

Her palms were sticky with sweat. She forced herself up, back to the kitchen, and held her hands under the taps, numb, not even sure if the water was freezing cold or scalding hot.

Instinctively, hopelessly, she finished making up the rolls.

Vicky's room was a prison, the walls edging in to crush her. But when, on the point of exploding, she rushed out, gulping the damp air, heading wildly down the road, she realised that there was nothing to do but keep walking. She had nowhere to go.

The Downs had offered her no answers in the morning, so she walked the other way, into town. It really didn't matter.

She found herself, briefly, at the gates of her old school, gripping the bars. Why had she come here? Because it had been a place where she used to learn, to feel in control. But it had no answers to offer this time.

She finished up in the town centre, marching through the shopping centre, up the High Street, round the town hall, down the High Street, through the shopping centre. She couldn't keep this up for ever. It wasn't helping, any more than the school gates had done. She emerged from the centre, into daylight, looking across the square with its patches of worn grass and its concrete tubs of bulbs, into the glass wall of the library. Her natural home, the place where she always sought answers.

The library.

It stared her in the face, the newspaper for the year of her birth, a great volume like the book of judgement, opened up to pronounce her fate. She'd hoped she might find some small snippet, some tiny clue, but there was nothing tiny

31

about it. The big story of 1990, it seemed. So obvious. The woman who claimed her baby was snatched.

She read, devouring every word, absorbed and yet detached, because it was too unreal.

The story unfolded. The woman claimed… The police suspected… The public thought…

It was true. Behind all the claims and suspicions, Vicky held the truth within her, like a hard, sharp jewel. She was the missing child. Snatched. That's what Gillian had done. Snatched her. Taken her home to Joan.

The library swam around her. Vicky shut her eyes, forcing her breathing to steady. The woman, her real mother – where was she now? In the hefty volume of the collected *Lyford Herald*, the story ran for a few weeks, then petered out. Was that all there was?

She enquired about the story and was directed to the clippings section of the local history library, with folders on every possible subject – factory closures, royal visits, council rebellions, accidents at sewage works. Pamphlets, articles, postcards even, collected, collated, indexed and cross-referenced. It was easy to find her story: it had a folder of its own. The same articles she'd just found in the *Herald* and other papers, with updates from later years. The latest clipping was less than a month old.

Vicky stood staring at it. It gave a name, a place. It was enough.

iii

Mrs Parish

'Mrs Parish.' The tone was hostile, struggling to be polite, as if the speaker would much rather have spat.

She stopped at the foot of the stairs and turned. Mrs Bone was peering round her front door, lips pursed. 'Mrs Parish. The graffiti. It's there again.'

'I didn't put it there.'

'No, well, I never said you did, but we all know why it's there, don't we. And it's not nice! None of it's nice.'

'It's not nice for me either.'

'Whose fault's that?' Mrs Bone slammed her door shut.

Mrs Parish continued up the stairs. Fifth floor flat. She could have taken the lift, but she'd made that mistake a month ago. She'd found herself trapped with a burly resident who felt obliged to make his feeling clear with his fists. When she escaped, someone called the police. Not an ambulance, just the police.

The latest incident in the park had set off the usual ritual – the tip-off to the local papers, the carefully legal tabloid sniping, then the abusive letters, the graffiti, the vigilante rage. Every few years it flared up, usually ending in an assault, a trip to the hospital. She knew by now how to handle it: wait for things to die down, then she'd quietly move on, find a new flat where her neighbours didn't know her.

The solution was simple. She knew it. Everyone knew it. She should move out of the area. But she wouldn't. Not till she had her answer.

She was out of breath when she reached her own front door. A red spray can had been used. Lots of it, randomly,

33

like blood splatter. The words 'Baby Killer' were scrawled across the door and onto the adjoining wall. Probably a dog turd shoved through the letterbox too. There usually was.

Then she noticed the figure.

Hunched, at the end of the corridor, hood up, rising from the ground now like an evil imp.

Her fingers fumbled with her key. She could feel the month-old bruises on her cheek flare up in anticipation, as the figure strode forward.

Then the hood went back. Not a hoodie but a cagoule, not a boy but a girl. A young woman, lank hair, long face white and desperate. No evident hatred, but the girl was strangely rigid.

'You're the one, aren't you?' the girl demanded. 'The woman everyone said killed her baby.'

She stood, equally rigid. 'I did not.'

'1990. It was you? The papers—'

'The papers got it wrong.'

'I know!'

It wasn't what she was expecting. Mostly, when she was recognised, her accosters said, 'Liar! You murdered her. We know the truth.'

She waited, her fingers twisting the key back and forth, something to concentrate on.

The girl lifted her arms, not to strike, but to reach out. 'I'm her! I'm your daughter. I was the stolen baby.'

Such insane eagerness. Of course, now it made sense. It was another of those deranged fantasists, or the heartless con artists. Every so often they popped up. She had given up trying to fathom why. Mad fixation, or some idea of wringing money out of her, or maybe just a hope of notoriety. Once, years ago, she'd have felt a wild lurch of hope, a racing pulse and a catch in her throat as she stupidly dared to believe. Now she knew better.

'No.' She spoke coldly, tired of the situation already. 'You are not my daughter.'

'But I am!'

The girl came forward, crowding in on her, as she fumbled and finally succeeded in opening the door. 'Get away from me. I know you're not my daughter, you understand? I know. I don't know what sort of freak you are and I don't care. Just go away.'

Mrs Parish shut the door in the girl's face. Through the panels, she could hear her, voice raised almost to a scream.

'Why? How can you know? Because you lied? Was that it? I wasn't snatched, you really tried to kill me.' She was thumping on the door. Would the lock hold? 'It didn't work! I didn't die!'

The hammering slowed, like a failing heartbeat. 'I didn't die.'

Mrs Parish waited for the silence to settle. It would pass, this episode of insane misery. She opened the cupboard under the sink, took out cleaner and a scrubbing brush, then put the kettle on. When she was sure the mad girl had gone, she'd deal with the graffiti.

iv

Kelly

'Just leave that for a moment,' said Kelly.

Roz laid the knife on the chopping board.

'Doc wants us to try this,' said Kelly, holding the cotton bud ready. 'A new way of testing blood sugar levels they want to check out. Might as well give it a go.'

'If you think so,' said Roz with comfortable unconcern, opening her mouth to let Kelly swab the inside of her cheek. 'It's all voodoo if you ask me.'

'Quack experiments,' Kelly agreed, with a shrug. 'But what the hell, if it keeps them happy.'

Keep everyone happy. Especially Roz, who trusted her implicitly. It was fine with her that her daughter was in charge. Control was something Roz had never been comfortable with.

Prompted by guilt, perhaps, Kelly's mind pictured her mother's face, thirteen years ago. A face so rigid with purpose that it had seemed to belong to a different person. Eight-year-old Kelly had been more disturbed by that look on her mother's face than by the cause of it. She could recall her mother treating the bruises on her cheek, but she could only vaguely recollect being hit.

She'd known that the shadow of violence lurked in the small terraced house in Milford Haven, although she had never witnessed it. She'd only seen her mother weeping occasionally, or dabbing make-up on a bruise. Until that day, Kelly had never been the recipient of Luke's drunken fists.

Luke Sheldon was a well-meaning man on good days. Even affectionate. Catch him in the right mood and there was nothing he liked better than to take Kelly to the swings, buy her ice creams, promise treats, everything a father was supposed to do. But when he drank there was no holding him. Everything irritated him and then the violence would begin.

Kelly, looking back, could understand her mother. Each time, afterwards, Luke would apologise, and each time Roz, incapable of contemplating a life alone, would accept his promise that it wouldn't happen again. But when he hit

Kelly, then the tigress inside Roz woke. While Luke went raging back to the pub, she packed a few things, bundled Kelly into her coat and walked out for good.

It had only been a brief moment of decisiveness, but it had been enough to wash mother and daughter onto a new track, first to a battered wives' refuge, where someone had helped Roz find a job at a supermarket. A proper job, with regular hours, fixed pay days and National Insurance stamps. Something so normal that Roz had always believed it utterly beyond her.

Kelly knew that her mother, after walking out on her husband, had desperately longed to return to the safety of their commune days, before Luke; those gilded days when they had lived first in tepees on the hills, then in an old farmhouse, with Roger and Mandy and Bo and Tig and Pete and Ieuan and Gish and all the others. It had been a glorious time for Kelly, thriving in the messy crèche, and it had given Roz all the reassurance and support she'd needed.

Roz's yearning to recreate the magic of the commune had been their eventual salvation. The commune had kept animals; Roz would do the same. To begin with there were three chickens in the backyard of their new council house. Kelly took charge of them, selling the eggs. Roz had helped with the commune's herbal remedies, so she started brewing them again, and thanks to her daughter's brazen salesmanship, found herself supplying some of the more quirky local shops. She had practised yoga with Mandy; Kelly urged her to take a proper course. When the instructor retired, Kelly prompted her mother to volunteer as teacher. Kelly set her up as an aromatherapy consultant.

It all worked perfectly. The adolescent daughter advertised, booked halls, paid the bills and took the money, and Roz serenely held her classes and consultations. Finally,

Kelly guided her, step by step, through all the complications of getting the lease on Carregwen. Roz Sheldon might never be able to own property, but she longed for a home, not just accommodation provided by the council. A patch of Planet Earth to make her complete.

Leaving Luke had paid off. And it had been for Kelly.

Kelly understood her mother better now. That fantastic suspicion planted by the nurses talking of mixed-up labels, explained Roz's anxieties. Roz had always nursed a paralysing fear of the 'Authorities', the men in suits, the women with thin lips and sharp eyes who were waiting to take away the only thing that really mattered to her. Only when they were finally installed in Carregwen, with their herbs and hay, and their sheep, two goats, three ducks and a dozen hens, had Roz at last begun to believe that the State might not snatch Kelly away.

By then Kelly had been old enough to resist any snatching. A girl who knew her own mind, who could organise without being bossy, who could keep the peace without rolling over.

Roz had even offered to let go, urging Kelly to try for university as her teachers had wanted. Urging with most of her heart and soul, and the little part of her that had hung back had rejoiced in a very shamefaced way when Kelly refused.

Kelly wasn't ambitious. She wanted what she already had – liberty, food to eat, enough money for today, time for tomorrow, friends and lovers, and a home so lost in the hills that no one was ever going to bang on the wall and tell her to turn the music down. To appease her mother and teachers, she had gone to the local college and taken a course in marine biology, on the strength of which she now worked part-time with the National Park. Reasonable

38

money by local standards, supplemented by work as a barmaid at the Mill and Tuppence, occasional demonstrations of willowcraft and help with a few boat trips in the summer. Why would she want more?

The problem was, she didn't want less either. She didn't want to lose her mother. Which was why she was determined to go to any lengths to sort this thing out. Solve once and for all this riddle of the switched labels.

Leaving her mother chopping parsley, she carried the precious swab up to her bedroom and slipped it into a plastic bag, pushing it, with the forms, under her bed. One down.

It was odd, considering how open and honest and forthright she was, that Kelly found it remarkably easy to lie.

V

Vicky

Nearly dinner time. Vicky had been out all day. Gillian breathed an explosive sigh of relief when she heard the door open. She'd been nursing the worry all afternoon that Vicky wouldn't come home at all. Now she had, and one good thing had come of her absence: it had given Gillian time to prepare. She was going to explain everything, put it right.

'Vicky!' she called up, as her daughter was on the point of disappearing into her room.

Vicky looked down at her over the banister, her face a mask of loss and misery, and, worse than either, hatred. Gillian's stomach tightened.

'Yes?' That cutting politeness.

'Can you come down, please. I want to talk.'

Vicky paced down, slowly, till she was eye to eye with her mother. 'You want to talk.'

'I want to explain. About the adoption.'

'Do you?'

'Yes, I know I've left it far too late. I was wrong. I should have told you, years ago, from the start. I wasn't trying to deceive you. I was just waiting for the right time, and it was always, always the wrong time.'

'I'm sure it must have been very difficult for you.'

'I didn't want Gran to upset you.' The bitterness Gillian felt for her own mother burst out. 'I didn't want her poisoning things, if I tried to explain!'

'Joan has been poisoning things all my life. I don't recall you ever stopping her.'

'I tried! I did try. I know things haven't been ideal.'

'*Ideal.*'

'If we could have afforded a place of our own, we'd have kept you right away from her. But we couldn't, and we had to make the best of things.'

'Joan isn't the best, she's the worst. She's evil! And you. Everyone. You're all evil!'

All civility was forgotten now. Vicky was shaking as Gillian had never seen her shake. What had happened? The mention of adoption seemed to have triggered a tidal wave of resentment.

Vicky breathed deeply, each breath a shudder. Then she ran back up the stairs.

'Vicky?'

The bedroom door slammed.

Gillian returned to the living room, sat down on the couch and rocked, her head in her hands. She wanted a cigarette. Never, in the last twenty-five years of abstinence, had she wanted a cigarette quite so much.

She should phone Terry at the garage. This was a family crisis, he should be here. But what was the point? Terry wouldn't know what to do. He had never understood any of it.

Tea. She needed tea and a Disprin. Put the kettle on, make a pot. Vicky must need one and it would be an excuse to speak to her.

She stirred the pot slowly, pushing tea bags round and round, when she heard Vicky's bedroom door open again. Gillian nerved herself and went to the hall.

Vicky was standing there, jacket on, suitcases at her feet, mobile phone in her hand, thumbing the keys.

'Vicky? What are you doing?'

'I'm going back to my digs in London.'

'But you've only just got here. I thought you'd be here for a month.'

'I can't stay here. Not with that evil bitch Joan. Not with any of you.'

'I'll speak to Gran, I promise. I'll make her—'

'You won't make her do anything. You'll curtsy round her like you always do. But she's not my Gran, just as you're not my mother, and I don't have to stay here anymore!'

Gillian floundered. This wasn't about adoption, this must be something more. She had to understand. 'Please, Vicky, don't go. You can't go like this. Let's talk, please. Tell me. Whatever it is, we can talk it through.' She followed her out.

'We had twenty-two years to talk it through. But you never talked. Just like you never listened and you never saw. Excuse me. I've got work to do. I need to concentrate. Goodbye.'

'No, wait!' Gillian followed as Vicky dragged her suitcases along the street. 'You don't want to go by bus. Your father will be home soon. If you really want to go back, Dad can give you a lift.' If she could keep her here, please God, another hour, two, surely she'd change her mind.

'I'm fine with the bus.' Vicky was almost at the bus stop and already a bus was heaving into view over the brow of the hill, ready to sweep down Drover's Way and scoop her up.

'Please, Vicky!'

'Just go home, Mum.'

'Come back with me, please.'

'No. I need to get away, okay? Go home.' Vicky sounded so bitter.

The bus drew up and the doors hissed open.

'I saw her.' She looked at Gillian just once, her face blank. 'My real mother. I saw her.'

Hiss. Doors closed. Gillian was left standing.

Vicky found a seat. She sat, back rigid, hands gripping the handles of her bags as if she would snap them off.

All that she'd kept bottled up for the last five years was roaring around inside her, ripping her apart. 'Get over it.' That was a phrase she'd adopted as her motto, cruel but intelligent. But it was a joke: she hadn't got over it at all. It had been waiting all this time to eat her up. Quiescent before, because there was nothing she could do, but now…

This new truth hung before her, blocking her vision. Everything she'd been through hadn't been inescapable fate. It should never have happened. She should never have been there, with Gillian and Joan. She should have been with another mother. Her first thought, that Gillian had been an evil child-snatcher, had made it easy. But no. She hadn't been lying about adoption. The lie had been in the tale of baby-snatching. A lie told by a woman who had wanted Vicky dead twenty-two years ago and who now slammed the door in her face.

She was just a piece of flotsam for them to discard and pick up at will, a toy for their evil games. How could she just get over it? She was hurt, she wanted to hurt back, to give voice to this sharp bright hatred that almost smothered the pain.

Almost.

The bus moved off.

Gillian stood there, remembering her daughter's face twisting in loathing: 'That evil bitch Joan.'

She turned, barely aware of what she was doing until she was almost back at the gate. Then she marched into the house. Upstairs, to the big room that should have been Vicky's. The room that needed fumigating and cleansing. Scent bottles. A porcelain figurine holding rings. Photos of Joan in younger days, with grinning men lost in the fog of time. The lewd glass clown Bill had given her. Silk scarves and fake fur. Apricot wig on its stand. Clutter that had no right to be here.

One by one, Gillian picked them up and threw them. She picked up a brass pot and thrashed at the glass, china, mirrors. Anything that wouldn't smash she ripped.

Then she sank down in the mayhem and sobbed.

CHAPTER 2

i

Gillian

20th November, 1989.

Gillian could see the date on the letter, clasped in the curate's hands, but his thick, strong fingers concealed the rest.

20th November 1989. Two days ago. Another wave of panic seized her. Had she got it wrong? Had she wilfully refused to see the word 'Rejected'? She read it five, six, seven times and still she was terrified she had it wrong.

But it couldn't be wrong, could it, or Philip would have said so when he'd read it? Perhaps he was praying that she accept her disappointment with grace. No. She must stop doubting. And she really ought to be listening to the curate, not itching to snatch the letter back, while he was addressing the Almighty. Giving thanks, he said. Thanks. Thanks. Thanks.

'Jesus, we thank you for seeing into our hearts and for your care of Gillian through this time of worry, of hopes and fears.'

He was always on such cosy conversational terms with his God. Her God too, she supposed, though she wasn't sure she believed in Him. This was absurd, celebrating her momentous news with this embarrassing chat with Jesus.

But she'd had to tell someone. As soon as she'd ripped

44

open the envelope and seen the words Adoption Agency, scanned down and read the verdict – Approved – she'd needed someone to tell her that she wasn't dreaming. But who could she go to? Not her mother, not yet at least. And not Terry, until he came home from the car plant. With the constant threat of redundancies she couldn't risk phoning him there. But she could tell Philip. He had, after all, been one of her referees for the agency.

'And we know that you will be with us, always, Jesus, holding us in your hand…'

This was the price for her hypocritical conniving. She had never been a churchgoer. Occasional visits to Sunday School at the corrugated Gospel Hall in Oswald Street maybe, when she was a child, so that Joan could get her brats from under her feet, but she had come away without any religious conviction, just some lurid imagery of lion's dens, loaves and fishes and flaming heads. She had, of course, dutifully sailed down St. Mark's aisle to marry Terry in her white polyester and her sprouting chrysanthemum of nylon netting, but she hadn't been near the church again until adoption had taken over her life. Then she'd started going to St. Mark's in earnest, even dragging Terry with her sometimes.

It would look good on the application, she had thought shamelessly. But it was plain superstition too. If some all-powerful God really was up there, she wanted Him on her side.

She wasn't the only newcomer to the congregation. The ugly brick St. Mark's, in the middle of Marley Farm, had moved in an Evangelical direction under Philip's enthusiastic guidance. Guitars and dance and drama, and impromptu shouts of 'Praise Him', from the congregation, which had tripled in recent years. Out with unctuous solemnity and in with loud born-again certainties.

'You know, Lord Jesus, what is best for each and every one of us. Give us your grace to believe and to trust. If it is your will that a child should be given into Gillian's care, we know you will guide all and give wisdom where it is needed, to the mother in her hour of doubt and distress, and to the authorities and to Gillian herself.'

Head bowed, perched on the edge of the sofa, Gillian found herself squirming. This wasn't what she wanted, to be told that they were all puppets of a God who might, if he chose, wrench a child from its mother for Gillian. She understood that her dream required some other woman to die, or be pushed to breaking point, or have her child snatched away by police and social workers, but just for now, she wanted to see the matter in less specific terms. She wanted to be told that all manner of things would be well. She wanted the mysterious quiet of an old church and a statue of the Virgin, eternal mother, holding out a child to her. Not Philip asking his chum Jesus to sort out the bureaucracy.

She waited for him to finish. '…and we put our complete faith in you, Lord Jesus, Amen.'

He was on his feet again, beaming down on her. 'You know that I don't encourage child baptisms, but when the time comes, I'll be delighted to hold a—'

She raised a hand in alarm. Superstition again. Bad luck to speak of it as fixed. 'Terry and I have just been accepted as potential adopters. It might be months before they match us to a child. It might never happen.' She forced herself to say it bravely. Merely to be accepted, after all those interviews and visits, all that desperate waiting, was a triumph in itself, but in reality she was still today what she had been yesterday – a childless woman, growing older, year in, year out, with nothing but desperate hope to see her through each day.

'Of course, Gillian, of course. But I have complete faith in the guiding mercy of Jesus and I know you have too. I'll pray for you, Gillian, and so will many others. We'll see you and Terry on Sunday?'

'Oh, yes. Yes of course.' There would be a special loud smug prayer for them, she knew, and many 'hallelujahs', and she would have to smile and endure. She would have to persuade Terry to come and share the embarrassment.

'And I'm sure your mother, Mrs Summers, is delighted for you.'

Gillian stared across the room at the cork-board over his desk. Church notices, a calendar, a wax crayon drawing of a camel. Done by one of his kids at the Jesus Club? 'I haven't had a chance to tell her yet.' Thinking: please, please God, give me a child to scribble camels with wax crayons.

And then she pictured Joan. She would have to tell her. Knowing that Joan would skilfully poison all the joy out of the day.

She went with Philip's blessing. And with the even greater blessing of that letter. Approved, accepted, approved, accepted. She repeated it over and over as she walked. Gillian Wendle had been accepted as a potential adopter. Neither Joan nor the malignant forces of the Marley Farm estate had destroyed her chances. That was the real miracle and she earnestly thanked God. For months now, she had lived in dread of the mistimed visit, the interview when Joan would show her worst, when the estate would erupt with drunken racist yobs and police sirens, or when Terry would walk in to say he'd been made redundant. But divine providence had been with her.

It seemed that the house in Drover's Way had worked for her, not against. It had been Gillian's home since the age of three, when Joan Summers, with a crippled husband, two

47

small children and a third imminent, had triumphantly claimed the brand new council house on the muddy building site that was hatching into Marley Farm Estate. Drover's Way was still extending along the hill, closes and crescents blossoming in the post-war drive to house the nation. Marley Primary Schools were rising from the mire, bright brick and glass and shiny tiles, amidst green playing fields. Parades of shops with maisonettes were springing up along Marley Ring. The sun was rising on a glorious new world.

Twenty-seven years later, when she and Terry moved back in with widowed Joan, to help buy the council house, the Marley estate had sunk into weary hopeless disrepute. Graffiti festooned the unkempt Marley Junior School, with its leaking Portakabins. On the Parade, barred windows protected seedy off-licences and video rental shops. Two houses had gone up in flames in the '81 wave of rioting. Shady deals were done on every littered corner.

Gillian simmered with quiet resentment about the house. Her wedding had been the most wonderful day of her life, not because she felt so beautiful or because Terry was the Romeo of her dreams, but because it meant escape from Drover's Way and from Joan. Now she was back, and trapped once more, because they had no choice. Council accommodation was no longer being allotted except to the most desperate, and with their savings all gone and rents rising, helping Joan with the mortgage was the only way they could keep a roof over their heads. If it meant living with Joan, then she'd just have to deal with it. Somehow. It was bad enough that the address would never impress an adoption agency. Joan's presence was a far worse blight, though Gillian had remorselessly painted it as a blessing, to anyone who'd listen.

She turned off Drover's Way into Ashley Close. Number 7. Sid Walker's house. Two cars parked up on the concrete, neither of them roadworthy. Gillian automatically went round the back. Only the police entered through front doors round here.

'Hello?' she called, into the cluttered, grease-smeared kitchen.

'Eh?' Sid appeared, unshaven and bleary-eyed, in string vest, a copy of the *Sun* in his hand. 'Oh, er, Gill, right.' He leaned back to call up the stairs. 'Joanie!'

An irritated, gravelly reply.

'Your girl's here.' He turned back to Gillian. 'Best come in then. She'll be down. Want a cuppa?'

'No thanks. I've just had one.' She was parched, but she wasn't going to sit drinking tea with Sid and her mother among the detritus of last night.

Flop, flop, down the stairs. Joan, hair on end, last night's heavy make-up smudged, her bony frame wrapped in a flowered dressing gown. 'Oh. It's you. Are you going to the shops? Get us some fags, will you?'

'I came to tell you we've had the letter. We've been approved.'

'Approved? Approved for what?' Joan was busy lighting her last cigarette, coughing over it. Deliberately obtuse.

'Approved for adoption. Terry and me.'

'Fucking hell, another bleeding brat around the house.' Joan opened the fridge and took out a bottle of sour milk. 'You got the kettle on then, Sid?' No love, of course, but no outburst of irate complaint either. It was as good as Gillian was going to get.

'Philip thought you'd be delighted for us.' When had she learned sarcasm?

'Oh the God Botherer, tell him before you tell your own

mother, do you? But then that's you all through. Always thinking of yourself first. Must have a baby. Never mind what anyone else wants. It's Terry I feel sorry for.'

Gillian took a deep breath. All her life she had been taking deep breaths. Gillian the appeaser, holding her tongue, not snarling back.

Joan slopped tea into a mug and shuffled back towards the stairs. 'Don't forget the fags.'

Sid scratched his belly. 'Well, it's good news, right?' He was never going to win prizes for charm – or cleaniness or grooming or humour – but he did have a grain of humanity in him. Not the worst of the men Joan had semi-permanently shacked up with since her husband's death.

Gillian forced a smile. 'Yes, it is good news. For me and Terry at least. I hope Mum will see it that way.'

'Oh she's all right,' rumbled Sid.

How exactly was she all right? wondered Gillian, walking home. What had Joan Summers ever done that was right?

She had come through the interviews with Claire, came the reply. What miracle had made Joan come across as a good-humoured rough diamond of a granny, offering all the support that Gillian would need? It must have been the hand of God, because it couldn't possibly have been intentional on Joan's part.

'My mother lives with us,' Gillian had explained, trying to sound positive. 'That's not a problem, is it?'

'It could be a big plus,' Claire had assured her. 'She's in good health?'

'Oh yes,' Gillian was able to say, quite truthfully. Not a hope in hell that some kindly plague would carry her mother off.

'If you were looking after an elderly invalid, someone housebound maybe…'

'Oh no, she's fighting fit.'

Claire had beamed. 'That's excellent. As long as she's enthusiastic about an adopted baby arriving in the household, of course.'

'Oh she is,' Gillian had rushed in, almost beating Claire about the head with her assurance, as if saying it with enough conviction would make it true.

But Claire had smiled, that official smile that always lurked behind her friendliness. 'Well, I'll be able to confirm that for myself when I meet her.'

Gillian's hopes had plummeted. Had she really thought she could get through all this without Claire meeting Joan? She was doomed.

And then, against all the odds, the worst had been evaded. On the first visit, Joan had just won on the bingo and was in an almost generous mood. A mild mocking of her daughter's urge to be a mother, no more. The second time, she had merely been silent. Bored probably, waiting for Claire to go. Gillian had spent three hours in advance making the house spotless, hiding the gin bottles and the cigarettes and the dozen ashtrays. Joan had pattered off in search of her fags without Claire noticing. The third…ah, of course, Claire had come with that man, Hugh someone. A man made all the difference to Joan. She had chatted and joked with him in an easy, mischievous sort of way. He'd actually been amused by her flirtation, probably thought she was the humorous spark that would lighten the household.

Well, however it had happened, that stage of the torment was over now. Approved. Not the end. Not nearly the end. But if Gillian could only hold out, if she could only receive a child into her arms, she could prove herself as the perfect, devoted, adoring mother she knew she was destined to be. Surely there was nothing Joan could do now to spoil it?

ii

Heather

Madonna and child. Some old master's idea of perfect womanhood – smooth serene face, small smile, soft doe eyes fixed on the plump dimpled child on her knee. Heather Norris blew a raspberry at the card and opened it. From the Library. *Merry Christmas from all of us, and wishing you a bumper harvest in 1990.* Hell, had she remembered to send a card to her old colleagues? She could ransack the bureau, hope there were still one or two charity cards in there somewhere.

The Madonna and child went onto the teak fire surround, between a glittery stagecoach scene, and an inflated cartoon robin. That was closer to the truth, Heather felt, easing herself onto the sofa; a big fat bird. A stuffed turkey. She'd put on weight after Bibs was born, and now she was like a barrage balloon. That serene Virgin had never suffered from swollen ankles and constipation.

'Brm, brm, brm brm brm.' Clatter, bang, scratch. Bibs came along the hallway with the plastic car they had bought him to keep his mind off the presents he wasn't allowed to touch until Christmas Day. How much paintwork had he taken off the skirting board this time?

'Bibs. Come in here, to Mummy,' she called, too heavy, too weary to get up and go to him.

Bang. The car hit the living room door, which swung open, sending a pile of magazines to the floor. She didn't want to have to bend and pick them up.

'Brm brm brm.' Tousled fair hair, and a bottom in blue shorts, up in the air.

'Not on my feet, Bibs!' Why did her son think it funny to run a toy car over her toes? Giggling, he did it again.

'I said no, Bibs. Do it again and I'll take it away.'

He looked up at her, his three-year-old face an open book – clear eyes, pursed lips parted, trying to make head or tail of those complicated adult responses. A little boy now, becoming his own person, no longer the helpless unformed scrap of herself that Bibs the baby had been.

And now she was going back to the start. Like landing on a snake and sliding back to the beginning, but this time without the novelty factor. No excited calls from relatives asking how she was doing, no aunts bombarding her with advice and horror stories, no parcels of hand-knitting. Even the midwife seemed less interested. Or maybe it was just her. She'd been there, done that, bought the t-shirt and now it was just plain boring.

The plastic car was thumping against her toe again. Bibs pushing his luck. He caught her eye, decided against it and swivelled round on the mat, busily motoring off to the window. A very quiet 'brm brm brm'. Had she quashed him? She didn't mean to. She loved him, adored him, sometimes she felt something burst inside her when she looked at him. Maybe she had never looked like that picture of the Madonna and child, but she had felt it, when he was born. For nine months she had sailed through the world, so intensely conscious of him within her that she had felt enclosed in a bubble of love. She hadn't needed him to be born to bond with him. It had happened the second the test showed she was pregnant. Or maybe even before.

Was that why she felt so equivocal this time round, she wondered. Was she feeling sibling rivalry on Bibs' behalf? Resenting this interloper who was waiting to come between her and her darling boy.

Well, it would sort itself out. It would have to. She hauled herself up and went into the kitchen to make Bibs some lunch. Fish fingers and baked beans. He was going through a faddy phase and she felt she ought to be doing something about it. Give him something bright and imaginative, but weighed down and aching, she didn't think there was much imagination in her at the moment. Certainly no brightness.

An hour later – the kitchen strewn with the pulverised beans that Bibs had refused to eat, the boy still snivelling after their screaming match, and the living room in gloom because the light bulb had blown – Martin arrived home to find her on the sofa with a wet flannel on her brow.

'Another of your heads?'

'Yes.' She peeled the flannel away and looked at the clock. 'You're early. What's happened? They're not cutting back again!'

'No, still got my job.' Martin looked in through the kitchen door. 'Shit. Bibs not eating again?'

'Yesterday he'd only eat beans. Now he won't touch them.'

'You being a bad boy then, my son?' He had Bibs up in the air, and the child was shrieking with delight. 'Giving your mother a hard time? Yeah!'

Oh yes, make a joke of it. She watched the two of them disappear into the kitchen then called after them, 'So why are you early?'

Martin was back at the door, his mouth full of fish fingers. 'Tie i lshiw.'

'What?'

He swallowed. 'Time in lieu – for Boxing Day?'

'I thought… Oh God, is it Christmas Eve tomorrow?'

'You wanted a last minute shop, remember.'

'Oh Christ, I don't want to go shopping. I just want to go to bed.' This time last year she had actually chosen to

go into London for the day for a bout of girly retail therapy
– as pleasure! This year the thought of squeezing into the
local newsagent's made her want to lie down.

'Do we actually need to go?' Martin was hopeful. 'Are we
desperately out of anything?'

'Yes of course we are! Vegetables. Milk. Endless stuff.'

'Okay, so we'd better go then.' Willing to make the effort
and take her, just not willing to do it for her. If he did, he'd
get all the wrong things. 'Den needs stuff, I suppose. Have
you got a list for him? How was he this morning?'

'Knew who I was.' She struggled up, resentfully. 'Still hid
the housekeeping though. But at least he didn't flush it away
this time.'

Martin chuckled. Her father had senile dementia and he
could chuckle about it. But then Den wasn't his father and
he wasn't the one having to deal with it every day. That was
down to Heather, of course. Her mother had died years ago,
when she was in her teens. No one to cope with Den's funny
ways except her. Like dealing with Bibs, day in day out. No
bloody end to it.

She was snarling as she pulled her coat on. Straining to
do it up. What was it she was carrying? A baby elephant?
Not that things would be any better in a couple more
months when it was out. Weeks of screaming and sleepless
nights and frayed nerves and sore tits and mopping up, and
Bibs having tantrums and Den having to be rounded up
and Martin's firm hovering on the brink, and Martin being
lovely to everyone because he didn't have to lift a sodding
finger. Peace and goodwill on Earth. Christmas spirit? Sod
Christmas. Sod the lot of them.

Next, the battle to get Bibs into his seat in the back of
the car. Cramming herself into the front, grinding her teeth
with irritation knowing that Bibs was trying to kick the

55

back of her chair, even if she could feel nothing because he couldn't reach. She had been dwelling on her superhuman love for her son a few hours back. Right now, she just wanted to shout.

'Sainsbury's then?' asked Martin, edging the car out of the drive. 'Don't need anything in the High Street?'

'If we do, we can go without.'

Trapped in a car five sizes too small, bracing herself for every speed bump. The Hopcroft was an intricate maze of mini-roundabouts, closes and pedestrian alleys, coiling into itself on what had been farmland little more than ten years before. New-build timber-frames that had not yet warped, picture windows that had not yet let in the draught, compact porches that did not yet leak, clipped shrubs that had not yet died; the aspirational British at their surburban best. Young families, drawn by the sparkling new primary school, the closeness to the new out-of-town supermarkets, and the semi-rural Marsh Wood station for that convenient commute to London. The would-be middle class, first generation professionals and white-collar workers, triumphantly escaping from council housing and greasy overalls. People exactly like her, she supposed. She recognised them as a mass, a type, but she knew none of them.

Her father was her closest connection here, in his so-called sheltered accommodation just across the roundabout from the Hopcroft; but most days he no longer seemed to know her, and when he did he was only interested in talking about the woman two doors down, who was trying to steal his photographs, or his tea caddy, or the pigeons he had ceased to keep twenty years ago. Nothing to say about Heather, but still it was almost the sum total of her social life now – the daily visit to see that Den hadn't wandered off, left the gas on or the taps running, or set the place on fire.

No one else to talk to. There were a couple of mothers at the nursery that she had chatted to briefly, but her friends were all three miles away, on the other side of Lyford town centre, in the grid of 1930s terraces where she and Martin and Bibs had lived until six months ago. She had thought she couldn't wait to leave, to move up in the world, to escape from the miserable pensioners, the loud football fans and the corner shop that had been boarded up since the Pakistani owner had been burned out by the National Front. Now she just wanted to be back there, with friends always ready with a cup of tea whenever she dropped in.

They shouldn't have moved here to Hopcroft. They'd been planning it since before Bibs was born as a distant project, but then, when Martin miraculously walked into a new job after the shock of redundancy, worry exploding into relief had prompted them to take the plunge.

They couldn't really afford it. Even with Martin's increased pay, they would be stretched with the mortgage, and just because he had a job today, who knew what would happen tomorrow? House prices were falling now and they were saddled with it, no chance of trading down as easily as they had traded up. In a couple of years, they'd thought, with Bibs safely at school, she could think about going back to the library, part time, earning a little extra to help them eke out the budget, but of course the new baby would put that timetable way back.

They hadn't planned this second child. One day, yes, but not yet. It was only after they had exchanged contracts and were committed to the move that she'd discovered she was pregnant again. Suspected, dreaded and then finally confirmed on the day when the *Marchioness* pleasure boat collided with a dredger on the Thames. She'd felt she was part of the disaster, drowning. A month later, the Duchess of York was crowing over the expected arrival of her second child. Heather had always liked the Royals until that day. Now she resented them and their bloody palaces and their nursemaids and their hand-picked gynaecologists. Let Fergie deal with a house move, a mortgage and a new bloody baby without any bloody help!

'Look on the good side,' Martin had said. 'We're going to be a mile nearer to the hospital.' It hadn't helped. He knew, as well as she did, that this second baby had come at the worst possible moment. Why hadn't they taken more care? She had even toyed with the idea of an abortion but didn't dare to raise it with anyone. You couldn't have an abortion just because you were moving house and you were terrified of not being able to pay the bills in a year's time. Martin hadn't shared her concerns. After an initial hour of grumbling, he had decided to delight in the idea of another child.

Out of the estate onto the dual carriageway, two more roundabouts and into the tarmac sea of Sainsbury's. Fairy lights, a luminous Santa, Christmas trees in their stocking wraps still piled up hopefully at the door. The car park was packed. The 23rd of December and everyone was out, spending money because that was what Christmas was all about. Spend, spend, spend. Alcohol that she wasn't allowed to touch. Food that would sit slowly decaying in an overfilled fridge. Presents that would be glanced at with a show of enthusiasm and then discarded. Toys that required a second mortgage. They couldn't afford all this. If other people thought they could, they were just insane.

The car park was full. Martin found a space at last, at the end furthest from the store. Heather bustled to get Bibs out. Why did he have to wriggle so much?

'Just keep still, will you! Hold my hand.'

A long long walk, not what Bibs fancied. He started to drag, leaning back until he was almost sitting on the tarmac. 'Bibs! Don't do that! Come on.'

'I don't want to!'

'Come on, old son.' Martin hoisted him on his shoulders. The easy casual solution as if her irritation was totally unreasonable.

Bibs was installed in the trolley-come-pushchair. This was the bit he always liked, being pushed up and down the aisles, while she plodded on with aching back and ankles. He was quite old enough to walk beside her, but it was safer having him in the trolley. At least she knew where he was.

Up and down the aisles – that was a joke today. Jabbing and squeezing into the first aisle was as much as she could bear. She picked up a bag of tangerines and stopped. Enough.

'You read the list, I'll get them,' said Martin.

'Bananas, grapes, onions, potatoes, carrots, Brussels.' Why Brussels? No one liked them. Why waste money on something no one liked and she didn't want to cook. 'Oh for God's sake, can't we just have beans on toast and have done with it?'

Martin chuckled, as if she were joking. She leaned on the trolley as he dropped a monstrous net bag of Brussels sprouts into it.

Milk, cream, cheddar, brie, Bibs' yoghurts, bread, biscuits, mince pies… Martin dropped a multipack of crisps into the trolley. Bibs, bored with singing and kicking, started to open it.

'Not yet, Bibs!'

He ignored her.

'Not yet!' Other shoppers, crammed against her, were

looking at her. 'Leave it alone!' She snatched the bag from him.

Bibs reached for it again. She held it out of his reach, nearly hitting an old lady beside her. Bibs jumped up and down in the trolley, then fished out a packet of biscuits and dropped it on the floor.

'Bibs! You're not a bloody baby!'

She wanted to hit him. She never hit him, she didn't believe in hitting children, but she wanted to hit him now.

People pushed past, no one stopped to help. She wasn't bending down to retrieve the biscuits; they could bloody well stay there and be trampled.

Triumphant in his victory, Bibs had a packet of eggs. She yanked them from him, feeling one crack inside. 'Stop it! Do you hear me? Just stop it!'

Was she screaming? Everyone seemed to be looking at her. Then Martin was there, with a pack of beer. 'Hey, hey, hey. Come on. Bibs, put that down now.' He removed the eggs to the front of the trolley, out of Bibs' reach. 'Be a good boy for your mummy, or she might not give you a little brother or sister.'

'Don't want one,' said Bibs.

'Of course you do.'

'I don't,' said Bibs. 'Don't don't don't don't don't don't.'

'Well, tough,' hissed Heather, 'because you're stuck with it, just like me.'

Martin was still chuckling. 'Don't put it like that. You make it sound as if you don't want it.'

'I don't bloody want it! Who ever bothered to ask me if I did? We didn't plan it and we can't afford it, and we're stuck out here, and it's all very well for you going gooey-eyed over another fucking baby, but I'm the one breaking my back here. I'll be the one in hospital having my insides ripped apart. I'll be the one stuck with filthy bloody nappies, day in day out, listening to the bloody thing bawl its head off.'

Was she shouting? Screaming? Shocked faces were staring at her. Martin stood open-mouthed. Look at them all, bloody strangers telling her that she didn't count, all that mattered was this thing inside her. She didn't want it. She just wanted to be rid of everything. In a rage she hadn't realised she was capable of, she thrust the laden trolley from her, sending it charging down the aisle.

Sailing between the parting shoppers, Bibs stared back at her, a whimper already beginning. His chariot collided with a pyramid display, sending jars of mincemeat flying with a sickening shatter of glass.

iii

Lindy

'Gi's a kiss then. C'mon,' he said, unkempt and unwashed, his stubble dark with dirt.

Lindy turned her head to avoid his whisky-soaked breath, and wriggled under his arm, braced against the wall. 'Geroff me, Tyler.'

'Aw, c'mon,' he said to the wall, not realising that she was no longer there. Pissed out of his tiny mind as usual.

Lindy was already climbing the narrow stairs to the first floor landing, and the safety of her own room. The lock was crap, but she could put a chair under the handle if Tyler followed. Time was, she used to bound up these stairs out of his reach, but today she was too weary. And too bulky. She hauled herself up, listening, ready to kick out if he tried to grab her.

Nothing. She looked back. At the bottom of the stairs, Tyler had slid to the floor and was mumbling into his chest. So maybe there'd be a racket and things flying when he woke up, but for now she'd have a bit of peace. No one else in the house was stirring. They didn't usually emerge until after dark.

She pulled back the curtains. Dark January gloom. She didn't like to have the lamp on in the day. Or the heating. It was fucking freezing, but the electric fire ate money up, and she only had one 50p left. When she saw him coming, she'd switch it on for a few minutes, but better without for now.

Her coat was good and thick. And voluminous. Wide enough to wrap round an army, which was the point of course. Anyone looking at her would think she was nine months gone with triplets. She unbuttoned it and began to empty the improvised sack beneath. Soup packets. Pot noodles. Biscuits. Three apples. They were healthy, fruit and stuff, she knew that, though she'd picked them because they were easy to slip inside. Like the packet of dishcloths she'd taken, because they had been there and easy.

She had a basket too, tinned stuff and a bottle of milk. You had to buy something if you spent half an hour wandering round a shop, or people would look at you funny when you came out. Fastest way to get stopped, that. So she had bought a tin of beans, a tin of ham and four cans of the cheapest lager. 50p left for the meter. If Gary did come home today, he'd find food in the cupboard, and a beer waiting for him. It made her feel competent, a useful little housewife. Maybe he'd be glad to be home with her again.

No need to think about what he was more likely to feel when he saw her.

62

She smoothed down the old quilt covering the mattress on the floor. With one of the new dishcloths she wiped down the formica table, the cupboard, and the one-ring Baby Belling. She used the worn brush to thwack the armchair free of dust – not too hard in case it lost more stuffing. She liked housework, this making-a-home game, even if she only had one room to play it in.

All she needed now was for him to arrive. It might not be today; the grapevine might have got it wrong. And he might be going somewhere else first. With a quiver, she thought: he might not choose to come here at all, ever again.

But no, she trusted Gary Bagley to come back to her because there was really no point in thinking anything else. You had to hope, or there was nothing.

Pulling her coat back round her, she dragged one of the vinyl-covered kitchen chairs to the window and huddled down, leaning on the rotten sill and watching the street for any sign of him. Gary Bagley, her man. Her family.

A family was what Lindy Crowe wanted. A nest, safe from the hostile world, with someone she could wrap herself around. There had been a family once, six siblings and Mum and Dad, though she had been too young to remember the drunken screaming and shouting that ended with her father knifing her mother. Maybe she hungered to find a family again because she couldn't remember. Foster homes hadn't counted, even when fosterers had meant well. They had just been alien beings who had separated her from her brother Jimmy. He was the next youngest and they'd been real friends, but no one cared about that. The Home was nothing like a family. Staff too busy for anyone, and Wayne Price and his gang doing whatever they liked to the younger kids, especially the girls. Lindy had run away at ten, then at twelve, then fourteen, and had been on her own since, living rough or in squats, getting by with shoplifting and begging and tricks. Then Gary. He hadn't made everything perfect, but she had never expected that. It was enough that he called her his girl and brought her here, to 128 Nelson Street, to a house that they could pretend was home.

In some distant past, someone had turned it into bedsitters. Someone must still be paying someone rent, because the electricity meters worked, and the water was still connected, though the dozen residents treated it as a squat. She and Gary had this room. They shared the bathroom, though the bath had no plug, and the people in the basement used the bog out back, and Tyler on the ground floor usually just peed in the hall.

It was all Lindy had ever hoped for. Nothing like spending a couple of winter weeks in a shop doorway down Almeida Lane without a penny in your pocket, with a broken heel and a black eye, to teach you that a roof, any roof, a bed, any bed, and something, anything to eat, is the best life has to offer.

Something to eat. She realised she hadn't eaten since the chocolate bar she'd nicked that morning. Must be the excitement of Gary coming back. She ought to eat. She took a couple of biscuits and one of the apples. Then she returned to her window perch to wait.

Nelson Road in the twilight. Lamps coming on, shifting it into a different dimension. All through the day it rumbled with traffic taking the short cut away from the endless traffic lights on Moreton Road. Hardly any pedestrians, drab old houses silent. Then at night the residents awoke. Where were they during the day, she wondered. Some must have jobs because at night the pavements were blocked with parked cars. Others collected like moths around the laundrette, the betting shop and the two pubs. At night, vans came and went from the yard that was padlocked by day, with Alsatians growling behind the metal gates. At night, figures gathered on the corner with Heighton Street and exchanged money and packets. Lindy knew them by sight if not by name. Gary used to send her with a wad of notes to deal with them for him. He'd let her try stuff with him sometimes, though mostly he only gave her a bit of weed. She didn't mind. It was just him she wanted.

A figure was coming down the street in the gloom. Hands thrust into pockets, feet kicking at anything within reach. Hood up. Hope, then disappointment. He passed under a street lamp and she could see it wasn't Gary.

Should she have gone to meet him? Last time she'd seen him, she told him she'd be here waiting for him, and he'd grinned and said, 'You'd better be.'

An old battered Cortina screeched to a halt in the middle of the road. A bloke climbed out of the back and smacked the top before the car hurtled on down the road.

It was Gary! Gary was home! She was up, leaning against the window, rapping on the glass, pleading for him to look up.

He saw her, raised a finger to tell her to wait, then turned aside to speak to Mick Crier who was passing with his Rottweiler.

He had seen her! She got up, switched on the fire and looked around wondering what else she could do to welcome him. She kept her coat on.

She heard swearing as he passed Tyler, kicking him out of the way. Running up the stairs. Door swinging open.

'Gary!' She rushed to him, wrapping her arms round

him. He brushed her aside, so he could push into the room. Cropped hair, stocky, less weight on him than when he'd gone inside. The same good looks though. The same cocky confidence in those looks and in his ability to survive. Her man.

'Gary, I didn't know if it was today or not. Drake said you was coming out. I would have come to meet you. Oh Gary!' She wanted to cling to him again, but he held her casually back, grabbing and swigging a lager. He wiped the back of his hand across his mouth and turned to look round. At her, briefly, with his old grin, then round the room, nodding, accepting that it would do.

'All right, all right. No need to fuss. Got out this morning. So, you pleased to see me then, girl?'

'Oh Gary, I been that desperate without you.' No, he wouldn't want to hear about her troubles. 'But you're home now. I'd have come more but when they moved you I couldn't afford the fare.'

He laughed. 'Always were fucking useless on your own. Never mind, eh. Home now. You going to give me a kiss or what?'

She rushed to him, arms thoughtlessly wide, coat swinging open.

She stopped, at his expression.

'You. Stupid. Bitch.'

'Gary…'

'Stupid fucking bitch. Who've you been screwing then, while I've been inside?'

'No one, Gary, honest.'

'Don't you lie to me. Don't try and tell me it's mine.'

'It is, Gary. I promise. I wasn't with no one else.'

'Oh no? How d'you get by then, without me, if you weren't on the game?'

66

'I got a job, Gary. Cleaning offices. Honest. Until I started getting sick and they dumped me. 'Cos of this.' She looked down at her swollen belly, pushing out the over-tight sweater.

'You stupid cow.' He snarled at her lump. 'It's not mine.' He stared at her with the look he used on customers who wouldn't pay up.

She didn't dare reply, just waited.

'Are you so fucking stupid you didn't think of getting rid of it?'

'I didn't know how, Gary. Didn't know what to do.'

'Stupid cow! Well, you can fucking get rid of it now.'

'I can't, Gary.' She was half crying, half pleading, knowing that neither would work with him. He didn't like whiney women. 'It's too late. They won't do an abortion or nuffin' now.'

'I told you, get rid of it, bitch.' Here it came. She could see the explosion rippling up within him, bursting out at last. 'Or I'll get rid of it for you.'

Even in the middle of the night it was never quite dark in the room, because of the street light outside and the thin curtains, but the light was softer tonight in the freezing fog. Lindy shivered under the quilt and tried to get more comfortable on the mattress, rubbing her feet up and down to warm them. No Gary to share his body's heat. He was out, she didn't know where. Didn't know if he was coming back. She'd asked but he was still too mad to reply.

Maybe it would make a difference if she lost the baby. She might. He'd punched her so hard she'd almost passed out. But she hadn't started bleeding or nothing. Now she didn't know what to do. There were ways of dealing with babies, other girls had told her, but that was for when you first got pregnant, not for when you were eight months gone. Things she just hadn't done. Like she hadn't accepted Carver's help. What if Gary found out about that? He'd be that mad.

Carver was the bloke upstairs. Top Dog. She was always a bit afraid of him. No, really afraid. Big black guy with eyes like bullets. Nobody messed with Carver, not even Gary. She'd delivered stuff for him now and again, because he'd asked, politely, and she'd pretended it was fine, too terrified to refuse. But mostly she ducked out of sight if she saw him first. Then one day he'd caught her on the stairs, looked her over, and asked her what she was going to do. Like she had choices.

She couldn't tell Gary that. Couldn't tell him that Carver had asked her if she wanted to him to fix something up for her. Or that she had shaken her head. Better let Gary believe she'd been just too stupid to know what to do.

Perhaps she was stupid. Lindy couldn't understand her own impulses. What happened in this world, or at least what happened to her, just happened. No rhyme or reason, no good or bad. So, lying alone on her mattress, she just hoped that Gary would forgive her and accept the baby because it was too late to put right her mistake. She never paused to think that maybe she had said no because she, Lindy Crowe, actually wanted the baby. She had been too useless to get rid of it, but not too useless, in her own small way, to look after herself and the spark of life within her. She'd stopped drinking – couldn't afford it, could she? Hardly ever smoked. Tried to remember to eat. Had dreams sometimes about holding her baby, cuddling it, having its fingers grab hers. Someone of her very own to offer her the one thing she had ever craved.

It was Gary's, whatever he said. She hadn't been sleeping

around while he was inside, at least not for the first four months. She hadn't slept around before, neither, not once she'd moved in with him, though he'd kept telling her his friends would pay good money if she gave them one. She'd hoped she wouldn't have to do that anymore. She would have done it, for him, in the end, but he was still bullying her about it when he'd got done for demanding money with menaces. Leaving her to cope all alone.

She'd started off well. Got a job, night cleaning. Greg paid her cash in hand and she'd enjoyed it, working through the night hours with old Sal, in brightly lit offices like another world. She was good at it too, sweeping, cleaning, polishing, making things neat and pretty. And even if Greg wasn't quite legal, it was like Christmas every week, knowing there'd be cash at the end of it. But then she'd starting throwing up and showing and Greg had told her to get lost and she was stuffed, in every possible sense. She was driven back to the inevitable round of prostitution and shoplifting. Not that many men were that keen for a fuck with a pregnant woman. Shoplifting was easier though. No one thought twice about her bulges.

She'd signed on too. She hadn't dared try before because they'd have just put her back in care. But now she was seventeen, they couldn't send her back, so a month ago she'd finally made it into the Job Centre, and found herself filling in a load of forms. Did she have a permanent place of residence? Yes! What rent did she pay? None. She shouldn't have said that. Did she have a partner? Yes, but he was in prison. Name, age, date of birth, National Insurance number… She didn't know nothing about half of it, all the questions and the boxes and the haranguing woman with big shoulders and steel glasses who looked at her like she was a worm. It was all just another of those processes that happened to Lindy, inflicted by other people, the usual round of meaningless battering. But she had emerged with the promise of a giro and leaflets on maternity welfare. Not bad for all that bother. The money didn't go far, but it was regular, enough for some food and light and weed, and a bit of heat if she was careful, and with an occasional bit of shoplifting, she got by. Waiting for Gary to come home.

She was stiff on the mattress. Aching. He really had hit her hard. She couldn't feel the baby moving tonight. Maybe it was dead. The thought left her numb with helpless grief, but there was nothing she could do about it. He was her man and if he chose to kill it, or kill her, or throw her out on the streets again, how could she stop him? She'd never said it, even to herself, but she'd known he would go mad when he found out. That was really why she'd stopped going to visit him in prison. Putting off the moment. She just hoped now he'd come round. Maybe he'd come home flush and feeling generous towards her. Maybe…

She was too cold to sleep, and yet she must have because she woke with a start when the quilt was snatched off her. It was still dark, lit by the glow of the street lamps, strong enough for her to see Gary standing over her. Staring down at her.

She shivered. She couldn't tell if he was still angry or what.

'Get us something to eat,' he ordered.

She struggled up. It was difficult in her state, getting up from a mattress on the floor. As soon as she was off it, he flung himself down in her place, dirty boots raking the quilt as he groped for his cigarettes.

She put the kettle on, opened cans, made tea and beans on toast with ham. Not much you can do with one ring and a grill that half works. She placed the plate on the table, but Gary grunted, so she gave him the plate where he half lay, half sat, on the mattress, and watched him shovelling the food into his mouth.

He wasn't talking, so she cleaned out the remainder of the beans from the battered saucepan, first with a spoon, then with her finger. The taste reminded her she was famished. She helped herself to another biscuit, then handed him the packet.

He grabbed her wrist, his eyes running over her, head to foot. 'Too late then, for an abortion.'

'I'm eight months, Gary. They wouldn't do it now.'

'Have you seen a doc?'

She shook her head. The local surgery, busy with old dears and bright mums with pushchairs had been too alien. She didn't like doctors. Too many memories of unfriendly examinations.

'Okay.' Gary nodded. Pleased? 'That's good. No one knows, right?'

What did he mean? She knew. He knew. Everyone who took one look at her knew.

'You listening? You haven't gone telling doctors you're pregnant. They haven't got you booked into hospital or anything like that. Right? So no one knows.'

The woman who fixed up her weekly giro knew. But no need to tell Gary that. Lindy shook her head.

'Right. So you keep your mouth shut about the baby, and when you've had it, we get rid of it.'

She went cold inside, colder than the icy fog. 'You wouldn't kill it, Gary.'

He laughed, cruelly, then like he was just laughing it off. 'We dump it, that's all. Leave it somewhere. No one need know nothing. Right?'

She wanted to say 'But I want my baby,' but she didn't dare, so she began to cry.

71

Tears never worked on Gary. 'Shut up, you stupid bitch. If you'd got rid of it in the first place, there wouldn't have been no trouble. Your own stupid fucking fault. If you want to stick with me, you dump it. And you want to stick with me, don't you, girl.'

She sniffed back her tears and nodded.

CHAPTER 3

i

Kelly

A long gravel drive led up to the house. Nothing like the farm tracks Kelly knew, but a farm it officially was. Some rare breed of cattle on one side, and an organic wheat crop on the other, sprinkled with wild flowers among the green spears.

Roz was looking out of the window, apparently serene, though her fingers were twitching on her skirt.

'Nearly there. We've made it.'

'Yeah. It's lovely.' Another twitch. Roz's old East-End accent, usually smoothed to the faintest nasal twang, reasserted itself. 'A bit posh, innit?'

Kelly laughed. 'Mum, it's Rog and Mandy. I don't suppose they've grown horns or anything.'

Roz smiled, nervously. She had lived comfortably with Roger and Mandy Padstow when they had been tepee-dwelling activists, dividing their commitments between Gaia, Wicca, road planning, and the ever-niggling internal politics of the commune, but here in Dorset she felt inadequate, all her old insecurities bubbling up again.

Kelly had no such qualms. People were people to her, wherever they lived, however they dressed or spoke. To her, Roger and Mandy would always be the couple with whom she grew up, models of easy confidence and kindly authority, with quirks that she could handle.

There had, of course, been no official leader in the commune, but Roger and Mandy had been the most articulate and rational of them all, the ones best at dealing with authority, perhaps because, whatever their radical views, they preserved the social confidence of their educated middle-class origins.

Raised in the commune, Kelly had no instinctive yearning for nuclear family structures. She had no grandparents, but she did have Roger and Mandy, and she imagined that grandparents must fulfil a similar role; wise people who could advise and support, and take over in crises. Except that grandparents would be much older. The Padstows' two children had been Kelly's commune siblings. It had probably been the children, Kelly thought, lacking any cynicism, that had led them to quit the commune a couple of years after she and Roz had moved out with Luke Sheldon. Now Mandy wrote books on life/work/health balance and Roger ran an IT company and together they farmed (organically) this estate in Dorset and produced (or their workforce produced) expensive brands of yoghurt and wild boar pâté.

They'd always kept in touch with Roz and Kelly. Not so much with others from the commune, who saw the Padstows as traitors to the cause – whatever it was. Roz had always been too needy for their approval to question the changes, but she did feel intimidated by their worldly success. Kelly was neither intimidated nor impressed, nor resentful. The Padstows were friends, in the commune or here in their six-bedroom semi-mansion in Hardy country, where their activism had transmogrified into buying the *Guardian* and donating to Oxfam.

Kelly steered the battered Astra down the drive, listening to the pop and rattle of the semi-detached exhaust as they rolled into the broad gravel between the house proper and the converted barns. She parked up between a Range Rover and a sleek black saloon with tinted glass. Roz's fingers were twitching at her skirt again, but Kelly was unfazed. She jumped out of the Astra, hoisting up the door to make it shut, just as Mandy and Roger appeared on the steps.

'Hiya!' Kelly waved happily, then hopped round to the passenger door to release her mother. 'Don't try to open it, Mum. I need to do it from this side.'

'Here, let me help.' Roger eased the door open with her. He crouched on the gravel, looking in at Roz. 'How's my dreamer?'

'Roger! It's really great to see you,' Roz said. The bone-rattling journey from Pembrokeshire had not been pleasant for her, but Kelly could see her relax at the sight of the man she had always trusted.

'Let's get you out then.' He smiled at Roz, still smiling as he looked up at Kelly, though she could see the alarm in his eyes. Roz was looking a thousand times better than she had a couple of months ago, but a hundred times worse than she had looked the last time Roger had seen her, a couple of years earlier.

'Kelly.' Mandy had joined them and hugged her, before reaching out to hug Roz too as she emerged from the car. 'Roz. My poor Roz. What has been happening to you? Let's get you into the house.

'Roger?' She looked askance at her husband.

Kelly kicked strategically to open the boot, so that Roger could haul out Roz's suitcase, a hessian bag of medications and herbal remedies, and Kelly's bulging kitbag. 'Thanks for asking Mum down. I can't get her to sit still at home. She thinks she ought to be doing things.'

'Well, we won't let her overdo things here, don't worry.

She can relax and get better. Mandy knows how to manage her.' He took the kit bag from Kelly as she was hoisting it on her shoulder. 'How are you doing, Kelly?'

'Oh, I'm managing fine. You know me.'

'Yes, I do.' He swung his arm, loaded with the suitcase, round her and gave her a squeeze. 'My sunshine soul. Always riding high on every wave. Trouble is though, Kelly, you're such a competent little manager it's easy to take you for granted. This couldn't have been easy for you. But you got her here.' He looked at the Astra. 'Just.'

'Don't think it's going to get through the MOT this time. It conked out on us once around Chippenham, but I got it going again.'

'Sure.' Roger ushered her towards the house. 'Kelly copes with everything.'

Gracious living at the Padstows'… Style with Feng Shui; designer porcelain with wholegrains; handcrafted woodwork with state-of-the-art electronics. Roz approved of the aromatherapy candles and Kelly loved the books and neither appreciated the market value of the Persian rugs or the bronze Buddha. They ate in the vast kitchen with its oak and granite, its Aga and Le Creuset casseroles, its immaculate quarry tiles and atmospheric under-lighting.

'I expect you are both still vegetarian,' said Mandy, busy with goat's cheese and rocket. 'We eat veggie quite often, don't we, Roger, even if we're not very strict about it anymore.'

Kelly, who had peeked inside a fridge the size of Belgium and seen a beef joint, two small partridges and a plate of Parma ham and chorizo, had already deduced that the Padstows had moved on from tofu and pulses, but if they were willing to pose as vegetarians again for Roz, that was very nice of them.

Afterwards, while Mandy fussed over Roz, settling her into her new quarters, Roger said, 'Come and see the Dexters.'

Cows, not neighbours. Kelly obliged. They walked together through the summer twilight, chatting as if their paths had never diverged. Roger was still, after all, Roger. He might wear a quilted gilet but he still had a ponytail. He talked of Dexters and White Parks and Maris Widgeon wheat, and Kelly talked of lambing and dyer's madder and St John's wort.

'So what are you going to do, Kelly?' Roger straddled a five bar gate as they looked out across the rolling landscape. 'How are you going to cope with Roz?'

'I'll do fine. She's much better than she was, you know. Not really an invalid. Just needs to take care.'

'Are you going to keep your smallholding on?'

'Of course!' The thought of leaving it had never occurred to her.

'It's a lot for you to cope with, if you're dealing with Roz as well.'

'I can cope.' She looked at Roger, trying to assess his reasoning. 'Why's it worrying you?'

'Because we worry about you. Both of you. We care hugely about Roz, you know we do, but we care just as much about you.'

'Yes.' Kelly laughed, swinging up onto the gate to sit beside him. 'I know you do. Thanks. I know how much you've done for us.'

'I wouldn't say that we did that much.'

His demurral was fake, so she brushed it aside. 'You know you did. Mum's always been, always will be, well, a bit flaky. She was just a kid, wasn't she, when she joined you. Without you, I don't know where she'd have finished up.'

He smiled, remembering. 'She was always fragile. I like to think we helped. We watched her blossom. But then she opted to leave with Luke and we thought that was it. We'd lost her. It was never going to work.'

'Happy families,' explained Kelly. 'I think that was it. She always had this fuzzy goal of something "normal" and she thought marrying Luke would be as normal as it could get.'

'We thought, to be honest, she was one of those women just doomed to fall for the wrong sort of man. I don't want to bad-mouth Luke, but we all knew he'd never be able to give her the sort of support she needed, and she was never going to be the sort of woman who'd stand up to him.'

'She did though, in the end.'

'Yes! Yes, she did. Well done her.'

'You see, your influence won through in the end, because she realised we could make it on our own.'

'You think it was down to us?' Roger laughed, with a hint of wistfulness. 'We all knew the Luke business wouldn't last and I thought she'd come back to us. Instead, she found her own feet. And you know, Kelly, that was down to you. She had you to care for, you to focus on, and even though you were a kid, you were there for her. Our little Kelly. Even now, I don't think she'd cope on her own. She's always going to be half in this world and half out.'

'In a very nice way.'

'Oh, a very nice way. Blind to all the nastiness of life. Does she still believe all your surplus lambs are living wild and free on the Preselis?'

Kelly laughed. 'She still believes Gwynfor takes them off our hands because he wants to give them a happy home. Well, he really did want to keep the first one. Rambo. Very productive, apparently. I haven't told her that the others go to market with the rest of his sheep, and she doesn't choose to ask.'

'That's Roz. I'm sure she could work it out if she chose but her motto has always been, "See what you want to see." Always in charmed denial over anything uncomfortable.'

'It doesn't hurt.'

'Except it's why she's in the state she's in now, isn't it…'

'Yes, I know.' Kelly picked at splinters of wood. 'Wouldn't dream of going to a doctor, but she must have known things were wrong. She's been dosing herself up with herbal stuff for years. But you know what she's like. It's a bit like the rates. If she refuses to acknowledge something, maybe it will go away.'

Roger ruffled her hair. 'Of course. You know exactly how she operates. Because you're the one who sorts it all out for her. But it's going to be a lot more than keeping an eye on the rate demands from now on, Kelly.'

'I know.'

'That's what's really worrying us. I know you can cope. No one can cope like Kelly. But what's happening to your own life? Are you going to spend it all as your mother's nurse and minder? Nothing for yourself?'

'I have plenty for myself. Everything I want. I'm very efficient; I can multi-task.'

'What about college?'

'I've been to college.'

'I mean university, getting a proper degree.'

'Why would I need one?'

Roger looked away, over his rolling acres, with a twinge of embarrassment. 'You can control her diabetes, but her kidneys are never going to improve, are they? At best, you're going to be managing it. At worst, she'll go downhill. Kidneys are tricky things.'

'I know. I wanted to give her one of mine.'

Roger grimaced. 'Of course you would, Kelly. Please don't rush into anything. I'm not saying don't do it, but think long and hard about it.'

'No need. I'm not suitable. They did tests – Mum didn't want it, but I needed to know, and there's no match, blood and tissue, so my kidneys are no use to her.'

'That's that then.' He was relieved. 'And I suppose she has no idea where her family is. She used to speak about a brother, but she never had any contact with him while she was with us. Any other relatives?'

Kelly rested her chin on the gate. 'The thing is, in a purely genetic sense, there might be.'

Roger sensed the hesitation, the way she was looking at nothing in particular, certainly not looking at him. Kelly always looked directly at the person she spoke to. He swung his leg over and jumped down from the gate. 'How do you mean?'

Kelly chewed her lip, still gazing into the middle distance. 'Mum's terrified there was a mix-up at the hospital.'

'With her treatment?'

'No, in the maternity ward, when I was born. A nurse told her labels had got switched.'

Roger opened his mouth to speak, thought better, shut it, then started again. 'You mean she thinks you're not her child?'

'Sort of.'

'Kelly, I wouldn't worry about it.'

'I don't!'

'I mean, I wouldn't give the story much credence if I were you. Seriously. Your mother has always been, well, a bit paranoid. That's exactly the sort of story she would hit on, like a focus for her fear. You were all she had, so she was terrified of losing you.'

'I do know how she works.'

'Yes, of course you do. And you must know how improbable it is. Things like that don't really happen. Not without people noticing, not without a huge furore and legal action and heads rolling. God.' He winced. Kelly could tell he was thinking now of his own children. 'It would be a parent's worst nightmare.'

'Would it?' She was Kelly again now, looking at him so directly he felt he was in the dock. 'Would you stop feeling like Tanja's dad if you discovered there'd been a mix-up at her birth?'

'God, I don't know. No, of course not, but – no, but I'd want to know, I'd need to know what had happened to my real child.' He saw the disappointment in her face and blushed. 'But of course Tan would still be my child. Hell, it's just not that simple. And listen, Kelly, don't waste your time thinking about it. It's not true. Roz is your mother, and she had half a dozen doctors and nurses in that maternity ward witnessing your birth. So there's not a blood match with your mother. That's bad luck maybe, but it doesn't prove anything.'

'No,' agreed Kelly. Why say more? Roger was not seeing this the way she saw it. No point in telling him that the blood and tissue tests might have proved nothing, but the other test had.

She thought about it as she lay in bed, in Tanja's room. Tanja was in London. After Cambridge she had got a job in television. Current affairs, nothing to do with animals. She had always liked animals as a little girl and, judging by the horsey theme in her fluffy bedroom, she had continued to like animals in her teens. Or at least she'd liked to hunt them. Not a glimpse left of the little gipsy Kelly had known.

81

Funny things, people. They never seemed to know what they wanted or how to be happy. Kelly had always found knowing what she wanted easy.

Except for this. Was this feeling dissatisfaction? She was determined to know. Determined enough to connive, to search the internet for maternity tests. All in secret. Even the tests Dr Matthews had arranged for the tissue matching had distressed Roz. The thought of a specific maternity test would have killed her. So Kelly had managed by subterfuge – the mouth swabs, the forged signatures.

She didn't feel guilty about it. Kelly wasn't paying for the test in order to reject or accept Roz. Nothing was going to alter their relationship. It was just the thought of that other girl out there. She had to know.

When Kelly had first jumped in with an offer of one of her kidneys, she had experienced a queer flutter of pleasure, the satisfaction of sainthood. She had mocked herself, but what was wrong with feeling good about self-sacrifice? And as she couldn't make that sacrifice, what if there was someone else out there who could? Would they? She would, she was confident of that. If a complete stranger approached her out of the blue and told Kelly that one of her kidneys could save an unknown woman, she was certain she wouldn't hesitate. That glow of virtue. Kelly had a strong sense of morality. Her own, based on her own values. A morality that would have urged her to save someone else if she could, but that didn't stop her tricking her mother over the maternity test.

The result had come on the day they'd heard from Roger and Mandy, inviting Roz to stay with them for a while to recuperate.

Roz was not Kelly's mother.

Kelly had read the report, put it aside and concentrated

on persuading her mother to accept the Padstows' invitation, making the arrangements, kicking the Astra into some sort of life, persuading Joe to move in for a few days to take care of the animals. Those were the things that mattered. The maternity test didn't.

But now Roz was here, it was time to think about the test. Somewhere out there was the child that Roz had carried for nine months, the girl whose blood and tissue might match. Kelly had arranged the test in order to know. What to do with the knowledge? She would have a week or two to think about it, while Roz was in Roger and Mandy's care, but she had no idea what steps to take. Somewhere in her imagination lurked a nebulous image of serendipity, an accidental meeting of two young women who recognised each other by magical instinct. But it was never going to happen that way. Any meeting would have to be engineered and Kelly had no idea how to begin.

This house seemed alien in the night, with its trappings of affluent chic. She needed to be back at Carregwen, mulling over the options with the chickens, discussing it with Eleanor and Rigby the goats.

Then in the morning everything changed.

Before breakfast, she carried her kitbag out to the car and found it gone. She returned to the house. 'Mandy, where's the Astra?'

Mandy, busy with dried fruit, hurried to reassure her. 'It's all right. Rog will explain. Roger!'

He came through from the conservatory, a wet towel round his shoulders.

'Explain about Kelly's car,' ordered Mandy.

He smiled and held up placatory hands. 'It's at Darnley's garage, Kelly. I arranged for them to come and take it. Urgent repairs.'

afford—'

rry about that. I'm dealing with it. Be honest,
ot safe, is it? How you got here without killing
od knows. I didn't want to see you driving off in
rage is going sort out the major problems. Can't
e they'll fix every rattle, but—'

w long are they going to be? I need it. It's all right
I know how to keep it going.'

m not letting you loose in it, the way it is. Don't worry,
re not holding you prisoner. The garage can work on it
ile you're gone, and it will be ready when you come back
o pick your mother up. And in the meantime, you can take
Mandy's Corsa.'

'No.'

'Yes,' insisted Roger, with Mandy nodding enthusiastic
approval.

She would have refused if it hadn't been too late. But the
Astra was gone, probably already disembowelled over some
pit and she couldn't wait forever. Joe couldn't be left in
charge of Carregwen indefinitely. A few days and then she'd
need to order more feed. And she had two jobs to get back
to.

She stayed for breakfast in the conservatory, and
reassured herself that Roz had slept well and that Mandy
knew exactly what to do with all the medications and the
dietary instructions, then she let Roger escort her to the
double garage where her new chariot awaited her. Electric
windows, air conditioning, a CD player and Sat Nav. It felt
like sitting at the controls of a spaceship. She hadn't been
in a car like this since taking her test.

'Don't worry about a thing,' Roger assured her, tapping
on the sunroof as she started the engine and waited for the
growls, grinding and whines that she associated with

internal combustion. They didn't come. It felt like cheating, letting the car roll softly out onto the gravel. Not real driving at all – nothing to fight. She manoeuvred it onto the drive, just to convince Roger she could handle it, then she stopped to say goodbye.

'You know how everything works? Lights there. Windscreen wiper. Sat Nav.' Roger leaned in to adjust it. 'It's on. Do you want me to show you how to use it?'

Kelly laughed. 'I'll manage. I usually get there in the end.'

'You always will, Kelly. Look, phone charger; you'll keep in touch, won't you?'

'Of course. Every day. Not that I don't trust you.'

He grinned. 'Don't worry, we'll mind her like our own.'

She waved, he waved. She headed down the drive, then sat back and began to get the feel of the ridiculously well-appointed car.

It was the Sat Nav that did it. Kelly navigated by instinct and memory; it had always worked in the past. But the Sat Nav on the Corsa's dashboard kept showing her the world that lay before her, the junctions, the forks, the crossroads. Constant temptations. She was heading north for the M4, and there on the map was the motorway running west for home. And running east. East to the M25 and the home counties, a world she knew nothing about but that was, in a sense, her birthright.

She pulled into a lay-by before the motorway and sat gazing at the map, zooming in, zooming out. East to London, the M25 and the satellite towns that clustered round the capital. Lyford. Turn off at that junction, the Sat Nav invited her; drive the twenty odd miles to Lyford and Stapledon General Hospital where, according to her birth certificate, she had been born. The hospital where labels had been switched.

Kelly nibbled the houmous and sun-dried tomato ciabatta that Mandy had given her. Maybe Joe could manage for another day or two. And she was owed some leave. They'd understand at work. Her mother was ill, after all. She looked again at the map, spreading its motorway tentacles out to her, as she sat in a car that would happily cruise anywhere, without being kicked or tickled into obedience. Fate, surely. How could she refuse?

She drove to the M4 and turned east.

Lyford. An urban sprawl, too big to be a mere town, but too formless, too lacking in identity to be a city. Too close to London to have any regional significance, and just too far out to share the capital's glamour. High rise blocks and concrete fly-overs superimposed on defunct car plants and forgotten gas works. Mushrooming housing estates and small-scale industrial complexes spilling out from a civic centre that had once had delusions of Art Deco style and that now nursed its pedestrian zoning under the shadow of a vast shopping centre and multi-storey car park. Kelly noticed narrow Victorian lanes and a gracious Medieval church as she strolled round the shopping precinct, wondering what it would have been like to have been brought up here. This was her place of birth but she felt no link to it. She'd been a couple of weeks old when she had left it behind.

Kelly had no affinity with towns, but she wasn't intimidated by them either. They were, to her, rather sad. Studying the well-stocked contents of the shops, reading the police notices seeking witnesses to a murder outside the Crown and Anchor, and chatting with the sellers of *The Big Issue*, she thought that, all things considered, fate had dealt kindly with her by taking her from here.

She asked in one shop for directions to the hospital and was sent to WHSmith's for a street map, but as that seemed a waste of money she returned to the car park where she had left the Corsa and tried the Sat Nav. So easy. Just follow the fly-over, then take the Stapledon link road past the football ground.

Lyford and Stapledon General Hospital. 1960s panelling in an ocean of tarmac. Busy, busy, busy. The sort of place where everyone was so rushed, the workload so heavy that surely mistakes could happen. Labels could accidentally be switched.

Kelly walked in through the glass sliding doors into the foyer milling with elderly hobblers, pregnant women looking hopefully for vacant seats, wan-faced children kicking concrete pillars, legs in plaster protruding from wheelchairs like battering rams, reluctant visitors buying flowers and magazines.

A man and two women staffed the reception desk, directing, snapping, pointing, furiously entering data into keyboards like a champion team at an advanced level of Space Invaders. Kelly mingled with others waiting for attention – there was no queue, just a mêlée of anxiety and irritation. She let others squeeze in before her. She had no urgent illness. Finally, she was face-to-face with one of the women at the desk, with sharp, pinched lips, determined not to give an inch to the barbarians. Her badge said Julie. She didn't look like a Julie. A Cynthia or a Selina maybe. Something serpentine.

'Any chance you can help me? I was born here, in 1990, and I want to speak to someone about it. Do you keep the records? Is there someone I can talk to?'

Julie stared at her as if she could see the bulge of a suicide belt under Kelly's jacket. 'What do you mean, records? You want your birth certificate?'

'No, I've got that.' Whatever paperwork Roz had started with had long ago been lost, but there had been some reason, later, why she had had to apply for a copy. After leaving Luke; one of Roz's first steps alone into the world of adult responsibility. Kelly could still remember her mother opening the envelope, expecting some sort of official reprimand, and then laughing with relief as the certificate emerged. Date, name, mother's name. No father's name, but that had never been an issue. Place: Lyford and Stapledon Hospital.

'There were problems when I was born,' she continued, watching Julie's eyes skirt past her towards the crowd behind.

'I don't understand. What do you mean by problems?'

'Stuff, you know. Do you keep records that far back? I just want to ask someone what happened exactly.'

A slight ripple of relief. This was outside reception business; a problem Julie could legitimately pass on to someone else. She spun round in her swivel chair and picked up a phone. 'I have someone here wanting to speak…' Her voice sank to a discreet whisper, drowned out by the crowds. Kelly could hear, 'Birth… problems… issues.'

Julie swivelled round again, picked up a pen and wrote quickly on a pad. 'Down the corridor, take the lifts to the second floor, first left and ask at the desk for Mr. Manderville. Thank you.' She brushed Kelly aside.

Kelly looked at the paper in her hand. Manderville. Right. That was a start.

Mr Manderville was an administrator. Jowly and unsmiling. He wore a suit, an aura of impatience, and an expression of extreme wariness. 'Miss Sheldon, is it? Yes. You have a query, I gather, about old records? I'm not sure

88

that we can be of any help to you. Records are, of course highly confidential, although if they pertain to yourself, the Freedom of Information Act may allow—'

'Oh sure, it's just about me,' said Kelly, looking round his office which was plush, any sign of activity organised into neat clipped piles. 'I'll tell you what it is. I was born here. I've got the certificate – March 13th, 1990. But it turns out that something went wrong.'

Before she could say more, she could sense a visor coming down, the wagons circling. 'I can assure you, Miss Sheldon, that if any problems arose during a birth, they would have been dealt with in an entirely professional manner. Complications can and do arise, of course, but the hospital cannot be held liable in any way without serious proof of malpractice. Do you have any reason to believe that the medical staff attending your mother were remiss in any way?'

'No, no. Nothing like that. Nothing wrong with the birth. Mum said the staff were very kind.' She felt his defences wobbling, so she added, 'Very professional.'

He sank back in his chair, fingers pressed together, nodding and frowning gently to show that he was willing to listen. For a couple of minutes at least.

'No, it's not about the birth, exactly,' she went on. 'It's just that Mum says a nurse told her labels had been mixed up. Labels on the babies. Wrong babies with the wrong mums.'

That floored him. He sat up again, shoulders broadening before her eyes, ready to charge. 'Absolutely impossible, Miss Sheldon. Your mother must have misunderstood. Believe me, there is no possibility that such a mistake could have occurred. We take the utmost care—'

'This was twenty-two years ago,' she reminded him. 'I

89

don't suppose you were working here then. Things could have been different.'

'You're quite right, Miss Sheldon, I was not employed at the hospital twenty-one years ago and not in any way responsible for any mistakes even if they had occurred. But I assure you the hospital would not have allowed such mistakes to happen even then. Procedures were in place. Errors, however improbable, would have been noticed and rectified immediately. Whatever your mother believes she heard, I assure you no nurse would have told her any such thing.' A twitch, resembling a smile, appeared at the corner of his mouth. He was sure here. Not confident about the switching of labels maybe, but confident that no nurse would have been fool enough to confess the mistake to a mother on the ward. His smile broadened. Perhaps he thought he was looking avuncular and reassuring. 'I believe that nursing mothers can be a little sensitive. Nervous. Quite understandable of course. Bearing a child for all those months and then the trauma of the birth itself. Very easy for the imagination to run riot. We find that many mothers suspect terrible illnesses, deformities, all manner of horrors. Our nurses do a fine job in reassuring them.' He didn't know what he was talking about, Kelly could tell, but he was an expert at talking without meaning.

There were few people that Kelly truly disliked, but she suspected Mr Manderville was going to be one of them. He was verbally hustling her aside, and she hadn't come all this way to be hustled.

'Yes, well, the thing is, it's all true,' she said. 'We've had tests done, DNA and all that, and they prove I really am not my mother's daughter. Not genetically. So that is why I want to see the hospital records and find out how the babies came to be swapped. She's sick, you see, my mum.

Diabetes and now kidney trouble, and it turns out I can't give her a kidney because I'm not genetically related. But someone else is, and I want to know who. All you need to do is give me the names of other babies, girls anyway, born at the same time, in the same ward, and then we can figure out who got mixed up with who.' She smiled brightly at him, watching his jowls quiver. 'That's all.'

'Quite impossible, Miss Sheldon,' he replied, a thin reedy note entering his voice. 'Such mistakes…unthinkable. There will be another explanation. Lyford and Stapledon General cannot be held in any way responsible…'

Kelly stood under the cantilevered canopy at the hospital entrance, watching grey clouds build up over the equally grey roofs of Lyford. The hospital and its management, terrified of any hint of legal culpability and compensation pay-outs, had slammed down the shutters, and pulled up the drawbridge, ready to man the battlements to the bitter end. In other words, they were not going to raise a little finger to help her. Well then.

Kelly was a tolerant girl, not easily provoked, but when she felt she had a just cause, she could be a terrier sinking her teeth in. If the hospital refused to give her the information she needed, she would find it by other means, and she knew just how to do it.

ii

Vicky

A knock on the front door. Gillian wiped her hands on her apron and hurried through to the hall. A special delivery?

She saw a shape behind the pixelating glass. An indistinct, obscure figure, but Gillian recognised it almost before focusing on it.

She flung the door open. 'Vicky!'

'Hello.' Suitcases at her feet, coat over her arm. Face emotionless as ever.

'What are you doing knocking? Here, let me take those. Give me your coat. Oh Vicky!' With arms weighed down, she struggled to embrace her daughter. 'Have you lost your key?'

'I didn't want to take anyone by surprise.' A sarcastic delivery but with a little girl's plea somewhere inside.

'It's the best surprise.' Gillian ignored the needling. 'Why didn't you tell me you were coming? Your room is ready, of course, but I haven't aired the bedding properly or anything. Oh, come in, come in. Vicky...' Her voice was breaking up. 'I'm so glad you've come home.'

'Well.' For a second their eyes met. She saw a brief glimmer behind Vicky's thick lenses, but of what? Something that wanted to come out, but Vicky wasn't going to let it. She looked away, hanging her coat up, depositing her suitcases neatly at the bottom of the stairs. It would be that terrible, unspeakable row. Perhaps she was embarrassed, or still too wounded. But she had come home, that was all that mattered. She hadn't disappeared forever.

'Is Joan here?'

'No. She and Bill are in Scotland. They tried to book a trip to Spain but the insurance – you know, their age and Bill's angina – so they've gone to Scotland. Can you imagine it? Your gran doing a coach trip of the highlands and glens?'

'It will be a trip round the distilleries, I expect.'

'Yes, of course. I hadn't thought of that.' Why were they babbling on about Joan, as if she mattered? But she did.

92

Her absence meant that mother and daughter could have a breathing space. 'Come through,' said Gillian, and firmly took her daughter's hand, leading her through to the living room. In the clearer light, she laid her hands on Vicky's shoulders and looked at her. Pale, but then she was always pale. Not noticeably sickly at least. She could feel how thin she was through the baggy sweatshirt. Was she eating properly? Was she coping? All that work, so many hours, so much studying.

'How are you, darling?'

Vicky shrugged.

'I wish you'd kept in touch more, let me know how you were doing. I didn't like to keep ringing.' Not after the first couple of weeks of ignored calls. 'You're over-working yourself, I know you are.'

'Work is fine.' Vicky took a deep breath. 'Is this what we're going to do then? Discuss my studies?'

'Not if you don't want to, darling. I am interested, you know I am, but—'

'And it will save us having to discuss the other thing. The thing you never quite got round to discussing for twenty years.'

'Oh Vicky.'

'I'll go up and dump my bag upstairs, shall I? Any chance of a cup of tea?'

'Yes! Yes, I'll make tea. You sort yourself out.' Gillian almost ran for the kitchen, where she could weep at her own cowardice. Where she could splash herself with boiling water as punishment for never getting anything right.

Vicky's arrival had been so unexpected. Gillian's instinctive desire to evade any nastiness – pour oil on troubled water – had kicked in before she could brace herself to do the right thing.

She was braced now. And the tea was brewed. It would be stewed if it wasn't drunk soon. She poured a mug and took it and a biscuit upstairs.

Vicky was standing at Joan's bedroom door, looking in.

'Thanks.' She took the proffered mug. 'What's happened here?' A clean room. White walls, new carpet, new curtains, new bedding, most of the old trash gone. An anonymous room, barely marked by Joan, although there were already tell-tale cigarette burns in the carpet.

'There was a bit of an accident,' Gillian explained. 'So we redecorated it.'

'Well, you can replace the fucking lot,' Joan had said, coming home to find the havoc. 'You can't expect me to sleep in that. Not safe in my own house with a mad woman. Lock you up, they should.'

So Gillian had taken her at her word, moving in like the guardian angel of house clearance, stripping, burning, consigning to the tip. An act of furious spite so unlike her that she didn't know how to present it except as an act of contrition, the sort of gesture that all her neighbours in the street would think so like Gillian.

Only Joan had understood it was an act of defiance. And two could play at that game. The cigarette burns had been deliberate. She wanted the room put right, at Gillian's expense, but she had barely used it since. She was virtually living with Bill now, talking about selling up, using the house money, with Bill's, to buy a place in Spain.

All talk. Joan couldn't sell the house from under them, Gillian was fairly sure. It had been their money, hers and Terry's, that had enabled Joan to buy the house. They had rights. Equity or something.

'Looks clean,' said Vicky. She sniffed. Air freshener. 'I wouldn't have recognised it.'

94

'No, well, it needed a make-over.' Stop it. Stop chattering. It had to be now. 'Vicky. If you want to talk… I know we should have talked years ago. I know it's all my fault, but if you want to talk about, you know—'

'My adoption.'

'Yes. I'll tell you anything you want to know.'

'I already know all I need to know.'

'You do?'

Vicky returned to her room, picked up the bag on her bed and rifled through. She held out a sheet of paper. 'I wanted to be quite sure the adoption wasn't a lie, so I got hold of my full certificate. The one I suppose you took care not to have in the house.'

Gillian put her hand to her mouth. She'd never admitted it, but Vicky was right. She'd kept the short version, the one that looked identical to a birth certificate, telling herself that there was no need to fuss with further paperwork. 'I was wrong.'

Vicky shrugged. 'Whatever. I applied for it. Thought it might give me more, but it doesn't. I'm a certified mystery. Legally, no one knows who my mother is.'

'That's right. You were found.'

'Yeah, yeah, that's the official line. But it was all there, wasn't it? The truth. In the papers. I found the story. In the *Herald*.'

'Oh. Yes.' Of course. It explained Vicky's last wild claim as she'd boarded the bus that she'd found her mother. She'd unearthed the old story in the newspaper. 'Yes, it was in the *Herald*.'

'I don't get it though. Why people didn't connect the dots. Too much bother? Or was it just that there were so many women around, wanting babies, like you, it was easier just to let it go?'

'I don't know.' Gillian couldn't understand her daughter's words, but she didn't want to risk another flaming row. 'I did want a baby. I wanted you. As soon as I read about you, I wanted you.'

Vicky smiled. 'You wanted a child whose mother left her for dead.'

'No!' Gillian threw her arms around her. 'Left to be found, to be given to me.'

Vicky's smile was almost a rictus of pain. 'You really do like to block out the darkness, don't you? You'd even give murder a rosy glow. She tried to murder me, but that's fine because it made things right for you. Or are you really asking me to believe that it made things right for me?'

How much could Gillian take without being stung? 'That's what it was all for, all my love and care – to make things right for you. If it didn't, I'm sorry. All right? I'm sorry if I wasn't the mum you think you should have had. I'm sorry if all I've done is make you unhappy and lonely and bitter. I never intended it to be that way.'

'Oh come on.' Vicky stomped downstairs. She was already in the kitchen, washing out her mug as if it contained elements of biological warfare, when Gillian followed her.

'What? I should have told you from the start that you were adopted? Yes, of course. But I was a coward. I didn't keep silent out of spite.'

'No.' Vicky turned away. She was willing to attack, but she wasn't so keen on being the one under fire.

'So just tell me where I went so terribly wrong,' insisted Gillian, following her into the living room. 'How did I make life so hateful for you? I nagged you, I pushed you. Is that it? I know. I shouldn't have pushed so hard. I should have been more concerned about you making friends, being happy, getting out and having fun.'

'Fun!' Vicky gave a shriek of bitter laughter. 'Oh yes, we all need to have fun. Good for us.'

'Yes! You should have made more friends. You should have got out more, gone places, the cinema...' Gillian groped for ideas, unsure where young people went these days. 'Discos. You should have been out meeting people instead of being trapped—'

'You mean *boys*. I should have been out meeting boys. A bit of how's your father, that's what a girl needs. Isn't that what Joan taught you? Well, don't worry about me being abandoned on a virgin shelf. I lost my sour little cherry a long time ago.'

'Vicky.' Gillian floundered. Sex wasn't something she had ever discussed with her daughter. She'd always had ideas of doing it properly, tenderly, but Joan's constant lewd remarks would have spoiled it all. A bit of how's your father, yes that was Joan. Surely, Gillian had told herself, the school would sort it out. When Vicky started showing an interest in boys, when she started bringing bashful young boyfriends home, that would be the time to speak more intimately. But Vicky never had brought a boy home, any more than she had brought female friends home. She had sat in her room with her books, that was all.

And now she was claiming sexual experience. Declaring it with scorn. Vicky was meeting people, loving people and Gillian knew nothing about it.

Or was Vicky's boast a sad little lie? She had never done anything to make herself attractive. A frump who had never caught the eye of any man, but who would say anything to avoid admitting it.

She reached out to put her arms round her daughter, but Vicky retreated across the room. 'I'd better unpack.'

'Yes, love,' said Gillian, in despair.

A jacket into the narrow wardrobe, underwear into its drawer, shoes neatly under the bed, laptop on the little desk. Vicky breathed deep. It was stupid to have come home. If it was home. She was better off at college, a different person. She was generally liked by Zoe, Drew, Caz, Jack and all the other happy normal students. Vicky, the asexual swot, never a threat to the girls, never a distraction to the boys, always available to help them out when they were too hungover to make head or tail of their assignments, but never missed when she failed to appear at the pubs and clubs, because everyone assumed she was someone else's friend. She could relax among them because they would never ask, they would never know.

But instead she had chosen to come home. Why?

It was stupid. She's been home for five minutes and the antagonism was all her own doing. She should get a grip, look on the bright side. Joan wasn't there.

Terry came home, glad to see his daughter. Gillian, hypersensitive to their inadequacies, was taken aback by Terry's cheeriness. Had he really not grasped their horrible quarrel and Vicky's flight? Probably not. Terry had always watched from the sidelines, this family stuff a bewildering puzzle. Perhaps he always reacted to Vicky with pleasure, but Gillian, so obsessive in her own love, had never seen it.

'You doing all right at that university then, girl?' he asked, as they gathered at the table. 'At the hospital and so on?'

'Fine,' said Vicky, letting him give her arm a squeeze.

'Doctor Vicky, eh. Well, well.'

'One day.'

'Me and your mum can't believe it, can we, eh, Gill? Doctor.'

98

Vicky shrugged. 'It's just a job. Same as yours.'

'Oh, I don't know about that. Hey, you come to the garage with me tomorrow, yes?'

'Er.' Vicky was caught off guard. It wasn't like Terry to invite her to the garage.

'Got something to show you,' said Terry, chuckling as he tucked into his cottage pie and peas.

Had they always communicated, Gillian wondered, watching Vicky climb into the car beside Terry in the morning? Normal father and daughter and she'd never noticed? No. She could see, as they drove off, that Vicky was as bewildered as she was.

Terry's repair garage, run with his buddy Colin, set up with their redundancy money from the car plant, was just like Terry really. Cluttered, unambitious, grubby, but getting by, ever hopeful and never demanding. Successful enough to keep the wolf from the door and what more could a man ask?

'Come on through,' said Terry.

So Vicky followed him into the corrugated workshop, picking her way round patches of black oil, coiled cables, abandoned nuts and bolts and worn tyres, out through the double back doors into the yard where cars were waiting for MOTs, new exhausts and respray jobs. She joined him as he fumbled in his overall pockets for a key.

'Here it is.' He fished out the key he wanted, gave her a big smile, patting the roof of a Mini. Lime green. 'I figured, you've done so well… Like to give my little girl something for it all.'

Vicky stared at the car. 'You're giving me this?'

'Yes. Why not? Not much, I know.' He patted it again. Twelve years old. He had worked hard on the rust spots, done as good a job as he could. 'But a little run-around, you know.'

Her throat caught. Not with gushing joy. She didn't know what she was feeling. A noose at her neck, snapping her back. 'Why?'

'Well, you work so hard and I'm that proud of you. Thought you deserved it. What's the point of running a garage if I can't find a car for my little girl?'

'But I'm not your little girl.' She had to say it. 'I'm adopted.'

Did he realise that this was a revelation to her? The focus of all her simmering bitterness? Apparently not. He must have assumed she'd always known. Gillian's business, that sort of stuff. 'Well, I suppose. Keep forgetting. Just think of you as my little girl.'

It wasn't a remark that she could deal with. 'You'd have preferred a boy, though, wouldn't you?'

'Oh.' Terry scratched his head. 'I don't know about that.'

Of course he would. He would have known what to do with a boy. Take him down the Rec every Saturday to play football. Help him build a train set. Terry was a simple soul who regarded women with respect and utter incomprehension. It was just the way he was. She couldn't blame him for that.

'So, you like it then?' he asked.

'It's…very nice.' And he was a nice man. Not her father, but a nice man, making a generous gift, to a child who wasn't really his and wasn't even a boy. 'I don't know where my licence is.' Not true. It was on her shelf where it had been since the day she'd received it. First driving lesson on her seventeenth birthday; a present from her quasi-parents. That first lesson had been such a thrill, liberating. Then the thing had happened and nothing had been thrilling

100

anymore. Not liberating, not even bearable. After that first joyous lesson she had forced herself to complete the course, taken her test and put her licence away. 'Not even sure I can remember how to drive.'

'Like riding a bike. You can't forget.' His face lit up. At last, something he could do with his little girl. Not football, not train sets, but something. 'I'll take you out in it. Let you get the feel of it.'

She laughed, bit her lip, killing the mirth because she hadn't come home to laugh.

'This afternoon? Col will be in—'

'No.' She wanted to be back in control. 'Tomorrow maybe. I've got things to do this afternoon. In town.'

'More books, eh?'

'People to see.'

iii

Kelly

'Yeah, you can give us the details now.' The girl at the desk of the *Lyford Herald* pushed a notepad and pen at Kelly. Her job was to deal with classified ads, and her day was one long stream of adverts for unwanted sofas, Ford Fiestas, fridge freezers. Hard to work up a decent show of enthusiasm for any of it. She went back to another call while Kelly wrote her message.

'*Lyford-Herald*-classified-ads-Emma-speaking-can-I-help-you?'

Kelly had poured through the classified section of last week's *Herald* in WHSmiths. Mostly cars, but two sunbeds and one set of disco lights. No hay bales and split logs, which was what she was used to. She'd looked at the *Evening News* too, but decided that a weekly paper would be a better bet. The *Herald* looked solid. Going since 1893, according to its banner. The sort of paper people would sit down to read properly, not just skim through and dump in the bin.

She smiled as she wrote. Did she know anything about newspaper readers? The nearest thing she read to a paper was the *Alternative World* news-sheet handed out at the wholefood store. Still psychology must just be common sense, and she had plenty of that. But not plenty of money, so she had to choose carefully where to put her ad, and this was it. The *Lyford Herald*.

'There.' She pushed the notepad back at the bored Emma, who counted the words.

'Wanted. Any girl born in Lyford and Stapledon General Hospital in the week March 13th-19th, 1990. Please contact…' She started to absorb the meaning. 'This is legit, right? Nothing, you know…' She was wary. She'd got into trouble once before for accepting an ad for youth performances, which, when it was vetted, was promptly passed on to the police. 'Kids. It's not some kind of – you know?'

Kelly wasn't entirely sure what the girl meant, but she recognised panic. 'Not kids. We'd all be twenty-two.'

'Oh yeah.' Emma grinned. She was only twenty-three herself.

Kelly explained, to put her mind at rest. 'That's when I was born, see? 13th March. 1990. It turns out there was some kind of mix-up, because we've had tests, and I'm not really related to my mother, not genetically, even though my birth certificate says I am. So there must have been a mistake in the hospital.'

'Oh, wow!'

'Which wouldn't have mattered really, except my mum's sick, might need a new kidney eventually, and because I'm not related, I can't give her one. So I thought I could find out who the other baby was.'

'Yeah!'

'I thought, if I put an ad in the local paper, perhaps the other girl is still living in Lyford. It's worth a try. I can stay another week, maybe, and see what pops up.'

'Right! So you're not from round here?'

'Pembrokeshire. We moved to Wales when I was a baby.'

'Oh, so you've come all the way to Lyford to search for this other girl.'

'Yes. To ask at the hospital really, but since they won't help, I'm going to stay on for a few more days. Mum is staying with friends for a couple of weeks.'

'Yes, I see.' Emma was a would-be cub reporter. She didn't like to jot down the details openly, but she was memorising fast. 'So, okay. We'll get this in this week. You've just made the deadline. And can you let us know if anyone responds?'

'Sure.' Kelly beamed. 'I'll come back and tell you all about it.'

A good, useful visit; two girls made happy by a few random words.

CHAPTER 4

i

Heather

Heather Norris went into hospital on the 24th February, 1990. Saturday, just as she had calculated, although it was two weeks after the doctor's prediction. Barbara Norris, her mother-in-law, had been summoned the day before, when Heather had decided to clean the house and shift all the furniture. She had been like that before Bibs was born, so Martin decided it was a sign. He was smugly pleased with himself when she had the first pains.

'I told you.' He rubbed his hands. 'Just as well Mum's here. Better get Bibs.'

'No. For God's sake, let him play. He won't have the first idea what's going on.'

'He knows he's going to have a little brother or sister. Can't wait.'

'Didn't show the slightest interest if you ask me.' She was determined to be argumentative, resenting the fuss that was about to mushroom around her. Her sheer bloody agony and being manhandled, legs akimbo, prodded and bullied and patronised by doctors and nurses who would insist on calling her Mother, as if her breeding function were all the identity she deserved.

'Well, anyway, Mum's here to take care of him. I'll get the car out.'

'Oh, no rush.' Heather plumped down, staking her claim to the sofa. A stupid move. It was too soft and deep; she'd be half an hour getting back out of it. 'I've had a couple of twinges. Hours apart. It's going to be ages yet.'

But Martin was already calling Barbara, who was tidying Bibs' room. Tidying it properly because she alone knew how to tidy a child's bedroom effectively. Mother-in-law. There were worse, Heather supposed. Most of the time, when there was nothing fundamental to fight about, they got on very well. Barbara had patronised Heather as she would have done any stray kitten her son had brought home, hoping that he would lose interest quickly. With their marriage, she had accepted that this kitten was here to stay, and had better be treated with affectionate tolerance. She was never overtly critical about the way her poor son's wife cooked or ironed, or dusted, or brought up their child, even if the criticism was there, in every firm, authoritative gesture.

'Now then, dear.' Barbara was in charge the moment she walked in, patting Heather on the head. No panic, no excitement, just a field marshall deploying troops. 'Calm down, Martin darling. There's no need to rush round like a headless chicken. Have you phoned the hospital to say she'll be on her way? Heather dear, I suppose you are sure. Definite labour pains? Not just indigestion? Constipation?'

'I do remember what it's like,' said Heather, heaving herself up. 'And there's no rush. I think I'll make a cup of tea. Do you want some?'

'Now dear, you just rest. I'll make it. Nice and strong. I may not have many talents but I do know how to make a *proper* cup of tea. Martin did say it would be today. You're lucky to have a husband who notices such things, but then he was always a sensitive boy. Caring. And we're both going to care for you now, so don't you worry about a thing.'

Barbara was already in the kitchen, determined to be mother. Shielding her poor sensitive son from the demanding needs of his flaky wife with her unnatural emotional outbursts. Barbara wasn't going to forget the fuss Heather had caused at Christmas. Other people could. The manager at Sainsbury's had decided that prosecuting an hysterical pregnant woman would be bad publicity, and the paramedics had decided, once she had calmed down, that if she let her GP sort her out she'd be fine. Just a bit stressed. Pregnant women often were.

Martin had been eager to forget, to get on with Christmas, to have fun with Bibs under the tree and not ever to mention all those terrible things Heather had let slip.

But Barbara, who had not even been there, had not forgotten. 'Poor Heather can be – well, I wouldn't like to say unbalanced, but I'm afraid she's finding it very difficult to cope. We'll just have to keep an eye on things, make sure she doesn't fly off the handle again.'

It had worked, in a perverse way. It made Heather determined to remain calm, to cope. She was not going to lose her temper or her reason again. Not if it meant Barbara Norris wrestling her into a straitjacket. So while her mother-in-law made the tea, Heather dragged herself upstairs, and checked through the bag she had ready packed. Nightdresses, dressing gown, slippers, brush, toilet bag, books – and baby clothes; some of Bibs' old things, and some new. Like doll's outfits. Once upon a time she would have gone gooey at the sight of the oh-so-cute little bonnets, bibs and babygros. Now she could only picture endless months of non-stop washing, and the washing machine was threatening to pack up.

'Heather?' Barbara appeared. 'Now you don't need to be

bothering with that. We'll sort out everything for you. I know just what a nursing mother needs.'

'I'm already packed, Barbara. See? Totally prepared. Dib, dib, dib.'

'Oh, good girl. Mind you, I'm sure I'll think of something you've forgotten. One always does. Not to worry; we'll be in to see you every day.'

'I'm not in for a month, you know. It's my second, so they'll probably turf me out tomorrow.'

'I wouldn't be so sure about that, dear.'

'They're always short of beds.'

Barbara tutted. 'We should have found a proper nursing home. You need time to rest. Believe me, I know.'

I know too, Heather swore to herself. She hated hospital, the smell, the lack of privacy, the discomfort, but hospital would mean having other people to take the baby, cook her meals, change her sheets; professionals, not interfering relatives trying to take over her home. As long as she was in hospital, she wouldn't have to worry about checking on her father or buying the milk or doing Martin's shirts or getting Bibs' tea. She could just lie and do nothing. But since Barbara thought she needed a week of doing nothing, Heather was determined to be in and out in twenty-four hours, just to prove her wrong.

Martin had phoned the hospital and was wanting to move, to get her safely inside. Bibs, aware that something was happening, sat down and screamed in terror. On another day, Heather would have fought for the right to comfort him. Now she let Barbara take charge. It would keep her occupied.

'Poor Bibsy Wibsy, is it all too much for you? But don't worry, we still love you, oh yes we do. Granny will always love you, my special weshal boy.'

107

'Go on, Bibs,' prayed Heather silently. 'Throw up on her.' Ah. The pains again. Getting more frequent. Shit. She remembered what it was like, she'd said, but it wasn't true. She had forgotten what a screaming torture it was. Get it over with, for Christ's sake. Epidurals, gas, any damn thing. Somebody just put her under and prise the bloody thing out of her.

'Come on,' she said, as the cramp receded, and she could look at Martin's anxious face without cursing. 'Let's go.'

He carried her bags to the car. Barbara stood with Bibs, making him wave as if, given the choice, he wouldn't wave to his mummy.

'Be good, won't you,' said Heather, kissing him before Martin shovelled her into the passenger seat. She delayed shutting the door, looking back at Barbara. 'I've left a couple of meals in the freezer. If they need more than that…'

'Oh good heavens, dear, you shouldn't have bothered with that. I'm here. I'll make sure they have *proper* meals, good home cooking. It will do them good for a change. Now off you go. Martin, you will phone, won't you?'

'You'll bloody eat those casseroles I've left, whatever she tries to feed you,' said Heather as they lurched out of the drive onto the street.

Martin laughed. 'Scout's honour.'

'And you will go round and see Dad as soon as you can, won't you? I know he probably won't understand, but you've got to tell him.'

'I'll call straight there on my way home. Right, let's hope there are no roadworks. Come on, come on!' A bus had stopped in front of them and he was itching to squeeze past.

'Martin, there's no…' She couldn't finish. The pain pounced on her again.

He was sweating with terror. He would be there, when she gave birth, because it was expected these days; he could cope with that, but the thought of her going into labour in the car was panicking him. He was crunching the gears like a learner driver on his first lesson.

'I'm all right,' she assured him.

He wouldn't believe it until he passed her into the care of the hospital staff.

Here she was again. First time round it had been huge, this event of events. She'd expected a fanfare of trumpets, every face in the hospital lighting up with awe at the thought of Heather Norris bringing a new life into the world. Surely the clouds were parting and crowds applauding.

That was then. Now there was no awe, no one to give a damn. Not even Heather herself.

The nurses who took charge of her joked among themselves, continuing conversations, barely registering her. She was one more parcel on the conveyor belt. A doctor was wheeled in, got her name wrong, inspected her like a prize cow. He watched dispassionately as the cramps took over again. At least the painkillers helped a bit, but as God was her witness, she was never ever going to go through this again.

Martin was no help. For an hour he got in the way, expecting instant fireworks, asking her if there was anything he could do.

'Have a vasectomy,' she ordered.

He winced. 'Let's just wait and see, eh.'

'No. It's an ultimatum. If you get me in the club again, I'm having an abortion.'

His wince turned into a full-blown grimace. Nerves and fear. He couldn't tell if she were joking or going to explode again with all that resentment he couldn't understand. 'You do want it, don't you, Heather? You were just kidding, that time. Weren't you?'

'Oh for Christ's sake, what does it matter what I want?'

She felt her body relax. It gave her space for sympathy. Poor boy, he couldn't help being useless. 'Look, Martin, it's going to be ages yet. I tell you what we've forgotten. A teddy bear.'

'Oh no, Mum's bought one.'

'No, I mean one from us. Just a nice squishy little bear. Nothing posh. I wanted to choose one but I never got round to it. You know I was eight hours with Bibs and you don't want to be hanging round here that long. Can you choose one?'

'Where?'

'There are shops just round the corner. Choose a nice one.'

'Right. A bear. Yes.' Did he know he was being shunted away, out of her hair? Probably as anxious to escape as she was to have him go. What were fathers supposed to do for eight hours? Bring back the civilised days when they were just sent off to smoke or boil water.

The door had barely swung to behind him when the pain was back and she knew this was it.

'Shit!' She slammed the button summoning the nurse.

Abigail Laura Norris was born at half past five after a very quick and uncomplicated labour. Seven pounds five ounces and wailing even as she emerged. A gasping mew. Heather was vaguely aware of it, through the pain and the sweating and a raging fury she couldn't understand and hoped no one else would notice.

'There we are,' said the nurse, presenting her with a raw red bundle with screwed up eyes. She had forgotten how small and ugly babies were. She dutifully had to hold it and feed it while they all looked on. What was she, an exhibit in a freak show?

'What a pity Father missed it. Never mind, he'll be so thrilled. Now let's get you cleaned up and sorted out and off to a nice fresh bed.' She was at the end of the conveyor belt. They wanted her out of the delivery room quick, and in with the next. She was wheeled to a side ward with five other mothers, three of them beaming as if they had fulfilled the divine purpose of the universe, one asleep, one muttering that she needed a fag. Maybe I could start smoking, Heather thought.

Martin turned up, with a blue bear, suitable squishy. He looked terrified and apologetic. 'I missed it! Will you ever forgive me? I didn't realise it would be so quick this time. There wasn't anything local so I drove into town, to Woolworths. So sorry, Heather.'

'Don't worry, I was too doped up to notice. There she is then.'

Granted permission, he turned to the cot, drooling over his baby daughter. 'She's so beautiful. Isn't she? Has your eyes. Oh God, she's lovely.'

'She'll do. You'd best get home to Bibs, give him the good news. But make a big fuss of him. Say it's a present for him. I don't want him to be jealous.'

But Martin wouldn't go at once. He had to go down to the foyer, phone Barbara, come back with flowers and chocolates and magazines, grinning as if he'd just won an Olympic gold.

'God, look at her, an absolute cherub. I've phoned home, told Mum.'

'Don't forget my father.'

'I won't. Oh poor Heather.' His attention was back to his

wife for a moment. 'I shouldn't have gone. How was it? Really bad?'

'No, I suppose not.' Absolute hell at the time, but the memory was already a blur. 'I just feel a bit sore. And tired. I want to sleep for a week. You don't mind, do you?'

Martin left and Heather slept. She woke in the middle of the night.

The gentle snoring and burbling of five other women and six babies, in the silence of a sleeping hospital. Distant clangs and soft feet in the corridor. Light, from outside, painting moving patterns on the ceiling. A twinge of deep depression. This was an alien place, and there she was, Heather Norris, forgotten, ignored, utterly alone.

Except for that one little fragment of humanity sleeping beside her. Her baby. Her one connection. Flesh of her flesh, bone of her bone, soul of her soul. Dependent on her.

She rolled over to study the little wrinkled face, and met a glimmer of blue eyes. Eyes without knowledge or fear, fixed on her, trusting. Eyes that knew her, that knew nothing but her.

She reached to ease the child out of her cot. 'Now you mustn't have baby in bed with you,' the nurse would say, soon enough. But the nurse wasn't here just now. No one was here. Heather was alone with her child.

'Just us, Abigail Laura,' she whispered, cuddling down with the child. 'You and me and no one else. Us two against the whole bloody world. God, I love you.'

ii

Gillian

'So where's this wonderful baby then?' Gillian's younger sister Pam looked around vaguely, expecting a baby to materialise out of thin air. 'I thought they'd have given you one by now.'

'They've approved us, that's all,' said Gillian. A letter of approval and then silence. How much longer could she wake each morning with a burst of hope that grew weaker and weaker each day? 'We're waiting for the right baby to come along. It's got to be right, for the baby and for us.'

'Oh.' Pam considered reaching for a biscuit but the tin was too far away and she couldn't be bothered.

Without thinking, Gillian got up and passed it to her.

'Ta. So you do get to choose then. I wouldn't like not being able to choose. I mean, you don't want a retard or something.' Pam laughed in horror.

'I don't care if it's handicapped.' She meant it. A handicapped child would need her even more than a healthy one. She could feel her heart swelling at the thought of being needed forever.

'Ugh.' Pam grimaced.

'You'll want a boy,' said Sandra, the eldest sister. She had been a dark pretty teenager, full of life, but at thirty-eight, she was every inch a second edition of Joan. Ironic, as she had spent her childhood screaming foul-mouthed defiance at Joan. 'Don't go for a girl. They're nothing but bother and pregnant before you know it.' She was qualified to talk. Bustled down the aisle at sixteen with hapless Dennis Taylor, because one had to in those days. Trevor had been born six weeks later. Now her daughter Sharon was

113

expecting her second child, at seventeen. The girl had been left to run wild, to live her life on street corners, getting drunk on cheap lager. Talked about the pill as if she knew it all, but never actually did anything about it. Sandra had done nothing to guide her and she'd doubtless follow the same route with four-year-old Dana.

'Ask me, they're never going to give her a baby,' said Joan, from the kitchen. She came through in a haze of smoke. 'Too old, in't she. Thirty-five? Looking for young mums, I reckon. Missed her chance.'

Gillian could feel tears prickling, not at her mother's unfeeling brutality, but the probable truth. Thirty-five was the age limit with the adoption authority. She'd been warned when she and Terry first applied.

Pam looked at her with sympathy. 'Well you won't be missing much, you know. They're just a fuss and a bother.'

'Bleeding pain in the arse,' agreed Sandra. 'Never a moment to think of yourself. Count yourself lucky you're out of it.'

'I want a baby!' Gillian's nails bit into her palms. 'Just because it's been so easy for you, even when you didn't want them.' They looked at her with incomprehension and contempt. Of course they didn't understand. Three Summers girls and only Gillian was truly capable of responsibility and love and caring. Why was she the only one denied the fulfilment they regarded as an irritation? Why was she condemned to this burning desperation?

She had always been the peacekeeper in the family, the good-humoured calming one, bowing to other people's egos. Sandra had been the rebel. There were still dents in the plaster where she and Joan had thrown things at each other. Pam was the baby, with the curls and the sweet smile. Cared for and pampered as a child, cared for and pampered as a woman. She had never had to make decisions or take charge in her life and that was how she liked it. Gillian had always understood by instinct. Sandra was to be calmed and obeyed, Pam to be worshipped and comforted.

Gillian had done whatever was asked of her, without complaint mostly. Looking back now, she could see just how much she had sacrificed. She had done really well at school. Probably as eager to please her teachers as friends and family. While Sandra played truant and Pam allowed others to do her work for her, Gillian sat and listened and worked and sailed through her eleven plus.

'That means you get to go to the girls' grammar,' said Aunty Doreen from next door, awestuck.

Joan, had laughed and said 'You kidding? She doesn't want to be stuck with that toffee-nosed lot.'

So Gillian had gone to Houghton Road Secondary Modern, like nearly everyone else on the Marley Farm estate, and she hadn't complained. Sometimes, the memory of her mother's laugh came back to her. If Gillian had put her foot down and claimed her right to grammar school, perhaps Joan would have given way. Not with a good grace certainly. With plenty of comments about hoity-toity and the sacrifices I have to make and you needn't think I'm going to wait on you hand and foot just because you've gone all posh. But she would perhaps have given way, complained about the cost of the uniform and sniffed with contempt in case anyone thought she might actually be proud.

But it was pointless wondering, because Gillian hadn't put her foot down. So she didn't go to grammar school and become a teacher, which is what grammar school girls did. She went to Houghton Road Secondary Modern, and she passed her O levels in English and Maths and she took her

115

commerce, shorthand and typing courses, and she got a secretarial job with the Gas Board, which was the acme of career success on Marley Farm Estate. A nice office job to see her through until she settled down to the proper business of a woman's life, getting married and having babies.

She did it all. She qualified, she worked, at twenty-one she married Terry, a nice undemanding lad with a decent job at the car plant, and she prepared to embark on motherhood.

And the needle stuck.

Why? How could life be so spiteful? It was all she'd ever asked. For a year after her marriage she'd stayed on the pill, while they worked on putting a bit aside, sorting themselves out, thinking about a proper home, instead of the rented flat over the florist's shop. Then they'd decided that now was as good a time as ever, and she'd come off the pill and waited for nature to take its course.

When nothing happened there was no great panic during the first year or even, really, during the second. Just a little uneasiness as time passed, as she lay awake in the early mornings, listening to Terry's snores and trying to detect the faint flutter of nausea.

In their third year of trying, she was determined. There must be something simple they were doing wrong. She borrowed manuals, wrote to advice columns in magazines, she insisted on new daring positions which left Terry struggling between titillation and embarrassment. She kept thermometers in the bathroom and demanded performance by the calendar clock, her husband grumbling.

And still nothing. In the fourth year she consulted a doctor, although it took another year before she could persuade Terry to go too. Fertility treatment. Poking and prying, living like a lab rat, and more humiliations than she had ever believed she could endure, and still nothing. Their savings dwindled and Terry was sympathetic and irritated in turns. He wanted a child, she knew. He didn't long to change nappies and attend parent's evenings, but he liked the idea that he might pass on the mysteries of the internal combustion engine to another generation.

But Gillian wanted a child in a different way. It grew and grew within her like a cancer, devouring body and mind, until it seemed the only thing she had ever wanted. Her only purpose was to carry a child, to protect and nurture it and watch it grow into some fabulous bird of paradise that would finally spread its wings and fly. Little by little, her sense of failure passed through worry, frustration and anger into aching, all-consuming despair.

Despite that letter of approval, if a baby wasn't available in the next few months, that door would close on her forever, and there would be nothing left except to die.

'You have no idea what they cost,' said Pam.

'And do you?'

Pam wasn't accustomed to being attacked. 'A lot! Ask Dave.'

Joan nodded. 'Eat you out of house and home. Want, want, want, that was all I ever got from you lot.'

'Yeah, and want was all we ever got from you,' said Sandra.

'Worked my fucking arse off for you, I did. Not that I ever got a word of thanks. Where would you all have been without me, answer me that.'

'In care and in bloody clover probably.'

Gillian put her tea down and left them to it. The washing was flapping out on the line, dry enough by now. Best to get it in before the skies opened.

Her mother and her sisters were terrible parents. What if it were inherited? All those months Gillian had spent trying to convince the powers that be that she would make a perfect mother. But what if she too were a failure, damned by the warped Summers genes? Should she withdraw? Warn the agency, for the sake of all children, to keep clear of her family?

For one bleak moment, she imagined it. 'Claire, it's wrong. This family isn't fit to have a child.'

'No!' She shouted it loud, though her denial was muffled by the flapping sheets. She couldn't do it. She wasn't that noble. And she wasn't Joan or Sandra or Pam. She was Gillian Wendle, a woman who wanted nothing but to be a mother. A good mother, if only they would give her a child.

'Crazy cow,' she heard Sandra laugh, back in the house. 'Who the hell wants a bloody baby?'

iii

Lindy

'Get that fat lump out of here, can't you.' Gary scowled at her. 'Got people coming. Don't want a great fat cow pushing herself in their faces.' He groped in the cupboard for a fresh packet of cigarettes. 'Look at that. Baked beans. Baby crap. Go get us some proper food. A pizza or something.'

'Yes, Gary, all right.' Lindy pulled her coat on without being asked twice.

Slumped at the table, Gary assessed her from head to foot. She wasn't really a great fat cow. Too skinny by nature. If she walked right and let the big coat hang, you wouldn't

118

even notice the bump. 'Watch yourself. Don't want the whole world knowing that thing's on its way. When is it due, anyway?'

She chewed her lip, like she was struggling to calculate. Dozy cow. 'I dunno. A couple more weeks, I think.'

'Okay. Just keep your head down. Couple of weeks, then we get rid of it, right?'

She looked at him, pleading. 'It's your baby, Gary.'

'Like fuck it is.'

'I swear.'

'Well I don't give a fuck, see. You stay with me – it goes. Got that, girl?'

She nodded.

'So don't go telling no one.'

'What about a doctor or something?'

'You don't need a doctor. It's natural, dropping a baby. Dogs and cats, they just do it, don't they? Just do it and no one need know. Now clear out. And bring back some beer.'

'Okay.'

Lindy knew she had to be out of the house while Gary did business, so there was no point in hurrying. No point in just trotting along to the local Spar and lifting a few cans and packets. Besides, she'd done it so many times now that Mr Patel was on the lookout for her. It would be better to go into town, the big department stores and the bustling shopping centre where no one would pay her any attention. She was a professional. She knew what to do.

Rain began to spot the pavement, gathering for a downpour. The voluminous coat was twice as heavy when it got soaked, and it took forever to dry in the damp flat. She was glad that she could slip into the shopping centre, where there was no rain or wind or sky. Always the same light, the same heat. Keep the customers focussed on the big glass windows. Boots, Debenhams, River Island, Next. It wasn't such a great place for food though. The Kentucky Fried Chicken and the Donut parlour were no use to her, unless she fancied trying to lift a couple of dozen sugar sachets. She could imagine how Gary would react to that.

She paused a moment, inhaling the smell of fried chicken. Not a good idea. It made her feel hungry, and she couldn't afford it. Forget it. There was a little Tesco's at the far end. That would do. Busy aisles and easily diverted check-out girls.

It would be tricky because she didn't have enough money to buy anything as cover. She'd had more cash, to be honest, when Gary was still inside. She'd been desperate for him to come back, to be her man, to take care of her, but now he never gave her any money, and he took her benefit, spent it all on fags. Still, she had him.

She plodded on. Wafted along by gentle skating muzak. People could skate here, the floor was that polished. Lindy had seen it being done. Working here for Greg, coming in through one of the unnoticed back doors beneath the multi-storey car park, in the dead of night, to join the cleaning crew, she had seen the polishers at work. No dirt and litter in the sanitised shopping centre.

She needed to sit down. It had been a long walk from Nelson Road, and she was feeling odd. Light-headed. Her back was breaking and her legs ached. She sat down on the island seats that were designed to be not too comfortable so the shoppers would be up and shopping again. Kept her coat clasped around her. A fat old woman sat down beside her, muttering at her disapprovingly for not being fat and old. Lindy wanted to give her lip. Wasn't her fault she was young. But she couldn't afford to get into a swearing match, because she had to keep her head down, Gary said, until the baby was born and they could dump it.

So after a minute she trailed on, leaving the fat old woman to spread herself. No rush to go round Tesco's. Try her hand somewhere else first. Didn't matter where. He could sell anything she nicked. Videos and records were good; there was HMV round the corner. Or here. Baby Garden, with its bright bubbly displays. Loads of stuff just asking for it. It didn't matter what.

Not many fat old women in here. Mums with buggies or dragging toddlers, or mums-to-be in frilly maternity dresses, edging their bulges round the displays. Baby clothes, soft and pastel and bright. Jackets and playsuits and tiny little bootees. Cots and quilts and changing mats and bottles and dummies and teddy bears and cloth books, and women thumbing through them all like this was expected, like this was what a baby had to have.

Just as well she and Gary weren't going to keep her baby, because she didn't have nothing for it. She stood watching a woman choosing between two tiny jumpsuits, one striped, one with stars. What would Lindy do? Wrap hers in newspaper? Gary was right, it was a joke, her keeping it. Stupid.

These women paid good money for this stuff. It must be worth nicking. Lindy picked up a gift set. Plastic mug and bowl, two plates, knife, fork and spoon, all with dancing bears, in rigid plastic wrapping. She'd take this. And that tiny quilted coat with the fluffy hood. Must be worth a bit.

The manager was looking her way. Suspicious. She could play it canny, put down the gift set and the coat and pick up something else, those cloth alphabet bricks maybe, keep mooching, choosing, edging out of sight until the manager's attention was drawn elsewhere. Then again, sometimes it worked just as well to play all innocent. Chin up, guileless, 'Course I've paid, do I look like I'm shoplifting?' That's what she'd do now. She slipped the gift set and clothes inside her coat and walked boldly for the door.

She heard the hasty 'Oi!' of the store manager, barely a second before a man's hand closed on her arm.

'Excuse me, madam, I believe you have items there that you have not purchased.' Polite preliminaries by rote. She looked up into his eyes and knew his courtesy had already run its course. No more of that 'excuse me' stuff for the likes of her. Big and burly, thick red neck, he was grinning with contempt, grabbing at the plastic packaging peeping from her coat. She fought him off, but he was stronger, dragging her back into the store.

'Geroff me!'

'Shoplifting. You're not going anywhere, my girl.'

'I ain't nicked nuffing.'

'What's this then?' Treating her like a rag doll, he pulled out the quilted coat.

'They're mine. I got them weeks ago.'

'Oh yeah?' He held them up to show the Baby Garden labels.

'Can we take this through to the office, please, Mr. Gilbert.' The manager joined them, nervous more than triumphant. She had spotted the probable shoplifting, but now they had an actual situation, a girl caught, an over-zealous security guard wanting to demonstrate his he-man qualities, she was just desperate to keep any unpleasantness from sullying her store. Customers were watching, uncomfortable and embarrassed, or tutting indignation.

The guard frogmarched Lindy through the store. 'Okay, don't you go making a fuss. Caught red-handed.'

The manager patted his arm, speaking softly to show him

that shouting wasn't a good idea. 'Just come through to the office, please, and we'll wait for the police there.'

'Stop pushing me! You're hurting me!' It was true. Lindy was hurting. 'I'm pregnant!'

'Ha ha, I doubt that,' said the guard with a lewd laugh. 'I know how these girls operate. Bit of padding in the right place. She's no more pregnant than I am. You see.' He thrust Lindy at the manager, who raised her hands to ward her off.

'I am, see!' Lindy flung her coat open. A pair of gloves, still with its Debenhams label, flopped out of one of the inner pockets, but her bump was evident. Painfully real on her thin frame.

'Then you should be thinking about your baby,' said a woman, prim cow. 'What sort of example are you going to set? Not fit to be a mother.'

'I just want stuff for my baby!' said Lindy hotly. Facing the hostility of the world was normal. She was born to be bruised and to fight back if she had to. 'I want stuff just like you and I ain't got no money, so there.'

'Yes, well, I'm sorry,' said the manager, ushering her on. 'I'm very sorry.' She sounded as if, left to her own devices, she would mean it. 'But that can't excuse shoplifting. We have a very strict prosecution policy; there's nothing I can do about it. You'll just have to tell your story to the police, when they get here.' She was breathing deeply. Why weren't the police here already, to relieve her of this embarrassment?

In the meantime, she needed Lindy out of sight, and Lindy knew it. The manager didn't want a pregnant woman kicking and screaming and making a scene.

'I ain't going no-where. Don't push me!' She could play hurt easily, because she was hurting. 'You shouldn't shove a pregnant woman.'

'Oh dear.' Another customer stepped forward, looking

anxiously at Lindy, then down at the floor. 'I think she's a wee bit wet.'

'Oh for God's sake,' said the manager, wincing in disgust.

'I think, maybe, her waters have broken,' said the customer.

Lindy watched the manager's jaw drop. 'Oh, Christ.'

All different then. Suddenly, she wasn't a sneaky little shoplifter. She was a helpless little mum-to-be, in need of urgent attention.

'Poor thing, she's only a child herself.'

'Are you with anyone, dear? Is there someone we can get for you?'

'Is there a doctor in the centre?'

'Hadn't you better call for an ambulance? She should be in hospital.'

'Ambulance.' The manager was hovering, hapless. 'Oh God, yes. Of course, I'll phone.'

'Here you are.' An assistant brought a chair. 'You sit down, dear. Someone will be along soon.'

'Best get the weight off your feet, eh?' It was the security guard, who told her he had a daughter who had just given birth. Funny what this business did to people, however threatening they had been before.

Everyone except Gary. He'd warned her to keep her head down.

There was nothing she could do about that now. They'd sent for an ambulance, and she was glad, because the pain wasn't easy like dogs and cats, whatever Gary said. It was real and Lindy was frightened. Terrified. This was all wrong and upside down and Gary would be mad, but what could she do?

Ambulance men appeared at the door of the shop, and a dozen eager shoppers directed them to Lindy.

'All right, love? Nothing to worry about. We'll have you in hospital in no time.'

The manager was on the phone, talking to head office, taking orders. A woman shoplifting was one thing. A woman giving birth was another. The Baby Garden chain had fourteen shops and the owners wanted their share of the Mothercare market. Right handling, right publicity, who knew how this could work out? The manager put the phone down, still nodding agreement, and raised a hand to the ambulance men, telling them she was going to attend to them as soon as she'd spoken with her assistants.

'So what's your name then?' asked one of the ambulance men, squatting down by Lindy.

'Lindy. Lindy Crowe.'

'All right then, Lindy. So how often are the pains coming?'

She looked at him helplessly. How often?

'I think she's got a while to go yet,' confided one of the spectators, who saw herself as an expert. 'But you can never tell, can you.'

'Well, we'll get you into hospital and the docs can have a good look at you, eh?'

How could she argue with them? She couldn't run away. As she was escorted out, the manager and her assistants stood at the door, like the three kings at the manger. Offering carrier bags bulging with Pampers, bonnets, bootees and babygros.

'Got to give Baby something to be getting on with,' said the manager, trying a tentative smile. 'Baby Garden believes that every child deserves a decent start in life.'

Lindy clutched the bags. She felt the softness of wool and towelling. She didn't know how to respond. She'd come to steal, hadn't she? And they had given her all this. So she'd got away with it. Was that how Gary would see it?

She didn't want to think about Gary. This was stuff for her baby, just like a proper mum would have. And she was going into hospital, just like mums did.

Lyford and Stapledon General. She had been here once before. One of Gary's friends had been in with an overdose last year, and she'd come to see him, because Gary wanted to make sure Pete wasn't saying nothing about where he'd got the stuff. She hadn't liked it then, too official, too full of people in uniform. Too many horrible smells, too much sickness and death. Pete was out of his head and she'd never liked him anyway.

It was different now. People were fussing round her, being nice to her. Nice but firm. When she'd been in care, firm sent her running. But now it was a relief. Nothing she could do, whatever Gary wanted.

'Now then, dear, let's have your details,' said the nurse who seemed to have taken charge of her. 'What's your name?'

'Lindy Crowe.'

'Lindy. Is that Linda?' As she wrote, the nurse checked Linda's hands, her fingers – no ring.

'Rosalind.'

'Oh what a pretty name. And your address.'

They wanted everything, her date of birth, her place of birth, her doctor. Wouldn't believe she didn't have one. Hadn't she had any medical check-ups while she was pregnant? No clinic? Nothing at all since she'd been at the home down in Barking? Who were her parents? Long gone. Mum dead, dad in gaol. Next of kin? Brother Jimmy, she supposed, but she hadn't seen him for eight years. Probably banged up too by now. She was too scared to name Gary;

126

he wouldn't like it. But she'd given her address in Nelson Road so maybe they'd find him anyway. She should have said 28. That way, if they did track her down, she could say it was a mistake. 28 instead 128. Too late now. She wasn't thinking straight because of the pain.

And then there was so much pain she didn't want to answer any more questions, and she didn't want to be here, with all these strangers, people in white coats, people with forms to fill in. No one was telling her that she shouldn't be here, and that was scary. But the pain was scary too and she just wanted it to end.

'Breathe,' the nurse said, panting at her. 'Like this. Don't push.'

And then, 'Push. That's right, push. Good girl, keep pushing.' She thought she was being ripped open, ripped in two, and soon she would be dead and she didn't care.

But then it all drained away, all the pain and the pressure drifting off in a blur. She was floating, and there was something on her face. Floating.

A hand on her brow, fingers on her wrist. 'She's all right now, aren't you, Mrs Crowe.'

Was she? The huge pain had gone. No, not all right. Something was missing. She was too groggy to think, but something was missing. Something vital taken away.

Then she heard it, the faint wail, and her eyes began to focus again. She fixed on the little wrapped bundle they were holding out to her. The baby. Her baby. Rosalind Crowe's baby, her family, her everything. She reached out.

'A little girl. A teensy bit underweight, but not too bad, all things considered. See? You've done all right. Now would you like to feed her?'

They wanted to help. They wanted her to breastfeed. She wasn't sure about that. Didn't seem natural. She'd fed babies before. Angie's baby, with a bottle. This wasn't right, this tit stuff. Not with all of them watching.

'Maybe you'd feel better with a bottle? Just for now.'

Then she was all right, even if one of the nurses looked at her like she was a lump of shit. This was what she wanted, to be here, all alone with her baby, feeding her, cradling her. Her little girl.

'Have you got a name for her?'

Lindy looked into the hungry blue eyes. No reason. It just came to her. 'Kelly,' she said.

CHAPTER 5

i

Kelly

'Joe?'

'What? Is that you, Kelly?' He answered at last, raising his voice over the music. After her mother's medical crisis, she'd had the landline reconnected in the living room. Joe must have his radio right by it.

'Course it is,' Kelly shouted, clamping the mobile between shoulder and ear while she unpacked. 'How's it all going?'

'Fine, you know. No probs.'

'Sheep okay?'

'Yeah, fine. And Eleanor and Rigby – well not Rigby; she ate my jacket.'

'Oh dear. All of it?'

'Na, just a bit of one sleeve.'

'Is she all right? Not choking or anything?' You had to be careful with goats. 'What about the chickens? Have you collected the eggs?'

'Yeah, yeah. They're fine.'

'That's great. Do you think you'll be able to manage for a few more days, Joe? Like, another week?'

'Week? Yeah, okay.'

'You sure?'

'You don't mind if I have a few of the guys round, do you?'

'No, of course not. Just try not to mess with Mum's things. You're going to need more feed. I'll order it if you can pick it up. Can you find the number? I've scribbled it on the fridge.'

Organising Joe over the phone was surprisingly easy. Of course, Kelly knew he might not remember to pick up the feed, or keep 'the guys' out of her mother's room, but she was sure that nothing could go seriously wrong. He wasn't likely to burn the house down, and the animals could forage for themselves at this time of year, if he forgot. There was a good chance of losing a couple of the chickens to foxes because Joe would forget to round them up, but that had probably happened already.

She phoned the feed supplier, then called Roger and Mandy.

'Kelly!' Mandy answered. 'Home safely? Did the car behave all right?'

'Perfectly. Just checking on Mum.'

Roz was fine. Everything in Dorset was fine, everything in Pembrokeshire was fine, the whole world was fine.

Joe was going to let them know at the Moon and Tuppence that she wouldn't be able to do her shifts for the next week. Too late now to ring the office. She'd do that in the morning, tell them she needed time off. They wouldn't query it, not with her mother being ill.

All sorted. She was free to go with this river she had jumped into. Had she been rash? She could see potential rapids ahead. But what the hell, she was a good swimmer. At best she would find herself a potential kidney donor and a sister of sorts. At worst, she wouldn't find anything. Nothing more disastrous than that. How could there be?

ii

Vicky

Vicky paced the street, watching, trying not to be seen. It was a part of Lyford she didn't know, so it had taken her a while to find it, but getting here had been the easy part. The woman had moved since their last confrontation, and no one at the old flats had been sure where. So Vicky had lain in wait for the postman. It gave her a sense of cool satisfaction when it paid off, although the postman had probably been breaking regulations in telling her that Mrs Parish had moved to Salley Meadows. He couldn't tell her which number though. They'd know at the sorting office, but that was far out on the other side of town. It was more tempting to take the number 16 bus to the Brookdale estate, hoping her luck would last, and she'd find another door sprayed with accusing graffiti.

No graffiti. Salley Meadows, the name promising lush grass and shivering willows, was just a dull anonymous street of dull anonymous houses and flats, not squalid enough to raise eyebrows, not deluxe enough to envy. Vicky walked up and down it twice. No sign of her birth mother. She'd recognise her. Even a glimpse from behind and she'd know her.

She returned, frustrated, to the bus stop, to wait for the next bus back to the town centre. Thirty yards away, across the street, the number 16 pulled up to let off passengers.

It moved on and there she was. The woman. Mrs Parish, gathering bags, heading for home. Vicky ignored her own bus, stepping back as it slowed, and the driver scowled at her indecision before accelerating again.

Thirty paces behind, Vicky followed her quarry back into

Salley Meadows. Twenty. Ten. The maisonettes. The woman put her bags down at the door of 28, searching for her key. Vicky speeded up.

Mrs Parish turned, alert, sensing the movement, looking Vicky full in the face. She recognised her. 'Oh. I see. You again.'

'Me again. Mother.'

'I'm not your mother. Just go away, will you?'

'No. I won't. I'll be here. Always. Just so you'll never forget.'

'Whatever your game is, I'm not interested.' She was in. Slam. The door shut. Vicky could hear bolts being drawn.

What was her game? Vicky wasn't sure herself. She knew she had to keep punishing this woman.

Someone had to be punished. Vicky wanted it to be Gillian, beaten and begging for forgiveness. But she knew that if she cast Gillian into outer darkness Vicky would be alone. She didn't have the courage. So it would have to be this woman instead. The one who'd failed to kill her, but left her to be fed to Joan. The one the whole world itched to punish.

Mrs Parish had moved, but she hadn't escaped. Number 28, Salley Gardens. No need to stay further today. Vicky would keep returning and returning and returning, because there was no way she could get past this thing.

iii

Kelly

The *Lyford Herald* came out on Thursday. Kelly bought it at the local newsagents and pored through it as she walked into town. Just a classified ad, in pages of others, under Personal. It looked nice and bold; Emma must have pulled some strings. Even so, maybe Kelly should have gone for something bigger, more prominent. Cost, that was the thing. She couldn't justify spending their money on a more expensive ad. But then she couldn't really justify spending their money on bed and breakfast in Colney Road either, so maybe it should have been in for a penny, in for a pound. There was always next week. If she got no response to this one, perhaps she would stay around long enough to put a bigger ad in the next issue. If she could endure Mrs Hanshaw's guesthouse that long.

She was sure the ad would be a waste of time, so when her mobile rang in the middle of the afternoon, she assumed it must be Joe or Roger, and was puzzled by the unknown number.

'Hello. Is that Kelly Sheldon? The one who put the ad in the paper? About kids born in March, in the hospital?'

'Yes! Hi. March 13th to the 19th, 1990.'

'Oh. Has to be 90, does it, 'cos I was born there March 16th but it was 1988.'

Kelly's pulse, which had started to race, slowed again. 'Sorry. It's got to be 90.'

'So I don't get it, then? The prize or whatever?'

'No, sorry. There's no prize.' Was a chance to give a kidney a prize? 'Just trying to contact people.'

'Oh. Well, it's not me then.'

'No. But thanks for phoning.'

After all, she thought, look on the bright side. It did show that someone had noticed it. There might be more.

There were more, that night and the following morning. Two people who'd misread the dates, two men who thought it must be a coded invitation to kinky sex, one who wanted to know what colour her knickers were, three who were convinced there must be some cosmic significance to those dates or evidence of extra-terrestrial landings and one a very vague old lady who wanted to talk about crochet patterns.

But also two people born in Lyford and Stapledon General, in the week of the 13th to 19th, March 1990. One of them, Christopher, was a man, and couldn't possibly be her missing phantom sister, but he sounded so excited by the idea of a post-cot reunion, as if he had been waiting twenty-two years for someone to suggest it, that she invited him along to the meeting she had arranged with Andrea, born on the 17th.

'So, anyway, it will be September next year.' Andrea sipped her drink and looked at her engagement ring. A large diamond. At least Kelly assumed it was a diamond. She only bought jewellery from the stall in the market that made stuff out of recycled tin cans. The diamond might be glass, but she guessed Andrea wouldn't be looking quite so smug if it were.

Andrea Marley. A girl born in the same week as Kelly, in the same hospital. And for all that, Kelly realised, not really on the same planet. She was getting married to her Matthew in fifteen month's time because apparently weddings took that long to arrange. In Kelly's world, weddings were a quick trip to the registry office. Or a bit of tantric chanting on Carn Ingli. Or once, at the old church by the beach, with the bride arriving along the sands on Maddy Davies' almost white pony in a high wind. Why did you need a year and a half to book church, flowers, dresses, morning suits, country house, photographer, hairdresser, manicurist, sunbed?

'Wow,' she said, smiling at Andrea, wanting to set her at

ease. Why was Andrea so stressed? She was beautiful and knew it. Beautiful with all the perfection of a boiled egg. She was dressed perfectly for this bar, Rick's Place, brushed steel and smoked glass, Space Age superimposed on Art Deco, with its tapas bar and continental beers and barmen doing little dances as they whisked up cocktails.

Rick's Place had ambitions to be somewhere other than Lyford. It wanted to be the place where people who were Somebody came to be seen, to be photographed on their arrival by lurking paparazzi. Except that there weren't any Somebodies in Lyford, or paparazzi either. They were all twenty-five miles down the motorway in London. But Rick's Place clung to the hope that one day, maybe, Somebody would walk in.

The aspiration had rubbed off on Andrea. For her it was *the* place. She had dressed up and Rick's Place was probably delighted with her, because most of the customers were increasingly loud topers working their way round the watering holes of Lyford's civic centre, before heading on to the Desert Dunes nightclub.

'And we're thinking of the Seychelles for the honeymoon, but we still need to decide on a hotel. It has to be just right, doesn't it?'

'Wow. Seychelles,' said Kelly.

'I don't even know where the Seychelles is,' grinned Christopher. He was just as excitable as he had sounded on the phone. Gawky, sandy hair that stuck up, and a tendency to jump up and down in his chair. He seemed genuinely impressed by Rick's Place. He'd seldom been to pubs. He spent most of his time on the computer, at work at J C Electronics or at home playing Warcraft.

There was a pause. 'They're islands,' said Andrea witheringly. She was sure of that, if nothing else.

135

'In the Indian Ocean, near Madagascar,' added Kelly.

'Oh Madagascar! Great film!' enthused Christopher.

Andrea sighed. 'Well, anyway, until the wedding, I'm working for Catterick and Mayhew's, but I'll probably quit when I get married.'

'To have babies?' suggested Christopher.

Andrea winced. 'No, not babies, thank you. So. Kelly. Do you have a partner? Someone special? Any plans?' She had been talking about herself since she came in, while desperately searching for clues. She knew exactly what to make of Christopher, in his Primark pants and his shirt with the egg stain, but she was at a complete loss with Kelly. How do you place someone in patchwork leggings, magic unicorn T-shirt, a velveteen waistcoat with feathers in its embroidery, a nose stud, a Buddhist tattoo on the back of her hand and a green streak in her hair? What sort of person would dress like that for a visit to Rick's Place? Either a *Big Issue* seller or – and this was the point – a real celebrity, someone so gloriously successful that she could set her own rules. Andrea's instinct, if they'd met in the street, would have been to step around Kelly as if she were a dog turd. In Rick's Place, she was more circumspect, just in case Kelly really was the Somebody the bar had been waiting for.

'Lots of special people,' said Kelly. 'And no particular plans. I just wait for things to happen.'

'What do you do then?' asked Christopher, and Kelly could see Andrea's ears prick. The question she had wanted to ask but hadn't dared.

'Bit of this, bit of that,' said Kelly helpfully. 'A bit of hill farming in West Wales. In a, you know, amateur sort of way.'

Andrea sipped her drink. That didn't help. Amateur hill

136

farming was just the sort of thing celebrities would take up as a hobby. 'So, then, I saw your ad. For a reunion. Any particular reason? Just to see where we've all got to in life?'

Kelly realised that was what Andrea had been doing from the moment she walked in. She had been presenting her CV, to prove that she too had been stunningly successful, in case they all turned out to be supermodels or millionaires or heart surgeons.

'It is kind of fun, isn't it?' Kelly suggested. 'Thinking of a bunch of babies that just happened to be born in the same ward at the same time, like an island in an ocean, and seeing where life has taken them.'

'Yeah!' agreed Christopher. 'Like, my brother went to Scotland.'

'But the real reason I put the ad in was this…'

Kelly explained, as concisely and undramatically as she could. It had never seemed particularly dramatic to her, but she didn't know how other people would react.

Christopher gaped open-mouthed. 'Like, you mean, they swapped labels, so we all got muddled up?'

'Not you, Chris.' Kelly smiled. 'At least, you certainly weren't muddled up with me, because my Mum definitely gave birth to a girl. But maybe Andrea…'

'No way!' Andrea was horrified. 'No! I don't care what you say! It's not true!'

'Well, it probably wasn't you,' agreed Kelly.

'I'm telling you it wasn't me!' As if she had been accused of something. She was determined to prove it, for her own sake rather than Kelly's. 'It's rubbish. I look just like my sister. Ask anyone. People used to think we were twins.' She half rose, her voice upping an octave. 'And I look like my mother. Anyone can see. So you got that completely wrong.'

A couple sitting nearby, by mutual consent, picked up

their drinks and moved to another table. A couple of men in suits at the bar swivelled on their stools to look.

Andrea was turning lobster red, torn between denial and her embarrassment at making a scene.

'Don't worry, it was only a chance,' said Kelly, hoping to calm her down. 'She's out there somewhere, but I wasn't really expecting miracles. It's just that, Mum being so ill and maybe needing a kidney transplant eventually, and I'm not a match…'

If it were possible for Andrea to look more horrified, she did now. 'You mean—' She almost choked on the words. 'You want to find someone so you can take their liver?'

'Kidney. Only one. And only if they want. They don't have to.'

Andrea looked at her as if she were a bodysnatcher with a big knife. 'You're sick. You're really sick. I'm not staying here!' She gathered up her coat and bag, heading for the door in such haste she almost tripped over. One of the men in suits held the door open for her, and put a hand on her arm in concern as she pushed past. She shook him off and was gone. The man glanced back at Kelly and Christopher with a raised eyebrow and a smile. Kelly liked the smile. Quirky.

'Oh well,' she said, and looked at Christopher. 'Do you think I'm sick?'

'No. No way. She really blew a fuse, didn't she? And all the time she might be your mother's daughter and you're her mother's daughter and… That's kind of crazy, isn't it?'

Kelly laughed. 'Nothing wrong with crazy. But I don't think it is Andrea. Seriously. She was born on the 17th. I know I put a whole week in the ad because I wasn't sure how long my mum was in hospital, but I don't suppose it was that long. Andrea was probably born way after Mum left. Do you think I should have explained that to her, set her mind at rest?'

'Oh. Er…' Christopher didn't get asked for advice very often. 'I dunno. Yeah, well, she wasn't exactly listening, was she?'

'No.'

'You should have grabbed her liver. Have it with fava beans and a nice chianti.'

'I should?' Christopher's Hannibal Lector impersonation was lost on Kelly.

'Yeah, you know. What are fava beans?'

'I don't know. I know a lot of beans, but not fava.'

'I thought, maybe they were like baked beans. But I don't like liver really, anyway.'

'Nor me, but then I'm a vegetarian.'

Kelly liked Christopher. It was possible to have a happy conversation without either of them having the first idea what the other was talking about. He needed to get out more, but he was okay. Unfortunately, he couldn't stay to see the evening out.

'I've got a raid. I've got to be there for nine.'

'The police? You know they're coming?'

'What?'

'A raid?'

'Oh, right. Not police. Warcraft. My guild.'

'Ah. Right.' She said goodbye with a big hug, which was the way Kelly said goodbye to most people. He ambled off while she sat with the remainder of her drink. A fabulously expensive continental lager.

She glanced at the people around her. A few couples, one of them snogging, the others intensely private, and a gang of rowdy youths, whose raised voices were turning to gibberish as they downed more drink. No, it really wasn't her type of place. She drained her lager and stood up.

'Eh, eh, look, e… eh, uh, ha ha!' One of the lads grabbed the fringe of her scarf. 'Look, she's got a tail.'

She laughed, tugged it back and stepped round him. Not difficult because he needed the support of a table to stay upright.

'Eh, eh. What's this then?' One of his companions blocked her path. Not belligerent exactly. Just some drunken illusion of having fun.

She stepped; he stepped.

'Come on,' she said.

'Come on, come on, cmon cmon cmon cmon.' His repetition turned to a chant that the others joined in. The game was to catch her tail.

'Hey!' An authoritative bark from the bar manager. Most of the lads stepped back, but one lunged again for the fringe, grabbed her leg instead and nearly sent them both toppling.

Kelly, who had wrestled worse, was prepared to jab him if he didn't move, but she found she had no need. An arm slipped round the lad and prized him away.

'Come on now. Leave the lady alone.'

It was the man in the suit who had smiled when Andrea left.

Kelly's half-hearted assailant looked at him as if debating whether to punch him in the face or throw up. The suit gestured to Kelly to follow him to the clear space near the door. That smile again.

She laughed. 'Thanks.'

'No damage?'

'I don't think so.' She examined the fringe of her scarf. 'I've been in worse at the Mill and Tuppence.'

'I thought you looked as if you could take care of yourself.' He grinned. 'But then how can I judge? You don't exactly look like anyone else I know.'

'Well, we're all different, aren't we?'

'Yes, but most of us spend our lives trying to be exactly the same.'

Did he? Was he the same as everyone else in the bar? In a sense. Mid-twenties, well groomed, smart but not flashy. But still unique. Nicely unique. She smiled. 'Thanks anyway. I'm Kelly.'

He held out his hand to shake. 'Hello, Kelly. I'm Ben. Can I buy you a drink?'

She had nothing else planned for the evening.

'How about a cocktail? A Margarita? Bloody Mary? Hairy Virgin, Angel's Tit, Hanky Panky…'

She was laughing with him. 'Are they all for real?'

'So the list says. Can't say I've tried many of them.'

'You choose. I'll try anything once.'

'All right. Let's think.' A barman was hovering, waiting. He knew a good customer when he saw one. 'A Satan's Whiskers for my friend here, and a Hanky Panky.'

'Yes, sir! Coming right up.'

'So is this your local?' asked Kelly, watching the barman go to work, wondering if she could pick up tips for the Mill and Tuppence. She wasn't sure cocktails would really work there.

Ben was looking round the bar. 'Not exactly. Used to come here a lot when I visited Lyford. That was with the old owner, Richard. He set it up, straight out of Casablanca. With a piano. Had us all singing the Marseillaise once. Even looked a bit like Bogart. Great entertainer but a lousy businessman. Went bust. Now, it's…' He shrugged despair. 'Gone horribly uphill. Lost all its charm. But it's close. I stay at the Linley.'

141

'That a hotel?'

'Yes. Just round the corner.' He pushed his stool back so he could see her from head to foot. 'You wouldn't know it if you're not from round here, and I'm taking a wild guess that you're not from round here.'

'Na. How could you tell?'

'Not many like you in Lyford. Where do you come from then?'

'Wales. Pembrokeshire.'

'You don't have a Welsh accent.'

'I could have, if I wanted,' she said, lapsing into west Welsh. 'Could talk all night like this if you want.'

'That's not proper Welsh. You have to say, "Indeed to goodness, look you, boyo."'

'That's Hollywood Valleys. So where do you come from?'

'I work in London, live out near Heathrow.'

'And you come here on business?'

'No, thank God. My mother lives here. I try to visit reasonably often.'

'Oh yes, of course.'

'How's your Satan's Whiskers?'

She considered. 'Interesting. How's your Hanky Panky?'

'Vile. Maybe I should have gone for the Painkiller.'

'Why? Are you in pain?'

He glanced at his drink, debating whether to laugh it off, then back at her. That little shrug again. 'Should be. My girlfriend's just dumped me. By text. That was why I came out tonight. Thought I'd need to drown my sorrows. But now, I'm not so sure they need drowning. I think I feel relieved. We were preparing to be getting engaged…'

Kelly shook her head in disbelief. 'This place!'

'What?'

'First I meet a girl who's taking eighteen months to plan

142

a wedding, and now I've met a man who was *preparing* to get engaged. How do you prepare? Don't you just say yes, no, whatever?'

He laughed, quite pain-free. 'According to Natasha, no. It's a big thing. Anyway, I'm just glad she got cold feet before I bought the ring.'

'Oh the ring. A diamond of course.'

'Almost certainly.' He met her eyes. 'I told you, most of us spend our lives trying to be just like everyone else. Glad there's someone who doesn't.'

'Are you really not upset?'

He took a deep breath. 'No. Which probably makes me a very shallow personality.'

'Or an honest one, snatched from drifting.'

'That I prefer. What about you? Married? Engaged? Significant other? Boyfriend in the wings?'

'Boyfriend, yes. Sort of. Joe. Yes, sort of.'

'But not the love of your life.'

She thought about it. No, of course Joe wasn't the love of her life. There had been other men who had aroused some vague emotional turmoil, but not Joe. 'He's a friend really. I think. Looking after my sheep for me while I'm away.'

'Sheep! Wales. Is it true what they—'

'No.'

He smiled, finishing his cocktail. 'So if Joe is just a friend, sort of, do you feel unattached enough to have dinner with me? Unless you've already eaten. I haven't and I'm starving, and I don't really fancy tapas.'

'I've had a bag of crisps.'

'Not enough.'

'Not nearly enough.'

What was she doing, she wondered, strolling the night

143

streets of Lyford with a man who drank cocktails and wore suits? They should have nothing in common. And yet, she liked him. She really liked him. Kelly generally liked everyone until they gave her good reason not to. But this was liking with a difference. Something visceral. A warmth. She felt she understood now what magnetic attraction meant.

He wasn't bad looking, but not a Hollywood pin-up. Pleasant. It was the smile, she decided. Or maybe just the willingness to smile. People in Lyford tended not to smile at strangers. They preferred to avert their eyes. Ben smiled and met her eyes, that must be why she liked him so much.

They finished up at an Indian restaurant, because it offered vegetarian options other than goat's cheese and rocket or glutinous vegetable lasagne.

'You would be a vegetarian,' he laughed at her.

'And you would choose the Taj Special lamb.'

'I would?'

'Hot enough to be seriously masculine but not pointlessly macho like a vindaloo.'

'I see, you think I'm not macho?'

'No, I think you're real.'

'Thank you.' He sat looking at her for a whole minute. 'Are you? Real?'

'Very. Feel.' She held out her hand. He laid his over it. Their fingers entwined.

'Is everything all right, sir, madam?' asked their waiter.

'Yes, great,' they both replied.

Comfortable. That was how she felt with him. Not as if she were being picked up. Nothing sleazy.

'So tell me about Wales.'

She told him about Carregwen and the sheep and her mother's yoga classes, about the Mill and Tuppence, and her job with the National Park, and how she was going to help her friend Mike run boat trips for the tourists in the summer. How her mother was ill and she was looking for relatives in Lyford, with no success. Leave it at that. While she was with him, she didn't want to dwell on the failure of her primary mission. Talk about him instead.

So he told her about his childhood in Coventry, and his time at university, and his blossoming career with an insurance company and his flat and his now ex-girlfriend Natasha.

'Brothers and sisters?' he asked.

'No. Just me and Mum. You?'

'A brother and two sisters. Sarah's just gone to York, the others are still at school. Am I going to see you tomorrow?'

'I hope so. If you want.'

'Oh yes, I want.'

He walked her back to her B&B on Colney Road where tight Victorian terraces gave way to houses with high gables and cellars and attics and steps to the front doors. Once upon a time, they must have been quite genteel, but gentility had moved out to the suburbs, and most of Colney Road had been converted into flats and bedsitters for the students of Lyford University, late Technical College. Since most students had disappeared for the summer, there were plenty of vacancies for anyone wanting to stay in Lyford on a budget.

They stopped outside number 47: The Balmoral.

'You're staying here?' Ben looked up the stuccoed façade with a grimace.

She laughed. 'It's dirt cheap. I'd ask you in, but Mrs Hanshaw probably has rules about gentleman callers. She has rules about most things.'

'It looks appalling.'

145

'Well, like I said, it's cheap.'

'Come back with me to the Linley.'

She hesitated. And he too, biting his tongue. As if they both felt this was too important to take casually. 'No, forget I asked that. But can't I find you somewhere better than this?'

'No, no. Seriously. I'm fine here.'

'All right.' He stood, lingering. Then he leaned forward to kiss her. Not a mad grab, not a wildly passionate embrace. A gentle goodnight.

She hugged him. 'I'll see you tomorrow.'

'I'll phone.'

'Yes.'

'Goodnight.'

They couldn't stand there dragging this out forever. She ran up the steps to the front door. A lace curtain twitched.

Ben raised a hand, then walked away.

Kelly lay on her narrow lumpy mattress, staring at the ceiling. She wasn't going to sleep, so maybe it was daft to lie there in the dark. She should sit up and read. Except that the forty-watt bulb wouldn't be much of an improvement on the glow from the street lamps. And besides, she just wanted to lie there and think.

About Ben.

She wanted to call him. It was three a.m. Maybe not.

Why couldn't she get him out of her head? Why did she feel her pulse racing at the memory of his face, his eyes, the touch of his hand? Why did she want to leap out of bed and run down the road to the Linley Hotel?

Was this falling in love? She'd been in love before, hadn't she? What about Geraint? She'd been quite hooked on him, moping round the house for days when he'd gone to college

146

in Bangor. No, that hadn't been love. Childish affection maybe. Not like this worm inside her.

How could she possibly fall in love, just like that, with a man in a suit, someone she had met just a few hours before? It was mad.

But, no, it wasn't. Kelly believed in Fate. She believed that there were kindred spirits who belonged with each other and destiny would bring them together. Perhaps this was what had really brought her to Lyford. How likely was it that she'd find the missing girl? There'd been another response to the ad, a text from someone whose friend Carrie had been born on March 15th, but she'd emigrated to Australia and did Kelly want her address? That was all. That was all there was likely to be. Fate had brought her to Lyford, brought her to Rick's Place, where Ben was sitting at the bar.

Could Fate be malign? She'd come, determined to focus on her mother's cause, and now this, messing with her big time, shaking up all her thoughts and feelings – and she didn't care. Other things should matter but tonight, they didn't. Nothing mattered except that she wanted Ben.

Crazy.

She woke wanting to phone him, just to say hello. Was six o'clock too early? Probably. She would wait a while, but not here, not in this gloomy little room. In this house with its lace curtains keeping the daylight at bay. Breakfast was served from 7.30, but did she want Mrs Hanshaw's breakfast? Reconstituted orange juice, soggy cornflakes, rubbery white toast, burnt sausage and shrivelled bacon. Kelly had said she was a vegetarian but it made no difference. Ahmed, one of the remaining student lodgers, told her that four of her long-stay guests were Muslims and still they were served bacon and sausage.

No. Kelly didn't want to start her day with lukewarm baked beans and tinned tomatoes. She got dressed and stepped out into a sparkling morning that lent even Colney Road a summer charm. Fresh air, that was what she needed. Heading back into town. She had been walking for ten minutes when her phone buzzed. Battery low: she'd need to charge it soon.

'Hello?'

'Kelly.' Ben's voice. 'Just wanted to see if you were awake. Thought, as you were a country girl, you'd be up by now.'

'Of course I'm up. Already milked the cow.'

'Had breakfast?'

'No.'

'Come and have it with me at the Linley.'

'Okay.'

'Shall I come and fetch you?'

'No need. I'm about a hundred yards from your door.'

He laughed. She had waited all night to hear that laugh.

'And you don't eat fish either? Scrambled egg with smoked salmon? It's very good.'

'I do eat fish, but only if I've caught it.' Plain scrambled egg was just fine. She sat back gazing at him, as warm sun poured across the dining room. He'd driven to Lyford the previous evening straight from work, but he was dressed more casually now; T-shirt and jeans. He was looking at her in the same way she looked at him, convincing himself that he hadn't been dreaming it all.

'Have you got plans for today?'

'Not really.' She played with her fork to stop herself reaching out to touch him. Not that he would have minded, but Kelly was bashful for the first time in her life. She wanted to be in private.

148

'So you can stick around with me. We could drive out onto the downs. Walk through the woods. I know a great pub.'

'Brill. Sounds as if you didn't have plans either.'

His lips twitched. 'Nothing urgent. I need to see someone later.'

She could feel his evasiveness. 'Your mother.'

'Yes, I'll look in on her afterwards.'

She glanced round the dining room of the Linley. Smart, gleaming, a hotel built for business travellers with generous expense accounts. There was a gym in the basement, a Japanese restaurant, laundry service. It was the sort of place a man would choose to stay if he had no friends or relatives in the area. 'If your Mum lives in Lyford, why don't you stay with her?'

He opened his mouth, shuffling lies. 'She's only got a small flat.'

What sort of a lame excuse was that? 'Sleep on the floor!'

Again he began a response, then winced, ashamed of himself. 'Truth is…' The wince became a grimace. 'We don't exactly get along. We weren't even in touch for years. It's – difficult.'

Kelly thought about this. The one fixed point in her happy-go-lucky universe was her mother. Roz could be difficult. Maddening. But still… 'She's your mother.'

'Tell her that!' A snap of anger and pain. He ran his hands through his neat brown hair. 'I know. This is me trying to accept that, like an adult. Put aside all that childhood resentment stuff. I'm doing my best.'

She grabbed his hands and squeezed them. She slipped round the table so that she could hug him. 'Sorry.'

People didn't hug or have emotional crises in the Linley's dining room. 'Come on,' he said. 'Let's get out of here.'

149

They walked on high open downs and they strolled in hushed beech woods, they ate lunch in a quaint pub by a duck pond, and they idled the day away as if the rest of the world did not exist.

Sitting in his car, his arm around her shoulders as they gazed at clouds drifting above interlaced branches, Ben sighed. 'I suppose we had better get back.'

He had to see his mother and he was doing his best. 'Yes,' she said, reaching for her seat belt.

They drove back into Lyford, to the Linley. 'I'll drop you here. Pick you up later for dinner. Stay in my room, if you like. Use the spa. You don't want to come with me for this.'

She put her hand on his arm to silence him. 'I'll come with you.'

'You won't like it,' he said. 'She certainly won't like you.'

Kelly smiled. 'I'm that hard to take, am I?'

'She doesn't like any woman I'm with.' He changed down a gear, manoeuvring into a different lane. 'She'll be rude. I'm just warning you.'

'Don't worry, I won't storm off. And I won't interfere. I'll just give you moral support.' She had tears in her eyes just thinking of him needing moral support to speak to his mother.

His fingers brushed hers.

After a hesitation at a crossroad, Ben performed a neat three-point turn in a side street. 'Have to get my bearings. She's only moved in recently. I got it wrong at the last lights.' They finally pulled up in a street of 1970s semis, garages and maisonettes. He sat for a moment, staring at one of them, then unbuckled his seat belt with a sigh and got out.

Kelly followed him up the path. He braced himself and knocked at a door.

A tired-looking woman emerged from the next property, pulling her coat on. 'You looking for Mrs Parish?'

'Yes.' Ben's inner conflicts disappeared behind a friendly smile. 'I'm her son.'

'Ah. Well, she's out, I think – gone for her walk.'

'Oh. Yes, of course, she would.'

'Likes her walking, doesn't she? Keeps fit, I expect.'

'Fit. Is that what it is,' said Ben under his breath. He still smiled at the woman but Kelly could feel his anger. She could feel it, but she couldn't understand it.

'Is it bad going for a walk?' she asked, following him back to the car.

Ben gave a hollow laugh. 'She knew I was coming, so she took a walk. To the park, of course.'

'Well, you've been out all day. You don't expect her to sit around waiting for you to show up, do you?'

He scowled then laughed. 'No. No, why should she?'

'Are we going to the park to find her?'

He settled in the driving seat, starting the car up again, staring at the wheel. What was the problem? He heaved another sigh. 'I suppose so. Stupid to leave without seeing her.'

Back down the main road, into a car park by a leisure centre. He pulled on the handbrake, oozing resistance. 'Do you mind another walk?'

'I'd love another walk.'

They went down a short lane to the park entrance. Ben stopped, staring a moment at the open iron gates, then shrugged.

Kelly slipped her hand in his.

Wide folds of lawn beyond the ornate railings, scattered with purple beech, horse chestnut and cherry trees, a serpentine lake and a distant bandstand. A relic of a former age. At the gates was a small wooden kiosk, and a uniformed warden looked out, an elderly black man with grey hair. He raised a hand in greeting.

'Hi.' Ben said. 'Lewis, isn't it? Have you seen my mother by any chance?'

Lewis strolled towards them. 'Mrs Parish? Yes, she's here. Down by the lake now, feeding the ducks.'

'Of course,' said Ben, through clenched teeth.

'Surprised she doesn't avoid the place,' said Lewis.

'Why?' asked Ben.

'There's been trouble.' Lewis's friendliness was qualified, Kelly realised. He was equivocating. 'Bad feeling.'

'There always is,' muttered Ben. 'Thanks anyway.' He turned to Kelly. 'You still want to come?'

'Sure,' said Kelly. He was hurting, for reasons she couldn't fathom, and his distress tugged at heartstrings she hadn't known she had, but she was with him and that was all she wanted.

The lake was grimier round the edges than it had looked from a distance. Ducks were outnumbered by floating litter. Still, there were a few weeping willows, a scenic bridge, and the paths were a pleasant enough stroll for the handful of elderly people who still thought a daily constitutional was a good idea.

The woman standing by the railings did not seem old – too erect, her shoulders too straight, her hands gripping the railings too strong for old age. But her short hair was grey.

Ben stopped, ten yards short, his jaw clenching. 'Mum?'

The woman turned, her jaw firm, her eyes glaring with anger, before she recognised him and broke into a distracted smile. She was not fat but well built. The sort who could deliver a killer left hook if she chose, and she looked as if she might. Yes, thought Kelly, she looks the kind of mother you would fight with. An eternal battle of wills. Was that how it was for Ben? How sad.

'Ben. It's you. I thought for a moment... That damned girl is here somewhere.' She looked away, across the lake, caught sight of a distant figure and nodded. 'I knew it. They just won't leave me alone. So, how are you?' It was weird, the way his mother spoke, neither surprised nor delighted to see her son again. 'I suppose you're still with that...' She stopped, seeing Kelly. 'Oh for God's sake, you haven't brought another one.'

'Hello, Mum,' said Ben resolutely ignoring her reaction. Keeping his distance. No kiss. 'How are you keeping? This is Kelly. She's with me.'

'Very nice, I'm sure,' said Mrs Parish, glancing briefly at Kelly then back at Ben. 'Nice to be able to move on.'

'Yes! It is! That's what I'm doing, Mum. Moving on. And hoping you might try it some time.'

'Just walk away, you mean.'

'Okay! I'll walk away!' He turned, hustling Kelly with him.

'Ben!' called Mrs Parish.

'Stop, Ben,' said Kelly gently, holding him back. 'Look, I don't know what it is between you, but you ought to sort it out and I'm not here to make things worse. She doesn't feel happy with me around—'

'Then she can do without me too!'

'No! That's not the way. Go back to her. Talk with her. I'll be fine. I really don't want to come between you.'

'It isn't really anything to do with you, Kelly.'

'No, I know. Whatever it is, go and sort it out.'

He hesitated, ashamed of his petulance. 'Dealing with it like an adult, eh? I don't know.'

'I do. Go and talk with her. I'll take a walk.'

He rubbed his hands over his face. 'All right. You sure?'

153

'Sure.'

He took a deep breath, then turned. 'I won't be long.'

'Don't rush.' She watched him march back towards Mrs Parish, who was still staring after him, hands clasped. Then Kelly wandered on through the park.

The solitary figure that had been watching across the lake disappeared into the far trees.

Kelly was chatting to an old lady when Ben returned, an hour later, anxious and apologetic.

'Kelly, sorry. Sorry!'

She laughed. 'You did talk with her? That's good.'

Ben sighed as they turned up the lane to the leisure centre. 'Yes, I suppose it's good. Or it could be. One day.'

'You're getting there. You're trying.'

'And you…' He kissed her on the cheek. '…are extraordinarily understanding. I bet you never have trouble talking to your mum.'

'No. Never. Sorry.'

'You don't know how lucky you are.'

'Yes, I do. We've always been best friends. Do you think you'll ever be friends with your mum?'

He laughed, less bitterly. Duty done, he was free. 'That would take a miracle and I gave up expecting those years ago.' He clicked his car keys as they approached and the locks flicked up. 'The sad thing is I can't actually remember when things used to be different. I can only remember that I used to remember. Maybe it's just as well.' He opened the door for Kelly.

She waited for him to settle himself in the driving seat. 'How long have you been at odds?'

'God, years. Look, Kelly, you don't want to talk about all this.'

'Yes I do. I want to know everything about you.'

He smiled at last. That smile again. 'Wish I were more interesting. What can I say? My family split up, that's all. I had a baby sister who died, that was what started it. It was – tricky. A bad time. Mum was upset, of course. Then more than upset. Obsessive. Lying.' He was back nursing his anger.

'Lying? That's a hard thing to say.'

'Oh, you don't—' He shook his head, shrugging himself clear. 'Yes. I shouldn't say it. It doesn't matter, because after that she was out of my life.' He switched on the car. 'Let's talk about happier things. Like dinner. Where shall we eat?'

Kelly believed in talking, exploring, but she saw his desperation to change the subject, so she laughed. 'Surprise me.'

'God. That means I'd better find somewhere special.'

'Anywhere with you is special.'

Brake off, foot hovering on the clutch, he turned to face her. 'You don't want to go back to the Balmoral B&B, do you?'

'No.'

'Stay with me tonight.'

Stretching the seat belt, she leaned across to kiss him. 'Yes.'

CHAPTER 6

i

Lindy

'Here we are, dear.' Marion, the friendly, plump, black nurse was helping a pale, fretful new mother into the vacant bed on the ward. 'And your baby's here. See?'

The woman looked to the cot, then shrugged off further attention without a word. She waited until Marion had gone, then looked across at Lindy. She pulled a face of exasperation that she obviously expected Lindy to share.

Lindy didn't share it. There was nothing here to exasperate her. There was an institutional feel, okay, but it wasn't like the home. No bullying, no watching your back, no scowling adults looming over you. The nurses could be quite pushy, of course, and one of them was a bit ratty, but she didn't feel lost with them. She felt special. She had her baby.

She wasn't even fussed about the food, although Lindy, by choice, would have gone for burger and chips not mash and cabbage but still, three meals a day, served up to her like she was a queen! A comfortable bed in a heated room, and baby Kelly beside her. Wanting nothing. Except Gary. 'Do you want us to let anyone know?' they had asked, and she had wanted to say Gary but didn't dare. He was going to be furious, she knew. She was supposed to have had it secretly at home, so that they could dump it. What would he do?

She reached out to stroke Kelly's tiny fingers, and smiled at the pale woman. Perhaps she'd had it rough in the delivery room.

'Are they all like that?' the woman asked, nodding at the door.

Like Marion? No, not all of them were that friendly and jolly. 'Some,' said Lindy.

'Is it a boy or a girl?' asked Jackie, an experienced mother of three, who was going home as soon as her husband and children arrived. She was dressing.

The pale woman lay back on her pillows. 'Boy. Just as well or my Kev would go fucking mad. When I had to give up work, he was that furious, said in that case it had better be a bloody boy.'

Jackie forced a smile. 'Have you got a name?'

'Anita.'

'For the baby?'

'Oh. Yeah, Kevin like his dad.'

'Lovely,' said Jackie. 'Very patriarchal.'

The door opened, Balgeet returning from the bathroom. She had the bed next to Lindy; her baby Deepinder had beaten Kelly into the world by forty minutes. 'Oh, a new baby! That is lovely. Is it—?'

'Don't touch!' said Anita, with a hostility that lowered the temperature in the ward by several degrees.

Jackie looked across at Lindy with raised eyebrow, then smiled broadly at the Sikh woman. Balgeet looked abashed, but only for a second. No point in making a fuss.

Lindy accepted it as natural. Race was an issue that had always surrounded her. Verbal abuse, violence, graffiti. For most of her life, she had hung around with people who thought nothing of chanting racist slogans or singling out Pakistani shops for vandalism. But for herself, she'd no real sense of tribalism, because she had no tribe. She was always the outsider. There were law-abiding respectable citizens, white, black, brown or yellow, and there were the outlaws, white, black, brown too, and she was lost among them, somewhere between Tyler on the ground floor and Carver upstairs.

So she was happy now in this pretend home with Jackie the white ex-teacher and Balgeet the Sikh lady and Marion the West Indian nurse.

Visiting time. Varinder Singh with two aunties, a grandmother and three children filled the ward with noisy delight, despite Nurse Patricia's disapproving reminder that only two visitors were permitted at a time. They knew how to handle Nurse Patricia. Suddenly, the entire Sikh family was having trouble with English, although they were fluent the moment the nurse was gone.

Jackie's beaming, slightly harassed husband arrived with their two children, a carrycot, and endless carrier bags. 'Good. You've got my jacket. And the shawl? Oh, Frankie! There was a brand new shawl your mother made. This is the dog blanket!' Laughter and bustle and they were gone, with one last hug and a kiss for Balgeet and Lindy. Lindy was sorry to see them go, to lose a part of her temporary family, though Jackie had only been in for twenty-four hours.

Anita's husband Kevin came in. No chocolates or fruit but a football for his baby son. Kevin had the thickest neck Lindy had ever seen. Red and raw and shaven. 'Fucking hell,' he said to his wife, glaring round the ward. 'You better not come home bleeding stinking of fucking curry.'

Peace. Visiting hours were at an end. Jackie had left. Kevin had swaggered away, on the firm insistence of a male nurse.

The Singh family had emerged from the curtains around Balgeet's bed, and Anita had drawn her own in response. Now Balgeet was sleeping and all was silence.

Lindy was alone with Kelly. The baby stirred, looking around with uncomprehending eyes. Lindy lifted her out of her cot and cradled her. All the rest, the illusion of home and family, was fake, a pretence that would vanish into thin air when Lindy was turfed out of this place, but Kelly was real. Kelly was for keeps.

Lindy's gift, or curse, was her ability to see and not see, to be selective in what she chose to know. It was her means of survival. The happy thought was enough – Kelly was for keeps.

No visit from Gary. He didn't know she was here. She wasn't going to think about what he would say when she arrived on his doorstep with Kelly. It was a long way off, because they were keeping Lindy in a bit. Anaemic, they said. And very young, and although she'd given an address, like a proper home, they would have to have a word with social services about her, make sure she had support.

'I've got my Gary,' she'd said, letting herself believe it.

That was a problem for another day. Today, she had Kelly. Such a pretty baby. And dressed like a princess too. Proper baby clothes, and bedding and nappies and a quilted Moses basket that had arrived at the hospital just after Kelly's birth, with a potty and bottles and rattles and a pink furry mouse and a rubber duck and a bunch of flowers. The manager of Baby Garden had been photographed by the press, handing them over to one of the admin staff on the hospital steps – Marion had told her about it, chuckling.

All this – for her baby.

Her hungry baby. She could ask for another bottle for her. Or she could try that other thing. While no one was

159

watching. She raised Kelly to her breast. Not quite sure how to arrange it, but after a minute they settled down together. It felt odd. Hurt a bit but it felt sort of – natural.

The baby slept again. Lindy placed her back in her cot, then padded out to the toilets. At the nurses' station in the corridor, Patricia was shuffling notes, while Marion stretched, hands pressed into the small of her back. 'Have security up here next time.'

'Shouldn't allow people like him in the place,' said Patricia. 'You could sue him, you know, for what he said to you.'

'Oh, men like him don't fuss me,' Marion laughed. 'But not very nice for the patients.'

'The wife's just as bad. You know what? We should do a quick swap of babies. Kevin Rainford for Adebayo in 3B. Black as the ace of spades, 'scuse my language. Switch the labels, and tell her he must have developed overnight. Wouldn't you give something to see her face?'

'Ah, no. Take pity on poor Adebayo, woman.' Marion saw Lindy and smiled broadly. 'You all right, Lindy?'

Lindy nodded, shuffling into the bathroom, disturbed. Nurses swapping babies; it didn't bear thinking about. She hurried back to her bed, where Kelly was lying alone and vulnerable.

She picked her up and held her tight.

The taxi pulled up on the corner of Heighton Road, because the kerb outside 128 was blocked by parked cars and a skip. A real taxi, not one of the minicabs that would have dumped her and made off at speed. The hospital had arranged it. They needed the bed after four days. The doctors had checked her over and a social worker called Caroline had promised to visit Lindy at home.

The taxi driver helped her out, with baby Kelly. Even carried all the Baby Garden stuff to the front door for her. Carver was coming out as she went in. He paused, watched the taxi driver dumping the Moses basket on the step, looked at the baby clasped to Lindy's shoulder. No smile, but then Carver never smiled. No frown either. He just took note. Then he picked up the basket and carried it upstairs for her.

'Thanks,' she mumbled, and opened her door.

Gary lay on the mattress, empty beer cans around him, smoking and dozing. Most of his work tended to be at night. He opened his eyes as she came in, propped himself up on his elbow to look at her. Then he saw what she was holding.

He jumped to his feet. 'You stupid bitch! Where the fuck have you been?'

'In hospital, Gary. Having the baby. See?' She turned the bundle she was carrying, hoping that seeing the baby's face would appease him.

'Stupid fucking cow! You were supposed to have it here. Not in front of half the fucking doctors in Lyford.'

'I couldn't help it, Gary. I got done for shoplifting, din' I, and it all just happened.'

'Shoplifting? You got done? Stupid cow. Stupid fucking cow. Now what? Whole bloody world knows now, don't they? Doctors? Police? Social Services? They'll never let up now, got their claws into you. Be round here all the fucking time, you stupid bitch.'

'I'm sorry, Gary. I couldn't help it.'

He stared at the basket and its contents. 'Where d'you get this crap? You nicked it?'

'They gave it me, Gary. The shop where it happened. They gave it me, honest.'

'Where it happened?' He grabbed her arm, pulled her round. 'You were in a fucking baby shop? You done it deliberately, din't ya? Stupid fucking bitch, I'll kill you!'

The first blow caught her round the ear. His fist was raised for the second, but then a hand closed round his wrist. A black hand.

'Calm down,' said Carver.

'See what she fucking done?' Gary was spluttering.

'You want to have the police round here? Think about it.'

There was a moment's silence, while Gary got control of his rage. Lindy wriggled free and carried her precious bundle across the room.

Carver stopped at the door, taking everything in. He glanced at Gary. 'Think about it,' he repeated, and was gone. Easy feet on the stairs. From the window, Lindy watched him stroll off down the road.

Leaving her with Gary. She loved him. But just now, she wasn't sure she wanted to be alone with him.

But Carver's words seemed to have done the trick. He was glowering, but no longer wild with rage. Just sullen. She couldn't blame him. He'd had it all planned and she had messed it up. But maybe, now, if he saw his baby properly, he wouldn't mind so much.

'She's called Kelly,' she said.

He grunted and kicked the basket across the room. 'Pick it up. Place is a fucking pigsty. Don't think I'm going to fucking wait on you, just because you come home with a fucking baby.' The rage was building up again, but he couldn't let it burst out as usual. So he grabbed his jacket instead. 'I'm going out. Clear the fuck up.'

Left alone, she tidied up. Set Kelly in her basket cradle, with her Baby Garden shawl and her Baby Garden quilt. Made the bed, cleared up the beer cans, the cigarette butts, the foul socks and underwear, washed the dirty crockery, stashed the baby stuff away in the cupboards. Her homecoming could have been a whole lot worse. Of course Gary was angry. Only natural. But he'd only hit her once, and he hadn't actually thrown her out, or taken a knife to her and the child.

All down to Carver, of course. If she weren't afraid of him, she'd have been grateful. Why had he told Gary to leave her alone? Maybe he liked her. She shuddered at that. Carver was dangerous; she'd heard things, that he had a gun, that he'd killed... He certainly had a knife. She was pretty certain he wasn't the sort of man who secretly liked babies. But whatever his reasons, he'd done the trick.

Gary came back late. She'd given up on him. She was lying in the dark, listening for the sound of Kelly's breathing to tell her she wasn't alone. He slammed the door. The baby stirred. He stood in the dark staring down at it.

'Keep it quiet,' he ordered, then began to pull his clothes off.

She did her best. For two nights she barely slept, listening for the first hint of a whimper from the cot. Even a sigh or a gurgle and she'd be up, slithering carefully off the mattress, settling on a chair in the far corner to feed Kelly, or carrying her, tiptoeing, up to the bathroom to change her.

Then the third night she was so dog-tired she fell asleep and missed the warning signs. Gary's foot woke her, kicking her ribs. Kelly was crying at the top of her tiny lungs.

Gary yanked her up. 'Shut the fucking thing up, okay, or I'll do it.'

There was a muffled yell of complaint from somewhere else in the house. Still half asleep, Lindy crawled to the basket and lifted the baby up. A wet nappy.

163

'Fucking stinks,' snarled Gary. 'Get it out.'

She staggered upstairs with a new nappy, dropped the old one in the plastic bag she'd left under the bath, washed and redressed Kelly, cooing incoherently over her. She didn't mind changing her, or feeding her, or doing anything the baby needed, but just now all she wanted was to get back to sleep. Back down to their room, pull off the wet bedding in the basket, put an old towel in instead; that would do for now. The baby went down without trouble. Kelly groped her way back to the mattress.

Gary had sprawled across it, arms and legs flung wide, snoring. She tried to edge in, to find enough space to lie down, but he woke and kicked her. 'Fuck off.'

'Gary, I need to sleep.'

He swore again, pulled one of the pillows free and threw it at her. So she took it, and her heavy shoplifting coat, and curled up under the table.

He was irritable next day, flying into a rage every time the baby made the slightest noise. He hit Lindy. She knew what he was like in these moods. Sometimes it was drugs, and sometimes it was nerves, but when he was like this he took it out on her.

He went for her again and tripped over the basket. She was sure he was going to turn on Kelly, shake her, slap her, hurl her round the room. Lindy crouched over the basket, taking his blows on her back and her shoulders, while he swore and snarled.

He got his foot under her, pushed her off, and stood with clenched fists over the cradle, his breathing halfway to a sob.

'Don't touch her,' Lindy pleaded.

He reached down, grabbed the baby's ankles.

Lindy sprang forward. 'You touch her, I'll tell Carver. I will!'

It worked. Gary stepped back as if the baby had given him an electric shock.

He soon got over it. Even managed a laugh. 'You think that's the magic word, do you?' He put on a silly whine. 'I'll go tell Carver.' He helped himself to a can of beer, leaning nonchalantly on the sink like he was the hard man of the street and no one dared mess with Gary Bagley. 'What you think, then? That Carver's got a soft spot for you? That thing's fairy godfather? Looking out for it? Stupid cow. He needs it quiet, that's all. Just for a few days. Got something big going down. I'm doing a job for him.' He said it proudly, like he'd been appointed Prime Minister or something, but he was scared too. Lindy could tell. That was why he was so on edge. He was in on something out of his league and he knew it.

'Don't,' she said. She didn't want her Gary in on it. A job for Carver was bad news.

'You what?' His lip curled.

'I'm scared, Gary. You do a job for Carver, what if it gets really bad?'

'Shut up! What do you know about it? I'm the man he wants, okay? You know what it's worth? You ain't got no idea.'

'All right, Gary.'

'Keep the fucking baby quiet too. Shit. If you'd kept your nose down and had it here, we could have got rid of it.'

Lindy cradled the baby. Imagined being here when the pain had started, imagined giving birth on this mattress, curtains drawn, Gary telling her to shut it. At least he'd have been there with her. Maybe he'd have held her hand like he did sometimes.

She held onto that comforting image, blocking out the darker ones she couldn't bear. They'd lurked at the back of her mind since Gary had come home. Get rid of the baby, he'd told her. Like leaving her on the hospital steps or something. That was what happened to a baby a year or so back. That was what Gary meant. She wouldn't let the other image in, the old newspaper and a brick and the stinking gully behind the garages in Heighton Street.

Gary slammed out. He came in late again, quieter. Let her share the bed this time, though he didn't touch her. She could sense his nerves, stretching him like a string.

The baby woke her, a fretful murmur, not yet a full-blown cry. She opened her eyes.

Gary was already out of bed. He stood, silent over Kelly in her basket, looking down on her, head on one side, like he was studying something fascinating. Not hostile, not angry, she could see that in the light of the street lamp.

He was holding his pillow, clutching it with both hands.

She switched the light on and he looked round at her. A stupid laugh. He'd taken something, that was why he was laughing.

'I'll take her,' she said, kneeling to pick up Kelly.

'I could make her go to sleep,' he crooned, gripping the pillow tighter.

'It's all right, she won't make a noise,' Lindy promised.

He was staring at them both as if he couldn't quite grasp what they were or why they were there. She rocked the baby, moving step by step away from him. At last, he staggered back to the bed and flopped down again.

Lindy switched the light off again, sat down on the chair by the door, and settled Kelly with a bottle. Kelly was a good baby, when she was fed and changed. It was easy to keep her happy. Easy because Kelly had everything she needed. Milk, warmth, love. How different was it going to be when she started needing proper food, and the nappies ran out, and she needed more clothes?

For a brief bleak moment, Lindy allowed herself to look into the future. What about when Kelly went to school? She wouldn't be such a good mum then, would she? Couldn't hardly read or write herself. Living here, with Gary, in this one room? Gary and his drugs, his rages, his pillow. What about when he'd done this job for Carver, and Carver didn't care about keeping things quiet any more? Lindy couldn't be awake all the time.

There was this heaviness in her gut. In her heart. Sadness that was never going to go away. Lindy was never going to be a good mum. She had nothing to give her baby. Kelly wouldn't make it, not here.

'We can discuss things,' the social worker had said, at the hospital. Like whether Lindy would prefer to put Kelly up for adoption. Lindy hadn't listened. She knew better than to listen to social workers. But she should have. She didn't want to have her baby taken away, but maybe that was what Kelly needed.

Except Lindy knew all about being taken away. The rush and noise and terror and big people treating her like she was nothing, and her sisters screaming, and Jimmy crying, and strangers all around her. So alone and helpless. She didn't want that for Kelly.

But if she kept Kelly here, it would happen. They'd watch over her, with their sharp eyes, for a year or two, noting bruises, stripping her, weighing her, bringing in doctors to poke her, and then they'd come for her, battering down the door. Snatching her away, no matter how Lindy screamed.

Better for her to go now, while she was a tiny baby, because people liked babies. Someone would want to adopt her, proper like, not just a foster home. A real family. Let them take her now. Lindy could do like that woman had done. Leave her somewhere safe, so that she'd be found quickly.

The bedsit was silent. Gary was asleep. Kelly was asleep in her arms. Lindy wanted this moment to never end. But they had to go.

She laid Kelly in her cot and got dressed. No noise. What time was it? Nearly four. Chilly out. Kelly would need to be wrapped up warm. Lindy picked the shawl up, the webbed design a grey veil in the darkness. This was no good. The baby that had been left at the hospital; they'd traced the mother because of something it wore. People might remember how she was given all this Baby Garden stuff.

What else did she have? No baby clothes of her own. Lindy stripped Kelly down to her nappy and wrapped her in a cheap vest top she'd nicked a year ago and never worn. Then in a towel. Their good towel, warm and thick. That had been nicked too.

Quietly, barely breathing, Lindy cradled the bundled baby to her, eased open the door, stepped out onto the dark stairs. Went down to the hall, opened the front door, drank in the clear cold air.

She was conscious of her footsteps ringing out on the empty pavement. No one was around to see or care. A couple of stray dogs running around, that was all.

She thought of returning to the hospital, but that was a really long walk, three or four miles. And the hospital wouldn't be quiet and dark like this. There were always people on duty, coming and going.

The police station? Same with that. It never went to sleep. And if Lindy didn't want anything to do with social workers, police were worse.

She reached the town centre before she knew what she was going to do. Then it came to her, because she had been here so many times before. Cleaners came in at night, through the little back doors under the car park, the doors that shoppers never saw. Came in, did their work, went out again.

She settled into a corner in Albert Street, near the door. They wouldn't look her way, a cul-de-sac for unloading trucks. They'd be heading the other way. Not so very long ago, she'd been one of them, earning her pay packet with a mop. She knew their shifts. Here and then on to the Town Hall, and the office block in William Street. Any moment now they'd be coming out.

Kelly was stirring. Lindy had changed her but she hadn't brought any spare. If the baby started bawling now, she'd be in trouble. She rocked the child, singing softly, and Kelly breathed a little sigh and settled down again.

With a blaze of light the door swung open, two women emerging, chattering loudly. Usually about eight of them, and then Stan. Always slow on his feet, Stan. Pausing behind them for a few swigs from the half bottle of whisky he kept in his pocket. By the time they left their last port of call, the minibus would be swerving all over the empty streets.

Four more women. A pause. Then a couple more, the door beginning to swing shut behind them. That was it. Now, before Stan followed them. Lindy slipped forward, caught the door. She knew her way. A sloping corridor, with a cupboard off it. She tried the handle, to be sure it was open if she needed to duck out of the way. Unlocked and empty except for a few cardboard boxes and crates. One of them was as good as a cradle really. She pulled it loose and crept on up the corridor into the empty, echoing, dimly lit expanse of the shopping centre. She could hear Stan singing. He liked the sound of his voice booming down the empty spaces. On his way, but still some way off.

She turned in the other direction. WHSmith's, she wanted really, because it opened early, but it was too far away. Debenham's was closer. There would be people around soon to find Kelly. She dropped the cardboard box in the doorway, then looked one last time at her daughter in her arms.

Lindy wanted to hug her and kiss her so much it hurt. But that would wake her. Carefully, gently, she laid her down in the box, swallowing the tears that were pouring down her cheeks. She mustn't sob, mustn't make any noise.

Forcing air into her lungs, she returned to the sloping corridor, as quietly as she could. Stan ambled into view as she slid out of sight. Had he seen her? He said nothing. His toneless singing didn't falter. She ran down the corridor, yanked up the bar of the door, fell out into Albert Street, ducked into the darkness of the cul-de-sac. Waited, heart beating.

The door eased open again. Stan came out. Door closed. He was locking it, walking away. Lindy couldn't get back in now. It was done, there was no going back.

And now she could cry in earnest, because the only thing she wanted in the world was to go back and undo it all.

'You stupid fucking bitch!' It was like being beaten round the head. When was the last time Gary had called her anything else? He used to be nice to her once. It did her head in. All of her hurt. Her stomach ached, her tits ached. She wanted to die.

'I told you we don't want no trouble just now, and what do you do? Dump the fucking baby in the shopping centre!'

'I thought it was what you wanted,' she pleaded. 'You said we should get rid of it.'

'Not this way! Stupid fucking bitch! What d'you think will fucking happen? Jesus fucking Christ!' He had his head in his hands. 'What if they come looking? You thought about that?'

'I didn't leave nothing on her to say where she'd come from, Gary.'

'Lindy, you stupid bitch, you was in the fucking hospital with her! You think they won't send someone round to check? Ask questions? Jesus! He'll kill us.' He turned on her, his fear crystallising into anger. 'I'm warning you, stupid cow! If anyone comes sniffing round here, if there's the slightest hint of trouble, I'll cut your fucking throat. Get that?'

She nodded. He wouldn't. He would hit her, because she was easy to hit, but he wouldn't do worse than that, because he wouldn't dare. But Carver – Carver would kill her, easy as blinking. The thing was, she didn't care any more.

ii

Gillian

Baby Found In Mall

Staff arriving this morning at WHSmiths in the Queen Elizabeth Shopping Centre were astonished to hear a baby crying, and traced it to a cardboard box in the doorway of Debenham's.

'We thought at first it was a cat,' said mum, Kathleen Morris, 38. 'We couldn't believe our eyes when we saw what it was.'

The baby, a girl thought to be less than a month old, was wrapped in a towel. There was no note, and police have as yet found no clue as to the identity of the mother.

'We need to find this lady, who may be in need of

medical attention,' said police sergeant Brian Hewitt. 'I urge her strongly to come forward.'

Staff at the Lyford and Stapledon Hospital have named the little girl Debbie, since she was found by Debenham's. She is thought to be in good health, though doctors are running tests.

Police and the management of the Queen Elizabeth Shopping Centre are at a loss to understand how the child came to be in the Centre, which is securely locked at night. Cleaning staff have been interviewed and have declared that no baby was on the premises when they were at work.

'If there had been a baby there, I'd have seen it,' said Stanley Turner, 63. 'It's my job to keep a sharp eye on things.'

This is the second illegal nocturnal entry into the Queen Elizabeth Centre in less than a month, although the break-in at Curry's on the 2nd was...'

Gillian didn't care about break-ins at Curry's. From the moment she had seen the headline in the *Evening News*, her pulse had started racing. It was galloping now.

Don't think about it, she told herself. Ten to one, they'll find the mother within a week. No point in raising her hopes. And yet...

Joan snorted over the story, before pushing the paper back across the Formica. 'Hanging's too good for them, you ask me.' She lit another fag. 'Hope they lock her up and throw away the key.'

'The mother?' Gillian snatched up the paper and put it in the bin, to stop herself rereading it obsessively. 'You want to lock up bad mothers?' Her sarcasm always sounded so apologetic.

Joan, having stated one emphatic opinion, was able to do a complete volte-face without batting an eyelid. 'Mind you, don't blame her. Times I wanted to dump the lot of you. Drain your life's blood, kids. Don't know why you're so set on having them. You'd think different if you were lumbered with one.' She coughed deeply, took another drag. 'Thinking they'll offer you this one, then?' She cackled. 'Not a chance. I told you, you're too old. Haven't got a hope in hell.'

'If I had no hope they wouldn't have approved us,' said Gillian. She needed to get out. It was one thing to tell herself she should expect nothing, another to have Joan ramming it down her throat.

'You wouldn't want that one. Some brat dumped in a box? Don't know where it's come from. It will have *needs*, you wouldn't want that.'

'Of course it will have needs!' Gillian snapped. 'All children have needs, in case you haven't noticed.'

Joan chuckled. 'And I saw to all yours, didn't I? Don't you go whining. Worked my knickers off for you, I did.'

Probably literally, Gillian thought. Though not for her children. Everything Joan had been, everything she had done and failed to do, was a model of the mother Gillian was determined not to be. A child with needs was exactly what she wanted. It wasn't about what she wanted, it was about how much she had to give. It would be so wrong for this little Debbie to be deprived of that.

No! Stop thinking about it. Stop trying to picture the baby. Don't use a convenient shop's name, invented by strangers. If the baby were hers, she'd call it—No! Forget it. It was never going to be for her.

The phone rang. *It's the agency, offering me the baby*. Why did she let herself think things like that? It was going to be nothing, for Joan probably. 'Hello, Gillian Wendle.'

173

'Oh there you are, Gilly.' Pam sounded almost excited. 'Did you see the *Evening News*? They've found a baby. You could have it, couldn't you? Isn't that what you wanted?'

'It doesn't work like that, Pam.' But why mock Pam for thinking it? Was it any dafter than her own silly hopes? 'The real mother's probably going to come forward in a day or two.'

'Why don't you tell them you are the real mother? Then they can just give it to you.'

Dear God, had that one crossed her mind too? 'No Pam. I think they'd want a bit more proof than that.'

'Oh, well,' said Pam, disgruntled. 'I thought it was good news.'

An abandoned baby was good news. Was that where Gillian's desperation had brought her?

She saw a leaflet that had arrived with the paper. An invitation to a vigil at St Mark's, to pray for a nurse imprisoned in Iran. Asking God to intercede. Apparently that was how God worked. He was sitting up there watching a nurse being imprisoned and refusing to lift a finger unless the congregation of St. Mark's begged Him. Well, maybe it did work that way. She could do that, get on her knees and pray for the nurse – a simple matter of right and wrong. Could she ask for divine intercession in this other matter? No, because there was no right and wrong, only her devouring need. And perhaps that need was more Satanic than divine.

iii

Heather

'Wa wa wa.'

What time was it? Half two. Surely it had to be later than that? Heather lay still, telling herself it was a dream. Less than an hour since Abigail had last had her up.

'Wa wa wa.'

It wasn't going to go away. Heather sat up. Instantly, Martin stirred beside her.

'Eh?' He gave a yawn. Lying bugger. He'd been awake, she knew. Just waiting for her to make the first move.

'I'm going.' She scrambled out of bed, across to the cot. 'What is it then, Abigail? Eh?'

Lifted her up. Felt her. Still dry. Hungry then. Surely Bibs had never been this insatiable? She flopped down into the chair to feed her. She hadn't wanted to get up, but now she had, her attention was all on the child.

So hungry! Greedy little guzzler. Heather looked down on Abigail, urgently working the nipple. This is me pouring into her, she thought. Like a vampire drinking blood. Except, did the victims of vampires find such visceral pleasure in being victims? My little Abigail, my daughter, my baby. She wanted to pour every ounce of herself into the child, to be fused with her, as they had been when Abigail had been in the womb. How had Abigail been within her and she had felt so little attachment? This child was her self, perhaps even more than Bibs had been, because she was a girl.

She crooned gently over the sucking baby. Very softly – she wasn't going to share this, even with Martin, who was deep asleep again, or pretending to be. Leave him to his theatrical snores. She had her little Abigail.

175

The baby stopped, already asleep on her breast. She would happily stay there, curled up in the chair, gazing down on her child, but her eyelids were beginning to droop again. And she needed to sleep. She'd be coping on her own from now on because her mother-in-law was going home at last.

Lower Abigail back into her cot. Cover her lightly over. Blue teddy bear where she would reach it. Very, very quietly raise the rail. Tiptoe back to bed, back to the warm quilt and the deep pillow, and sleep…

'Wa wa wa!'

It couldn't be happening.

'Wa wa wa!'

What time was it now? Half three? No! No, she needed to sleep. She loved her baby but she needed to sleep.

'Wa wa wa!' More and more strident. Damn it. Don't play bloody games, Martin, I know you can hear it.

'Wa wa wa!'

She lay rigid, determined that this time she would not be the one. Even Martin could not pretend unconsciousness through this. No. Here it came. A heavy roll over, arms wild, hoping that his thrashing would rouse her if the baby hadn't.

A half-asleep grunt came out of the darkness.

Still she lay rigid

'Wa wa wa wa wa!'

A big show of struggling up into a sitting position. Big yawn. He turned, blinking, and saw her eyes were wide open.

'Heather?'

'Yes?'

'You all right? Baby's crying.'

'I know the baby's crying.'

'What, do you just let her cry then?'

'No, we don't just let her cry. We get up and deal with her, like I've done three times already tonight. So maybe, this time, it's your turn.'

Martin glowered. 'I do have to work in the morning.'

She said nothing, still locked rigid.

Grumbling, he staggered over to the cot. She could see his silhouette, raising the child in what he hoped would look a cack-handed manner. He knew perfectly well how to hold a baby.

'She's wet,' he said.

She said nothing.

'She needs changing.'

'The nappies are by the changing mat.'

He was angry now, trapped into it, shuffling things in the darkness. In his arms, Abigail stopped crying, and Heather could see him hesitate. Yes, he would actually put Abigail back in the cot in a wet nappy if she didn't cry.

'Wa wa wa!'

He put her on the mat and peeled off the dirty Huggie. What was he going to do with it? Leave it there for her to deal with in the morning of course. He wouldn't think of putting it in the bin that was standing there.

Grunts and mutterings and a lot of rustling and a weary sigh. Was he wiping her down? Too difficult?

'Look,' he said at last, dangling a nappy in the darkness. 'I don't know what to do with this. You'd better come—'

'Don't.' He'd raised his voice so she would damn well raise hers. 'Don't you dare pretend you don't know how to change your own child!'

'Right! You want me to make a crap job of it just so you don't have to get out of bed?'

'No, I want you to make a good job of it, just for once. Just for once pretend you're responsible here, as well as me.'

'I am responsible. I'm out every day earning a living. You think that's not responsible? You want to swap? You go out to work and I'll stay home and change a couple of nappies and do my nails all day.'

'You think that's what I do? Two children to care for, my father to look after, the housework, the shopping, the washing, cooking your bloody meals, and you think I sit around doing my nails? No, I am a twenty-four hour a day nursemaid with no time off for good behaviour. That baby is our baby, Martin. Ours, not mine. Three times I've been up for her tonight, and three last night, so I reckon you can manage it just once!'

The bedroom door creaked open. Bibs toddled in, pyjamas askew, his face screwed up in distress. Crying at the nightmare of his parents arguing in the middle of the night.

Heather forced her rigid limbs to relax. Arms extended, she swung round out of bed, reaching for him, but Martin was there first, leaving Abigail on the changing mat and racing for his little boy.

'Now see what you've done,' he said, lifting Bibs up. 'You really want to upset everyone in order to make a point? For God's sake see to the baby before we have the police round.'

'Is everything all right?' Barbara, hair in curlers, quilted dressing gown wrapped round her, poked her head round the door. 'I thought I could hear a bit of a rumpus. Should I be calling a doctor?'

'The baby needs changing and Heather's refusing to deal with her,' said Martin, all his attention fixed on Bibs, who was hugging him.

'For God's sake!' began Heather, but Barbara, tutting, was already on her way to the changing mat.

'Can't have little Gigi going wet, can we? Oh no no no.

Leave it to poor old Granny, shall we, pet. Who's a lovely girl, then? You just want someone to take care of you, don't you, and it looks as if it's going to have to be me.'

Martin made a great show of comforting Bibs who, by now, had completely forgotten his distress. He glared at Heather. Barbara glanced at her with silent disapproval.

Heather rolled back into bed and pulled the duvet over her head. To hell with the lot of them!

CHAPTER 7

i

Kelly

'Miss Sheldon? Kelly Sheldon?'

The voice on her mobile was masculine, pushy, smug, but she said, 'Yip, that's me.'

'Great! This is Jim Matthews, *Lyford Herald*. How are you?'

'I'm fine.'

'I see you put an ad in our paper last week. Looking for your fellow babies?'

'Yes…'

'Great! Our girl Emma told us all about it – eventually. Silly girl!' He chuckled. A clerk keeping a story to herself? Whatever next. 'Didn't want to miss you. Just to get this right, you've got evidence that babies were mixed up, right?'

'Yes.' Kelly didn't like him.

'Great! And your mum's ill. Human interest story and a hospital foul-up. We want to do a follow-up, big spread, get your story in full, front page maybe.'

'I see.'

'So, Kel, let's fix up for a proper interview, a few pictures, yes?'

She hesitated. A couple of days earlier, this would have been fantastic news. But her universe had slipped to one side since then. Everything was wonderful, aggravating, unnerving, but most of all, confusing. She'd accepted that finding her phantom sister was impossible, a daft idea from the start, and with nothing else to keep her in Lyford, she'd been planning to head home this morning.

But an article. A big article with a full explanation, that everyone would read; that might make the impossible slightly more probable? It was worth a try. One last go.

It would mean an interview with this slimeball. But hell… 'Okay,' she said.

'Great!'

'With Emma.'

'Er, sorry, what? Emma?'

'Emma, the lady I spoke to when I placed the ad.' Kelly smiled at the phone. 'She can interview me. I'll tell her all about it.'

So she'd have to stay another day.

Ben had gone back to his apartment near Heathrow and his job in the city. Reluctantly, furiously, but he'd had to go. She had his mobile number, his home number, his work number, his email address, and he'd already phoned her once this morning and sent a dozen texts, but she felt amputated without him near.

If she couldn't be with him, she certainly didn't want to be here, in dreary soulless Lyford, nursing this weird fierce emotion.

It wasn't just sex. Their one night together hadn't been an explosion of rampant passion. Almost the opposite; it had been tentative, exploratory, nervous, as if it had been the first time for both of them. Two babes in the wood. But it had been matchless. Why?

Because she was in love, and love, it seemed, was strangely like grief. Numbing. She would do her duty for her mother; give her story to the *Lyford Herald* and hope the publicity would help trace Roz's birth daughter. But

181

after that, Kelly had had enough. If she couldn't be with Ben, she just wanted to go home.

The Sat Nav ordered Kelly off the M3. Fortunately. She knew where she was going, but she was finding it difficult to concentrate on the road. It was just as well it was there. Probably take her the wrong way up a one-way street or off a cliff or leave her marooned in a service station in Lincolnshire, but she would take the risk. Better than trying to picture a map in her head when the only image she could conjure up was Ben.

It didn't hurt anyone, did it, this obsession? And it didn't really alter anything between her and Roz. Roz was still her mum, would always be her mum, they would still do anything for each other. Kelly would still do everything realistically possible to find the girl with those all-significant genes. Her mobile number and her home address were on record with the *Herald*, and she had given her story to a desperately nervous probationary Emma, under the guard of the cocky Jim Matthews, nice and plain, all the facts as she knew them, dates and details, without embellishment despite Jim's fishing. So there it was. Forget it until the paper came out in a couple of days. If there were no useful response, she'd think about a new approach. But just for now, she could concentrate on Ben.

What was he doing? She knew what he was doing; he had told her half an hour ago. He was in a meeting. What was he saying? How was he looking? Was he concentrating on his presentation or thinking about her?

Stop! A car slowed in front of her and she was nearly up its exhaust pipe before she noticed. Leave it. Put Ben on hold, until she was at the Padstows, with her mother, telling Roz all about him.

She turned into their lane at last, crunched to a halt on the gravel outside the house. Roger strolled over to greet her as she opened the door.

'Hi, Roger.'

'Hello, Kelly. You're looking extraordinarily bright-eyed and bushy-tailed.'

'I'm in love.'

'Ah. That would explain it.'

'She's been good,' said Roger. They were standing, after dinner, on the banks of the river. Slow drifting water, paling in the evening light. 'A bit of a crisis the second day, when you'd gone, but other than that, just fine. Eating well, getting plenty of exercise, keeping her spirits up. I think she'll come through it, don't you?'

'She had you taking care of her.'

'And you'll do just as good a job, I've no doubt of that, as always.'

'I hope so.' It had been her mission since she was ten, taking care of her mother. Of course a grown woman, not yet forty, should be able to take care of herself, but most grown women were not like Roz. Few had Roz's ability to block out problems. Left to manage alone, could Roz be trusted to pay the rent, remember her appointments, take her pills? Or would she think that everything could be solved by an hour of yoga and meditation?

For the first time it crossed Kelly's mind that being a caring daughter might be incompatible with being a lover. She had a foot in two worlds, and suddenly her balance was precarious.

'Could be a bit of a hindrance with the great love affair?' suggested Roger.

'Oh, don't say that!'

He laughed and put an arm round her. 'I do understand. It's never easy. I can see it from both viewpoints. Your mother needs you and you need your life.'

'Yes but…' Kelly took a deep breath, furious with the confusion fate had thrown at her. 'They can go together, can't they?'

'Why not?' he agreed.

'He has a mother too; he has to sort things out with her.'

'A caring sort.'

'Yes. Trying to be.'

Roger hugged her, reassuringly. 'It will work out all right, don't worry. You deserve it, you and Roz. It's an order. Neither of you are to be unhappy.'

'Yes, Boss.'

'You're our mission, you know that. Our daughters almost. We have a vested interest in seeing you both come good.'

She nearly said, 'Daughter and granddaughter, you mean.' Then she realised how right he was. It wasn't a mother and daughter that Roger and Mandy and the others had offered a refuge to, twenty-two years ago, but two children, equally vulnerable, equally in need.

She had a memory, so distant it was almost formless, of the warm oil-lamp glow in the half-ruined farmhouse, of being in a nest of cushions between Roz and Mandy, as they shared a book, Mandy's finger following the words as she read aloud, hieroglyphs that Kelly could not yet understand. Roz's head bent over to follow the finger just as Kelly's was, her hair tickling Kelly's cheek. Roz learning to read.

While Kelly had grown from baby to toddler to happy curious child under their guidance, Roz had grown too, moulded by her surrogate parents so that, one day, mother and daughter could step out into the world together and survive.

What would have happened if Roger and Mandy had not been there for them? 'We owe you,' she said. 'Big time. Really. I do know it.'

Roger chuckled. 'As long as you're both happy, that's all that counts. Now, tell me about this Ben. You could talk about nothing else at dinner.'

'So he's going to come this weekend and you'll love him, I know you will.'

'Of course I will, if you do,' said Roz.

'He's twenty-five and he comes from Coventry but he works in London—'

'Yes.' Roz laid a hand on Kelly's arm to redirect her attention to the road. 'You told me.' At least thirty times. She wasn't puzzled by her daughter meeting a man from Coventry who worked in London. All sorts turned up in Pembrokeshire in summer.

'I should have taken a photo. Why didn't I?' Kelly wasn't one for photographs. She looked with her own eyes, at the here and now.

'I don't need a photo,' said Roz. 'He's—' She laid a hand on top of her head. 'About this tall. Brownish hair, hazelish eyes, quirky smile—'

'All right.' Kelly laughed. 'But that doesn't do him justice, you know. He's altogether lovely, and I can't stop thinking about him and I think I'm going to die without him.' She paused for breath.

Roz gazed at Kelly and smiled. Could she really be feeling such excitement and intensity? Roz tried to equate it with what she had felt, for husband and lovers. There had been something overwhelming when she had been young, but had it really been love? Need. That was all. Clinging to any arm that offered to hold her up. She'd fulfilled some sort of fantasy by marrying Luke Sheldon, but that wasn't the same, nothing like the love Kelly had for this Ben. She had wanted someone, anyone, and when Luke had shown such a clear, flattering liking for her, she had stuck to him like a limpet. Until the tide of his drunken violence had touched Kelly, and washed them both off the rock. The occasional lovers that had followed had been friendships, brief touches in moments of loneliness. Her need had gone, quenched by the only love that really mattered to her, love for her child. Mutual dependence that would last forever.

Why hadn't she known that one day love might steal her daughter away? 'I'm looking forward to meeting him.'

Kelly pictured it with an inner glow. Her mother and Ben together in Carregwen. Ben walking with Kelly on the hills, feeding the sheep with her, retreating to her beautifully eccentric bedroom with her.

Ben, with his smart suit and his perfectly cut hair. Ben with his well-paid graduate job, and his gleaming new car and his place near Heathrow. Kelly felt a twinge of panic. He was far away and the gulf between them was so very vast. Their worlds were so alien, so incompatible. How could it possibly work?

It would be enough to see him again. Just bring the threads together and hope they would weave themselves into something manageable.

A junction ahead.

'Where are we?' she asked. No Sat Nav now. They were back in the Astra, so smooth and soft-spoken that it no longer felt like their car, but the garage had not fitted Sat Nav and Kelly was really going to have to concentrate. Get her mother home, that was the first step. Then check on the animals, get in some groceries, and only then think about Ben.

After she had thanked Joe for his help.

Ah. She had forgotten about Joe.

'No, it's been great,' Joe assured her. 'Everything's fine, like, you know. Cool. Except I've been missing you.'

Kelly hugged him. That was all right, she owed him that. And he'd understand. Or at least he wouldn't be too badly hurt. They were friends, never really more than that. Not lovers in any meaningful sense, she could see now she knew what love really was. He'd move on, no trouble. But maybe she'd explain tomorrow. She didn't want to be dishonest about it, but it wasn't really fair to leave him looking after her farm for her for more than a week, then come home and tell him it was all over between them.

'Are you coming up the Mill tonight, then?' he asked.

'Not tonight. I need to sort Mum out. But tomorrow. I'll come round to your place tomorrow.'

'Great! Black Amber on in Swansea, this weekend. I got tickets when you said you were coming home.'

'That sounds – great. I'll see you tomorrow, and we'll talk.' She kissed him on the cheek. Couldn't he tell? No, not Joe. She watched him mount his motorbike and rumble away down the rutted track. Then she went inside to clear up his beer bottles. Clearing up a stage of her life that was gone for good.

ii

Vicky

Gillian looked at the lime green mini, tucked up against the wall of the house. Vicky had only driven it a couple of

187

times. Preferred to walk or cycle. Never mind. Exercise was good for her. Gillian, washing the windows, gave the windscreen a quick wipe over. Might as well keep it sparkling for the girl.

She tipped the dirty water down the drain, and went back in, wiping her hands on her apron as she took it off. How was Vicky? She wished she knew. Gillian was living on broken glass. Vicky was a whirlwind inside, driven by some inner obsession, but burning herself up in her determination not to show it. She had always been like that.

Hadn't she?

Gillian pictured Vicky walking to Junior School, her hand in her mother's. Yes, she had been quiet, no running and shouting, no naughtiness, but she had not seemed unhappy back then. Not defensive, determined to keep Gillian out.

Adolescence made such a misery of lives. Was that it? The angry self-assertive teenage years turning a quiet happy child into a sullen unhappy woman? Unhappiness made worse by Gillian's stupid silence about the adoption, but surely not caused by it? Exacerbated by Joan, of course. That went without saying. Gillian could remember her own teen years, the endless fights and tussles. Joan would make anyone sulk and storm.

Maybe every family went through this. Every mother left yearning for the time when her child had been young and dependent and cocooned in her nest. Gillian made herself a cup of tea and sat down, pulling the old photograph albums out. Vicky as a baby, gurgling contentedly in Gillian's arms, rolling on a rug in the garden. Vicky's school photographs, the little shy smile gradually becoming more confident, the soft round baby features altering year by year into the future woman. Vicky smiling broadly at the camera, looking pleased, almost cocky. In the back garden. Cosmos and scarlet runner beans. Gillian could remember that shot. It had been the summer after her GCSE exams. She had just had the results, she'd done so well, everyone had been so proud. Only Joan had scoffed, but Joan would.

Vicky on her seventeenth birthday, surrounded by cards and holding up the car keys triumphantly. The more controlled smile of a teenager, who didn't want to be so uncool as to whoop like a baby, but still a smile, still genuine. And then...

Gillian flicked through pages, first with a pang, then with alarm. So few pictures of Vicky, as if she were determined not to be photographed. And when she was caught, she was looking away, or head down, or her long hair shaken to conceal her face. No more smiles, happy or haughty. Just blank eyes.

What had happened? Gillian was holding in her hands evidence that all her daughter's happiness had vanished in a puff of smoke. It was there, on the page for anyone to see, so obvious, yet she had lived with Vicky every day and she'd noticed nothing. She'd been irritated by the increasing antagonism and isolation, yes, but she'd never noticed that it had all begun then. Just like that.

What was it she had missed? God, how terrible a mother had she been? So desperate to adopt and an utter failure. Frogmarching a child into a career far beyond the dreams of anyone else on the Marley estate – was that really successful motherhood?

A rattle and thud at the door. The paperboy. Automatically, she went to the door, picked up the *Lyford Herald* and unfolded it without reading a word. She could only think about Vicky and her own failure.

Back to the photographs. She went through them again. It was so screamingly obvious. What had happened? Vicky had been at Sixth Form, taking A levels. She had worked hard, aiming for medical college – and that was all her life had been. Up, to school, home, upstairs to study. At weekends, breakfast, upstairs to study, down for dinner, back to her room.

'So responsible, so dedicated,' Gillian had said. But it hadn't been dedication, had it? Vicky had been turning herself into a recluse, and Gillian had stood by and let it happen.

Was it the illness? After she'd discovered that she had a condition she could never cure? It would be understandable. But no. It hadn't been diagnosed until Vicky had started university. And she had taken it well. She had almost seemed to welcome having something that she could take charge of and control. So not the diabetes then.

A boy? It must have been. Puppy love and then cruel disappointment. Had that sad little claim to sexual experience been Vicky falling for some spotty youth, being spurned, breaking her heart? Why couldn't she have talked to her mother? Gillian could have helped. She could remember what teenage infatuation felt like. All joy one moment and the end of the world the next.

Gillian sighed and closed the albums, putting them back on the shelf. Tidied the room, plumped up the cushions. Picked up the *Lyford Herald* again. Began to read.

Missing Daughter Quest: Hospital Rapped.

The typical *Herald* tabloid style. She looked at it with just curiosity at first, until the details began to blare at Gillian. *Kelly Sheldon…her mother Rosalind who suffers from a form of diabetes known as MODY, Maturity Onset Diabetes of the Young…trying to find her mother's lost baby…March 1990… There was someting about a mix-up at the hospital, but that must just be a cover story.* Her heart was thumping

190

so loudly, she didn't hear the footsteps on the stairs at first. She rolled the paper up, thrusting it behind a cushion on the sofa.

'Vicky!' she said, flustered. 'Finished up there? I'll make some tea.'

'You okay?' Polite, guarded.

Was she concerned for Gillian? It was Vicky who mattered, not Gillian, and not this Kelly Sheldon person. 'I'm all right. But how about you?'

'Me? I'm okay. Why?'

'If you had a problem, you could talk to me, couldn't you?'

'What?' Vicky's face twisted. 'Talk?'

'If anything happened, if you were upset—'

'We don't talk. Like you not telling me I was adopted for twenty-two years.'

It was never-ending. Every day. Like some scab she had to pick.

'Anyway.' Vicky opened the bureau drawer, searching for an envelope. 'I've got a letter to post.'

'No, don't take it yet. It can wait a moment. Sit down. I want to us to talk now.' That touch of firmness that might have made her a good teacher. The mother daughter ties were still there. The girl sighed and sat down, folding her arms.

Gillian pulled out one of the old albums. Not to open, just as a prop. She perched on the sofa and stroked the closed book. 'I've been looking at our old family photographs.'

'Family.'

Gillian ignored the jibe. 'Looking at pictures of my little girl. You were a happy child, Vicky…'

A bitter smile.

191

Gillian went on. 'I know we had upsets and sulks and tears, sometimes with good reason.' Mostly the days when Joan was around. 'But you were happy. You knew how to smile.'

No smile now, just a closed book.

'And then you weren't happy. You were doing your A levels and you stopped being happy.'

'You wanted me to work, didn't you? You made that clear often enough.'

'I nagged you, I know. I wanted you to do well and I pushed too hard. I'm sorry. But that doesn't explain it.' She drew breath. 'Was it a boy, maybe?'

Vicky's lip curled.

'Did you fall for someone and he didn't want you? Was that it? And you never told me?'

'For Christ's sake, no, I didn't fall for anyone.'

'You can tell me, Vicky. You could have told me then. I know it would have been – not easy, bringing a friend here, with Gran—'

Vicky laughed. A harsh burst of outrage. 'Joan!'

'I know she'd have said something – Was that it? Did she say something cruel? Did she make you feel no one would want you?'

'Listen, will you? It isn't a question of whether some silly boy or some slimy man wants me, it's whether I want them, all right? I've had enough of that, and that bitch Joan can play her games with someone else!'

Gillian turned cold inside. Joan. 'Vicky, what games did Joan play? What did she do that made you so miserable?'

'I am not miserable!'

'You're not happy.'

'Happy? How do you want me to show I'm happy? You'd feel better if I dropped my studies and went out whoring each night, is that it? That's what happiness is?'

'Of course not.'

'Oh really? Because I thought that was exactly what everyone wanted. Well, don't worry, I've tried it. Joan saw to that. And...' She stopped.

'What? For God's sake, Vicky, what are you talking about?'

'You really don't know, do you?'

'No!' Appalled, Gillian braced herself for what was coming.

Vicky, trying to be disdainful, was going to talk, it seemed she couldn't help herself anymore.

'That time, just after my seventeenth birthday, when Granny Wendle was ill?'

'Yes, I remember. Terry and I went...' She and Terry had gone to see his mother who was dying in Romford. Stayed over a couple of days until she'd passed away. They hadn't taken Vicky. She had her studies and she was old enough now. It wasn't like leaving a baby with Joan. A seventeen-year-old girl would be safe enough, surely?

How could she have been so stupid?

'What happened?'

'What do you think? Joan thought it was time I had some fun and she'd better arrange it. She called Dana round and Gemma and Jade.'

Joan's willing lieutenants, Sandra's youngest daughter Dana, and her granddaughters by Sharon. Hard bitten, hard biting girls, as unlike Vicky as it was possible to be.

'She told them to take me out,' Vicky continued. 'Show me "a good time". That's what she kept calling it. Gemma and Jade made me put on all this stupid make-up and some of their clothes, and I could see Joan and Dana laughing in the mirror. Except that I couldn't see much because they took my glasses away. I thought, "Okay, put up with it, go out for one night and maybe they'll shut up and leave me alone." So when they'd got me all tarted up, they took me out. Joan was on the doorstep, winking at them, saying, "You make sure she has a good time, eh. Poor kid doesn't know nothing. You show her what it's all about."'

Gillian covered her face with her hands.

'They took me to a pub, kept trying to get me to drink but I didn't want to. I expect they put something in my Coke though. They were laughing as if they had, so I didn't drink that either.'

Vicky had started her account in an almost conversational tone, treating the episode with contempt. But she couldn't keep it up. The underlying hysteria was welling up, and she spoke now in staccato bursts, on the verge of hyperventilating. This was it, Gillian knew. It would all come out. Nothing could stop it now.

'They produced this boy. They kept telling me he liked me. Pushing me at him. He was laughing, in on the joke with them, pulling faces at me. Making obscene gestures. It was disgusting. I ran. Locked myself in the toilet. Jade came to get me out and I said I was going home, so she said, "Yes, all right, we'll all go home with you." But he came too. Craig.'

'Craig Adams?' breathed Gillian. She knew him, him and his leering mates, the estate's future pimps, if they weren't already.

Vicky shook the question off. 'When we got home, Joan pretended she couldn't see anything was wrong. Said she could tell everyone was having a great time. I tried to go to my room, but they wouldn't let me in. Kept saying how mean I was. To poor Craig. They pushed me into Joan's room with him and held the door shut. Joan watched telly. They locked me in with him so he could show me what was what.'

Gillian could feel her knees buckling. That drumming

in her ears again. She was dreaming this. She must be dreaming. 'He raped you.'

'Oh no. We were having a good time.'

'He raped you!'

'No!' Vicky leapt to her feet. 'No! He didn't have a gun or a knife. I decided to go along with it. It wasn't rape.'

'It was! It was rape.'

'No, I am not a rape victim!' Vicky pressed her hands to her chest, flinching from the word.

'And Joan knew?'

'Of course she knew. It was her little birthday treat. Make a woman of me.' Tears now, burning on Vicky's cheeks. Gillian could see them through the blur of her own.

'Oh God, oh God.' She couldn't stop shaking. She wanted to vomit. 'You didn't tell me.' She reached out, but Vicky turned her back.

The girl had been raped and hadn't said a word and Gillian had noticed nothing. She thought back, trying to recall. Her mother-in-law's funeral. Vicky had been silent, moody, but Gillian had been preoccupied, stressed with the arrangements and upset about the death of old Nora. She had put Vicky's sullenness down to teenage stroppiness and maybe the trauma of the first funeral she'd attended. But it hadn't been that at all. It had been the worst thing a mother could contemplate, barring the actual death of a child, and Gillian had done nothing. She had snapped at the girl.

And now, how was she to make up for it? She had wanted to put things right, but not this. Nothing could mend this.

She swallowed hard, took a deep shuddering breath and crossed to her daughter. 'Vicky. I didn't know, I didn't know.' Again she put her arms out to hug her.

'No!' Vicky fought her off, shoving hard. 'Don't touch me! Don't touch me.' She was rigid, her hands claws.

'Oh Vicky, I'm so sorry. Forgive me, I should have realised, but I was just so selfish! Oh God, and I was so determined – I was going to be such a perfect mother, give you such a perfect life and all I did was ruin things for you. When I read about you being found, that day, it was like a wonderful flower bursting open in front of me and all I've done was trample it down.'

'Must be me, mustn't it,' snarled Vicky. 'Mothers take one look at me and want to kill me.'

'What?'

'The first one did! My birth mother. At least she didn't drag it out for years.'

'Oh Vicky, no one thought she wanted you dead. She left you, so carefully, where you would be found.'

'No. No that's not right. What do you mean, no one thought? You… She… No, she left me for dead!'

'I promise you, she didn't. I still have the cuttings, when you were found, when I first thought – hoped… She'd wrapped you up, and when I read it, I thought, I'll wrap you up cosily, too, I'll make everything lovely for you, just as she must have wanted to, but all the time—'

'No! There was nothing about me being found. It was just about her, that woman, trying to kill me.'

'Kill you? No, no, you've got it wrong, Vicky. I'll show you. I've got it, 20th March, 1990. I thought it was the beginning of a whole new world.'

'20th? No. No. I've seen her! I've read the story. It was the 23rd!'

Vicky backed away. Gillian couldn't get her head round what her daughter was saying. Vicky had been abused, horribly, and telling the truth seemed to have unleashed total chaos in her mind.

'I saw the woman,' Vicky insisted, in a whisper. 'She claimed her baby was snatched, but no one believed her, because she made it up. I believed her story. I found her. Here, in Salley Meadows. I told her I was her daughter, and you know what? She slammed the door in my face. She thought I was lying, because she knew I should be dead. She gave birth to me, she tried to kill me and now she won't speak to me.'

Gillian steadied herself on the back of the sofa, trying to pin down one small fact in this whirlwind. 'I think your birth mother is in Wales.'

'What!'

Gillian groped among the sofa cushions and produced the rolled-up newspaper.

'I think this must be about her.' Shaking, she held it out.

Vicky took it as if it would burn, unrolled it and stared at the front page.

Bright, attractive Kelly Sheldon, 22, is in Lyford on a mission...

'I think it must be her,' said Gillian, faintly. She couldn't stand it any longer. She groped her way to the kitchen sink and threw up. Shivering, she ran the cold tap, soaked her face. She had no idea how to handle this. She ought to know what to do, driven by maternal instinct, but she was no mother. She was a selfish cow who had wanted a child. This was no house to bring a child into. She'd known it, always, even back then. You don't bring a child within a mile of Joan. If she had had a true mother's love for Vicky, she would have let another family take her.

She straightened, still shivering, and groped her way back to the living room.

No Vicky. The *Herald* lay on the floor, its first page ripped off. The front door was standing open.

Of course Vicky had to get out. They all did. Get out, away from here.

Gillian walked. The air was warm, cloying, not fresh. Traffic fumes hung in it. She couldn't breathe. Past the electricity substation, surrounded by broken wire. A nasty place.

It had been a nasty place forty odd years ago when she had lost her virginity in the long grass behind it. Learnt what it was all about, according to Joan. Arranged by Joan. Gillian's disgust and misery, and Joan's evil cackle. 'Had a good time, girl? Always knew there was a slut in you.'

Why hadn't she seen it as rape back then? Why had she just endured, because it was one of those things? If she'd seen it straight, seen her mother for what she was, she'd never have left Vicky to suffer the same.

She stumbled on. St Mark's church. She hadn't realised she was coming here. Hadn't been in the place for fifteen years. She'd been regular to start with, with her new baby, guiltily giving thanks, but in the end, Philip Coley's soul-battering enthusiasm had been too much for her. And then he had gone and the congregation had withered, and there was no more sense of guilt to nag her.

By luck the door was open; she could hear voices in the vestry, some meeting going on. Usually, these days, the place was kept locked. There were no treasures to steal, but anything that wasn't fastened down would be ripped up or sprayed.

She walked up the central aisle. Plastic chairs and the smell not of sanctity but of polish and disinfectant. She stopped before the crucifix with its pink writhing Christ. A crown of iron thorns. Vivid glistening painted blood. Let the thorns bite deeper, she thought, staring up at the dead image. Let them hurt you like you hurt me. Why did you let it happen to my little girl? I hate you.

But there was nothing here to hate. Sitting down on one of the plastic seats and staring at the image, she knew; there was no God. There was only hell.

iii

Kelly

'Oh,' said Joe. Hangdog. It occurred to Kelly that Joe always looked slightly hangdog, so there wasn't really much change. A shift from aimless contentment to bewilderment. 'So, that means, we're not, like, together any more.'

'But we're still friends. Just not – you know.'

'Yes. Sure.' Joe stood up. 'I'm going out. Need to get my head round this.'

He sidled out of the door, shoulders hunched. What should she do? Give him space to come to terms with it, or follow him? Either way, she could hardly stay in his digs while he mooched off. She grabbed her bag and hurried after him.

He hadn't got far. He was standing staring at his bike, hoping it might give him an explanation.

Kelly swore inside. She hadn't meant to hurt Joe. She had never meant to hurt anyone in her life, but perhaps that had been more the easy-going goodwill of laziness than innate virtue. She wasn't feeling virtuous now. She was feeling cruel and heartless, and that wasn't fair because she hadn't planned this. It had happened, this tsunami. Why did there have to be this flip side to finding her soulmate?

'Joe, I'm sorry. It just happened. It's not like anything I've ever felt before.'

'Not for me, you mean.'

'Not for anyone. It's not about liking someone, or fancying them. It's something I didn't even know existed.'

He looked at her, a hint of puzzled curiosity in his misery. If she had discovered something entirely new, perhaps it was some weird exotic thing, like Lassa fever, and she couldn't help it.

199

'I am so sorry, Joe. I really do like you, I want to be friends, especially after you've been so great with my mum being ill – looking after the animals and all that.'

He shrugged, perhaps feeling the self-satisfaction that she had hoped to inspire. He'd proved a true friend when she'd needed him. Never mind that for him it had actually been a rent-free holiday with minimal responsibilities and a chance to drain someone else's larder. 'Yeah, well, that's okay.'

'We still friends?'

'Yeah.' He sounded resigned. She couldn't really expect him to sound enthusiastic. 'You still want to come to see Black Amber?'

Damn. 'I can't, Joe. Ben's coming...'

'Oh. I've got the tickets.'

'What about Maddy?' Inspired thought. 'She was really keen on them. I bet she'd love to go. Ask her; she'll buy a ticket off you.'

'Maddy? You think? Yeah, maybe.'

He could offer to sell Maddy a ticket or, if he had any gumption whatsoever, he could just invite her. She was unattached at the moment, and even if she were more interested in Black Amber than in Joe, it would salve his dignity a little. It was up to him; Kelly wasn't going to pull any more strings.

'Yeah, maybe, I'll go see her.'

She watched him get on his bike, stamp hard and turn out onto the road.

It had been painful, but it could have been worse. The decks were clear now for Ben to arrive on Friday night. She'd topped up her mother's prescription and done the shopping. Bought a steak. She might convince him in time that the vegetarian option could be just as good, but baby steps, no need to rush it.

She'd just got to wait out the next twenty-four hours. She turned the Astra for home, feeling that warmth growing as she bounced slowly along the track to the cottage. Just twenty-four hours between her and ecstasy. The office and the pub weren't expecting her back at work until next week. Nothing else to worry about.

Except that they had visitors.

She didn't recognise the car. A green mini, parked by the wheelbarrow near the front door. Jehovah's Witnesses? They usually stopped at the top of the lane and walked down, in their misplaced Sunday best.

She carried the corn to the bin in the shed, gathered up the bags of shopping, slipped into the house, expecting to hear the anodyne murmur of religious platitudes.

She heard her mother's voice, high with panic.

'But I don't understand. It can't be.'

'It's here, in black and white,' accused another voice, as Kelly, dropping the shopping without a thought, burst into the kitchen.

A girl, her own age maybe, short lank hair, angular face, heavy glasses, slamming a sheet of newspaper down on the pine table at a terrified Roz.

'Who the hell are you?' demanded Kelly, grabbing the girl's wrist.

She turned, wrenching herself free.

'Who are you?' repeated Kelly.

'My name is Victoria Wendle.' The girl straightened her cuffs. 'Allegedly.'

'What are you doing here?'

'Doing what you wanted, aren't I? Come to visit my mummy.'

'What?' Kelly looked across at Roz, who was standing, hand to her throat, scarcely able to breath. 'It's all right,

Mum.' She looked down, at the torn sheet of newspaper unfurling on the table. The front page of the *Lyford Herald*.

It wasn't supposed to be here. She hadn't calculated on anyone showing a copy to Roz. This was Kelly's private scheme.

'You're Kelly Sheldon, I suppose?'

'Yes, but...' She had asked for contact from the missing girl. An exchange of notes, testing the waters, before they decided where to go next. Nothing sprung on them like this. This was that girl? No phone call, no questions, she'd just driven straight here, on the basis of one newspaper story? She must be a crank. 'You think you're the baby I was swapped with?'

'Oh yes, "swapped" all right.' Vicky jerked her head in Roz's direction. 'I wasn't quite what she wanted so she swapped me.'

'I don't know what story the stupid paper has printed,' said Kelly, 'but you've got it all wrong. My mother had nothing to do with it. There was a mix-up at the hospital.'

'Oh yes!' A harsh laugh. 'Labels swapped. Is that really what she told you?' Vicky flung her accusation straight at Roz. 'Is that what you said?'

Roz raised her hand to her mouth, biting her finger. 'I don't know. I heard the nurses – I don't know. I don't remember.'

'It's all right, Mum.' Kelly was beside her, guiding her to a chair, but Roz refused to sit down.

'Don't get upset. She has no right to come in here, attacking you like this.'

'No?' asked Vicky. 'No right to ask the woman who gave birth to me why she dumped me in a cardboard box and exchanged me for a better model?'

202

'I don't know where you got this idea from—'

'From the *Lyford Herald*!' Vicky picked up the sheet of the *Herald* and slammed it down again.

What on earth had it said? Kelly picked it up, her fingers trembling with anger.

Kelly, a marine engineering graduate of Pembroke University...

'There isn't a Pembroke university. And I never said I had a degree.' It wasn't the issue, she knew, but it told her exactly how it was going to be. She read on. Had her mother seen this? 'I didn't say half this.'

Roz gazed in bewilderment at Kelly. 'I don't understand. You said?'

Kelly put her arms round her and squeezed. 'I'm sorry. But you were ill and I thought if I couldn't give you one of my kidneys there might be someone out there who could, so I went to Lyford—'

'Lyford?'

'Where I was born?'

Across the table, alone, Vicky was looking at them with loathing, her hands clenching and unclenching.

Kelly was appalled. Why was the girl so angry? Kelly hadn't pictured their meeting like this. She had imagined shock, maybe, even denial, but not this fierce fury.

Well, never mind Victoria Wendle. An irrational crank. It was Roz that mattered now, and Kelly could feel the life draining out of her mother.

'Why did you go to Lyford?' Roz whispered.

'I thought I could find the other baby. I put an advert in the *Herald*, and then they wanted to follow it up so I gave them an interview. I didn't stay to see what they printed. I wish I had. I didn't say anything about you dying, having just a month to live. I never said anything like that. I just

203

said you'd developed kidney problems, but they've made it into a stupid sob story.'

'You just said kidney problems?' demanded Vicky. 'They invented the bit about Maturity Onset Diabetes of the Young?'

'No, no, I explained that bit—'

'Well then!'

'Well what?'

'That's what I have. That's what I have to deal with for the rest of my life. Inherited. Thank you, Mother. Diabetes and a cardboard box were all that you ever gave me.'

Roz was biting her lip, shaking with panic, eyes wide.

'You have the same condition?' Kelly tried to think. She had never thought of the probability of them sharing the illness. 'So you wouldn't be able to give a kidney anyway?'

'Give a kidney? You seriously think I'd give up a kidney for her, when she threw me away? I'd rather give her arsenic!'

'Look, stop it!'

Whatever was going on here, Kelly could sense the girl's anger eating into Roz like acid.

'I don't know why you're so mad, but it's not Mum's fault. She didn't know she was giving you diabetes. She didn't know she had it herself until a few months ago.'

'But she knew enough to decide I wasn't what she wanted.'

'You're talking nonsense.' Kelly stared at the paper again, searching for some clue to this cardboard box stuff. There was nothing about that in the article. Crap about Roz being on the point of dying and Kelly's desperate quest and the mix-up in the hospital. The rest was a diatribe against the Lyford and Stapledon Health Trust, hospital incompetence, careless disposal of hospital waste and stuff about a body wrongly labelled in the morgue. Nothing about a cardboard box.

'Go on,' said Vicky to Roz. Despite her iron self-control, Kelly could sense shivers running through her like the tremors of an earthquake. 'Tell her the truth. Tell her how you decided I wasn't good enough, so you dumped me in a shop door and chose another baby instead.'

Kelly expected Roz to be outraged by this, but Roz's face wasn't registering denial. Shock yes, but the shock of awakening, as if cold water had been flung in her face. She gasped.

'I didn't think that!' Roz's eyes flicked from Kelly to Vicky to Kelly, as if she couldn't comprehend which was which. 'No, it wasn't like that!'

'Mum?' Kelly said. She too was looking from Roz to Vicky to Roz, chilled – two faces so entirely different and yet, in some appalling way, so much the same. Mother and daughter. The same jaw and cheekbones, the same hair colour. Kelly had never worried that there might be another girl entitled to her mother's love. Was it the similarities that hurt now? Or the way Roz was focusing on the other girl, with tear-washed pleading eyes?

'I loved you,' said Roz. 'You don't understand. I was frightened. I was only 17. I thought Gary was going to kill you. I couldn't protect you. I thought you'd be safer, happier, if I gave you up. I put you where I knew you'd be found.'

'In a cardboard box.'

'For warmth, yes. I thought you'd be safer without me. Only after I'd done it, I couldn't bear it. I wanted you back so much, and there you were, and when I had you back, I knew I could never be without you again.'

Kelly stood frozen. She couldn't understand what her mother was saying.

205

Vicky stood silent too, for a moment. The shaking was subsiding, the anger losing its needle-sharp intensity. 'You didn't have *me* back though, did you?'

'I – yes. I did. I got you back.'

'Not me.' The girl pointed at Kelly. 'It was her. Another baby. Say it. You took another woman's baby.'

'No. No! There was no other woman! There was just a baby. Just my Kelly.' A door opened in Roz's brain, a door that had been barred and bolted and padlocked for twenty-two years. A door opened and a terrible truth was creeping out. 'I wanted you back so much.'

Kelly stared at her, feeling something inside herself shrink and shrink until it shrivelled away. 'You took a baby? Is that what she's saying? You just took me?'

Roz's face was grey. 'You were there. Waiting for me.'

'Oh God. Oh no. What did you do?'

'Nothing. You were there, so I picked you up and carried you home.'

Kelly swallowed hard. 'You thought I was the same baby you had given up?'

'Yes!'

They both looked at Roz, staring at her, challenging her to tell the truth.

'I don't know. I don't know what I thought. It was all different then. Everything was frightening. I thought Gary would kill you. I thought they would take you away from me. I don't know!'

It was true. Roz didn't know. A voice within was telling her she could know if she chose. She could look at it straight and recall it all, cut through the muddle and desperation and see the cold cruel truth. But that would mean letting go of all she had. All her life she had been clinging to someone or something. For years she had clung to Kelly and if she looked straight at the truth now, that one beacon, her daughter, would be lost. Everything would be lost. 'I don't know!'

Kelly pulled away. She had no words. She wasn't Roz's daughter, not by birth, or by monumental clerical cock-up. She was someone else's stolen child. This was so different from anything she had imagined, so awful that she couldn't cope with it. She stared at the girl across the table.

Vicky said, 'What was wrong with me? What was wrong with you? You loved your baby so much? You're trying to tell me you were frightened for me? Did you ever, ever bother to think what might become of me? Where I might finish up? Did you?'

'I'm sorry,' whispered Roz.

'Or perhaps it really didn't matter what happened to me, just as long as you had something to cuddle. Why didn't you just get yourself a doll? Or a pet? Yes, help yourself to someone else's pet. Why not? Better than being stuck with me.' Her bitterness beat around Roz.

Roz flinched.

'Leave her alone.' Kelly gripped the back of a chair to keep her balance. 'She didn't know what she was doing, all right? It was terrible, but she was upset, confused. And now she's ill. She can't cope with this now, with you accusing her. I'm sorry, but just go, will you?' It probably wasn't right, leaving this mess like this, but Kelly needed time to find the ground beneath her feet. 'Please leave us alone.'

Vicky looked at her. 'Yes, I might as well. I wanted to know who this woman was who threw me away and took another baby in my place. Now I know. She's nothing,' She turned and walked out.

The slam of the door. 'Oh Kelly...' Roz was in tears.

No. Now the girl was gone, it was Roz that Kelly wanted

to shut out. 'Don't. I can't believe this. I can't believe you could just—' She wanted to be sick.

She bolted for the door, flew across the yard as Vicky was getting into her car. 'Stop!'

Vicky clicked her seat belt into place, inserted the key into the ignition.

'Don't!' Kelly clung to the Mini's door, holding it open. 'I didn't mean it. We can't leave it. I have to know.'

Vicky looked at her. 'Know what?'

'Know what happened. Don't you see? I thought I was Kelly, but I'm not. You're Kelly. So who am I?'

Vicky switched the engine on. 'I am not Kelly. I am Vicky. She left me to my fate. Right, I'm leaving her to hers. As for who you are, well, you can find that out for yourself, the same way I did. I told you, I found it all in the *Lyford Herald*. March 1990. Go and read it if you care that much. I'm not sorting out your life for you.' She pulled the door shut.

Kelly stood staring after the Mini as it drove away, concentrating on the glimpses of lime green through the hedgerow, the fading engine, so that she wouldn't have to think about that other thing.

Not think about it. Just like Roz. Was it a talent she had learned from the woman who had taken her? No. She did face up to things, and she would face up to this.

She marched back to the house.

CHAPTER 8

i

Lindy

Gary didn't want her any more. That was the truth. She was nothing but trouble, he said. A slag who tried to palm another man's baby onto him, and now she had the whole fucking police force out looking for her.

She knew he would have been rid of her before this, but Carver didn't want screaming women being kicked out onto the street and nosy neighbours calling the police. Not yet.

She hid behind the door, as Gary signalled her to do, when Carver knocked, oh so politely.

'Baby's been quiet,' Carver said. 'Not a cry, not a whimper for two nights now.' Carver noticed everything.

'Yeah.' Gary tried a laugh. 'I kick Lin out to deal with it every time it starts up. Don't want to wake the whole fucking street.'

'That's right.'

A pause. Holding her breath, Lindy could tell, from the jerk of Gary's head, that Carver was looking at the empty Moses basket.

'She's taken it out. Walk in the park.'

'Is that so?'

Gary tried to make a joke of it. 'You know, fucking women and babies, reckon they actually like them.'

'She's a mother,' Carver responded, his deep voice thick with sarcasm.

'Yeah, well—'

'So leave her to it. Keep your hands to yourself. No blue lights, no trips to casualty, no questions asked. Right?'

'That's right, Carver. No trouble. I'll see to that.'

When Carver had gone, Gary was almost wetting himself. Terrified, wanting to hit her and not daring. Not for now, anyway. He stormed off to get drunk, leaving her alone, soaked from aching, swollen tits, in the room cluttered with baby things.

Carver's job was going to be soon, she guessed, and then this life of hers would be over. Gary would throw her out no matter how she begged. Or more likely he'd get nicked. He was the sort who always was. Carver would get away but Gary would get caught, and whatever it was, this job, it would be serious, not just a bit of pushing, or something. It would mean big time for him.

A month ago, Lindy would have grieved. He had been everything to her, her Gary. But now— Now she couldn't get fussed, because the bit inside her that got fussed wasn't there any more. There was just a great big hole. Empty as the Moses basket.

That was what she wanted – not Gary, her baby. She wanted to be feeding her, changing her, washing her. All those little things for her Kelly.

She could still do the washing and cleaning. She brought out all the Baby Garden stuff, hugging each piece of soft white clothing, because she didn't have a baby to hold. She even hugged the Pampers.

She heated water, unearthed the soap powder, filled a bowl in the sink and started washing them all. Stripped the Moses basket of its precious bedding, breathed it in to catch the last of Kelly, then immersed it in the soapy water. Everything should be really clean. That's what babies needed. No germs or stuff like that.

She thumped and rubbed and squeezed, and then she rinsed. She wrung everything out, till she couldn't get out another drop of water, and then she tied string between the two chairs, and hung it all up to dry. She put 50p in the meter and put the electric fire on. Breathing in the steam. It was like a proper baby laundry. Showed she was a good mother. They couldn't fault her for this.

It kept her busy, so she didn't feel the ache so much.

So busy she didn't hear footsteps, the click of heels.

Tyler must have let the woman in, in one of those rare moments when he was sober enough to stand. A sharp rap on the door of her room made her jump. She grabbed a wet sleepsuit defensively as the door opened. Lindy knew what that meant. Authority. People who didn't think they had to wait to be invited in.

'Rosalind Crowe?' The woman was brisk, with the sort of official smile that wasn't friendly at all. A 'let's keep this as pleasant as we can, shall we?' smile. 'Caroline Rothsay, social services. Do you remember me? We met at the hospital? Can I come in? The door seemed to be open.'

'What you want?' Lindy said, still hugging the sleepsuit, its dampness spreading across her T-shirt. 'I ain't done nuffing.'

'Please, don't worry. I said I'd call, do you remember? Just to see if we can help.'

'Well you can't!'

'You never know.' The Rothsay woman was looking round the room, beady eyes taking in every detail. The steaming washing on the improvised line. The empty basket. 'You have just had a baby, my dear, and we all know

211

what a difficult time that can be for a new mother. Especially one without support—'

'I got support!'

'The baby's father? He lives here too, does he?'

'Yeah. Gary. And he won't want no social services nosing round here.'

The inevitable tightening of that false smile. 'I'm afraid that's not up to him to decide. I have a duty to make sure you are all right. You and little—' She paused long enough to glance at the notebook she was holding. 'Kelly. I need to know you're both fine, doing well, being looked after properly.'

'I know what social services does. They take kids away. Well, you're not taking my Kelly away! I can look after her, right!'

'Yes, I'm sure you can. Doing the washing, I see.'

'Yeah! Anything wrong with that?'

'Nothing at all, my dear. It's excellent.' She was looking at the empty basket again. 'And where is little Kelly?'

'Out,' retorted Lindy. 'Gary's got her. Gone to his mum's with her, so I can do the washing. What's it to you?'

'Ah. No, no, that's good. Family support. Gary has a mother helping out. That is very good.' The social worker was jotting down notes. Then she smiled again at Lindy, with a trace more humanity. 'You know, Rosalind, we are not all bad. You were taken into care yourself, weren't you, and I'm sure that must have been very traumatic for you, but sometimes it really is necessary.'

'Yeah but—'

'No one is saying it's necessary this time. As long as little Kelly is being looked after properly, receiving all the attention she needs – and you too – it's my job to help, not to hinder. And we can help, you know. In all sorts of ways.'

That couldn't be true. No one helped Lindy.

'Just think of me as a friend,' Caroline Rothsay assured her. 'You can call on me if you ever need me. And I'll call on you to see if everything is all right.'

'No need!'

'No, my dear. I am afraid I shall have to call again. I will need to see little Kelly. When she's not with her grandmother. Tomorrow. Will you try to be in with her, so I can see her?'

'You're not taking her away!'

The social worker patted Kelly's arm. 'Don't you fret. I promise I'm not planning any such thing. I'll call tomorrow, and we'll talk things through. Fill in a few details, complete a few forms. No need to worry about a thing.'

She was going. Kelly wanted to kick the door shut behind her, but instead she listened to the woman's shoes click-clicking down the stairs. She went to the window, and looked out as the Rothsay woman emerged into the street, with a backward glance of faint disgust at the house.

Caroline Rothsay paused, opened a case, produced a clipboard and a pen. Lindy, looking straight down on her, could see the sheet of names. Hers, *Rosalind Crowe — 128 Nelson Road — Kelly*. Lindy could read her own name and address easily enough. There were other names too. A couple had already been crossed out. The woman was beginning to cross Lindy's out too, but she stopped, put a question mark instead. Then she put her clipboard away, glanced at her watch and marched away.

Lindy looked after her with loathing. No social worker was going to take her baby away.

She looked back at the clothes drying, the empty basket. They couldn't take Kelly. She didn't have Kelly. Kelly was gone, and no matter how hard she wished it otherwise, Kelly wouldn't come back.

What if she asked for her? She'd heard people talking about it on the local radio. The abandoned baby. A policeman asking the mother to come forward, saying she wouldn't be in any trouble, they just wanted to help. Yeah, like the social services wanted to help. Lindy had heard other people on the radio too, calling in, saying she should be strung up, forcibly sterilised, she wasn't fit to have babies. That was what it would really come to if she did come forward. The police snarling at her, doctors, social workers looking down on her. Probably just put her in prison. She'd never get to keep Kelly if she went to them.

What if that woman started checking up. Gary didn't have a mother. What if she came back and Gary was here and there was still no baby? She was coming back. It was only when you really needed them that those people didn't show up. She'd be back tomorrow, with forms and orders, and maybe a policeman in tow, and a thin-lipped cow with hard eyes to seize the baby and take it away.

Lindy wouldn't be here. Had to shop, didn't she? Had to go out, and take the baby with her. She could stay out all day if she needed to.

ii

Heather

'You really should let me take you, dear.' Barbara Norris was insistent. She had moved back to her own home but still she couldn't resist coming round each day, with another knitted jacket for Gigi, or a toy for Bibs, or yet another hotpot. Just to see if Heather needed her help. 'It won't take me quarter of an hour to run you in. And I could always—'

214

'Look, thanks, Barbara, but really, I'd prefer to go by bus.' Heather was determined to keep it pleasant. Having her mother-in-law under their roof had dangerously strained their relationship. Things needed to get back onto tolerant separate tracks. 'I know you think I'm daft, but I just want the chance to manage on my own again. I can cope fine with the bus.'

'I thought managing on your own was becoming a teensy bit of an issue?' Barbara could smile and smile and still be a mother-in-law. 'Poor Martin has begun to feel quite guilty about leaving you alone all day, although Lord knows what he's supposed to do about it.' Yes, she was going to nurse every complaint, reasonable and unreasonable, that Heather made. 'I just thought I could help, in his place.'

'Thank you, really. But, today, I'm fine, and I want to prove I can manage.'

Not that getting into town for a dental check-up was going to be a doddle, on the bus, with a frisky toddler and a new-born baby, but Heather could cope. She was sure of it. The new buses were easier, more accommodating, and she was going to be well clear of rush hour. Of course, when they'd moved here she should have changed dentists, like the doctor, found a nearer practice, but she hadn't got round to it. Maybe next time.

And maybe a baby sling next time. She'd seen a mother in the next street with one and thought what a wonderful way it was to carry her baby. Against her breast, feeling her all the time against her own body. But maybe a bit avant-garde for the Hopcroft. The mother did draw a few disapproving stares and sniggers. Anyway, Heather couldn't afford to think about buying something new, when she had the old fashioned but perfectly serviceable carry-cot pram that Bibs had used, donated by Martin's sister when her three had done with it.

A bit of a handful, but Heather had learned how to have it up and down in no time when a bus appeared.

Eleven o'clock. The buses weren't crowded at this time of day, so no jostling. The driver was relaxed enough to give her a hand, and most of the passengers were old ladies, keen to inspect the sleeping infant. Abigail, under their scrutiny, was as good as gold. Bibs was not. A bus was a place to run up and down, if a little unsteadily, making aeroplane noises. Or was it supposed to be a mechanical digger?

'Bibs, come here and sit down!' said Heather for the twelfth time, trying not to let her irritation show. Bibs clambered onto the seat opposite her and jumped up and down, looking out of the window. A few frowns of disapproval now from the old ladies. Well, what was she supposed to do? He wasn't molesting them, was he?

The bus was busier by the time they reached the town centre. Reassembling the pram in the general rush to exit, she barked her shins, and nearly lost hold of Bibs.

A brisk walk to the dentist's. Not far, but uphill. Other pedestrians staked their claim to the pavement as if gold had just been discovered there.

'Take a seat in the waiting room,' said the receptionist, and Heather was glad of the chance to sit, though she was up every few minutes to drag Bibs back. Then Abigail woke and wanted a feed. Faced with a grumpy old man and two leery teenage boys, Heather retreated to the cramped toilet, begging Bibs not to start whining.

Abigail was hungry, not to be rushed. When Heather emerged, she had missed her go, and had to wait another half an hour. Her check-up would have been quicker if the dentist's nurse had not spent most of the time trying to keep Bibs from helping himself to all the instruments. What had got into the boy? Was he being deliberately difficult?

No, she admitted. He was being his usual self, exploring his potential, pushing his limits. He was just like this at home, but at home it didn't matter. It gave Barbara something to tut about, but Heather could cope with him. Out in town, with things to do, it was another matter.

This was a mistake, she thought, emerging at last onto the street, this pointless bid for freedom. She should have accepted Barbara's offer of a lift, or left the children in their grandmother's care. Why had she had to be so obstinate? Still, it was done now, and there was nothing for it but to tackle the bus again and get them all home. Maybe when she was back at her front door, she would feel suitably triumphant. But for now, with no Barbara to notice, she just felt weary.

At least the walk back to the bus stop was downhill. Bibs decided an old iron bollard at the entrance to Miller's Lane was exactly what he needed to clamber on, but there was a number 42, the last of the queue just boarding.

'Bibs! Come on!' Could she do it? Run with the pram and a toddler?

Bibs would not budge.

'I said come on!' She grabbed him and tugged him howling behind her. She would do it if the bus driver chose to be generous. He could see her hurrying, surely?

Maybe he could, but it wasn't his generous day. The doors hissed closed and the bus swung out into the traffic.

'Shit!' Heather came to a halt, ignoring a look of disgust from an old lady. 'Please shut up, Bibs!'

The boy continued to howl.

What now? Wait here another half an hour for the next 42? Walk to the bus station? A hundred yards down the road was the shelter for the number 43. Every quarter of an hour, to the other side of the Hopcroft estate. Take that and deal with a long walk home at the other end?

Bibs was bawling still, dragging back towards his chosen bollard.

'Listen,' said Heather. 'How about we go to the park? Swings and roundabouts?'

Bibs stopped crying instantly.

Forget the buses. If they were going to have to wait, they might as well enjoy it. Walk through the park, give Bibs his half hour of playtime, and there was always the number 16, which ran down Buckingham Road. It didn't go into the Hopcroft, but it stopped close to the roundabout, less than half a mile from Linden Close.

Problem solved. Pleasanter than waiting here. They would go to the park.

iii

Lindy

Gary was hungry. Lindy fried him eggs and bread, but they didn't have any bacon or sausages. He curled his lip at that, but how was she to know he'd want a cooked breakfast? He usually rolled off the mattress at about midday and just groped for a can of beer and a cigarette.

Today he was up by eight, looking important, like he had a proper job to go to. 'Got things to do,' he announced, rubbing the eggs off his mouth.

'All right, Gary.'

'I'll be out. Mind you keep things quiet here, remember?'

'Yes. Are you going to be out all day?' It was good that he was going to be out early, because that Rothsay woman could come calling any time. Gary wouldn't give her the time of day, probably just throw her out, but best if he weren't here to see her. Or for her to see him.

'What's it to you? Mind your fucking business and keep your mouth shut.' He was playing the big man, throwing his weight about. She knew, when he did that with her, he was worried, needed to give himself a boost. It was going to be very soon then, this job. Maybe today even. And who knew what would happen then? She wanted to put her arms round him and kiss him but he pushed her away. He was a man, about men's business; no time for all that kissy stuff.

As she watched him swaggering off down Nelson Road, her own criminal instincts told her he was doomed. Bound to muck up. And then he'd be answering to the police or to Carver. Which would be worse?

It was sad but she had other things to think about. The Rothsay woman would be coming here demanding to see Kelly. If Lindy wasn't in, she couldn't see her, so Lindy would be out, with Kelly, till dark if she had to be.

She picked up the shawl, donated by Baby Garden. Soft and white and lacy, with a fringe, so pretty. The weather wasn't that warm. Kelly would need to be wrapped up.

There was no Kelly. No baby to wrap up. Again that huge devouring emptiness. It only went away when she pretended it wasn't true. All these baby clothes, dry now, ready for the baby that wasn't here.

Lindy took up a sleepsuit, hugged it to her, rolled it. Rolled another round it. A jacket, a dress, she wrapped the shawl round them all. It felt like a baby, wrapped and hooded in the shawl, clasped to her aching breast. She stood for a moment, rocking back and forth on her heels, soothing it to sleep.

Better go, or *they*'d be here to take her baby away. She

clomped down the bare dirty stairs, clasping Kelly to her as Tyler, with bloodshot eyes and four days growth of stubble, lurched across the hall.

'C'm here.'

'Geroff! Don't you touch her!' She edged past him, prepared to kick, and made it to the liberty of the front door. Out into Nelson Road. It stretched forever. Lindy didn't want to be walking along it as Caroline Rothsay drove down. She ducked into a side road, kept walking, anywhere, it didn't matter. Nothing mattered as long as she wasn't at home when the Rothsay woman called.

Headed for town. It was okay except that nosy cows kept trying to look at her baby. She wasn't having none of that. She was starving too, but stopping for something to eat was a problem. Women at counters, they wouldn't keep their eyes to themselves.

Maybe town wasn't such a smart idea. She climbed up on the footbridge that crossed high over the Stapledon link road, with its roaring traffic. It was like being up in the sky up here. She'd stood up here with Gary once, when he was pissed. He'd dropped something on a car below. What had it been? Half a brick probably. She remembered the loud crash as it hit a car roof and they'd both run, haring off the bridge into the alleys beyond, before anyone could catch them.

Seemed stupid now. Now she was here on her own and she didn't have anything to drop. Except the baby. Supposing she dropped Kelly, down in all that traffic. It would be horrible. Better move on. Where? Where could she while away the day?

The park maybe. She could hang around there and no one would notice. Sit on one of the benches. Or on the swings. No wardens any more. No nosy bastard in uniform yelling at her for playing on the swings because she was too old. There were the toilets. People hung around there, with stuff. Something to make the day pass easier. Except that she wasn't supposed to be touching stuff any more because of Kelly. But she could sit on the swings.

Like being a kid again, instead of a seventeen-year-old. She liked it, the feel of swaying backwards and forwards, the creak of the chains, letting her heels drag on the broken tarmac. Get up a nice rhythm. Twirl round even, winding the chains together until they were tight and she was on tiptoe, then lift her feet up and whiz round till she felt light-headed. That was great.

But maybe not so good for the baby. And there was only so much you could do on a swing if you were holding a baby. You couldn't go up really high because that needed both hands and she didn't want to put Kelly down. So she left the swings and took a couple of turns on the roundabout. It would be good, sitting there with Kelly, watching the world go round and round, but she had to keep dropping down to push it on. The gears were rusty.

What else? Round the lake maybe. The boatyard. That would be great, taking Kelly out on a paddle-boat. They could drift under one of the weeping willows and hide there like it was a fairy house, and snooze the day away. Except that the boat man would come prodding them with his long pole when their time was up. Anyway, she couldn't afford a boat and they only ran the boats at the weekend. The yard would be locked up.

Unless there was a way to sneak in. But the lock wasn't smashed for once, the wire fencing was intact and all the boats were drawn up on the tarmac, upside down to drain. Lindy would never be able to drag one down to the water, not holding Kelly. And anyway, there were too many people

221

around. Office people, eating their sandwiches, reading newspapers, finishing off their lunch break.

There was the crazy golf, up the other end of the lake. She walked up but the kiosk was shut. She climbed over the fence – all the office workers had gone back to work – and mooched around on the empty course, littered with cigarette butts and empty cans, but it wasn't any fun with no ball. You couldn't pretend to hit a ball.

You couldn't pretend…

She ran, like someone was after her, heart pounding. She might trip, running. Must be careful, with the baby. There was the summerhouse. She could sit in that. Sit and watch and wait. With her baby.

She sat there for a bit, but it smelt too much of pee, so she went and lay down on the grass among the trees and she knew she was dead tired. She let herself doze off.

She woke feeling stiff; the grass was damp. Better go back to the swings maybe. She walked round, through the trees, among the squirrels. Gary chucked stones at them; he got one once, killed it, and kept wanting to do it again. He made Lindy throw stones too, but she always missed. She was glad. She liked the squirrels, she liked anything furry, if it didn't bare its teeth and snap at her, but she didn't tell Gary that. She had hated seeing the squirrel dead, however proud Gary was.

Plenty of squirrels today, dashing across the grass, darting up the trees, afraid of her. That was sad. She would have happily picked one up and cuddled it. Cuddled a squirrel. Cuddled her baby. Sadness twisted inside her.

Out of the trees, onto the rolling grass, past a clump of bushes. Some of them had little red flowers. And there was the pram, and the baby.

Blue eyes peeking open, the head stirring as the baby woke from contented sleep.

Like a great slap, it winded her.

Lindy held her Kelly closer, but she knew it was no baby at all. Just a shawl. Kelly had gone. Where?

Panic filled her. Her baby was gone. No. No she wasn't. She was here. Here in the pram. She must have slipped out of the shawl. Pick her up, wrap her up safely again. There she was, safe and sound, heavy against Lindy's breast. Just where she belonged. So quiet. Such a good baby. She probably needed feeding and changing by now. Maybe it was time to go home.

Yes, she'd do that. Take Kelly home. She'd had enough of the park.

iv

Heather

They'd stopped at a Spar, one of the small shops on the periphery of the town centre. Bibs wanted sweets, and Heather was tempted to buy him his usual chocolate buttons, but she had just been to the dentist, and the threat of dental misery was still fresh in her thoughts. She shouldn't be giving him sweets, should she? Fruit maybe. How about a banana? But Bibs didn't want a banana. Never mind that he usually loved bananas, today he wanted sweets. Biscuits then. Were biscuits better for his teeth than sweets? At least they looked more wholesome, so she wouldn't feel so bad. She could have bought him a Penguin or a Kitkat, but she knew that once it had been devoured he would have been pestering for more, so she bought a packet of chocolate digestives. Not intending to give him more, but as long as he knew they were there, in the bag slung from the pram handle, he could be bribed into good behaviour.

A packet of chocolate digestives. Looking back, afterwards, she thought, why didn't I buy him the chocolate buttons?

The park was quiet, a few wanderers distant among the trees or across the lake. A weekday, lunch hour over. A couple of office workers lingered over the last crust of their sandwiches, before hurrying off. The playground was abandoned. She'd been afraid it might be occupied by a mob of truant teenagers, but today they were nowhere in sight. Bibs had it all to himself, the baby swings, the roundabout, the see-saw, the smaller slide.

She was getting good at this, a uniquely maternal form of ambidexterity. Pushing a swing with one hand and rocking a pram with the other. Encouraging words to Bibs and coos to the baby. Wipe the chocolate from round Bibs' mouth while tucking Abigail's blanket round her.

The baby was awake, but not fretful, blue eyes gazing on a world that as yet meant nothing to her. Was it wonder at the sight of the swings, the grass, the trees, the glint of water? Or was it merely contented incomprehension? At least she liked the rocking of the pram, Heather could see that.

'Come on, Bibs.' He had had his quota of fun, surely. A full half hour of swinging and sliding and spinning, and two biscuits.

'No!' He was running from her, back to the roundabout.

'All right. Just this and we go.' She heaved the roundabout into motion for him while he squealed in delight. Nothing else would make his life worthwhile. What would make mine worthwhile, she thought, was a cup of tea. She grabbed Bibs as the roundabout slowed and he prepared to dive off it for the slide.

'That's it. Time to go home now.'

'No! No!' Dragging her back.

She wasn't going to have it. 'No, Bibs. That's enough. You've had a nice play. Now we're going home.'

'I want—' He was straining, pointing at the slide.

'You've had plenty of goes on the slide. Now. Don't make me cross. Be a good boy.'

Petulantly, he fell into step beside her. Her grip loosened as he stopped yanking away from her. He was still pouting, but he was holding her hand and trotting beside her, accepting defeat.

Abigail, drifting back into sleep, stirred a little, shifting the blanket, and Heather released Bibs' hand to pat it smooth.

Only a second, but it was enough. They were on the path leading to the back gate and the number 16 bus stop. Bibs had seen the lake, worse, the ducks on the lake, and all else was forgotten – swings, slides, going home. Released from her hold, he gave a shriek and ran tumbling down the grass to the lake's edge.

'Bibs! Come back! Come here now!' She had a moment of panic. There were railings round the lake, but was he small enough to squeeze through? In a flash, she pictured him falling in, drowning. 'Come back to Mummy, Bibs. Please. Not down there! Come back and you can have another biscuit.'

But he was not listening. The ducks had his full attention and, seeing him approach, they turned in the water like a well-trained cavalry charge, heading for him and whatever bread, buns or bird food he might have to offer.

She would have to fetch him back. She turned the pram, felt its wheels skid in the mud that edged the tarmac path. There had been so much rain lately. Today's weak sun wasn't enough to dry out the waterlogged grass. She didn't want to get bogged down, wrestling with the pram as well as Bibs. Abigail was sleeping, peaceful and oblivious; she would be all right. Heather parked the pram up on the path, in the shelter of a bush, slipped the brake on, grabbed the packet of biscuits and hurried down the slippery grass to retrieve her son.

Bibs was reaching through the railings offering grass to the ducks. A dozen were waddling out, up the bank to investigate. He laughed in delight. What child would not, at the absurd sight, the waddling bottoms, the thunderous chorus of quacks, the eagerness? Heather couldn't be cross with him.

'Come on now.' She crouched down beside him. 'They'll nibble your fingers. You don't want that, do you?'

But there was nothing that Bibs wanted more than having his fingers nibbled by ducks.

Heather glanced back. The pram, partly concealed by the bush, was safe enough. There was no sound of crying. Abigail would sleep on unaware. 'All right, but they don't want grass.' The ducks were already telling Bibs that in no uncertain terms. 'Here, see if they'd like this.' She had brought the biscuits as a lure for her son, to bribe him to follow her back, but now she broke pieces off a digestive, and let him toss them through the bars to a raucous clientele. Grass no, biscuits yes. The ducks liked them. Oh yes, very much, indeed.

'There.' The biscuit was finished. And then another.

Bibs stamped his foot and grabbed the railings. This spectacle was too good to leave.

'All right, one more, but just one.' She was going to make sure he understood this time. 'Just two pieces, Bibs, and then we're going.' The armada of ducks was being followed by a small flotilla of swans, gliding disdainfully towards the source of the excitement. Ducks she could cope with, even in Hitchcock numbers, but swans were alarming. Beautiful at a distance, but far too frightening close up. 'Last piece, Bibs. And I mean it, this is the last one. Who are you going to give it to? What about that poor one at the back?' She held his hand, helped him throw the last crumb to a lone drake, and on cue the horde of ducks turned and speed-waddled in pursuit. That would do.

'Come along now. No! No arguing. Be a good boy. I let you feed the ducks, now we're going back to Gigi.' A pout, a show of resistance, but he bowed to her superior strength, trotting with her back up the slope to the waiting pram.

Afterwards, she thought, had there been a time warp down by the lake? Had hours flown past, while they had fed the ducks? She could have sworn it was a minute, two, three at most.

The pram was where she had left it, brake still on, the bag suspended from its handle. Inside, the blanket was pulled loose, rumpled. There was no baby.

V

Lindy

It was such a long way home, back to Nelson Road. It had seemed no distance this morning, but Kelly had grown heavier. And more fretful. Cradled in Lindy's arms, she had slept at first, but now she was showing distress. She needed changing. Well, she'd have to wait until they got home.

So long, Nelson Road! 128 was a million miles away. But she was there at last, as Kelly began to bawl in earnest. Let

the door be open, please. She didn't want to have to thump
and get Tyler to open it.

It was ajar.

'Miss Crowe. Ah good, I caught you. I was disappointed
to find you'd gone out. I said I'd call, remember?'

That woman, Caroline Rothsay, with her smart jacket
and her smart shoes. Wanting to take Kelly. Lindy clasped
the baby tighter to her.

'What you want?'

'I just want to talk, my dear, to see how you're coping
with little Kelly there. To see what help we can offer.'

'Well, I can't talk now.' Edge in through the door, hope
the woman would go away. 'She's wet. I've got to change her.'

'Of course, Rosalind.' She was following. 'You see to
Kelly. Don't worry about me. I can wait.' Coming up the
stairs after her. 'When you've changed her, we'll have our
little talk.'

Lindy knew women like this. No keeping them out. But
she had to think about Kelly, poor wet little thing, still
bawling. Lindy grabbed a clean nappy from the cupboard
then took the baby upstairs, locked the bathroom door on
them. Could she stay here until the woman had had enough
and left? Maybe, if she took her time. Not that she wanted
to linger here. She was the only one who ever gave the
bathroom any sort of a clean, and it stank. The floor was
wet with shaving water and pee. The bath was okay though.
Old green stains under the tap and round the plughole, but
no one ever used it, so it could be worse. Lindy laid the
baby down in the bath, unwrapping the shawl to let her
little arms thrash around. Stripped off her clothes. Lindy
didn't like those clothes. They looked all wrong. Stripped
off the sodden nappy, dropped it into the plastic bag she
left tucked out of sight.

228

The baby was gurgling now. Was there any hot water? Sometimes, someone put money in the meter. She let it run. Not hot, but lukewarm. She'd have liked it hotter but it would have to do. Tenderly, she wiped the baby down. There was baby talc on the shelf. Just a tiny bit left. Where had the rest gone? Some wanker had been using her baby talc.

Kelly was quiet now, letting Lindy dress her in the newly washed clothes that had been wrapped in the shawl with her. There, she was almost like her old self. A bit bigger. A little bit more fair fuzzy hair. But babies were like that. They changed every day.

'There you are, Kelly. My little Kelly.'

The baby looked at her. No recognition. Well, of course not, she was too young for that. But there was something she would recognise, surely. Lindy put the lid down and settled on the toilet, lifting the child to her breast. She still wasn't used to this, the bottle felt more decent, but this would keep her here, in the bathroom, away from that woman.

Then the baby was asleep again. She couldn't sit here forever, rocking Kelly in her arms. She'd have to go down. Maybe the woman would have gone by now. She stuffed the old clothes out of sight in the bag with the dirty nappy. Deal with them later. The shawl would need a wash. She snatched it up and headed downstairs.

Caroline Rothsay was waiting for her. Poking round the bedsit, prodding at the window frame. Who did she think she was? Lindy ignored her, laying Kelly in the Moses basket, covered her up, put her little pink mouse next to her.

When she turned, Caroline was smiling as if she had just witnessed a cute nativity play. 'I'm sure you take great care of her. But we do need to consider—'

'No you don't. I don't need your help. I can look after her. You're not taking her.'

'I am sure you are a wonderful mother.' The woman was trying to reassure her. 'But we need to think about other things. Are you receiving the proper benefits you're entitled to, for instance? And is this really the best environment for your baby? I am sure you and – Gary, was it? – are doing your best, but perhaps we could find you somewhere better to live.' Her glance was taking in every facet of the miserable room – the mattress on the floor, the rotting window, the peeling wallpaper, the seeping damp stains on the ceiling. 'I can help you apply to the council. Wouldn't you like that? A nice clean council flat maybe on the Nanwell estate?'

Lindy's fingers clenched on the shawl. A real flat, somewhere proper for her and Kelly to live. Enough benefits so she wouldn't have to keep nicking things and a home when Gary kicked her out. But it was a trap. It had to be. They'd say things like this so she wouldn't make a fuss and the moment she complied, they'd have Kelly in care.

'Let me just take a few details,' Caroline was saying, opening a case full of papers. 'You are Rosalind Crowe… yes? I have your date of birth and Kelly's details. Your partner, Gary. His name is?'

'Gary Bagwell,' said Lindy reluctantly. She didn't want to be answering this woman's questions. Certainly not questions about Gary.

'Is he employed?'

What was she to say? Yes, he's doing a job for Carver upstairs? Next it would be all about his mother, and where she lived, and how she could help with the baby. Then this woman would be off investigating and find there was no mother.

'What's it to you?'

230

'I just need to know what help you need, Rosalind. If Gary is supporting you both—'

'I'm not staying here.'

'Ah?'

'No. I'm not staying with Gary. I got family, in Barking. I'm going to them, going to take Kelly with me.'

'Ah. I see.' The woman was scribbling notes. Would it stop her asking questions? She went on, wheedling, and Lindy went on prevaricating. It wouldn't work, not in the long run, but at least it would get rid of the woman today.

The Rothsay woman went at last, with her notes, and her smile, leaving Lindy alone with her baby.

She stood looking down on the Moses basket, at the baby, her baby, asleep so peacefully. It was like Peter Pan and that fairy. You just had to believe. If you believed hard enough, then it would be true. Everyone would believe it was true. But if you stopped believing, then it would die.

All she had to do was believe.

vi

Heather

There was no baby. The world had stopped moving. Clouds were frozen in the sky. The noise of everyday life was switched off – drowned out by the roaring in her ears. Heather shut her eyes, gripping the pram handle, knowing that she was having a stupid nightmare. When she opened her eyes, she would find the baby there, safely tucked up under her blanket.

She opened her eyes. No baby. Just a rumpled cover.

It wasn't possible. It was not physically possible for

Abigail to have wriggled her own way out of the carrycot. She was only three weeks old. What had happened? A gust of wind, sharp enough to tilt the pram, and throw the baby out?

Pushing Bibs aside, Heather fell to her knees. It would be all right. Abigail would be down here, under the bush, lying happily. Please, don't let her be injured by the fall.

There was no Abigail under the bush. Nothing but an empty cigarette packet. No sign, anywhere, of the baby.

This was stupid. She would be kicking herself in a minute, laughing at her own stupidity. She hadn't looked properly in the pram, that was it. Abigail had somehow jiggled around, under the blanket. Heather got to her feet, pulled the blanket off. Nothing. A bare mattress. She pulled up the mattress, revealing the bottom of the carrycot. Nothing.

She couldn't breath. It wasn't happening. She was confused. There was something here she wasn't understanding.

Bibs tugged at her sleeve.

'Not now, Bibs!'

'I want a biscuit.'

'Not now! Be quiet! Please be quiet.' She was having to gulp for air. Her shins were turning to jelly, collapsing under her. She had to cling to the pram for support. How could Abigail just vanish?

Someone had taken her. It was the only explanation. Heather stared around. Nothing would focus properly. The nearby trees were swimming, boughs moving in the breeze. She blinked hard. No one in sight. No one anywhere. Just a couple of dogs running wild on the far side of the lake.

Dogs! Dogs could have taken her baby. Like dingos. She let out a scream. A small scream already stifled in her throat. She wanted to shut her eyes again. She wasn't really here in

232

the park with an empty pram. She was at home asleep and dreaming. A nightmare.

'I want a biscuit,' whined Bibs.

'Shut up, Bibs! Shut up, shut up, shut up!'

What could she do? She wanted to run, shouting and screaming, to search the entire park, find her baby, find the person who took her baby.

But what if she had it all wrong? What if Abigail were around here somewhere? She had to be. Somehow she had fallen. If Heather moved she would be leaving her.

She couldn't cope with this. No one could cope with this.

A man. There was a man coming her way. Big black overcoat, hurrying through the park towards the Buckingham Road gate. Brisk walk, eyes fixed ahead, deliberately not seeing her. That was how people behaved in public. No eye contact, no need to share this universe. He would pass without a word.

'Please.'

He was almost on them, preparing to skirt them without altering his stride.

'Please. Help me.' She lurched to grab him.

He recoiled. His hostile eyes glance over her then he hesitated.

'Help me,' she repeated. She mustn't be hysterical, mustn't scream and sob. She must be calm. 'Help me please. My baby's gone.'

And then she couldn't help herself.

CHAPTER 9

i

Kelly

Roz was sitting at the kitchen table, crying.

Kelly was supposed to rush to her, hug her, comfort her at the first sign of her tears. Every instinct told her to do so now, except that this monstrous knowledge swept away everything.

'Don't cry. Stop it. Tell me what happened.'

'I don't remember.'

'Yes, you do. Don't go all vague. You stole me. You stole a baby from another woman. Who was she? What happened to her?'

'I don't know,' wailed Roz. 'Truly, I don't know. I never saw any woman. I just saw you. I took you away, we left Lyford, I don't know what happened. I never meant to hurt anyone.'

'No.' Kelly forced herself to be reasonable. Of course Roz hadn't meant to hurt anyone. But someone had been hurt. Horribly tortured, in a way that couldn't just be brushed aside. 'I'm going upstairs. Okay? I need to think this through.'

Roz was up, groping for her, pleading, but she would just have to cope. Kelly needed space. She shut her bedroom door and slid down onto the rug.

Why couldn't it have been a hospital mistake? A slip-up,

two mothers left in blissful ignorance. But this— So much hurt. Everyone was hurt. That bereaved mother, surely. And that hard, angry, accusing girl. Yes, Kelly could see she had been hurt, because this should have been her home, her life, Roz should have been her mother, and she had been denied it all. It had been Kelly's instead.

It was so confusing. What was she supposed to do? Until now, there was one person who had not been hurt – Kelly herself. But now it turned out that all that she loved, the mother she cherished, the life she had drifted through in charmed contentment, was not hers. She'd stolen it from that girl, just as Roz had stolen her. She should have had another life, family, mother – and she didn't want any of them. The only emotion left was guilt. Guilt that she had grown up loving not the woman who had borne her, but the woman who had stolen her away. She could not undo that love, redirect it on command. She loved Roz. They were mother and daughter in every way that mattered; but it was all wrong because it hadn't been about loving, but about stealing and hurting.

What now? Roz was her mother, and Kelly had to help her, forgive her even. She couldn't just lash out. However wrong their relationship had been in the start, neither of them were complete without the other. Kelly had to try to understand.

Roz had been seventeen. Girls could be so vulnerable at seventeen, still children. Kelly herself had been mature and confident, but then Kelly had a home, a mother she could always turn to. Roz had been an orphan, in care, living rough, lost. Kelly had heard that much from Roger and Mandy, though Roz never spoke about it. A sad life. Kelly knew girls who had been through much the same and had emerged hard and strong, but not Roz. Crushed or on top

235

of a wave, she had always been the sort to be swept along, used and abused so easily.

But the trouble with wisdom and understanding was that it was two-edged. Kelly understood just how vulnerable Roz was, how adrift, but it dawned on her now that this vulnerability was not just a weakness, it was a weapon. There was manipulation in there somewhere, a deliberate helplessness. Things just happened that Roz could not be responsible for but somehow they were what she had wanted to happen. Her mind could rearrange itself to block out what it didn't want to know.

If Kelly followed that line of thought, she would find herself hating and despising Roz. Was that what she was supposed to do? Was that just? Crap. Whichever way it turned, there was no justice in a situation like this, so there was no point in punishing Roz.

What was she to do? She didn't have Roz's capacity to rearrange her feelings to order, even if she knew what her feelings were. She needed to find out the unadulterated truth. Not from Roz. She knew better than to try and screw facts out of her mother. It was all in the *Lyford Herald*, Victoria had said. Well then.

The loathsome *Lyford Herald*…

Kelly had a goal again, pumping strength into her legs, lifting her from the floor.

Roz was still in the kitchen, no longer crying. But staring out of the window. She looked like a woman, not like the half-child she could so easily be when it suited her. That was good. She was going to have to be a woman now.

'Kelly.'

'You're going to have to cope for a day or so, Mum.' Kelly grabbed her bag, her purse, her phone. 'I've got to go, to Lyford.'

236

The look of infant panic on Roz's face would normally bring Kelly quickly to her side. Then it vanished. Roz nodded. 'Yes. Of course.'

'You'll be all right? Take care of things? Take care of yourself?'

'Yes.'

Kelly opened the front door. Why wait?

'Kelly…'

She turned.

'It was in the park,' said Roz. 'You were in the park.'

Her eyes begged forgiveness. And Kelly would have to forgive. Just not yet. She nodded. 'All right,' she said, and left.

ii

Vicky

A motorway service station. An oasis of stillness, as the daylight faded and the shapes of cars began to disappear behind the brightness of their headlights. Across an ocean of tarmac, the warm cluttered service area glowed yellow, intensifying the gloom outside.

Vicky sat, staring out. She had needed to stop. She'd needed the toilet, she'd needed food, the right food, because she would always have to take care. She needed her medication. The rational part of her brain had put itself to work sorting out those needs. Simple problems that could be resolved, neatly and efficiently. Now she sat back in the car, alone in her little metal bubble, a hot drink on her knee and miles of motorway before her. Stretching away into infinity.

There was a tightness in her chest, an ache in her head. It had gripped her all the way across Wales. Would she ever be free of it?

She looked out at other people, milling in the car park, and caught her own reflection, a flicker of a ghost in the windscreen.

'I am not a victim!' she had shouted at Gillian, and she had been shouting it at herself for so long now. But that was precisely what she had let herself be. Something had damaged her, five years ago. It wasn't the physical thing – she refused to call it rape – the bruising, humiliating unpleasantness of the moment. It was her family's betrayal. She was trapped in it, with no hope of escaping it, because it was the way things happened in her family's world.

That was how she'd have always felt, if she hadn't discovered, through one chance overheard remark, that she didn't belong in this family after all. That changed everything. The lead seal of her coffin had melted away. The sticky strands of Joan's web had snapped. She'd been dragged into this family. If she had been the one stolen, she could have made a triumph of all this. But she wasn't the prize. She was the one cast away, so that Gillian could pluck her up like a toy and inflict Joan on her. Misery and anger. How she'd wanted to hate them, to punish them all, mothers, betrayers.

She was their victim.

'No!' She slammed the steering wheel. Her fist tightened on the paper cup, sending scalding tea flying sideways, towards the open road atlas on the passenger seat. She lunged, and the tea-soaked atlas toppled to the floor, pages fanning and crumpling as it wedged itself under the seat's metal framework. She grabbed a page and it ripped from the binding.

'Can't anything bloody well go right!' She threw herself back in her seat, fighting back tears. She mustn't cry. She would not cry!

Taking a deep breath, she reached again for the atlas. Smoothed the ripped page. Where did it fit? She studied its confusion of meandering roads connecting the scattered villages and towns. Wroughton. Ogbourne St. George. Winterbourne Bassett. Each isolated place woven into the whole by the threads of those roads. Swindon. The torn page fitted under Swindon. You had to see the whole to make sense of it.

All those little places on the map – none of them existed in isolation. Winterbourne Bassett was not a mythical point on a shred of paper. It was on a road coming from somewhere, going somewhere. Like her. Like everyone.

It was what she should have grasped long ago, if her determination not to be a victim had not locked her in. She had been damaged, but they had all been damaged, all the women whose roads connected with hers. There was really no point in hating them.

That Roz Sheldon woman, who had left her in a cardboard box. Seventeen years old. Vicky had been seventeen when the thing had happened. It was young, seventeen. Terrifyingly vulnerable. Roz wasn't some wicked witch, just a pathetic child. And now she was ill. Possibly quite seriously ill. The medical student in Vicky, the girl who could speak so compassionately with patients, writhed uncomfortably, remembering her bitter outbursts. She should never have let her pain explode in such callousness.

And Gillian. The woman who had so zealously tried to protect an abandoned child and failed miserably. For five years now, Vicky wanted to attack Gillian, to beat her with her fists and howl. The violence had been lurking behind every sullen look, every polite rejection.

But Gillian hadn't failed her because she was evil, or callous, or a part of Joan's twisted plot. Her tragedy was simply that she was an ordinary inadequate woman. A woman who tried her best in the face of overwhelming odds.

Joan, she was damaged all right. Vicky couldn't even try to humanise her.

But the other woman, the other hamlet on the map... Vicky covered her face with her hands, remembering. Rounding in her own savage misery, she'd embraced a story that wasn't her own and stalked the woman, wanting to make her suffer. As if she hadn't suffered enough. She was the real victim in all this. A victim beyond imagining, and Vicky had made her suffering worse.

There were emotions she needed to acknowledge now. Before they had been wrong, and she'd let anger and hatred drown them out. But this time they were justified and they were shouting at her.

Guilt and shame.

She could refuse to be a victim if she liked, but someone else could not.

iii

Kelly

What the hell had Kelly thought she was doing, driving off like that so late in the day? And getting lost. Was she surprised? She should have stuck to the motorways.

But they were too inhuman. The human being in her, frail and vulnerable, wanted human contact, someone to talk to, someone to reach out and touch across this disintegrating cosmos.

She wanted Ben. Under the trees, in the dark lay-by, she ached for Ben. But he was about love and happiness, her Ben. He didn't belong in this dark place. How could she even begin to explain to him what it was all about?

But she wanted to. She had the phone in her hand. No, not yet. She had to get it straight in her own head first. Then she would turn to him. Besides, it was the middle of the night. She couldn't wake him. He had work to go to. But not the journey to Wales; that was out now. No blissful weekend playing meet the family. She'd better text him. *Don't go Wales. I'm going Lyford. Speak tomorrow.*

Now she needed to work out on this stupid map where exactly she was. The Midlands? She'd got onto the wrong road somewhere. There was a sign to Stratford-upon-Avon. Way out. Get an hour's sleep, start again with a fresh head. No point in arriving too early anyway, not before anything was open. She'd grab some sleep. Don't think about talking to Ben. Not yet.

iv

Vicky

The blank walls and ceiling of a Travelodge. Headlights moving across it. The low rumble of heavy lorries edging onto the slip road. A muffled moan of never-ending traffic on the motorway.

Vicky lay in the dark, staring at nothing. She needed this, a white alien bed in a nowhere place, where she could stop and think. She kept conjuring all the faces dotted

241

around the peculiar road map of her life. Gillian. Roz. Kelly. Mrs Parish. People hurting. All pieces on the board, as she had allowed herself to be. Liberation was taking charge of the game, and she could do it. She could make something right.

V

Kelly

At five o'clock, Kelly drove along to the next village, found it on the map and figured out where she was. Too far north but she could see her way. Cross one major road, head south on the next, get on the motorway. She stopped at a service station, bought herself a serious shot of caffeine. Gone six now, late enough; Ben would be awake, surely. She tried his number. His phone kept ringing. He was probably in the shower. Then it stopped ringing. Hell! Battery low. It needed charging and she hadn't brought the charger. How could she be so bloody incompetent?

She was in Lyford long before the office workers and shop assistants. Early enough to find the car park over the shopping centre almost empty. Should she find a payphone? Except that Ben would be on his way to work now. She couldn't discuss all this while he was squashed in with other commuters. Give him time to reach the office.

She started walking towards the concrete headquarters of the *Lyford Herald*, then changed her mind. Old editions, she wanted; twenty-two-year-old news, not this week's bullshit. They'd have old copies at the town library. Much better. No chance of her giving someone a punch in the eye in the library. If she visited the *Lyford Herald* again, she might just be tempted to make her feelings understood. The utter crap they'd written…

But it hadn't all been crap, that was the problem. They'd added and subtracted, but they had worked on the story Kelly had handed them on a plate.

She found the library, in Queen's Square. A couple of hundred yards from the Linley hotel and Rick's Place. Beacons in that other life, when the mystery of her birth had been an exciting adventure.

A façade of glass etched with open books, quills, music notes. Double doors waiting to open at nine o'clock and not a moment before. She sat in the square outside, among the clipped ornamental trees and the pigeons, and was first through the doors, the moment they opened.

There were microfilm readers in the reference library, if she wanted old copies of the *Lyford Evening News*. Or bound copies of the weekly *Lyford Herald*. She settled for the *Evening News*. If the story was there, she wanted it day by day, blow by blow. And she wanted the privacy of the cubicles that housed the microfilm readers. She didn't want to sit at a central table exposing her history to the whole world.

Start with her own birth date. Alleged birth date. Tuesday 13th March, 1990. Lorry jack-knifed on the bypass, an engineering firm closing, football club scandal. What was she expecting? Roz would hardly have put an announcement in the papers. Wednesday, Thursday – nothing through the entire week. Into the next, and there it was, Tuesday 20th March.

Baby found in Mall.

God, it was true. Roz had really abandoned her baby. This was that Victoria. *A girl, thought to be less than a month old, was wrapped in a towel.* Kelly could see Roz doing it, thinking it was the best thing to do. Poor Roz, poor helpless young mother. Kelly could understand what had driven her. But she could see, too, why Victoria Wendle had been so upset. To know that your mother had just left you in a doorway – and then taken another child.

That was the really terrible thing: the taking of another child. And it hadn't been a fantasy, not Victoria putting the wrong two and two together. Roz had admitted it. In the park, she had said.

Kelly scrolled on. Friday.

Baby Vanishes in Park.

Kelly covered her face with her hands. Could she bear to read on? She had to. Not that there was much to read. A large headline to make up for a scant article. Stop-press stuff, the paper trying to put something together quickly with nothing to work on. A blurred picture of 'the park' as if that would help.

> *Police are searching urgently for a baby snatched from her pram today by the lake in Portland Park. The mother, named by the police as Mrs Heather Norris, of Linden Close, is understood to have left the pram briefly, while attending to another child. When she returned, the baby girl, Abigail Laura, was missing. Police have as yet no clues as to the identity of the person or persons who might have snatched the child, and are appealing urgently for witnesses. They would like to hear from anyone who visited the park today, between 1.30 and 3.30 p.m.*

Abigail Laura. Was that who she really was? And Mrs

Heather Norris. Was that her real mother? The woman left with an empty pram. A terrible crime.

She had to go on. The next day the paper was full of it. Parents were *too distraught to give a statement.* Distraught. Kelly's parents. People she didn't know, who had been no part of her consciousness until now. Heather and Martin Norris. What had happened to them? Where were they now? How long had they been distraught? How long before dull acceptance had driven out the worst of the pain? What do you do if someone steals your baby?

Police had spoken to people who had been in the park, but as yet there were no leads. An interview with a mother who had noticed a suspicious stranger loitering around a nearby infants' school. Fear stalks the streets of Lyford. There was a summary of previous abductions and some distasteful speculation on the intentions of the abductor.

More on the Monday – photographs of Heather and Martin Norris, snapped as they were bundled inside their home by police officers. Kelly sat staring at them. Grainy photographs, even more indistinct on a ghostly microfilm, but there they were. A totally normal couple. Nothing to set them apart from all the other couples who lived in that suburban street. That should have been her home, that house, with its tile-hung walls and cramped little porch, and its clipped pocket-sized front garden, indistinguishable from the houses to either side. They should have been her parents, that sad couple. He was just an average man, nothing heroic, nothing villainous. Wavy hair. She could see that much. And a face that would probably have been quite nice if his jaw was not set and his eyes were not glassy and unseeing.

Daddy.

She was even less clear, Kelly's mother, Heather Norris.

245

Shoulders hunched and head bowed, her hair falling over her face. Broken.

'Mum. Roz. What have you done?'

'Find what you were looking for?' asked a librarian, passing her cubicle.

'Yes, thanks,' said Kelly, hurriedly. This was private. She didn't want to share it with a librarian.

She wanted to share it with Ben. He'd be safely at work by now. She could ring him, pour it all out. She left her bag and coat by the microfilm reader and went down one floor to the rank of public telephones by the newspaper room. Tried his mobile. It was switched off. He did that, she knew; switched it off when he was in a meeting. Maybe she could try his office, leave him a message.

A woman answered, bright and businesslike. 'Good morning, Claims, Jane Danby speaking.'

Kelly tried to collect herself. Office Speak. 'Hi. Good morning. Is...' How stupid that she didn't know his surname. She racked her brain, trying to remember what his mother had been called. Parish. 'Is Mr. Parish there? Could I speak to him please?'

'Parish? Sorry, no one of that name here.'

'Ben Parish?'

'Sorry.' Kelly could hear Jane Danby's strident voice away from the phone. 'Anyone know anyone called Parish working here?' Back to the phone. 'No, sorry, you've got the wrong number, I'm afraid.'

'Okay, thanks.' Kelly put the phone down. It was all part and parcel. Parallel worlds. She'd slipped through, and Ben was in another world, no longer part of hers.

She went back to the *Evening Post*. Tuesday. A plea from the father, her father, for whoever had his child to come forward. More biographical details of the parents. Heather

Norris was twenty-seven, born in Nottingham, had worked in a library. This one. Kelly looked around. This one or its predecessor. It looked like a new building. Martin was twenty-eight. A stock controller. Kelly pictured him rounding up cattle. Born in Lyford, he had been a champion sprinter for his school and his mother Barbara was a stalwart of the St Michael's Amateur Dramatics Society.

Details. Snippets that she should have known all her life. She wanted to see their faces.

She found them on the Wednesday edition. Someone had given the *Post* a wedding photograph. Martin and Heather cutting the cake, he beaming broadly, she, with veil pushed back, revealing a slightly anxious smile. The tone of the article had changed. Quotes from neighbours about how stressed Mrs Norris had been, long before Abigail had gone missing. Hints of a nervous breakdown.

On the Thursday the gloves were off.

Police have confirmed that they have taken Heather Norris in for questioning about the fate of missing baby Abigail. No charges are imminent at this stage. Grandmother of the child, Mrs Barbara Norris, said, 'I cannot bring myself to believe that Heather could have harmed her own baby, but if she has, I beg of her to tell us the truth now, so this agony can end.'

Pages, day after day, of evidence and rumour and innuendo. Diatribes in the letter columns. A solitary plea from a vicar to bear in mind that we are all innocent until proven guilty. And then the story petered out.

Police have confirmed that Heather Norris, mother of missing baby Abigail, is not being charged, although in-

247

vestigations will continue. 'The case will remain open
until the fate of the child is finally uncovered,' said Su-
perintendent Barry Trufall.

It was all there, and it wasn't enough. She wanted more. She
asked for the old bound copies of the *Lyford Herald*. A weekly
paper, with more considered coverage. Not more enjoyable
reading though. At least the pictures were clearer. A more
recent photo of the husband and wife. Her father and
mother, and their little son. Barbara Norris, her grandmother.

A map of the park, showing where and when. A
photograph of the lake.

She really needed Ben now. Try again. Try his office once
more. There were no parallel worlds, just this one. One
world screwed up in an unbelievable knot.

'Can I speak to Ben, please.'

'Hang on. Ben! For you.'

His voice, at last. 'Hi, Ben Norris here.'

She had known. A growing suspicion – her previous visit,
those photographs, the faces, that lake. She'd known.
Perhaps, secretly, she had known from the moment Roz had
mentioned the park. 'It's me, Kelly,' she said, astonished
that the words came out.

'Kelly! Where are you? I've been trying to reach you. Got
your text this morning but I couldn't get through to your
mobile.'

'Battery's out. I couldn't recharge it.'

'Where are you though? In Lyford? What's going on? I
thought—'

'What are your parent's names?' she interrupted. 'Their
Christian names?'

'Christian names? Martin and Jacky my step-mum – and
Heather my mother. Why?'

248

Why had she even asked? 'Your mother's Mrs Parish.'

'Yes. They both remarried. Why? Kelly, what's up?'

'Can you come here?'

'To Lyford? Now? I don't know – No, of course I can come. Something's wrong, isn't it?'

'Something's wrong. Yes. Something bad.'

'You're all right? Are you hurt? Is it your mother? Tell me, Kelly.'

'I'm all right. Upset, but not hurt. Please come. I can't explain this on the phone.'

'I'm coming,' he said. 'Give me a couple of hours. I need to get back to my car.'

'I'll be here. Outside the library. I'll wait.'

And that was all she could do now. Sit and wait.

Ben, in his suit, ran across the square, searching the lunchtime crowds. Kelly raised her hand and he saw her.

She watched him coming, Ben Norris. Pictured that photograph in the *Lyford Herald*. Heather and Martin Norris and their young son Ben, known as Bibs.

Her brother.

'Kelly!' He hugged her, reassuring himself she was in one piece. 'I didn't know what to expect. What's going on?'

She stared at him. Lightish brown hair, hazel eyes, just like her. Just like her. Was that what she had seen, in Rick's place? Was that what Ben had seen in her? 'You had a baby sister who died.'

She felt his flinch of withdrawal, the defences against past pain. 'What? Yes. She died.'

'Abigail Laura.'

'OK, she was called Abigail. What have you been digging up? Because I wish…'

'I'm Abigail.'

249

'What?'

She drew a deep breath. 'I'm Abigail. I'm your sister. Mum...Roz took me, from the pram in the park.'

'No!' It wasn't shock or surprise. It was denial, absolute and unconditional.

'She admitted it. I discovered I wasn't her natural daughter. That was what brought me to Lyford in the first place. I wanted to find the other girl, the one she gave birth to. I thought... Never mind what I thought.'

Kelly took his arm, led him to a bench. He sank down, dazed.

'I was just trying to help. Mum was ill and – she'd said something about a mix-up in the hospital, labels being switched, two babies accidentally swapped. God knows where she got that idea from. The truth was, she had a baby, she gave it up, and then – then she wanted it back. So she took a baby, from the park, convinced herself it was hers. She admitted it. I've found the whole story in the newspapers. March 1990. It means I'm your sister, Ben. I'm Abigail.'

He was staring at her, drinking in the words, trying to shuffle them into an order that made sense. Still refusing to believe. 'This is some kind of con? A joke? Do you have any idea what you're saying? Abigail is dead.'

'No. She was taken. By my – by Roz.'

'It isn't true.'

What could she say? Keep repeating the facts? This was all too much for him. It was too much for her and it had been creeping up on her gradually all morning. He didn't want to believe. They were lovers. And now she was his sister. How cruel was that?

'We're still—'

'No!' He jumped up, away from her touch. 'You don't understand.'

'We didn't know we were related. I love you, Ben.'

His eyes met hers, staring into them, wanting to feel what he had felt before, wanting this all to stop, now. 'You don't understand,' he repeated.

'We met and fell in love. That hasn't changed, has it? Being brother and sister, it's just—'

'It isn't that! God! It isn't a matter of incest!' He put his head in his hands, then walked away, stumbling as he went. He reached the first fluttering tree and leaned against it for support.

Kelly rose to follow him, then stopped. There was nothing to do but watch and pray. It couldn't end. No matter what evil, vile trick fate was determined to play on them, it couldn't just end.

He raised his head at last, lowered his hands, straightened himself. Then he marched back.

'I'm sorry. Kelly. It's not the incest. It's just – you see – if you really are Abigail, you can't understand how much – all these years – how much I've hated you.'

It wasn't what she had expected. It hit her in the solar plexus.

He looked away. Shut his eyes a moment, then sat down beside her, staring down at his feet. 'You wrecked my whole life and I hated you.'

She needed him to explain, but all she could say was, 'Sorry.'

He flashed her a brief, bleak smile, before looking down again. 'I thought you were dead. We all did. Dad was so sure. So certain Mum had killed you.'

'She didn't.'

'God! All these years! He was so convinced. Everyone thought it. Everything fell apart. They divorced. Dad kept asking me, "What really happened, son? What did she do? You must have seen something." But I didn't see anything.'

I couldn't remember anything. He told me you were dead, and I believed him. I couldn't believe her, you see? Because she didn't want me, she just wanted you. Abigail, Abigail, Abigail. And I thought it was because of me. Something to do with me. My fault.'

'No!'

'I thought she blamed me. Maybe she did, I don't know. I just remember Gran telling me, again and again, "Don't you worry, Bibs, whatever anyone tells you, it wasn't your fault." So I thought it must have been. And all these years I've hated you for causing it all, and I've hated her for messing things up.

'You know what Dad couldn't forgive? It was the fact that she wouldn't admit it. He could see the guilt in her eyes, but she wouldn't admit it. Kept insisting someone had taken you. So that was what I came to hate. The lie. Her refusal to say what she'd done.

'I remember—' His eyes were screwed up, recapturing the image. 'Being in the car with Gran, driving past and seeing my mother standing on a street corner, handing out leaflets. "Have you seen this baby?" Not in the car with me. Standing there while I drove by, asking people about you. Trying to pretend it was all true, that story about you being taken. That was all she did, pretend to look for you. They divorced and she never came to see me.'

'I'm so sorry, Ben.'

'They had blue teddy bears on them, those leaflets.' He bit his lip, breathing hard. Then he turned, ready now to look at her again, ready to cope with the knowledge shifting the ground under his feet. 'She never came to see me. Why? God, you know I think it was him. Dad. He wouldn't let her come. I hadn't thought of that. I only knew she didn't want me, she wanted you and she wouldn't admit that she'd

252

killed you. We didn't have any contact for years. Dad and I moved north, and he started a new family. When I came to find her again, a few years ago – do you know why? I didn't want to make it up with her. I just wanted to plague her into finally admitting what she'd done. Just say it, just once. I wanted to shake her and shake her.'

Kelly looked at her fingers, plaiting them together. 'She didn't do it,' she said.

'No.' He covered his face. 'All these years she was right and we were wrong.'

He was blaming himself. She couldn't have that. 'None of it was your fault, Ben. You were just a baby yourself. What else could you do but believe what they told you?'

'I could have believed her.' He was arguing with himself, not with her. 'I was wrong to hate her. I can't deal with this.'

'You need time. We all need time.'

'Yes.' He looked at his hands, then across at hers. He reached out to touch them. 'My sister. Abigail.'

'And Kelly.'

'Which? You can't be both.'

'Can't I? In that case, I don't know who I am.'

They sat silent for a while.

'Twenty-two years not being believed,' said Ben at last.

'Someone believed, surely?' Kelly, ever hopeful. 'She remarried. Someone had faith in her.'

'Keith Parish? Yes. He was a campaigner, Keith. Helped her with the leaflets. Enjoyed the challenge. A creep. I remember him at the house. Don't know why she took up with him.' He laughed, bitterly. 'Yes I do. There wasn't anyone else. In the end he stopped believing too. Got bored with it. He got a job in Bristol and Mum wouldn't leave. She was going to stay in Lyford, prove her case, find her Abigail. I was never sure if she was bad or just mad.'

253

'I would be mad, I think.'

'Yes.' He stood up, his face in his hands. 'Enough to drive anyone mad. Oh God.'

She reached to touch his hand. 'Can we go there? To the park. I know we've been there, but it meant nothing to me then.'

'Funny. It means a hell of a lot to me.'

She was quick to withdraw her suggestion. 'If it's too painful—'

'No. Come on.' It was a chance to walk, to expend energy, anything other than stand there drowning.

So they walked. Hand in hand, because she gripped his hand, never wanting to let it go. Knowing that it would never be the same again. There was a barrier between them now. A Perspex barrier that they could see through but never touch.

The park again. An innocuous bit of urban greenery, just like any other. Now it was transfused with significance. Parallel worlds again? Two worlds had brushed together here, and separated and everything was changed. A baby had come here twenty-two years ago, in one universe, and had left in a different one, and here she was again now, and how could all the destruction of that brief collision be undone?

She stared around at the lake, the grass, the trees, waiting for something. But she felt nothing. Nothing but compassion for Ben.

He was taking deep breaths. 'Sometimes, you know, I think I remember it all, everything that happened. Then I realise I'm just remembering what I've been told. What Dad told me, what Gran told me, what Mum kept trying to tell me. The truth is, I have no memory at all of that day. I was three. I didn't understand anything. I didn't even understand that you'd gone. If only I'd been a bit older, a year or two, maybe I would have seen something, I'd have been able to tell them—'

'None of it was your fault, Ben. You were—' Kelly stopped in her tracks.

Ahead of them, gripping the railings by the lake, was the woman. Mrs Parish. Ben's mother. Her mother. Heather Norris. The stocky figure stared into the murk of the lake and then turned abruptly to face the trees, expecting – what?

Kelly couldn't go on. It was the next step, wasn't it? Reunion? But she didn't want it. She didn't want to have her whole life washed away, condemned as fake. She didn't want to be claimed by a total stranger. She wanted to run. Except that she was Kelly, and Kelly didn't run away.

Ben had frozen too, staring at his mother with guilt and anguish. 'Sorry. I should have thought. She would be here. She's always here. My fault.'

'No.'

'Yes, it is. When we made contact after all those years – I told you – I really just wanted to confront her, make her acknowledge the truth. But when it came to it, I didn't have the courage to say it outright. She thought I was trying to help her remember some vital clue. She took it into her head that if she retraced our steps some detail would come back to her. I wanted to torment her with this place. Instead she's tormented me with it. I should have known she'd be here.'

Kelly licked her dry lips. 'I've got to meet her, haven't I?'

Ben stared at her, as reluctant as she was. It had to happen, but it was something neither of them wanted.

Kelly stepped forward.

Ben followed. 'Mum.'

Heather was frowning, lost in her own thoughts. She didn't hear.

'Mum,' Ben repeated, his voice strengthening.

Heather turned, face briefly lit by delighted surprise as she focussed on Ben. Then darkened with irritation as she saw Kelly.

'Ben, darling, what a lovely surprise. I wasn't expecting you today. Can you come back for tea with me? Or are you too busy with your friends?'

'Mum.' Ben's voice was croaking. He cleared it. 'Mum. This isn't just a friend. It's Abigail.'

Heather flinched. Her eyes flashed angry hurt. 'Ben, please don't tell me you think that makes a difference! I don't care what her name is. Call her what you like. She's not *my* Abigail.'

'Mum, she is. She's your daughter. Your baby, who was taken here, in the park.'

Kelly took a step forward.

Heather stepped back, staring at her with repulsion. 'No!'

'Yes, Mum.'

'No. How dare you! All these lunatics who keep claiming to be Abigail, I can cope with them, but how could you, Ben? You can't be this cruel to me. This horrible joke. She's not my Abigail.'

'Mum, I'm not joking. It's real, please.'

Kelly wanted to cry. Heather was looking at her with hatred. This woman, her mother, hated her. Her brother, her lover, hated her.

'No, she's not Abigail. You're lying!' Heather retreated, as Ben advanced, raising her hands to ward him off. 'No! This is wicked. This is a lie. You're not to do this. She's not Abigail. Abigail is dead.'

Ben stopped, shell-shocked. The admission that he had

wanted to wring from his mother had come at last, just when he knew it could not be true. He looked after his mother as she ran from him, then back at Kelly, aghast. 'I don't know what to do.'

Kelly swallowed. 'We shouldn't have met, not this way. It's my fault. Everything's my fault. I'm sorry.'

He paced, helpless.

'You must go after her.'

'You'll wait here?'

'Yes. I'll wait.'

What else could she do but sit there and wait, alone on a park bench? So recently she'd discovered love. Now she understood despair. There was no hope in this, she knew.

Somewhere, in this park, was the lonely ghost of the Abigail she had once been, imprisoned here since the day she had become Kelly, abandoned here, except in the memory of the woman who had refused to let go. Kelly wasn't that ghost. She had become someone else. There was no going back.

She sat watching the ducks, pecking at the rubbish on the water. Eyeing her in passing, just in case she had something for them. But she had nothing to offer them or anyone. She was a fake, an illusion.

vi

Heather

'Mum!'

Heather Parish could hear him calling, but she walked faster. This cruelty was beyond belief. Her own son; she'd never forgive him.

257

'Mum. Please. Listen. It's not a joke. I swear. She is Abigail. It was all a terrible, terrible mistake, crime – I don't know what, but it's true.'

'No!' She turned to face him as he caught up with her. 'It's a sick lie. Abigail is dead. You hear me? She's dead.' The words she had fought for years not to say, bearing her denial like martyrdom. 'I don't care what she says. You're cruel, or you're a fool. I can't believe you'd do this to me. Go away. Leave me alone!'

She walked on, and this time he didn't follow.

Furious, head down, hands twisting in her pockets, she walked on.

'Mrs Parish.' The voice was soft. Embarrassed. She couldn't equate it with the girl who had been tormenting her these last months, but there she was, following as she reached the gates of the park, haunting her, the same as ever.

Not the same. No hatred now.

'Go away! For God's sake!'

'I've got to speak to you. I'm sorry. For what I did before, what I said. I thought I was your daughter, but then I learned the truth. Let me talk. Please. Let me explain.'

'Explain? Explain what? I know what you are, you're all liars and frauds.'

'Please. That girl. I saw you with her. I was coming to find you because I wanted to explain, and I saw you all. That girl, and the man – is he your son? Her brother?'

'No! He is my son, but he is not her brother, because his sister is dead. Now leave me alone, or I'll call the police.'

The girl hesitated. 'Yes. Yes maybe it would be best if you called them, because they'll be able to confirm my story, and clear your name. Won't you let me explain?'

Heather walked on.

'She was trying to tell you she was your missing daughter, wasn't she,' the girl continued, keeping pace.

'Another one like you!'

'But this time it's true. I knew he was her brother. You can see it. They look so alike.'

'And you think, just because some girl makes herself look like my Ben, that I'll believe this hogwash? I'm not stupid, even if you are.'

'I don't believe it because they look alike. That just confirms it. I know the whole story now. I got it wrong at first. I'm involved too. We're all involved, and none of us knew it. Let me explain. Please. So that something can be put right at last.'

Heather stared at her, searching for the smirk, the sly amusement, not finding it. 'Tell me what you like. I can't stop you, can I?'

vii

Kelly

Ben sank down on the bench beside Kelly, hands thrust deep into his pockets and looked at the ducks. Silent.

Kelly looked at her hands.

'Confronting her like that; of course it wasn't going to work.' She sighed. 'Is she still upset?'

'I don't know. What is she? Crazy? In denial? She doesn't want you to be Abigail. Can you understand that?'

'Yes.' Kelly shut her eyes. 'The truth is, I don't want her to be my mother.'

'She said you were dead. All these years she's insisted you were alive, snatched away, and now she says you're

259

dead. She can't cope with it, can she? I'm her son, why can't I help her? I've spent so long hating her, blaming her and now I've got to admit I was wrong and be there for her. I don't know how. All I can do at the moment is hate myself instead.'

'Don't. I understand. You can't just switch off the feelings you've felt for years. It doesn't work like that. Roz took me from your mother, and I know she did something terrible, and I should be feeling – I don't know what, but I can't just stop loving her.'

Ben snarled. 'You love her? The woman who did all this to us?'

'She's my mum.'

'No! She's a criminal! She's worse than a murderer! How can you even speak about her without wanting to—' His hands were clenched.

'Because I can't just wipe out the last twenty-two years any more than you can. Do I excuse what she did? No. She was seventeen, she had no family, and maybe she didn't really grasp what she was doing. Maybe. None of that makes it excusable. But she's still my mum. She's been my mum in every way that matters. She's loved me.'

'I don't get you. You can sit there and talk about that monster as if she matters more to you than we do.'

'It isn't that simple!' She could be angry too. 'Are you finding it simple? It's hard. Roz *is* my mother, she's cared for me all my life and now she's ill and needs someone and her world is falling apart—'

'Like ours fell apart. Good. Now you know how it felt.'

She couldn't reach him. 'You really do hate me, don't you?'

Ben said nothing.

'I thought love would conquer all.'

He was crying. 'Nothing can conquer this, Kelly.'

She wanted to fight. And then she didn't; there was no fight left in her. She turned and walked away.

'Where are you going?' he called.

She stopped. 'Home,' she said, and walked on. He didn't follow.

viii

Heather

Heather Parish closed the door of her maisonette. Calmly, she placed her bag on the side table, took off her jacket and hung it up, then walked into the living room.

She sat down. On the floor. Then curled herself into a foetal ball on her side, arms round her head, blocking out light, sound, everything. She played and replayed the story she had been told as she marched home, that strange insistent girl dogging her footsteps.

The story was absurd.

The story made sense of everything, if only it were true.

She thought back to the park, the other girl, the one with Ben. The one who looked like Ben. She could see her, plain as day, nothing like the Abigail of her imagination, nothing like the child she had pictured in her dreams and nightmares, and yet there was a thundering voice in her head, a roaring in her blood, saying, 'Yes! Yes! Yes!'

Was it possible that after all these years of longing for her, she hadn't instantly recognised her own daughter? The weird girl, Vicky Wendle, had seen it, so why hadn't she?

Because she had been offered so many false promises before

that, she had grown immune to them, shutting herself off from the cruelty of a hope that was sure to be torn to shreds.

But another answer needled her. An accusing answer. She hadn't recognised her daughter because she didn't want to. She was Heather Parish, the searcher, the suspect, the pathetic self-deceiver, the contemptible child murderer, the woman who couldn't get on with her life because she had this thing stamped on her. Her quest, with all its horrors and tortures, had become her identity, and now, if it were all over, what was left? Nothing.

The carpet was scratching her cheek, its smell beginning to clog her nostrils. The buckle on her shoe was biting into her flesh. Her blouse was rucked up, pulling uncomfortably.

She sat up, straightened her clothes, heard sparrows twittering outside and blinked at a ray of sunshine. Suppose this earthquake was not an end of her, but a beginning? The trapdoor of the dungeon that she'd been in for twenty-two years was sliding open. It wasn't easy to step out into the light, but there was the door. She had borne so much, more than she had thought possible. She had been burned to the bone by it all and yet she had carried on, so surely she had the courage for this now?

'Think about it,' the strange Vicky Wendle had said, when they had finally reached Heather's home. 'I know it's too much to take in at once. You don't know how to cope with it. I've been through it. I know.'

Another wounded soul. Heather could remember the aching anger. Vicky Wendle had been through her own mill. Heather wasn't the only victim here. But Vicky had no anger now. Just a determination to face it and sort it out. They had shaken hands on Heather's doorstep.

'Of course I'll think it through,' she'd said.

And now she had.

She got to her feet, retrieved her bag, flipped open her phone and rang the only number recorded.

The ringing stopped. Someone was taking the call, but wasn't saying a word. Probably he couldn't.

'I need to see her again, Ben. This – Abigail. I have to see her, don't I?'

ix

Vicky

The minicab drew up on the curb, one tyre on the pavement. Gillian watched from the living room. Home from Scotland. So Joan wasn't going straight back to Bill Bowyer's then. Come to dump her luggage here first before carting her free whisky samples back to his place. You had to admire the old girl. Never a dull moment. Plenty at her age would be sitting in an old people's home, tucked under blankets, dribbling quietly, but not Joan. It would take more than age, arthritis and a weak bladder to keep her down. A stake through the heart, maybe.

'Well, what d'you expect with the bleeding Jocks,' Joan was saying, as the front door opened. The cab driver was carrying her bags in for her. 'You just going to stand there gawping, girl? Pay the bloke.'

Gillian paid him. It wasn't worth fighting over. She looked at the cabby, unsmiling. 'You'd better leave us now.'

He ambled out, pulling the door shut behind him.

'What's up with you, girl?' Joan was groping for her cigarettes. 'Face like a wet floor cloth. Nice welcome I come home to, I must say. What you been doing? Trashing my house again?'

Gillian didn't reply.

'Well, I'm not dragging them bags up the fucking stairs.' Joan flopped down on the sofa, puffing her cigarette, scrawny legs splayed. 'Make us some tea.'

Gillian ignored the order. 'I've been talking to Vicky.'

'Huh. That sourpuss. What's she had to say for herself? Can't be bothered to come down to say hello to her gran.'

'You're not her grandmother.'

'Never thought I was. It was you always wanted to play that game.'

'Vicky told me what you did.'

'What I did? I never did anything to her. A clip around the ear occasionally. You going to be all namby-pamby and say I shouldn't have laid a finger on her? I don't hold with that modern crap. You have to discipline children. It was the way I brought you lot up.'

'Oh yes! I remember how you brought us up!' She wasn't going to be distracted by that. It was Vicky who mattered. 'Nothing changes with you, does it? I'm not talking about you smacking her, although God knows that was bad enough.' Keep calm, keep it cold. 'I'm talking about what you did to her that night, sitting down here all innocent and letting the girls lock her in upstairs with that pig.'

'Pig? What pig? I don't know what you're talking about. You need to see a doctor, my girl, getting hysterical, trashing things, all this shouting. You need seeing to.'

'Oh, yes, that was one of your expressions. I remember. Is that what you told Dana to do? Get Craig Adams to give her a seeing to?'

'What's the silly cow's been saying? Fucking lies, all of it. Can't get a man so she makes stuff up. Pissed off that he never came back for more? 'Cos if she told you it was rape,

264

she's leading you right up the garden path. Couldn't get enough of it, from what I heard.'

'Don't you dare say such filthy things when you know damn well she was terrified and she didn't want any of it! You arranged the whole thing. You make me sick!'

'Hey, hey, you keep off me!' Joan was fighting her off and Gillian hadn't even realised she was shaking her. She had been so determined not to lose her temper, to be cold as an iceberg. Couldn't she do anything right?

Joan pushed her off, snorting indignantly. 'If you think I'm going to sit around in my own house, being insulted like this, you can think again.'

She made to rise but Gillian pushed her back down. 'Oh no you don't. You don't just walk away, not this time. I left her in your care for one night. One night! And that was all you needed for your filthy little games. One night for you to hurt my girl, destroy her childhood, make her feel wretched and degraded.'

'You're bloody barmy.' Joan was angry, and then suddenly cautious. Afraid. 'I'm your mother. I'm an old woman. You want to listen to a pack of lies about me? Your own mum?'

Of course Joan was afraid: of the brass poker in Gillian's hand. When had she picked it up? She couldn't remember, but the urge to use it was so strong she was frightening herself. And glorying in the terror in Joan's eyes. But Joan couldn't simply be afraid. Even in terror she had to scoff. 'You wouldn't dare.'

'What makes you think that, eh? I'm your daughter. Is there anything you'd be too ashamed to do? You sat round smirking like a disgusting old brothel madam, while my daughter was raped—'

'I did not! How was I to know what they were doing up there?'

265

'You knew exactly what they were doing. You planned it.'

'I did not!'

'I know you did! Just like you planned it with me! I should have killed you then, forty years ago, before you could hurt anyone else. But no, I left you to hurt my daughter, and I'm damned if you're going to hurt anyone else!'

Joan stared up at the round brass knob of the poker handle, raised over her. Would she still be staring when Gillian brought it down?

She was going to. Her arm was aching with the force with which she gripped the poker. Her whole body was rigid. She could smash the witch's skull, or skewer Joan like the pig she was.

'Don't.'

A voice in her ear. A hand closing round her wrist, holding her and the poker.

'Don't, Mum. She's not worth it.'

'Vicky?' How was she here? Vicky had left. Gillian had been so certain that this time she'd gone for good. But here she was, holding the poker back.

'If you kill her, you'll go to prison and she's not worth it. Don't let her destroy anything else.'

It was enough to ease Joan's panic. 'That's right, you stop her. Ought to be locked up. Waving a poker at me.'

'Shut up,' said Vicky, quite quietly, almost politely.

'Don't you shut up me. This is my house. And don't you go bad-mouthing me, telling your lies, young madam.'

'Shut up!' screamed Gillian, clutching the poker again.

'Shhhh,' soothed Vicky. 'She's a bag of wind. Don't let her hurt you.'

'But she hurt you.' Gillian sobbed, gulping for air, feeling the violence drain out of her. 'I should have known, because

266

that's what she does. That's what she did to all of us. Why?' Vicky had taken the poker from her hand, but Gillian could still grab Joan and shake her. 'Why, you evil old witch?'

'Witch? And after all I've done for you?'

'What have you ever done for anyone? Don't you dare call yourself a mother! You have never cared about anyone. Why? What's wrong with you? Why can't you care for anyone else?'

'Why should I?' spat Joan. Now that Vicky had pulled Gillian back, she had room to rise. 'No one ever fucking cared for me. I had to manage, didn't I? I had to go through it all. I had to learn the hard way. Why should it be any different for any of you? I had it a bloody sight harder than anything you've gone through.'

'Oh. Is that it?' Gillian stepped back, staring at Joan. 'You were abused? Your father beat you? Your mother put you on the game? And your revenge is to hurt us in your turn? Your own children, and your grandchildren and your great grandchildren? You sick, sad, old woman!'

'Yes, she is a sick, old woman,' said Vicky, so calm and quiet. 'Don't let her hurt you any more.'

'I'm the one hurt here,' snapped Joan. 'Being attacked with a poker. Assault, that's what it is. I'll have the police on you!'

'Call them!' retorted Gillian. 'Go on, call them, and I'll tell them what you did to Vicky.'

'I didn't do anything. You've got this bee in your bonnet about rape. They were kids having fun. If she told you it was rape—'

'Vicky didn't say rape. But that's what it was and I know, because I went through it, all those years ago, you pushing me on Michael Ridgeley that night, locking the door so I couldn't get back in, sniggering through the letterbox, "You

267

show her a good time, Micky, you show her what's what eh?" I was fifteen!'

'Fifteen? So what? I was bloody twelve!'

'I don't care! I don't care what you went through as a child. You forfeited my pity forty years ago. But instead of spitting in your face, I just accepted you as the poison I was stuck with. And I brought another child under your roof and I let you hurt her in exactly the same way!'

'It's a cycle,' commented Vicky, as if conversing about the weather. 'She was abused, she abuses. But you didn't. You've broken the circle.'

'No,' wept Gillian. 'Because I left you with her and that was as good as abuse!'

'No! She's the abuser. Rapist by proxy. They could do an interesting study on her. Sociopathic responses to—'

'You and your bloody long words. You think you're so clever.' Joan's chin was up now, the last trace of fear gone. 'You're no granddaughter of mine. That stupid cow there ain't your mother—'

'But she is,' said Vicky. 'Though I agree you're not my grandmother. Mum should disown you too.'

'Disown! I'm the one doing the bloody disowning. Get out. I don't want you in this house. It's my house. I say who lives here, and I want you out.'

'No,' said Vicky, putting her arms round Gillian, only partly to restrain her. 'You're the one who's going to go, Joan. You're going to pack up your things and get out. Move in with Bill. This is our home, it's my parents who have paid for it, and you're the one who isn't wanted.'

Joan laughed. 'My name on the deeds, girl. Just because I offered my useless daughter a roof over her head, when she'd chucked all her money down the drain, doesn't give you any right.'

'Well, rights, you know, Joan, are just a matter of applied or implied force, in the end. Give a man all the rights in the world, and it's meaningless if he's too scared or weak to assert them. It doesn't really matter what legal rights you have in this house, because you are not going to assert them. You are going to move out and leave us alone.'

'Like fuck I am.'

'Yes, you are, because if you don't, I am going to the police to report exactly how you organised and supervised my rape.'

Joan laughed again, blustering. 'You couldn't. Kids mucking around, that's all. You weren't underage. You can call it rape now, but you didn't say nothing back then. You think the others will back you up? The police will know you're crazy.'

'But there's evidence. Plenty of it, in my medical records. I went to the doctor, remember? But I don't suppose you do. You'd had your fun, so you weren't interested in what I did next. I went to the doctor, next morning, scared I might be pregnant or infected. I let him examine me. He could see exactly what had happened and his records prove it. He was all for going to the police then but I wouldn't. I felt dirty. Ashamed. I didn't want anyone knowing, so he agreed to keep quiet, but the records are there. The police aren't going to argue with them.'

'Maybe it was rape, I don't know. How am I supposed to know what kids get up to? It was nothing to do with me.'

'It was everything to do with you,' said Gillian. She felt as if a weapon had been put into her hands at last, a real weapon, not a decorative brass poker. 'And I'll tell them exactly how you operate. What you did to me, and the others.'

'There'll be plenty of corroboration,' added Vicky.

'Doctor White probably still has the semen sample too. DNA. That will be enough to prove who it was, and what do you think Craig Adams will say when he's questioned? He'll drag in the others and they'll blame it all on you. And of course it will get out and the whole estate will know about it. Remember how they blew up when Noel Ashford was suspected of being a paedophile? It doesn't take much to get the mindless hypocrites going. Your choice, Joan. What would you prefer? To be charged or lynched? Or would you rather just move in with your toy boy and leave us alone? One way or another, you're out of here.' Vicky smiled her contempt, in command.

Joan's thin lips were working. 'I tell you something, I'm not staying in this house tonight. Not with a couple of lunatics like you. Murdered in my bed, likely as not.' She marched to the door, picked up her case, dropped it again in favour of the bag with the whisky bottles. 'Don't you think you're having it all your own way. I'm getting the police onto you, right enough. You don't scare me.' She was already out of the door, sparrow legs hurrying down the path.

'I'm hoping Mum and Dad will sell and move,' called Vicky after her. 'If they do, we'll pass on a quarter share. That sounds reasonable. Consult your solicitor.' She shut the door and moved the suitcase disdainfully out of the way. Then she looked back at Gillian.

Gillian embraced her, her voice thick with emotion. 'Oh God, oh my darling, I thought I'd lost you.'

'No,' said Vicky. 'It seems not.' She let herself be embraced. Tentatively, experimentally, she hugged Gillian back. 'She's gone, you know. She won't dare try coming back, whatever she says.'

Gillian held her closer. 'I'm sorry, Vicky, so sorry. I should have been there for you. You had to deal with it all alone.

Thank God you thought of going to the doctor.'

'Don't be daft. Of course I didn't. I went to my room and locked the door.'

'But – if she goes to the police—'

'She won't. Don't you know her well enough by now? She's out, gone, and we're rid of her. It's all right, Mum. It's all right. I can deal with anything now.'

X

Kelly

Kelly took the motorway home. Fast and inhuman. That was all right, she didn't feel human anymore. She was an advanced primate with vocal chords, language skills and opposable thumbs. No emotions. Emotions hurt too much.

Who was to blame for all this? Roz, of course. Her sublime determination not to think of the consequences of her actions or inaction. Roz was to blame for the past. But the misery of the present, that was all down to herself. Why had she had to interfere? Why had she had to investigate, stumbling in with a big smile, expecting everything to fall into place around her? For what? Who had reaped one tiny grain of benefit from her interference? No one. Not Victoria Wendle, not the Norris family, not Roz, and certainly not Kelly herself. She had begun with the whole world, and now she had nothing.

Nothing except Roz.

When she got in, Roz looked at her, shut her eyes, looked again, not daring to believe. 'You've come back. I didn't think you would. I didn't think you'd want me any more.'

'Well, I do,' said Kelly, dully. 'It looks as if you're all I've got.'

271

CHAPTER 10

i

Heather

'Now, Mrs Norris…all right, love? Can you answer some questions? About what happened? Can you talk? We need you to tell us as much as possible.'

He was a policeman in plain clothes. Heather found that easier to cope with. At first the police uniforms had been reassuring. Authority, people who could put things right, make this nightmare go away. But then the uniforms just seemed to make it all seem more surreal. She could no longer tell what part she was supposed to be playing in all this.

She was in a house. How had she come to be here? Wide window with horizontal bars curving round the corner of the room. She could see through it the Buckingham Road gates of the park. This must be that weird cubist house she often saw from the bus, the sort they kept featuring in *Poirot*. Often wondered what it must be like inside—

Why was she thinking about architecture? For God's sake! She should be thinking about Abigail. Except that she couldn't think any more.

They had brought her here, the nearest place. A la-di-da woman, magistrate type, standing on the doorstep ushering them in, Heather and a policewoman. Other officers were in the park, questioning the man in the black coat. Where was the policewoman now? Oh, she was with Bibs.

'Bibs. My son. Is he all right?'

'Yes, Mrs Norris, he's fine. WPC Line is looking after him.'

'Don't let him have any more biscuits. He's had too many, they're not good for him.'

'Don't worry, no more biscuits. Now, can you tell me about Abigail?'

He was very gentle, very kind. Like a doctor. She couldn't remember his name. He had introduced himself but she just couldn't remember.

'Tell me what happened, Mrs Norris.'

For the hundredth time, and each time it became more unbelievable. Heather looked down at her hands in her lap. They were shaking. Not as badly as they had been, when she had collapsed in the park. 'We missed the bus in town, so I thought we could catch one in Buckingham Road. We'd been at the playground. Keeping Bibs occupied. We were going, and Bibs saw the ducks on the lake. He ran away, down to the lake, do you see? And I didn't want to push the pram through the mud, so I left it on the path. Abigail was all right. I swear, she was sleeping, she didn't even notice I was gone.'

She put the back of her hand to her mouth, biting flesh and bone, hoping the pain would drive away that deeper agony. Abigail was gone and she hadn't even said goodbye.

He leaned across and patted her hand. 'All right, Mrs Norris.'

Parker. That was it. DC? DI? She couldn't remember, but his name was Parker. Thunderbirds, Lady Penelope's chauffeur. He did look a bit like him.

'So you left Abigail asleep in her pram.'

'It wasn't far,' she explained, trying to show with her hands how small the distance was from the path to the lakeside. 'Just across the grass. I could still see the pram, always, when I looked back. But Bibs wanted to feed the ducks. We weren't there long. I swear. A minute or two. He didn't want to leave the ducks, you see. But I took him back in the end, and when we got back to the pram—' She tried to get her mouth round the words and could not. She could not say it. She could feel the hysteria rising within her again.

'And when you got back to the pram, the baby was gone,' Parker prompted.

She could only nod.

He gave her a moment. 'Now, try to think about this, Mrs Norris. Did you see anything?'

She shook her head, violently.

'Anyone? No matter how innocent, how far away. There must have been other people in the park.'

'No! There was no one! I looked. There was no one in sight. Just a couple of dogs. The dogs took my baby, didn't they?'

'I don't think so, Mrs Norris. Just think once more. You are quite sure about this? You didn't see anyone afterwards.'

'Not until the man in the black coat.'

'Alan Gregory, the man who called us after you found Abigail missing?'

'Yes!'

'What about before? Think, Mrs Norris. Try to think back. While you were pushing the pram along the path, before your son ran down to the lake, do you remember seeing anyone then?'

'No.' She did what he said, tried to think, dredging her memory. She hadn't noticed anyone on the path. She had had Bibs and Abigail to concentrate on. 'There might have been. I wasn't looking! In the trees. Maybe. Something. I don't know. I don't know!'

'All right.' He patted her arm again. 'Is there anything else you can tell us, anything at all?'

She shook her head, her shoulders heaving. How could something like this happen without any warning?

'And you were down by the lake for no more than a minute or two, you say.'

'Just time to feed the ducks. It couldn't have been more than five. No, no, it couldn't have been. It wasn't ten.'

A door opened and Parker stood up. 'All right, Mrs Norris, we're going to get you home.'

'But I can't leave. You've got to find Abigail.'

'We will look for Abigail, Mrs Norris, don't you worry. We've got men searching every inch of the park. The moment we have any news, you'll be the first to know. But for now, it's best if you go home. We've contacted your husband; he's coming home to be with you. And a doctor. So you go with PCs Michaels and Line here and leave the searching to us.'

They took her and Bibs home in a police car. Bibs liked that. He liked it even more when PC Michaels put the siren on for him, just for a second. People in the street jumped, stopped and stared at the woman and her son being driven by in a police car. Under arrest, probably. Yesterday, she would have cared what they thought. Now she couldn't care. Even so, she saw them all. One of them must have Abigail. Her eyes were fixed, waiting to focus on the one human form she sought. One glimpse of her baby would be enough.

Twice, her stomach rose, and her heart and lungs and liver, jolting upwards at the sight of a baby, only to plunge because it was the wrong baby. WPC Line kept talking to her but she didn't listen. She had to concentrate.

Martin was already home. He looked ill, but he put his

arms around her, led her into the house. 'Jesus, Heather,' he whispered. 'How could this happen?'

'She's very distressed, sir, naturally,' the policewoman explained. 'We've called a doctor to give her a sedative.'

'I don't want a sedative, I want my baby,' said Heather.

'Yes, dear, of course you do.'

But when the doctor came, she let him give her something to calm her. Was this calm? This sluggish detachment? They were controlling her, so she wouldn't make a fuss and embarrass everyone. The man in the park had been embarrassed. She was sorry if she was embarrassing people.

'I just don't understand,' Martin said, to anyone who would listen. 'How could someone just take our baby? What sort of monster would do this?' He was pathetic and angry in turns. Mostly angry. That was the only way to deal with it. Be angry. Heather wanted to be angry but with whom? If only she'd seen someone. Again and again she ran it back, ran it back, ran it back. Office workers hurrying away after a late lunch. Who else? There must have been someone. In the trees. Surely she had seen movement. Someone lurking. If only she could think straight.

Barbara Norris. Where had she come from? Someone must have sent for her. 'Martin! My poor boy, oh I can't believe it. Where is little Bibs? Come to Grandma, darling. Oh you poor poor thing. Heather, Heather, why oh why would you not let me give you a lift this morning? Why did you have to insist on going alone? I just knew something like this would happen.'

'Mum.' Martin steered her away. 'This won't help.'

'She just had to have her own way. Why are there so many police here?' She turned on PC Michaels. 'What are you doing, standing round here? Why aren't you out there

276

looking for my grandchild? Why isn't anyone doing anything?'

It kept them occupied, heaping soothing reassurances on her. Leaving Heather to sink into the nightmare and disbelief. Oh God, oh God, whoever had Abigail, let her be all right. Let her still be alive.

ii

Lindy

Kelly was fretful. More fretful than she used to be. Like there was something she missed.

'Here you are.' Lindy crouched over her, waving the little pink mouse for her. She just wanted her baby to be happy. Mouse wasn't good enough. Kelly's face was still screwed up and troubled. Lindy picked her up to cuddle her. That would work, eventually. If she just sat here rocking her.

She could sense the door opening behind her, though it did so silently. Not Gary. He never did anything silently.

She turned. Carver was watching her like a statue. His eyes were very dark. Usually dark eyes were soft, but his were hard.

'That woman,' he said. He didn't sound angry or anything, but Lindy knew trouble. 'Who was she? What was she doing here?'

'Social worker,' said Lindy. 'The hospital sent her to check up on the baby, make sure everything's all right. And it is. She said I was doing fine. Said she'd let them know there was no need to keep checking on me, I was a good mother.'

Was that a smile in those black eyes? Possibly, but it

wasn't a smile Lindy found comforting. She watched Carver's gaze move from her to the baby. Her flesh crawled.

'This isn't a suitable environment for a baby,' said Carver. 'You should find somewhere else to live.'

'Yeah.' She nodded agreement. 'I'm going to have a council flat.'

Carver's gaze was back on her. 'Good,' he said. 'Best thing.' He pulled the door silently shut.

Lindy's heart pattered. He hadn't said anything bad. Hadn't threatened her, or Kelly. Not with words. But there had always been something about Carver that terrified her, even when he was being nice. Perhaps even more when he was being nice.

He wanted her gone.

She really needed to think now. Carver had as good as ordered her out. She'd told the Rothsay woman she was going back to her family in Barking. Maybe she really could do that. Except that she didn't know where any of her brothers and sisters were, not even Jimmy. She'd seen him once or twice after they were separated, but not for years now. She couldn't be sure he was still alive.

She might try it though. Hitch a lift into London. Easy to get lost in London. Not that she fancied living rough again, not with a baby. It was getting dark outside, reminding her of nights on the street, of how much safer this room was.

No, not really. Shelter from the rain, that's all it was. Not safer. Not with Gary. Not with Carver upstairs.

Street lights on. Nightlife creeping out, Nelson Road creaking open its coffin. A yellow glow from the Duke of Wellington. A few voices raised, a long way off the sound of shattering glass. But no sound in the house. It was like everyone in it had been told to stand still and hold their breath. No trouble, Carver had said, and everyone obeyed him, always.

It was going to be tonight then. She should go to bed and pretend not to notice anything. Innocent as little Kelly. No, she couldn't hide under the quilt yet. She had to wait up for Gary. She always waited up for Gary.

Nearly eleven.

'Out of my fucking way.' Gary's voice, slightly slurred, from the hallway. Never any trouble hearing him coming. She could always tell what sort of a mood he was in from his footsteps. Sometimes they staggered, sometimes they were, like, frisky. Today they were fast, heavy, like he was playing a tough guy. Trying really hard to convince himself. She'd seen him shouldering people off the pavement in the street, because he wanted to act like a gangster. Most people were convinced. She'd watched them step out of his way before he reached them. She knew better though. She had heard him whimper in his dreams.

He shouldered open the door. She'd be nice to him, get him something to eat, and maybe he'd settle down.

'Geroff me.' He shook her off, turning to shut the door as if there were werewolves out there. She could see sweat on his neck.

'I got you a beer, Gary.'

'No time—' He changed his mind. 'Yeah, give me a beer. I need my gear. Going out, all right? No need for you to fucking fuss over me. I've got—'

The noise woke Kelly. She gave a little gurgle and began to cry. She would keep crying.

Gary froze in his tracks. He stared at the baby in her basket.

'It's all right, Gary, she just needs a feed. I'll keep her quiet.'

279

'You... You...' He was lost for words. The words he usually used were so overworked, they had no value left. He could do nothing but mouth silently.

He was petrified.

'What have you done, you stupid bitch?' His voice was a squeak. 'What have you done?' He shook her by the arms.

'Nothing, Gary. I didn't do nothing.'

'Where did you get that from?'

'My Kelly?'

'She's not your baby. Are you mental or something? You dumped your baby in the shopping centre!'

'Yeah but it was a mistake. I didn't mean it.'

'What the fuck do you mean, you didn't mean it?'

'I got her back.'

'It's not the same fucking baby! It can't be! You stupid—' His voice rose, his hand entwining in her hair, ready to hit her. Then he froze, as his terror overwhelmed his anger. He mustn't raise his voice, or hit her, or do anything to make a fuss. Keep it quiet. He released her, pushing her away like she had leprosy. 'Jesus, Jesus. You're going to kill me, you know that? Are you so fucking thick that—' He had his face in his hands.

Then he pulled himself together. 'You keep it quiet, right. For tonight. You keep it quiet and you keep your head down and you don't say nothing to no one. Carver's not going to know about this. All right? You hear me?'

She nodded.

'All right. Just shut it.' He turned away, wiping his mouth, packing his gear, pretending that his hand wasn't shaking. His leather jacket and his baseball cap. The bag that he'd kept stashed under the sink, telling her not to touch it. She hadn't touched it. If it terrified Gary so much, it wasn't something she wanted to know about.

280

He was running cold water in the sink, splashing his face with it. Then he finished his beer, opened another, swigged hard. Turned to look a fleeting second at the baby cradled in Lindy's arms, then screwed his eyes up and turned away. He really was shaking.

The door opened.

'Ready?'

'Yeah. Sure, Carver.'

'You've got it?'

'Yeah. Here, safe and sound.' Gary patted the bag, hoisting it up, putting the beer can down and missing the cupboard, so it fell to the floor, its contents foaming over the threadbare carpet.

Lindy moved.

'Leave it,' snapped Gary.

'No,' said Carver. 'Let her clean it up. Do what she does. Come on.'

'Right, Carver.'

Lindy put Kelly back in her basket and reached for a cloth in the sink. She dropped to her knees to mop up the spilt beer.

The front door clicked quietly shut, and she could hear Gary's heavy boots in the street. She couldn't hear Carver's at all. He walked like a cat. She heard muffled voices though, several of them. A couple of doors shutting, engines revving, cars moving off. Then silence.

Kelly was still stirring, still wanting something. Attention. Lindy picked her up again, rocking her back and forth. Just letting instinct take over. That bag of dirty nappies up in the bathroom. She should chuck it, and all the other crap in the flat, empty cans, old newspaper and such. Letting Kelly lie on the empty mattress, she gathered up every scrap of rubbish that she could find, fetched the bag from the bathroom with its smelly load of strange baby clothes, crushed in the other trash and took it down to the front step. Tied a knot so it wouldn't spill out. Pushed it into the skip blocking the pavement, in amongst the broken tiles and rubble, an old suitcase and a dead cat. Everyone dumped stuff in it.

She went back upstairs to her baby. Lay down beside her. It was her home, this place. Crappy though it was, it was all she had. But Carver had told her to go. If she refused, she'd finish up floating in the sewer, and Kelly with her. She didn't want to lose Gary; he was her man. But Kelly was her baby. She didn't want anything happening to Kelly.

Besides, if Carver's job went wrong, this place would be swarming with police, asking questions, turning everything upside down, and they'd bring in the social workers again, and Kelly would be gone. Better to go now, before the whole world of Nelson Road came crashing down. How long could she leave it? She didn't want to go out into that dark night, but she couldn't stay until morning. Another hour or so, maybe, here in the warmth of what had been home.

She could pack. Kelly's things, mostly, and some of her own clothes, into a carrier bag and the big canvas shoulder bag she'd nicked last year. Some food. Hitchhiking could take forever. A packet of biscuits, that would do, and a bottle of coke and a bar of chocolate. It would see her through till she got to London. What else? What about cash? She had three pounds fifty, but Gary had some. Never gave her any, but he had some somewhere. She'd seen him flashing notes around.

Probably had it on him, but you never know. She searched the pockets of his abandoned clothes, struck lucky. There was a fiver in his jeans pocket, so dirty and crumpled people would think twice about accepting it, but it was money, wasn't it? A few pennies, a bit of silver. And then, joy, a crisp new tenner and a fifty pence piece in the pocket of his denim jacket.

A car screeched down the road. She rushed to the window. Was it Gary and Carver back already? No, it couldn't be. Just a joyrider out to annoy the area. The streets were more or less clear now. Silence, except for a dog barking. Lights out at the Duke of Wellington.

Half two. Could she risk staying for another hour? Back on the mattress with Kelly. Just a little longer—

She must have dozed off. Woke with a start, hearing a siren. Just a quick blast, a long way off, but it made her jump. What time was it? Gone four. She scrambled up in a panic. They could be back any moment. She had to be gone before they came back.

And Kelly was waking. Another feed? Now? Well, the baby didn't know better, did she? Better now than out in the dark. Then she had to be changed again, but that was all right, best to start off clean and dry. Just as long as Carver didn't come back. Lindy's fingers moved like greased lightning.

'There's my little girl.' Into the Moses basket. It would be a bit awkward to carry far, but it held most of Kelly's stuff, as well as the baby.

Down the dark dirty stairs one last time. She met the cold blast of night air, and out into deserted Nelson Road.

A long walk, across to Moreton Road, past the foundry, and the garages, under the railway bridge, down Weston road, skirting the council estate, out to the edge of town. Not so long ago it had petered out into open fields with a few trees. Now the bypass cut across the farmland, a tarmac girdle for Lyford, sweeping lorries and commuters down towards the motorway.

The sky was grey in the east by the time she got there. Even under the yellow lights of the intersection, she could see the silhouette of distant downs and trees.

Weary now, ankle sore, she stood at the slip road, thumbing hopefully at the passing traffic, but no one stopped. A lorry slowed, but then accelerated past her. She saw one car hesitate, a driver in shirtsleeves. Then he passed her by.

It was Kelly. Lindy had never had trouble cadging a lift before. Had to fight the drivers off sometimes, and once or twice she'd failed, but that risk went with the territory. Usually, if they made eye contact, they'd stop. Girl on her own, they'd stop without a second thought. But now she had a baby with her. That must be putting them off.

Traffic thundered past. Where did they all come from? Mostly trucks and vans, but the cars were starting. Commuters in their posh saloons, some of them shaving at the wheel, or tuning their radios, none of them pausing for a girl and her baby basket. Every passing lorry enveloped her in a mini-hurricane. Kelly was beginning to cry.

Maybe Lindy should play it the other way. Flaunt Kelly, look like a plaintive mum, and hope someone would take pity on her. She picked the baby up and cuddled her.

It worked. Eventually. Daylight now, and at last a lorry stopped, edging in onto the curb ahead of her. She hoisted up the basket again, her carrier and her canvas bag, adjusting her balance, and scrambled for the lorry.

The driver had the passenger door open.

'This is no place for a little babby, girl. You'd best get in here.' He looked OK, burly like truckers were, but pretty old, grey hair and all. Someone's granddad; that's why he'd stopped. 'Where're you going?'

'London. See my brother.'

'You'd be better off on the train, thought of that?'

'Ain't got no money for the train.' That wouldn't have stopped her, but hitching was a habit. She always hitched.

'Well, I'm heading for Oxford, but I can't leave you standing there. I'll take you to the lay-by, drop you there. At least you can get yourself a nice cuppa.'

'Thanks.' She was ready to struggle up into the cab, with the baby and all, but he jumped down to help. Yeah, someone's granddad, no doubt about that.

'So, you're off to the big city then,' he said, checking his mirrors and back into the traffic. 'Show the little one the sights, eh? What is it, boy or girl?'

'Girl.'

Kelly blew a raspberry.

'She got a name?'

'Kelly Crowe.' Lindy felt her. Kelly needed changing again.

'Well, little Kelly, you listen to Freddy here, and you tell your Mum it's a dangerous world and she shouldn't be hitching rides with a babby.'

'Just to London,' insisted Kelly. 'Then I'll be all right.'

He shook his head, but it wasn't really his concern. They were coming to the lay-by. He'd done his bit, getting her off the slip road.

It was a big lay-by, with toilets at one end and a kiosk selling hot tea and sausage and bacon butties at the other. A couple of cars and half a dozen big lorries already parked up. Freddy drew up alongside and she opened the door.

'You take care now,' said Freddy. 'Don't you go climbing in with just anyone.'

'Thanks,' said Kelly, dropping down, taking her bags from him, moving out of the way as he drove off again, still shaking his head.

The smell of frying, over the diesel fumes, drew Lindy

285

like a magnet. She could afford a bite, couldn't she? Wouldn't cost the earth, not in a place like this.

But Kelly came first, before she started bawling in earnest. Change her in the toilets that stank of pee and disinfectant. Pathetic little steel basins and no hot water, but it was all there was. Lindy gave her the bottle she'd brought with her in the basket.

Then she bought herself a bacon bun. Great, the warm grease dribbling down her chin. All she had to do was wait for the next lift that would take her the twenty odd miles to London.

But no one was offering. Not even when she asked them direct. It was the baby, no doubt about it.

She had been there nearly two hours when they arrived. A camper van, painted with leaves, like it was advertising a garden centre. Or just gipsies. Lindy watched a man get out, long hair tied in a ponytail, embroidered waistcoat. Then a woman, long hair, long skirt, helping a toddler out and a little boy, shepherding them to the toilets. The man went round the back, prodding at the exhaust. It had been making a racket as the van had pulled in.

Lindy sidled towards them. A family with children, safe enough. She was fed up with drivers looking at Kelly like she was some alien. And she needed the bog. That bacon bun had got her insides churning.

The man smiled at her as she carried Kelly past. In the toilets, the woman was wiping the toddler's bare bum. She smiled too. 'Hi.'

Lindy chewed her lip, dropped her bags and then laid the basket down. 'Can you watch her while I go in?'

'Surely.'

Sitting in the stinking cubicle, looking at the scratched steel door, Lindy could hear the woman talking. 'Aren't you a sweet little thing then? Come on, come to Mandy. Let's give you a cuddle.'

She could hear Kelly's gurgle. Contented. There was this great upheaval inside Lindy. All sorts of feelings fighting each other. Jealousy that Kelly was responding to someone else. Anger and worry, that gut terror that someone else was going to take her away. And this strange warm longing, to have someone just smile at her and Kelly.

She emerged, to find the woman crouching on the floor, long skirt splayed out, showing Kelly to the two kids. The toddler was reaching out to touch her.

The woman smiled at Lindy, and laid the baby back in the basket. 'She's lovely. I love kids. Is she yours?'

Lindy snatched the baby up. 'Course she's mine. She's my Kelly. I got the papers to prove it.'

The woman put her arm round Lindy. 'Oh I'm sorry, I didn't mean... I just thought how young you were, her big sister maybe. I do apologise.'

She spoke posh, weird with her looking like a gipsy.

The little toddler was still reaching up to the baby. As a token of forgiveness, Lindy let her touch.

'Tanja likes her too,' said the woman.

'Where you heading then?'

'Oh, west. We're going to join friends over in Wales.'

'Right.' If only they had been going to London. Lindy could have asked them for a lift and she was sure they'd have said yes.

'And what about you and Kelly?'

'London. Don't know when though. I'm not getting much luck with lifts.'

A flash of alarm, hastily stifled. 'You're trying to hitch-hike with a baby? That can't be easy. Sorry, I assumed you were with someone.'

'Going to stay with my brother.' With Jimmy, who might or might not be in London, who might or might not remember her. 'If I can find him. Got to go somewhere, haven't I?'

The woman looked at her in sympathy and concern, then she smiled. Not a social worker's smile at all. 'Sure you wouldn't prefer to come with us to Wales?'

It was like balancing on the middle of the see-saw back in the park. One step to the left and it tilted one way, to the right and it went the other. She didn't have to go to London. She could do anything she liked. Head off with this woman and her family. A real family.

'Yeah, all right.'

iii

Heather

One second of bliss, emerging from drugged slumber. Then something gnawing within her, even though she couldn't remember what it was. Something was wrong. Maybe it had been a dream, and now she was waking and she'd find it wasn't true…

Heather opened her eyes, willing the nightmare to be gone. Martin stood by the window, staring out at a grey dawn. He was going to turn and smile, and say, 'Hello sleepyhead, ready for a cup of tea?' And Bibs would come padding in with his blanket, and Abigail would give a little gurgle from the cot.

Martin turned, his face bleak and grey. He attempted a smile, so feeble it barely gasped for air before dying. But he wasn't looking at her. Not quite looking at her.

There was no gurgle. There was no cot. She struggled up. 'Where's the cot?' Panic. 'Where's the cot gone!'

'Ssh.' Martin tried to calm her. 'It's in the spare room. They thought it would upset you.'

It vanished, the last shreds of that kind illusion of a dream. Her baby was gone. The memory came back and all the anguish and gut-churning terror. 'No!'

Martin drew a deep breath, then put his arms round her. 'Just...go back to sleep.'

'How can I? My baby's gone! I've got to do something, I've got to find her.' She could hear the words clearly enough in her head, but she knew that mere gibberish and sobs came out.

She grabbed his arm. 'Something's happened, hasn't it? There's news. They've found her. She's—' She couldn't say the word, couldn't even think it.

'There's been no news,' said Martin. 'They're still looking.' He let go of her. 'I'll make us some tea.' Eager to be gone.

Tea. Yes, she needed something to drink. Her mouth was like sawdust. She couldn't lie here looking at the spot where Abigail's cot had been. She groped for clothes, fresh ones, not the ones that someone had folded neatly and laid on the chair. She never wanted to wear those clothes again. They could go in the incinerator, along with all her memories of yesterday.

Maybe yesterday was the last day of her life with Abigail.

No, Abigail would be found. It couldn't be much longer. Maybe they had already. Maybe the police were already bringing her home. Heather had to be ready for them.

She groped her way downstairs. Martin was in the sitting room holding the blue bear. He had been crying. She wanted to go to him, comfort him, but she had barely taken a step into the room when Barbara's voice, gritty with anger, cut through from the kitchen. 'Why wouldn't she listen to me!'

Martin looked up sharply. 'Mum, leave it. Heather, we're just making tea.'

She took the bear from him, hugging it.

Barbara emerged with a tray. Silently, she laid it on the coffee table, pressed a mug into Martin's hands, giving him a squeeze of sympathy, then handed one to Heather without looking at her.

'Thanks,' Heather whispered.

Martin sniffed, then picked up a plate and offered it to her. Chocolate digestives.

Heather picked one up, staring at it with loathing, crumbled it in her clenched fist. 'Bloody bloody biscuits. Why didn't I buy him sweets? We wouldn't have fed the ducks sweets. Oh God! Oh God, oh God, oh God. It's not happening. I only left her for a moment.'

'A moment! What sort of a mother walks off and leaves—' Barbara was hissing.

'Mum, please...' Martin guided her away. 'This won't help. Go and see to Bibs. I don't want him frightened.'

Barbara was snorting. 'I notice *she* hasn't rushed to him.'

'Please.'

'Oh yes. I'll go. You can rely on me to take care of my grandchildren.'

Martin watched her out then turned back to Heather. She had folded her arms round herself, rocking on her heels.

'How could you do it, Heather? How could you just leave her?'

'She was there! I didn't go far, just after Bibs. I could see the pram.'

He clenched his fists to keep control. 'You didn't see, though.'

'I've got to do something.'

'What?'

'What are the police doing?'

'Searching. With dogs. Door to door enquiries.' He turned away. 'They're going to dredge the lake.'

She pictured the lake, the wide water with its ducks, and its mud and garbage, the willows brushing the scum of cigarette butts and used condoms. She wanted to be sick.

'He wouldn't have done that.'

'Who wouldn't have done what?'

'The man who took her.'

'You said you didn't see anyone. That's what you claimed.'

'I didn't. But someone took her. He wouldn't harm her, would he? No one would take a baby just to harm her.'

'How would I know? I don't understand any of it. All I know is that you took Abigail to the park and turned your back on her, and now she's gone.'

'Yes! And I wish I was dead!'

At last she had broken through his anger to his compassion. His arms were round her, holding her, hugging her to him.

'What are we going to do, Heather? What the hell are we going to do?'

They stood together for a while, trying to block the world out. Then she felt his grip loosen. She felt his chest rise as he drew in breath, in preparation.

'Heather. Listen. You would say, wouldn't you, if something happened?'

'Say what? What do you mean?'

'If something had happened to the baby. If there had been an accident or something. If you'd done something to her—'

She stood back, pushing him away, not believing what he was saying. Already his face was contrite, wanting to take the words back. But it was too late. They were said.

iv

Heather

Lyford Police station. Always busy. It would be. Lyford was a typically dysfunctional town. 'A regrettable lack of social cohesion,' the vicar of St. Bartholomew's had said recently, after his church had been torched. Racial tension increasing daily, drugs and football hooliganism, unemployment at dangerous levels, one pub a known haunt of IRA activists, crime spiralling out of control according to the local press; all the usual urban stuff. Most of it finishing up here, pinned on the walls of incident rooms.

'Are we definitely discounting the girl seen in the park?' Inspector Trip scratched his head, looking at the board. Not puzzlement, just dandruff.

'Fraid so, sir. Wrong time.' DS Parker yawned, desperate to get off early for once. 'Definitely seen on the swings with a baby, between twelve and one. That was at least an hour before Heather Norris was anywhere near the park.'

'What about this woman, hitchhiking on the ring road with an infant?'

'Another dead end, sir. A lorry driver's come forward. Fred Ableman. Says he gave her a lift, and she told him the baby's name. Kelly Crowe. We checked with the hospital and they've got her on their radar. So have social services. Juvenile mother, talked about heading for London, apparently. She was visited a couple of times and it was all regular and above board. Passed the notes on to Carradine.'

'Carradine? He's not on this case.'

'No, sir, but he's liaising on the Watford warehouse job.'

'Armed robbery, fatal shooting? What's he want with the girl?'

'Seems the girl, Rosalind Crowe, was shacked up with one of the gang. The one that got shot, Gary Bagley. She probably knew there was going to be trouble, legged it before the shit hit the fan. Anyway, if they want her, she's their baby now.'

'While ours is still missing. We're not getting anywhere with this, are we?'

'Not anything tangible as yet sir, no.'

'Beginning to look as if we're left with one obvious conclusion, doesn't it.'

'I'm afraid so, sir.'

'Better have her in, then.'

'Thank you for coming in, Mrs Norris. We need to go over the details of the day Abigail went missing, one more time. You left the pram on the path, and you followed your son down to the lakeside. Is that what you're still claiming? How long were you there, Mrs Norris? Two minutes? Five? Ten? You don't seem to be able to decide.

'You say you saw no one in the park. Then you thought perhaps you did see someone in the trees. Which was it, Mrs Norris?

'You claimed dogs had taken her. Then you changed your mind.

'What really happened, Mrs Norris? An accident, was that it? You didn't mean it. Abigail fell, perhaps, or the blanket smothered her and suddenly she wasn't breathing?

293

You were frightened, you didn't know what to do, so you hid her body, and told everyone she'd been snatched.

'You have to see it from our point of view, Mrs Norris. It's a question of evidence. And there is no evidence that anyone took Abigail. Just your word. Very distressing, having a baby snatched, but Alan Gregory tells us you didn't seem at all distressed – not until you'd stopped him and got his attention. Then you turned the waterworks on. His words, Mrs Norris. There was no abduction, was there? The truth is, you killed your baby.

'You never wanted this baby, did you? You've been stressed. Money worries. Your father a bit of a burden, isn't he? Must be a terrible strain. And now a new baby. Screamed your head off in a supermarket at Christmas, telling everyone how much you didn't want it. You resented her, isn't that true? Hated being left to cope with screaming kids. You refused to get up to change her, just left her to cry.

'Your mother-in-law offered you a lift into town that day, didn't she, Mrs Norris? Offered to take you to the dentist, offered to look after the children for you. But you insisted on going alone. On the bus, with a toddler and a month old baby in a pram. You chose to do that rather than accept a lift. Why was that, Mrs Norris? Why did you walk through the park, Mrs Norris? Your bus stops in Williams Street. That's the nearest stop to your dentist. Why did you choose to walk another half a mile instead, through the park?

'Where is Abigail, Mrs Norris? What did you do with her?'

There wasn't anything she could say. Nothing to be said except an endless repetition of all she could recall. The trouble was, the recollection was so indistinct, because there was nothing to give it substance. Abigail had been there in her pram and then she had been gone. Nothing else, except Heather's imagination painting in horrors, and as the days passed, she found it more and more difficult to be sure what was real memory and what was imagination. What she had seen and what she had feared were so muddled, she could no longer be sure of anything. No longer certain in her own head, and there was no one to reassure her. Only a husband who looked at her with doubt in his eyes.

They were hammering her, these men, with accusations she could not refute. Not even to herself. Was it as they had said? Had she killed her child? She wanted to shout at them. She wanted to reach across the desk and seize their lapels and shake them. No! We were in the park, feeding the ducks and she vanished! But all the while, there was this little voice in her head, this little cold sharp pinprick, whispering, 'Maybe it's true. Maybe you did kill her.'

V

Lindy

Wet grass under foot. Olive green hills rolling on in all directions. Fir forests like that ought to have wolves in them. Sheep. Birds that looked like eagles up in the sky. When it was night, away from the sparking campfire, there weren't any street lights. Just stars, like she'd never seen before.

With bare feet, Lindy splashed in the ice-cold foaming water of the stream. No, not Lindy. She was Rosalind from now on. A new name for a new world. And she liked the way Roger said it, though she couldn't understand half of what he said. Talked about her Orlando and the forest of Arden and laughed. He was probably making fun of her a bit, she could tell from the way Mandy scowled at him, but she didn't mind. She didn't mind anything any more. She'd never even imagined a world and people like this, but she had dreamed of a family, and this was a real family, for her and Kelly. It was going to be all right.

vi

Gillian

'Mrs Wendle? Gillian! This is Claire Dexter. I think we may have some good news for you…'

Gillian was trying to jot details down, but she couldn't hold the pencil. She held the banister instead, gripping it to stop herself sliding to the floor. Was she dreaming this? No, it was Claire's voice, loud and clear, even if Gillian couldn't make out the words.

Why hadn't she had more faith? She had been waiting for this, ever since that first article in the paper about the abandoned baby. She had sensed, deep down, that this was it. Her destiny. God answering her prayers. The baby had been abandoned for a purpose.

'…so we'll see you and Terry this afternoon?'

'Yes,' whispered Gillian. 'Yes.' She had to gasp for breath. She put the phone down, forced another deep breath, picked up the receiver again. Rang the works.

'It's Gillian Wendle. Can I speak to my husband, Terry? Is it possible? It's quite urgent. I wouldn't ring but—'

They weren't worried about her excuses. It must be a good day at the plant. Someone was going off to find him.

Keep breathing. And keep calm. She couldn't be a gibbering idiot when he came on the phone.

'Terry here. That you, Gill? What's up? Something wrong?'

'Terry, they've got a baby for us.'

Silence. Oh God. Terror gripped her. Why was he silent? Did he no longer want a child? Was this the final twist of fate?

'I'm coming home,' he said, indistinctly.

He was coming home. Home. From now on it was going to be a real home. A home with parents and a child. She had been right to decorate the little room, to buy the cot, the teddy bear, the mobiles, the pretty curtains. She hadn't been mad. She had known, deep down, this was it.

All her prayers answered.

Joan was standing in the living room doorway, fag in hand as usual. 'Just remember whose house this is,' she said. 'Don't except me to babysit. I'm not holding some snivelling brat while you two go off and enjoy yourself.'

Gillian laughed. Blissful release. Chains falling off her. 'Don't worry, Mum. I'll take care of my own baby. It's the only thing I want to do. I promise you'll never have to babysit.'

CHAPTER 11

i

Kelly

'Hello.'

Kelly hesitated. She'd answered the phone and now she wasn't sure she should have. She couldn't take any more buffeting. But she wasn't one to walk away. 'Ben. Hello.'

He was hesitating too. He needed to think what to say. 'I'm so sorry. All the things I did and said, I'm sorry. I can't believe I just let you go like that.'

What was that, fluttering inside her? Hope? For a fleeting second she felt like the old Kelly, ever optimistic and generous. 'You were upset.'

'That was no excuse. I was stunned, yes, but – how must you feel? You came back to us, and we drove you away.'

'I did spring it on you out of the blue.'

'It was a lot to take in. I wanted to tell you I've taken it in now. I've talked about it with Mum. She's – you do understand, don't you? It was so much to hit her with, the way we did. She just needed time. She's getting there. And I've told Dad. He's – look, I know it's a lot to ask, after the way we treated you, but can you come back to Lyford? Meet us again?'

Not so long ago she would have jumped in the car then and there. Fools rush in... She was beginning to develop an angel's fear of treading unwisely. But she had started all this, she would have to finish it. 'Yes, all right. When?'

'Whenever you like. I'm going to take some time off work. I'm with Mum. Trying to repair things.'

'That's good!' The flutter again. He was still her Ben. 'I am glad. I'll come tomorrow if you like.'

'Thank you! Could we meet—?' He paused.

'In the park?'

'Yes. Would you mind?'

'No. I don't mind. I'll see you there.'

Roz was leaning on the gate, looking at the sheep.

'I've got to go back to Lyford,' said Kelly. 'I've got to see them again.'

'Yes. Of course you do.' Roz's fingers closed on the gate, her arms bracing with determination. 'When are you going?'

'Tomorrow.'

Roz nodded. 'Will you take me with you?'

'To Lyford! Why? You can't undo any of it, you know.'

'I know. But I keep thinking about her, them, all of them. That family. That girl, the baby I abandoned.'

'You can't go and see Victoria.'

'I didn't realise how much I hurt her. She was so angry. The baby I gave up.'

'You gave her up because you thought, in your muddled way, it was for the best. Yes, she is angry, but it's not for you to try and put things right. It wouldn't work. You gave her up then, you have to give her up this time too. She knows where you are. If she wants to make contact again, she'll come to you. You can't ask anything of her.'

Roz smiled bleakly. 'You can't be my daughter, can you? Far too wise. No, I won't force myself on her. But I need to go to Lyford. Please take me. I'm going to go to the police.'

'Don't be crazy. What good would that do after all these years?'

'Everyone thought she'd killed you, didn't they? Heather Norris.'

'She was never charged.'

'Just suspected. All these years. At least I can set the record straight.'

'And be taken to court?' Was there a statute of limitations on child abduction? Kelly had no idea. 'You want to go to prison?'

'I should, shouldn't I? I did all this. I did so many bad things. I ought to pay in the end.'

'Look. I'm not going to excuse everything you did, but you were a child, trying to survive. Who's it going to help if you go to prison?'

'It will clear her name.' Roz smiled. 'Please Kelly. I'm going to do this. It would be easier if I came with you now.'

'You realise if they see you, they'll probably lynch you.'

'I wouldn't blame them.'

Kelly looked at her. The final step of growing up, for both of them maybe. 'All right. I'll speak sweetly to Joe, see if he'll chicken-sit again.'

'I never intended to hurt anyone, you know. Least of all you, Kelly. And you've been hurt so much, haven't you?'

'I'll get by. Not sure how, but I will.'

It was dry at least, sun glinting through occasionally, a bit of a breeze fluttering the leaves. Sunday and the park was busy. Not as busy as it might have been on a Sunday fifty years earlier, but not the ghost park it was on weekdays.

'I remember it,' said Roz. 'There was crazy golf over there. And the boat-yard. That's still there.' Children were out in paddle boats, and one cocky teenager was trying to look cool in a canoe. Her eyes moved round, across the lake, following the line of the fence.

Kelly was ahead of her. She had already seen the woman and the young man.

Roz said, 'Is that them?'

'Yes.'

Roz squared her shoulders.

'No.' Kelly put a hand on her arm. 'Don't come now. Let me see them first. I don't know how things are going to work out this time, but let's take it one step at a time. Me first.'

'Yes, of course.'

She left Roz by a willow tree, and walked round the lake. She didn't have hopes or expectations any more. She just wanted to get it over with.

Heather watched her approach, scarcely breathing. How had she not realised before? Take away the green streak in Kelly's shaggy hair, the nose stud, the tattoo, and anyone could see she was Ben's sister.

He was standing back, nervous, hurting, saying nothing.

Heather took a step forward as Kelly came up to them. She forced herself to reach out, touch her cheek. Experimental. The girl might just dissolve, like all the girls in her dreams. 'Abigail.'

'Yes. I was Abigail.'

Heather nodded. Closed her eyes. Took a deep breath. 'Yes, you are.'

Kelly forced a laugh that was anything but humour. 'Well. Hello.'

Heather tried a smile. 'You look like a gypsy.'

'I am a bit of a gypsy, I suppose.'

Ben came forward at last. 'A farmer, aren't you, Abigail. Sheep and chickens and goats called Eleanor and Rigby.' Proving he remembered every word.

'It sounds like fun,' said Heather, her voice half strangled.

'Pretty much fun,' agreed Kelly. 'At least when the weather's good.' Was this it? No fireworks of denial this time, but then no fireworks of any description. A mother and daughter separated for twenty-two years and they had nothing to say. Impulsively, she took Heather's hand. She should try to relate to this hurt woman. She couldn't yet, but perhaps they could make it happen.

Heather looked at Kelly's hand in hers, then gripped the girl's shoulders. Forced back the sobs that were clawing at her.

Ben put his arm round his mother and smiled at Kelly, a smile of pure relief. 'Thank you. I wouldn't have blamed you for refusing ever to speak to us again.'

'I'd never refuse to speak to you, Ben.'

'No.' He looked down.

'Is this her?' Another man's voice, abrupt. Kelly looked round. A middle-aged man, overweight, thinning hair, was striding down on them with a newspaper under his arm. 'You're telling me this is Abigail?' He said it as an accusation.

'Yes, Dad.'

Martin Norris looked Kelly up and down. She guessed she was not quite what he wanted to see. 'Hello,' she said.

'What proof do we have?'

'Dad!'

'No, no, some girl appears out of nowhere, and asks us to believe that she's the daughter we lost as a baby? You expect me to believe that without evidence?'

Heather turned to her former husband. 'She is our daughter, Martin.'

'Oh yes, of course you'll want to claim any girl that throws herself in our way, Heather. Anything to get you off the hook, prove you the martyr, but I'm not falling for every junky con artist that tries it on. A genetic test will prove it. Are you willing to be tested?'

Kelly looked at him, confronting his anger. Why should she help this man out? 'No.'

'No? In that case, I would say point proven. Because there's no earthly reason why I should believe you. If you refuse to take the test—'

'I refuse, because I'm not here to prove anything to you. I am your daughter, and if you don't like it, or you're not convinced, then that's your problem, not mine. I came because Ben asked me to come. If you don't want to acknowledge me, that's fine by me.'

'She is our daughter,' repeated Heather.

'She's Abigail,' confirmed Ben. 'She's told me exactly what happened.'

'Anyone could make up a story. It doesn't make it true.'

'It is true,' said Roz.

Kelly span round.

Roz was coming along the path towards them. 'It is true. I took the baby, from her pram by the bushes. I took her.'

'You!' Martin's suspicions of Kelly turned to outright spluttering fury at Roz. His face deepened to dark red. 'You come here, after twenty-two years, and coolly announce that you stole our child!'

'I took her,' repeated Roz.

'Right! Hold her! I'm calling the police. I want that woman locked up!' He was groping for his mobile.

'Stop it,' said Ben, a hand on his father's arm. 'Calm down.' But the sight of Roz made him too angry to say more. Angry and desperately trying to contain it.

'Damned if I'm going to stop it. I want her prosecuted. I want her punished!' Martin stepped up to Roz, hand out to stop her escaping. 'You know what you did? To us? Why?

Why did you think you could destroy our lives for your amusement? Eh? Tell me that!'

'I can't,' said Roz. 'I wanted my baby back. I thought she was my baby. Or I wanted to think she was my baby.'

'Tell that to the police, and see how they like it! You're dying, that right? I hope so, because it means you'll die in prison, where you belong.'

'Leave her alone!' Kelly stepped between them. 'She's not dying, but she is ill. She's going to the police anyway.'

'You defend her? She stole you!'

'She loved me.'

'Love!' Martin, trembling, was guided back by his son. Ben could not look at Roz, but he was trying to keep it together.

Martin jerked free, raising his finger to jab in Roz's face. 'You dare to say you loved her! You're not fit—!'

'Martin,' said Heather. A quiet authoritative voice.

He turned towards her, resentful of being diverted.

'I know what all this fire and fury is about. You feel guilty, don't you? Guilty that you never believed me. So guilty, you won't even accept your own daughter now she's come back.'

'I didn't say that. But how can she be my daughter if she defends that woman!'

Heather took a deep breath, then took a step towards Roz, forcing herself to look at her. 'You looked after her?'

'I tried,' said Roz.

'You made her happy?'

'Yes,' said Kelly.

'Thank you,' said Heather.

'Thank you?' repeated Martin.

'I don't thank her for taking Abigail, or for putting us through so much misery. No, I'll never forgive her for that. But I can thank her for keeping my baby alive and well and happy. I thought whoever took her might have killed her. I thought I might have killed her.' Heather looked at her hands, as she had in secret so many times over the years, expecting spots of blood. 'Everyone told me I had. I began to believe it myself.'

Her voice broke. 'Someone just tell me. Can I stop being mad now?'

'Yes!' said Ben and Kelly together, seizing her hands.

Heather looked away, out over the lake. 'Try to remember, Ben said, when he came back to me. So I kept coming here, hoping that one day it would happen, I would trigger some memory I must have blocked out. Whatever it was I'd done, if I could just remember…'

'Mum.' Ben was crying, tears on his cheeks. 'I should have believed you.'

'Someone should have.' Heather shot a look of accusation at Martin, then a smile of consolation at her son.

Finally, she turned once more to Kelly, looking deep into her eyes. 'Yes. You are Abigail. I have missed so much. It should have been mine – your whole life. I've missed it.' At last the sobs broke loose.

Kelly's instinct was to hug her. But Roz needed hugging too. Roz had stood by, taking their abuse. She deserved it maybe, but she was trying to do the right thing now. Which mother was Kelly to turn to and comfort? And Ben. It was Ben that Kelly wanted to hug more than anyone. Ben her lover. But never again.

'We'll have to see if we can fill in the pieces,' she said.

First they had to pick them up. No one seemed to be sure how to do it.

'Will you come back to Mum's place?' suggested Ben.

'Sure.' Go back to a house and resolutely play happy families with bright fake smiles. She would have to do it,

305

but not yet. 'First I'm going with Mum…with Roz. To the police station. That first.'

ii

Vicky

The curling wave of the downs was scarred with white streaks in the dry grass where the chalk etched through, with, here and there, a scattering of stunted thorn bushes. From the foot of the escarpment, a panorama of home counties countryside rolled out to a distant haze. Behind, on the dip slope, the lush green of beech woods. Up in the sky, three hi-tec kites fought for supremacy.

'We used to come here and fly kites, didn't we,' said Vicky. 'I'd forgotten. Dad made me one.'

'And I painted a face on it,' Gillian reminded her. 'A cat.'

'It was a tiger, I thought.'

'It was supposed to be a tabby cat.'

'All right. And we'd always have an ice cream from the van by the car park.'

'The van's still there. Shall we…' Gillian hesitated. 'I suppose you shouldn't really eat ice creams.'

'What the hell,' said Vicky. 'I can manage one.'

It was all slightly artificial still, this fellowship, but they were working at it. Arm in arm, they walked back along the downs to the ice cream van, dodging frisbees and small children rolling down the hill. Then they walked on, licking their cones.

'It's such a terrible story, baby snatching, the whole thing.' Gillian shaded her eyes to focus on a distant church tower. 'So much hurt. And you've met all of them.'

'Sort of. I talked to Heather. I tried to help. Think I got through to her.'

'And your real mother too.'

'Rosalind gave birth to me. That's not what being a mother is. That's what Joan did, give birth to you.'

'Yes, you're right. That's not being a mother. Did you sort things out with Rosalind too?'

'Not really. I was too angry, too eager to blame her. I shouted at her. She cried.'

'Did she explain why she'd left you?'

'She was very young. Just a child who couldn't cope.'

'I thought it would be that. And I was so old. I used to worry that it would matter, me standing with the grannies at the school gates, instead of with the young mums. It was never that I should have been worrying about, was it?' Gillian stared up at the sky, her fist clenching. 'Why couldn't I see?'

'Because you were Joan's victim too. Another little project.' Vicky contemplated her ice cream. 'I can't believe it never occurred to me. Of course she'd done the same thing to you. You got over it. I'm over it too. Or I will be. I'm going to be a doctor, sort out other people, heal their pain. Got to start with myself, haven't I?'

Gillian hugged her, ice cream smearing her cheek. 'I was so selfish, bringing you into that house.'

'No! No, believe me, you did me a favour. If it hadn't all happened, I'd be living in a shack down a muddy lane, with a tattoo and a nose stud.'

'And instead you had Joan.'

'We all had Joan. And now we don't.'

'Is it too vindictive, getting Dad to change the locks?'

'I don't see there's anything wrong with a little vindictiveness.'

Gillian squeezed her daughter. A new relationship, one she still had to learn, but it was wholesome. The poison had been sucked out. 'And he was delighted to do it, wasn't he? I can't remember your father looking that ferocious and determined.'

'Dad the warrior.' Vicky smiled. 'Come on, let's go home and see how he's getting on. Give him some moral support.'

They turned back towards the lime green Mini. 'Are you going to see any of them again, do you think?' asked Gillian.

Vicky thought about it. 'I suppose. Some time.'

iii

Early morning in Portland Park, the sun sparkling on the lake, dew on the grass, a few ducks still with their heads tucked under.

It was the best time of day, Kelly always thought. Everything fresh, nothing smudged yet.

It would be smudged soon enough.

She leaned on the railings, watching the breeze whip up a scurry of ripples on the opaque surface of the lake.

'Hello.'

'Hi,' Kelly responded, without thinking, before she'd had time to look at the solitary walker. Then she recognised the girl. 'Oh.'

'Do you mind?'

Did she mind what? The girl being there in the park with her? In the world with her? Or in her life, shattering it apart. 'No.' There were yards of vacant railing, but Kelly shifted along as if to make room for her.

Vicky came forward, touching the rail, running her

fingers along it. 'I thought you might be here. I almost caught you yesterday, but you were just leaving. I thought you must be an early bird.'

'A bird who's not sleeping, at any rate.'

'Yes. Of course. It's all…' She shrugged. 'Sorry about the way I behaved at your house.'

'You were upset,' said Kelly. 'Of course you were. I didn't understand then. I didn't know the full story. It must have hurt so much.'

Vicky's eyes were fixed on the surface of the lake. 'I wanted it to hurt.'

'To hurt Mum, you mean.'

'No, to hurt me.' Vicky shook her head, clearing it. 'It's complicated. Never mind that. Did you honestly know nothing? You didn't even suspect?'

'No. Why would I?'

'Never thought you didn't really belong?'

'Is that how it was for you?'

'Yes. Not now.'

'Will you ever be able to forgive her, do you think?'

'I expect so. What's the point in not? Will you?'

'Oh yes. But it's not for me to forgive, is it? I didn't lose anything by it – at least I didn't know I had.'

'Your parents. Your brother.'

'Yes. My brother.' Kelly cleared her throat. 'I didn't know I had a brother to lose. But it turns out I did, and I lost him then, and now I've lost him again in a different way. Not sure about my parents. Heather – she told me you met her, gave her the whole story. Convinced her I wasn't just an impostor.'

'Yes, well, she's met plenty who were, I think. Me included. So the whole family is reunited at last.'

'Not really.' Kelly gave a hollow laugh. 'We're jointly

309

occupying Lyford, you might say. Mum and me at a guest-house, Mr. Nor— my father at the Linley, my brother and my – other mother at her house. And you. Do you live here too?'

'Yes. With my mum and dad. Just the three of us. No one else. What's going to happen, do you know? About your – my – our mother.'

Kelly shook her head. 'She went to the police, and fessed up. They're still trying to decide whether they should be bringing charges. Heather said no. Brave, don't you think? Maybe that will count for something. It seems so pointless now, making a big legal thing of it. There are far more important things to deal with.'

'Like getting to know your lost family.'

'Yes. A week ago I thought I was Kelly Sheldon, in love with this lovely guy, and now I'm supposed to be Abigail Norris, with a mother I don't know how to talk to, and a father who can't decide if I'm a devil or an angel, and the lovely guy I was in love with turns out to be my brother, who has trouble even looking at me now.'

Vicky winced. 'I was thinking of us on interconnected roads. Now it's as if, at one of those random junctions, there was an almighty car crash. I am so sorry.'

'Yes, a crash, all right. Would it have been better or worse, do you think, if we'd never found out?'

'Worse for me. Worse for Mrs Parish. But better for you. That is sad. I am sorry. What are you going to do? Stay here? Go back to Wales?'

'Attempt both, I suppose. Try to build bridges. Stick by Roz, at least until we know what happens next. I've got a friend, a family friend, Roger. I phoned him yesterday, told him all about it. He's coming over from Dorset. Quite comforting, actually, to think of someone coming to take control.'

'Yes.'

'He says I should think about university. A means of getting away, starting afresh on my own. Finding my feet as Kelly Sheldon, no one's daughter or – sister. Just me. It makes sense, I suppose. If I can find a university near a prison.'

'I'm sure she won't go to prison. Not now.'

They were silent. A duck came swimming towards them. Followed by ducklings, hurrying to keep up with their dam. Captured in their mother's wake.

'I wouldn't be able to give her a kidney, you know,' said Vicky.

'No. I realised that.'

'I really am sorry there's no simple happy ending for you.'

'I don't think there are any endings, happy or unhappy. We just move on. On our diverging roads.'

'Yes.' Silence again.

'Well. Keep in touch, do you think?'

'Yes. Why not.'

They parted, two girls, walking in different directions. On the lake, behind them, the ducks paddled aimlessly. Ripples circled out around them, meshing, separating, out and out and on and on forever.

More from Honno

Short stories; Classics; Autobiography; Fiction

Founded in 1986 to publish the best of women's writing, Honno publishes a wide range of titles from Welsh women.

In a Foreign Country *Hilary Shepherd*

Anne is in Ghana for the first time. Her father, Dick, has been working up country for an NGO since his daughter was a small child. They no longer really know each other. Anne is forced to confront her future and her failings in the brutal glare of the African sun.

ISBN: 9781906784621
£8.99

Left and Leaving *Jo Verity*

Gil and Vivien have nothing in common but London and proximity, and responsibilities they don't want, but out of tragedy something unexpected grows.

*"Humane and subtle, a keenly observed exploration of the way we live now...
I am amazed that Verity's work is still such a secret. A great read"*
Stephen May

ISBN: 9781906784980
£8.99

About Elin *Jackie Davies*

Elin Pritchard, ex-firebrand, is back home
for her brother's funeral. Returning brings
all sorts of emotions to the fore, memories
good and bad, her own and those of the
community she left behind.

"...unsettling and evocative"
*"...a deeply moving novel from a new Welsh
talent."*
Cambrian News

ISBN: 9781870206891
£6.99

Dear Mummy, Welcome *Bethany Hallett*

Despite a successful City career, there is a
void in Beth's life, a void that only a child
can fill. Newly on her own, she is
confronted with the inevitability of a
childless future and so embarks on a
journey to adopt the child she has always
longed for.

Poignant, honest and intimate, *Dear
Mummy, Welcome* is the true story of one
woman's fight against the odds, and a little
girl's journey to find a mother.

ISBN: 9781906784300
£8.99

All Honno titles can be ordered online at
www.honno.co.uk
twitter.com/honno
facebook.com/honnopress

Jill *Amy Dillwyn, ed.Kirsti Bohata*

Jill is an unconventional heroine – a lady who disguises herself as a maid and runs away to London. Life above and below stairs is portrayed with irreverent wit in this fast-paced story. But at the centre of the novel is Jill's unfolding love for her mistress.

"Jill's experiences are told in a style of quiet power, and with a dry, almost grim, humour." The Academy

ISBN: 9781906784942
£10.99

Here We Stand *Ed. Helena Earnshaw & Angharad Penrhyn Jones*

A fascinating and unique anthology about contemporary women campaigners and how they were changed by the process of changing the world.

'A beautiful and necessary book full of passion, humour, encouragement, information and hope. This is the kind of writing that saves lives.'
A.L. Kennedy

ISBN: 9781909983021
£10.99

All Honno titles can be ordered online at
www.honno.co.uk
twitter.com/honno
facebook.com/honnopress

ABOUT HONNO

Honno Welsh Women's Press was set up in 1986 by a group of women who felt strongly that women in Wales needed wider opportunities to see their writing in print and to become involved in the publishing process. Our aim is to develop the writing talents of women in Wales, give them new and exciting opportunities to see their work published and often to give them their first 'break' as a writer. Honno is registered as a community co-operative. Any profit that Honno makes is invested in the publishing programme. Women from Wales and around the world have expressed their support for Honno. Each supporter has a vote at the Annual General Meeting. For more information and to buy our publications, please write to Honno at the address below, or visit our website: www.honno.co.uk

Honno, 14 Creative Units, Aberystwyth Arts Centre
Aberystwyth, Ceredigion SY23 3GL

Honno Friends

We are very grateful for the support of the Honno Friends: Jane Aaron, Annette Ecuyere, Audrey Jones, Gwyneth Tyson Roberts, Beryl Roberts, Jenny Sabine.

For more information on how you can become a Honno Friend, see: http://www.honno.co.uk/friends.php